Pennac, D

WRITE TO KII

D0625821

0169202

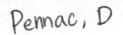

Also by Daniel Pennac in English translation

The Belleville Quartet
THE FAIRY GUNMOTHER
THE SCAPEGOAT

Essay
READS LIKE A NOVEL

Daniel Pennac

WRITE TO KILL

*Translated from the French
by Ian Monk*

WEXFORD
COUNTY
LIBRARY

F/451941

THE HARVILL PRESS
LONDON

First published with the title *La Petite marchande de prose*
by Editions Gallimard, 1989

First published in Great Britain in 1999
by The Harvill Press
2 Aztec Row, Berners Road
London N1 0PW

www.harvill-press.com

1 3 5 7 9 8 6 4 2

Copyright © Editions Gallimard, 1989
English translation copyright © Ian Monk, 1999

Daniel Pennac asserts the moral right to be
identified as the author of this work

A CIP catalogue record for this book
is available from the British Library

This translation is published with the financial
assistance of the French Ministry of Culture

ISBN 1 86046 535 8 (hbk)
ISBN 1 86046 536 6 (pbk)

Designed and typeset in Minion at
Libanus Press, Marlborough, Wiltshire

Printed and bound in Great Britain by Butler & Tanner Ltd
at Selwood Printing, Burgess Hill

CONDITIONS OF SALE
All rights reserved. No part of this publication may be
reproduced, stored in a retrieval system, or transmitted
in any form or by any means, electronic, mechanical,
photocopying, recording or otherwise, without the prior
permission of the publisher

This book is sold subject to the condition that it shall not,
by way of trade or otherwise, be lent, re-sold, hired out or
otherwise circulated without the publisher's prior consent
in any form of binding or cover other than that in which it
is published and without a similar condition including this
condition being imposed on the subsequent purchaser

For Didier Lamaison

In memory of John Kennedy Toole,
who died from not being read,
and of Vasily Grossman,
who died from having been.

*"I is another,
but it isn't me."*
CHRISTIAN MOUNIER

The author would like to thank

Paul Germain, Béatrice Bouvier and Richard Villet,
who respectively guided him through
the forests of the printing world,
the notation of Pinyin Chinese,
and the passageways of surgery.

I

THE GOAT'S HARNESS

You have a rare vice, Malaussène: you sympathise.

Chapter 1

IT ALL STARTED with a sentence trotting through my mind: "*Death is an on-coming process.*" The sort of snappy sentiment you'd expect to come across in some trendy Yank airport novel. I was just wondering where I'd read it, when the giant burst into my office. Before my door had even had time to slam shut, he was already towering over me.

"You're Malaussène, aren't you?"

A massive bone structure wrapped up in vague contours. Bones like shillelaghs and a scalp covered with crew-cut bristles.

"So, are you, or aren't you?"

Bent like a long-bow over my desk, with his huge hands throttling my armrests, he was holding me prisoner in my chair. Prehistory in person. Crushed into my seat, with my head shrinking down between my shoulders, I was incapable of saying whether I was me or not. All I was wondering about was where I'd read that sentence: "*Death is an on-coming process.*" Had it been in English, in French, from a translation?

That's when he decided to put us both on the same level. With a mighty heave he hiked us up, me and my chair that is, right up off the floor and onto the desk. Even then, he still stood a good head taller than me. Beneath the prickle bushes of his eyebrows, his wild eyes ferreted around inside my brains, as if he'd lost his car keys there.

"Do you get off on torturing folk?"

His voice sounded strangely childish, with an agonised tone that was supposed to be threatening.

"You do, don't you!"

While up there on my throne, all I could think about was that sodding sentence. It wasn't even elegant. It rang false. Like a Frog trying to croak like a Yank. Where the hell had I read it?

"You never worry that some day someone'll come along and smash your face in?"

3

His arms had started to shake. Like a drum roll foretelling an earthquake, a deep vibration from his entire body was being transmitted through the armrests of my chair.

It was the phone ringing that let all hell break loose. The phone rang. With one of those musical trills of today's phones, phones that have memories, phones you can programme, status-symbol directorial phones for the masses . . .

The phone shattered under the giant's fist.

"Shut it, you."

I had a fleeting vision of my boss, Queen Zabo, upstairs on the other end of the line, buried waist deep in her shag pile by that shillelagh blow.

Upon which the giant grabbed hold of my beautiful almost-director's lamp, snapped its exotic wood in two across his knee, then asked me:

"The thought that someone'd come along and smash your entire office to smithereens has never occurred to you?"

He was one of those loonies who always hits before they speak. Without giving me time to answer, he swung the leg of my lampstand, which had now been reduced to its primal state of a tropical wooden club, down onto my computer, smashing its screen into a spray of pale shards. Neurons popped out of the collective memory. As if that wasn't enough, my giant started hammering at the keyboard until the air was full of symbols that had been reduced to primordial chaos. Christ, if I didn't do something we were all going to end up back in the Stone Age.

His attention had now drifted away from me. He overturned my secretary Mâcon's desk and took a kick at a drawer stuffed full of paper-clips, rubber stamps and nail varnish, sending it crashing down between the two windows. Then, armed with the ashtray, whose leaded hemisphere had been wobbling merrily on its legs since the 1950s, he started working over the volumes in the bookcase facing me. The ashtray's leaden legs ripped into them violently. This bloke obviously had a knack for using primitive weapons. At each blow, he gave off a boyish yelp, the sort of frustrated cries that must accompany most crimes of passion – while sobbing like a baby, I beat my wife against the wall.

The books took off then flopped down again, dead. There was only one way to stop this massacre. I got to my feet. I grabbed hold of the coffee tray which Mâcon had brought in to softsoap my previous batch of moaners (a group of six printers whom my charming boss had put on the dole queue because they'd delivered six days late) and chucked the whole lot through the glass doors of the bookcase in which Queen Zabo displayed her finest bindings. The empty cups, the half-filled coffee pot, the silver tray and the shards of glass made a good enough racket for our man to go still, with the ashtray brandished above his head, before turning round and asking me:

"What are you doing?"

"The same as you. I'm communicating."

I threw the crystal paperweight that Clara'd given me for my last birthday over his head. The paperweight, a dog's head that looked vaguely like Julius (sorry Clara, sorry Julius) demolished the face of good old Talleyrand-Périgord, the secret founder of the Vendetta Press in the days when, like now, people needed paper to settle their scores.

"You're right," I said. "When you can't change the world, you can at least change the decor."

He dropped the ashtray onto the floor. And then, the inevitable finally happened: he burst into tears.

His tears made him fall apart. He now looked like one of those wooden puppets which collapse when you press a button under their base.

"Come over here."

I had sat myself down once more on my chair, which was still perched up on my desk. He swayed over towards me. Between the cables in his neck, his Adam's apple was bobbling up and down, pumping out his agony. This sort of suffering was familiar to me. I'd seen it all before.

"Come closer."

He took another couple of steps forwards, till he was right in front of me. His face was streaming. Even his hair was soaked with tears.

"I'm sorry," he said.

He dried his eyes with his clenched fists. His fingers were hairy. I laid my hand onto the nape of his neck and drew his head against my shoulder. After half a second's resistance, the whole lot gave way. With one hand I cradled his head in the hollow of my shoulder, while with the other I stroked his hair. My mother was very good at doing this, so there was no reason why I shouldn't be as well.

The door opened to reveal Mâcon, my secretary, and my friend Loussa de Casamance, a five-foot-six-inch Senegalese with eyes like a cocker spaniel's and legs like Fred Astaire's and who is by far the greatest expert on Chinese literature that Paris has to offer. They saw what there was to be seen: a literary director sitting on his desk and comforting a giant who was standing in the middle of a bomb blast. Mâcon's eyes were aghast at the extent of the damage, while Loussa's were asking me if I needed help. With a back sweep of my hand, I gestured to them to be off. The door closed again with a sigh.

The giant was still sobbing. His tears were pouring down my neck. I was drenched to the waist. But I was in no hurry, so I let him cry his eyes out. The patience of the comforter came from the fact that he had troubles of his own. Cry, my old mate, we're all in it up to our necks, a little bit more won't make any difference.

And while he was pouring himself out into my shirt collar, I thought about Clara, my favourite sister, and her engagement. "Don't take on like that, Benjamin, Clarence is an angel." Clarence ... how can anyone be called Clarence? "A sixty-year-old angel, sweetheart, he's three times as old as you." My sister's velvet laughter. "I've just found out two things at the same time, that angels do have a sex and that they're ageless." "All the same, my Clarinette, an angel who's the governor of a prison . . ." "But who's made his prison into a paradise, Benjamin, you mustn't forget that!"

Girls in love have an answer to everything and the big brothers are left on their own to fret: my favourite sister is marrying a head screw tomorrow. Not bad, eh? If we add that my mother pissed off a few months ago with a copper, so head over the heels in love that she hasn't even phoned since, then you can get a pretty good picture of the Malaussène family. Not to mention my other brothers and sisters – Thérèse with her star-gazing, Jeremy who burnt his school down, Half Pint with his rose-tinted glasses, whose slightest nightmare turns out to be true and Verdun, the latest arrival, screaming like the battle of the same name from the moment she was born . . .

And you, the tearful giant, what sort of family have you got? None, maybe, and you've been investing everything in your writing. Is that it? He was now calming down a bit. I took the opportunity to ask him a question, even though I already knew the answer:

"They've rejected your manuscript, have they?"

"For the sixth time."

"The same one?"

Another nod of his head, which he had finally unstuck from my shoulder. He then shook it slowly.

"I've worked it and reworked it so much that I know the thing off by heart."

"What's your name?"

When he told me, the hilarious look on Queen Zabo's face when she'd commented on the manuscript in question immediately flashed before my eyes: "Someone who writes sentences like *'Pity!' he hiccuped, backing*. Or who thinks it's funny to call Selfridges Shelfridges and then stubbornly lays the same thing on six times over in six years. What sort of prenatal disease did he suffer from, Malaussène, can you tell me that?" She shook that huge head which nature had

6

planted on her anorexic body and repeated the sentence, as if it was a personal insult: "'Pity!' he hiccuped, backing. . . . Why not 'Hello,' he said, *inning* or 'Cheerio,' he said, *outing*?" Then for a good ten minutes, she reeled out an astonishing series of variations on this theme because, if there's one thing Queen Zabo doesn't lack, then it's talent . . .

So we wound up sending back the manuscript without reading it. I signed the slip with my own name and now chummy was almost dying of a broken heart in my arms after having turned my office into a municipal dump.

"You didn't even read it, did you? I put pages 36, 123 and 247 in upside down and that's how they came back."

A classic ploy . . . And yet smart-arse publishers like us still get caught out like that! What can you say, Benjamin? What can you say to this man? That he's slaving away over a piece of outdated, childish claptrap? And since when have you believed in *maturity*, Benjamin? I don't believe in anything, for Christ's sake, except that typewriters are fatal to babblers, that white paper is bullshit's winding sheet and that the person who could sell this bollocks to Queen Zabo hasn't been born yet. That woman is a living manuscript scanner. Only one thing in the world brings tears to her eyes, and that's the death of the imperfect subjunctive. So what are you going to suggest to our giant, then? That he takes up painting watercolours instead? Good idea, if you want him to blow what's left of the building away . . . He must be a good fifty years old, and it's now been thirty years at the very least that he's been consecrating himself to letters. Blokes like that are capable of anything if you try to knock the lead out of their pencils. So I took the only way out open to me. I told him:

"Come this way."

And I leapt straight down from my chair onto the floor. I rummaged through Mâcon's gutted desk till I found the set of keys I was looking for. I edged across the room. He followed me like he was picking his way through the desert. A post Israeli-Syrian conflict desert. I knelt down in front of a metal filing cabinet, which slid open at the first turn of the key. It was stuffed to the gills with manuscripts. I grabbed the first one that came to hand and said:

"Here, take this."

It was entitled *Without Knowing where I'm Going* and was signed Benjamin Malaussène.

"It's by you?" he asked me when I'd closed the filing cabinet.

"Yes, and all the other ones, too."

I went and put the set of keys back into Mâcon's wreckage, exactly where I'd found them. He'd stopped following me. He was staring at the manuscript with a puzzled look.

"I don't understand."

"It's perfectly simple," I said. "All my novels have been rejected far more often than yours have. I'm giving you this one because it's my latest offspring. Maybe you'll be able to tell me what's wrong with it. Personally, I reckon it's great."

He gawped at me, as if the dancing furniture must have driven me gaga.

"Why me?"

"Because we're all far better judges of other people's work than of our own. And what you've written at least proves that you're a good reader."

Upon which, I coughed, turned round for a second and, when I stared back at him, my eyes were brimming with tears.

"Please, I beg of you, do it for me."

I think he went pale, then it was his turn to open wide his arms, but I dodged his embrace and led him to the door, which I pushed wide open.

He dithered for a moment. His lips had started quivering again. He said:

"It's terrible to think that there's always someone worse off than you are. I'll write and tell you what I think, Monsieur Malaussène. I promise. I'll write to you!"

He gestured at the wrecked office and said:

"I'm sorry . . . I'll pay for the damage, I'll . . ."

But I shook my head whilst manoeuvring him gently through the door. Then I closed it behind him. The last image he took away from our little meeting was of my face running with tears.

*

I wiped my face with the back of my hand and said:

"Thanks a lot, Julius."

As the dog didn't react, I went up to him and repeated:

"No, really, thanks a bunch! There's a dog who defends his master for you!"

As much good as talking to a stuffed pooch. Julius the Dog just sat there in front of the window, watching the Seine flow by, with all the patience of a Japanese painter. Pieces of furniture had flown round his ears, his own effigy had plastered Talleyrand, but Julius the Dog didn't give a toss. With his twisted gob and dangling tongue, he was watching the Seine flow by, with its barges, crates, old boots and lovers . . . So motionless that our giant must have mistaken him for a piece of primitive art, sculpted in stone, that was too cumbersome even for his raging fury.

I had a sudden suspicion. I knelt down beside him. I gently called:

"Julius?"

No answer. Just his smell. "You're not having another fit on us, are you?"

The entire Malaussène family lived in terror of his epileptic fits. According to my sister Thérèse, they were always the sign of a coming catastrophe. Then there were the after-effects: twisted gob, dangling tongue . . .

"Julius!"

I took him in my arms. No, he was full of life, all warm, greying fur, stinking from every pore: Julius the Dog in perfect nick. "Right," said I. "Let's come down from the clouds, get your butt in gear and off we'll go to give Queen Zabo our resignation."

Was it the word "resignation"? He got to his feet and reached the door before I did.

Chapter 2

"THIS IS THE third time you've resigned this month, Malaussène. I can spare just five minutes to put you back on the rails, and not a second more."

"Not even a second, your Majesty, I'm resigning and you're not going to talk me round."

My hand was already on the door handle.

"Who said anything about talking you round? All I want is an explanation."

"No explanations. I'm fed up and that's an end to it."

"You were fed up on the previous occasions as well. You're chronically fed up, Malaussène. That's the trouble with you."

She wasn't sitting in her chair, she was planted in it. Her frame was so skinny that I was always expecting her to vanish between the cushions. Stuck on top of that body, like on a metal stake, an extraordinarily obese head was gently wobbling – a tortoise head in the rear window of a car.

"You sent back some poor bugger's manuscript without even reading it and I'm the muggins who had to sweep up the shit again."

"Yes, I know. Mâcon told me. The poor little thing was rather shaken up. So he pulled the upside-down-page trick on you, did he?"

She was starting to chuckle between her jowls. When the explanations began, I always ended up being had.

"Too right. And it's a miracle he didn't burn the place to the ground."

"Well! Then we'll have to sack Mâcon. Turning pages the right way round is her job. I'll take the damages out of her severance pay."

At the ends of her scrawny arms, her hands, too, were pudgy. Something like a baby's hands rammed onto screwdrivers. Maybe that's what made me all emotional. I'd seen so many babies' hands! Half Pint's hands were still baby hands. Verdun's too, of course. Tiny little Verdun, the One to End all Ones. And Clara's as well, in a way, Clara who was getting married tomorrow, she too still had baby hands.

"Sack Mâcon? Is that all you can come up with? You've already put six printers on the dole queue today, isn't that enough for you?"

"Listen up, Malaussène . . ."

The patience of she who thinks she's above making explanations.

"And listen good. Not only did your printers deliver the album six days late, but they also tried to pull a fast one on me. Take a sniff at that!"

Without a word of warning, she opened a book and stuck it under my nose: a sort of coffee-table commemorative production, Vermeer of Delft looking truer than life, overpriced and under-read, an essential addition to every dentist's waiting room.

"Very classy," said I.

"I didn't ask you to *look* at it, Malaussène, I asked you to *smell* it. So, what can you smell?"

It smelt like a nice new book, a publisher's hot cake.

"It smells of glue and fresh ink."

"Not that fresh, in fact. What sort?"

"Sorry?"

"What sort of ink is it?"

"Stop playing silly buggers, your Majesty. How on earth should I know?"

"It's Venelle 63, my lad. In about seven or eight years' time, it'll start making lovely little reddish tints around the edges of the letters and our book will be fucked. It's a piece of chemically unstable shit. They must have had an old stock of it and tried to offload it onto us. Oh, and by the way, how ever did you manage to get rid of your psycho? The way he was coming on, it looked like he was going to take you to pieces!"

A swift change of subject. That was her technique. One bit of business sorted. On to the next bit.

"I turned him into a literary critic. I slipped him one of our unclaimed manuscripts and told him it was by me. I asked him for his opinion, for his advice . . . I turned the tables on him."

(This was my favourite ploy, in fact. I wound up receiving letters of encouragement from authors whose novels I'd turned down: "There is a true sensitivity at work in these pages, Monsieur Malaussène! You'll make it one day, just do as I do – keep at it. Writing means having infinite patience . . ." I answered by return of post, giving them my heart-felt thanks.)

"And it works?"

She was staring at me with incredulous admiration.

"It works, your Majesty. In fact, it never fails. But I'm fed up. I'm resigning."

"Why?"

Good question, that.

"Are you scared?"

Not even. That sentence about death being an on-coming process was nagging at me a bit, but our jolly rabid giant really hadn't scared me.

"Is it the inhumane nature of publishing that's getting to you, Malaussène? How about trying real estate, then? Or the petrochemical industry? Or banking? In fact I reckon you should go for the International Monetary Fund, I can just see you cutting off aid to an underdeveloped country because it can't keep up with its debt repayments. With millions of deaths as a result!"

She was always taking the piss out of me in that macho-maternal way. And she'd always ended up getting me back. But not this time, your Majesty, this time I'm off. She must have read that in my eyes, because she half got up, with her pudgy paws leaning on her desk and her huge head about to tumble down like an over-ripe fruit onto her blotter:

"For the last time, just listen to me, you little twit . . ."

She worked at a pathetic little metal desk. The rest of her office looked more like a monk's cell than a governor's holy of holies. Nothing like the Louvre ante-chamber where I slogged away, or the glass and aluminium structure that belonged to Calignac, the sales manager. In terms of office space, everyone else was far better accommodated than she was; in terms of clothing, you'd have mistaken her for a recently taken-on press attaché's part-time secretary. She made a point about her workers being able to labour in luxury and fart into pure silk. She'd perfected her trick of being the soberly dressed little Napoleon, surrounded by her marshals with gilt and gold dripping down to their arseholes.

"Now listen, Malaussène, I took you on as a Scapegoat so that you would get bollocked instead of me, so that you'd wash away the shit with your timely tears, so that you'd solve the unsolvable by opening wide your martyr's arms, so that, in a word, you'd carry the can. And you are, indeed, a wondrous can-carrier! The greatest! No-one alive carries a can like you can, and do you know why?"

She'd already explained that one to me umpteen times: because I was, to her mind, a born Scapegoat, that it was in my blood, a magnet where my heart should have been, which attracted arrows. But that day, she piled it on higher and thicker:

"Not only that, Malaussène, there's more: sympathy, my lad, sympathy! You have a rare vice: you sympathise. Just now you were suffering for that infantile giant who was demolishing my furniture. And you felt his pain so clearly that you had the brilliant idea of turning the victim into the executioner, the failed writer into the all-powerful critic. It was exactly what he needed. You're the only person capable of sensing such simple things."

Her voice was like a high-pitched rattle, somewhere between an ecstatic little girl and a world-weary witch. With her, it was impossible to distinguish between enthusiasm and cynicism. She didn't give a damn about anything, all she wanted was to understand.

"You're the true man of sorrows in this vale of tears, Malaussène!"

Her hands were fluttering under my nose, like bloated butterflies.

"Even I make you feel for me, and that's really saying something!"

She stuck her chubby index finger into her hollow chest.

"Every time you set eyes on me I can hear you asking yourself how such a monstrous head could have grown on top of such a rake!"

Wrong. I had my pet theory about that one: successful psychoanalysis. Her head had been healed and her body eliminated. Thanks to the cure, her head alone now benefited from the good things in life.

"I can just hear you working out the history of my personal suffering: an unhappy love affair to kick off with, or an overly acute awareness of the absurdity of the world, with the final remedy being psychoanalysis, which rips out the heart and puts armour-plating round the brains. The magic couch trick, that's it, isn't it? The pay-as-you-earn Ego, aren't I right?"

(Well, swipe me . . .)

"Look, your Majesty . . ."

"You are the only one of my employees to call me your Majesty to my face – the others all do it behind my back – and you really think that I'm ready to lose you?"

"Look, I'm fed up, I'm leaving, and that's it."

"What about books, Malaussène?"

She'd screamed that out while leaping to her feet.

"What about what books?"

With a broad sweep of her hand she took in the four walls of her cell. They were bare. Not a single book. But it still felt like we'd been plunged into the heart of the Bibliothèque nationale.

"Have you thought about the books?"

She was steaming. Her eyes were bursting out of their sockets. Her lips had gone purple and her chubby fists ashen. Instead of falling to pieces in my chair, I too leapt up and started into bawling as well:

"Books! Books! That's all you can talk about! Just name me one!"

"What?"

"Name me a book, the title of a novel, any old one will do, something from the heart, go on!"

Her few seconds of suffocated astonishment were fatal to her.

"See?" I gloated. "You're not even capable of coming out with a single one! Had you said *Anna Karenina* or *Bibi Fricotin*, I'd have stayed."

Then:

"Come on, Julius, let's go."

The dog, who was sitting facing the door, lifted up his fat arse.

"Malaussène!"

But I didn't turn round.

"Malaussène, you're not resigning, I'm firing you! You stink worse than your dog does, Malaussène, when you talk from the heart, people can smell what you had for dinner last night! You're a piece of fly shit, a pathetic little worm who's about to get swept away into the gutter, and don't think I'll lift a finger to help, so just fuck off home then and sit and wait till I send you round the bill, for the wrecked office!"

II
CLARA GETS MARRIED

I don't want Clara to get married.

Chapter 3

I T TOOK ME half the night. Only then did I understand why I'd left Queen Zabo clutching an empty goat's harness.

I'd taken shelter in Julie's arms, my head had nestled between Julie's breasts ("Julie, give us a lend of your mammaries!"), Julie's fingers were dawdling in my hair, and it was Julie's voice that brought it all home to me. Her beautiful Savannah growl.

"If you ask me," she said, "you only resigned because Clara's getting married tomorrow."

*

Jesus, how right she was! It was the only thing I'd thought about all day: "Tomorrow, Clara's marrying Clarence." Clara and Clarence . . . just imagine Queen Zabo's expression if she'd come across that one in a manuscript! Clara and Clarence! Even Mills and Boon wouldn't dare to print such a cliché. But, leaving aside how daft the situation was, it was the situation itself that was doing me in. Clara was getting married. Clara was leaving home. Clara, my little sweetheart, my soul sister, was going away. No more Clara to separate Thérèse and Jeremy when they had their daily slanging match, no more Clara to comfort Half Pint when he woke up from one of his nightmares, no more Clara to cuddle Julius the Dog in epilepsy land, no more *gratin dauphinois* either, and no more legs of lamb *à la Montalban*. Except on Sundays, maybe, when Clara would visit her family. Jesus Christ . . . Jesus sodding Christ . . . Yes, that was all I'd been thinking about during the entire day. When that slimeswold of a Deliure had come round complaining that his works weren't being delivered to airport bookstalls rapidly enough (it's because the booksellers don't want them any more, you little cretin, you've worn yourself out bragging on the box instead of staying in and sharpening your quill, can't you see that?), what I was thinking about was Clara. I started sobbing: "It's my fault, Monsieur Deliure, it's my fault, don't say anything to the boss, I beg of you . . . ". Meanwhile I was saying to myself: "She's going tomorrow, tonight is the last real time I'll see her . . . ", and that's what I was still thinking about when the sextet of conmen from the printer's works arrived to plead their untenable case and, when our Cro-Magnon man was demolishing the place, what really got to me was that Clara was going away. Benjamin Malaussène's life could now be neatly summed up as follows: his little sister Clara was leaving his home for someone else's. That's where Benjamin Malaussène's existence came to a halt. And Benjamin Malaussène, suddenly submerged under an infinite sense of world-weariness, swept overboard by a huge wave of sorrow (steady on there!), gave his boss, Queen Zabo, his resignation, while putting on all the airs and graces of a moralist, which suited him about as much as a chasuble suits a lifter of poor-boxes. I'd committed suicide.

Outdoors, when Julius and I had gone for a walk, all puffed up with stupid pride at this victory-cum-defeat, Loussa de Casamance, my friend in the world of publishing, had drawn up next to us in his red van, chock-full of the Chinese books with which he flooded New Belleville's *Les Herbes Sauvages*, and took us aboard. He was the one who started to screw my head back on the right way, what with the commonsense outlook he had from being an ex Senegalese infantryman who'd come through Monte Cassino. For a few minutes, without saying a word, he'd let his library on wheels roll on. Then he'd glanced across at me, his eyes swivelling round, lit with exotic green glints, and said:

"Allow an old negro who loves you the privilege of informing you that you really are a shit-for-brains."

There was a mocking gentleness in his voice. But, then too, I was thinking about Clara's voice. In fact, it was probably going to be Clara's voice that I would miss the most. Even when tiny, from the moment of her birth onwards, Clara's voice had protected our home from the city din. Such a warm voice, so full, so like her face that, if you looked at Clara when she was silent, busy developing her photos under the red lamp, for instance, you could still hear her, still wrap yourself up in her lamb's wool on some cool spring evening.

"Pulling the book among books trick on Queen Zabo was hardly playing fair," said Loussa. "If you want my opinion."

Loussa was a quietly loyal subject of Queen Zabo. He never raised his voice.

"'Name me one . . . just one', that was a snide barrister's ploy you came up with there, Malaussène, nothing more."

He was right. I'd flabbergasted her, then made the most of her paralysis to deliver the death blow. A nasty piece of work.

"That's how to win a trial, but it's also how to smother the truth. *Fan gong zi xing*, as the Chinese put it: examine your conscience."

He was a particularly bad driver. But he reckoned that, after the carnage of Monte Cassino, he was immune to traffic. Out of the blue I said to him:

"Loussa, my sister's getting married tomorrow."

He didn't know my family. He'd never been to my home.

"Then her husband's a lucky guy," he said.

"She's marrying a prison governor."

"Oh!"

Yup, "Oh!" was my opinion, too. He went through a couple of red lights, across a couple of dangerous intersections, then asked:

"Is your sister old?"

"No, she's going on nineteen. He's the one that's old."

"Oh!"

Julius's stench made the most of the silence to make its presence felt. Julius the Dog always wafted his way to people's attention. With a simultaneous hand movement, Loussa and I wound down our respective windows. Then Loussa said:

"Look, either you need to talk, or else you need to remain silent. Either way, I'll buy you a drink."

When it came down to it, maybe I did need to tell it all to someone. To someone who wasn't already in the know. Loussa's right ear would do perfectly.

"Ever since my left eardrum exploded during the war, my right ear has grown far more objective."

THE STORY OF CLARA AND CLARENCE

Chapter One: Last year, while the old ladies of Belleville were having their throats cut and their savings stolen, my friend Stojilkovicz, a sort of Serbo-Croat uncle to our family, got it into his head to protect the old dears who the coppers had left to the mercy of the wolf.

Chapter Two: In order to do this, he armed them to the teeth by resurrecting an ancient stock of firearms which he'd hidden in the Montrouge catacombs since the end of World War II. Once he'd trained them up in the full range of shooting techniques in a specially laid-out area in the above-mentioned catacombs, Stojilkovicz had quite simply let them loose in the streets of Belleville, as unpredictable as heat-seeking missiles.

Chapter Three: The slaughter, of course, only escalated. A plain-clothes officer, who'd tried to help one of these sprightly ladies across an intersection, ended up laid flat out on the tarmac with a bullet between his eyes. Whoops. Grandma'd been too quick for him.

Chapter Four: At that, the force swore to avenge its fallen hero and really got its act together. Two inspectors, who were a little less dumb than the rest, rumbled what was going on and Stojilkovicz ended up in the can.

Chapter Five: (a little parenthesis, the *in petto* of life's music): During the course of their inquiries, the two inspectors had got to know Belleville in general and the Malaussène family in particular. The younger of the pair, a certain Pastor, fell head over heels in love with my mother, who thereupon decided, for the eighth time, to start all over again with a brand new lover-boy. Exit Mum. Exit Pastor. Off to Venice and the Danieli Hotel. Oh yes.

As for copper number two, Inspector Van Thian, a Franco-Vietnamese on the verge of retirement, he'd copped three bullets during their attempts to nail the old ladykiller and was spending a pleasant convalescence under our roof. Every evening, he told the kids a chapter of this story. He was a strangely moving storyteller. He looked like Ho Chi Minh but sounded like a gravelly cop in a black and white movie. Sitting on their bunk-beds, the kids listened to him, their nostrils dilating at the smell of the blood and their souls swelling at the promise of love. Old Thian called his story *The Fairy Gunmother* and gave us all highly flattering parts to play in it. Which "pulled in the listeners", as they say on the air.

Chapter Six: The only snag was, no more Stojilkovicz, no more Serbo-Croat uncle with a voice of bronze, no more opponent for my games of chess. As we aren't the sort of people who abandon an old mate, Clara and I decided to visit him in jail. He'd been locked up in the Champrond Detention Centre in the Essonne Département. Métro to the Gare d'Austerlitz, train to Etampes, taxi to the prison and, there, amazement: instead of finding a block sealed off by cliff-like walls, what we encountered was an eighteenth-century country manor. Admittedly, it had been converted into a prison, with its cells, caps and visiting hours, but it also boasted French-style gardens, fitted shag carpets, beauty all around you and the hushed silence of a library. Not the slightest jangle of a key. Echoless corridors. A haven. Then a second surprise: after we'd been shown to Stojilkovicz's cell by an ancient turnkey, as discreet as a museum keeper, our old friend refused to see us. We just managed to glimpse his small square den through the half-open door, its floor smothered with crumpled sheets of paper, with a desk rising up in the midst, which was groaning under the weight of dictionaries. Stojilkovicz had decided to translate Virgil into Serbo-Croat during his stretch, and the few months he'd been given were not going to be long enough for him. So, off with you, then, kiddies and put the word round: no visits to Uncle Stojil.

Chapter Seven: The vision occurred in the corridor on the way back out. For, the first meeting of Clara and Clarence was truly a sort of vision. It was a spring evening. Russet sunlight was gilding the walls. The ancient turnkey was showing us out. Our footfalls were muted by the silence of a long ceremonial carpet. All we needed now was for a shower of Walt Disney sparks to hit us before Clara and I were whisked away, hand in hand, to some Never-Never Land of eternal bliss. To tell you the truth, my feet were itching to get out of there. This prison looked so little like a jail house that, as far as I was concerned, the natural order of things had been upset. And I wouldn't have been at all surprised if the diesel-engine cab that was waiting for us in front of the gate hadn't been transformed into a crystal carriage drawn by a special breed of winged horses which never shit.

That was when Prince Charming put in an appearance.

Standing there, tall and straight, a book in his hand, at the end of the corridor, his white head splashed with gold from a diagonal sunbeam. An archangel in person. The lock of immaculate hair which tumbled down over his eye did in fact look pretty much like an angel's recently folded wing.

He raised his eyes towards us. Eyes that were heavenly blue, natch.

There were three of us standing there in front of him. But all he saw was Clara. And, that smile appeared on Clara's face which I'd been dreading for so long. The only thing was that I'd always imagined she'd dedicate the first edition of it to some vague pimply character – with trainers and a personal stereo – who'd fall under big brother's command even as he was succumbing to little sister's charms. Or else Clara, who'd never done that well at school, would bring us home a stuck-up brainbox who would be gobbled up raw by our family's eccentricities. Or a greeny, who I'd convert by bringing on the shoulder of lamb. Not a bit of it. An archangel. With heavenly blue eyes. Who was fifty-eight. (Fifty-eight, pushing sixty.)

A prison governor. The earth had been glued to the heavens by the intensity of those two stares and had stopped turning. Somewhere along those silent corridors, the plaintive voice of a cello started up. (Don't forget, this is all going on in a prison.) As though giving a signal, the archangel flicked back his mop of white hair with a graceful sweep of his hand and said:

"So we have visitors, do we, François?"

"Yes sir," the ancient turnkey replied. And Clara's bags were already packed.

*

"So tell me," Loussa said, putting down his glass. "What exactly do your lags get up to in this dream prison of yours?"

"First off, they aren't my lags and it isn't my prison. Secondly, what they get up to is everything artistic imaginable. Some of them write, others paint, or else sculpt, there's a chamber orchestra, a string quartet, a theatre troop . . ."

Yup . . . Saint-Hiver's pet theory was that *a murderer is a creator who hasn't found his outlet* (his italics). He had the idea for this prison during the 1970s. First as an examining magistrate, and then as a judge, he'd been able to see all the harm that a normal jail does, had dreamt up this solution, had little by little forced it onto the system and, lo and behold, it worked . . . and had been for almost twenty years . . . *the conversion of destructive energy into constructive will power* (still his italics) . . . a good sixty killers transformed into *aar-ists* (Jeremy's pronunciation).

"All in all, a nice little place for me to retire to."

Loussa was dreaming.

"The rest of my days spent translating the Civil Law Code into Chinese. Who do I have to kill?"

Our empty glasses were refilled. I turned my one round between my fingers. I was trying to read Clara's future in the crimson depths of my Sidi-Brahim red. But I wasn't gifted like Thérèse.

"Clarence de Saint-Hiver. How can anyone be called Clarence de Saint-Hiver?"

Loussa didn't find it that incredible.

"It's an island name, that is. From Martinique, maybe. In fact," he added mischievously, "I can't help wondering if what's really getting your goat is that your sister's marrying a white nigger . . ."

"I'd rather she was marrying you, Loussa, a black nigger with a red van full of Chinese literature."

"Oh, I wouldn't be up to it any more. I lost my left ball in the Monte Cassino bone orchard, along with my left ear . . ."

A gust of wind sent us a whiff of Belleville. A blast of Merguez sausages and mint. Next to our table, a rotating spit was gently sizzling. At each turn of the roundabout, a sheep's head, skewered like a chicken, eyed up Julius the Dog.

"What about Belleville?" Loussa suddenly asked.

"What about Belleville?"

"What do your Belleville mates make of all this?"

*

Good question. What did Hadouch Ben Tayeb, my childhood friend, and his father Amar, the restaurateur, in whose eatery the Malaussène tribe had dined since the year dot, and Yasmina, a mother to all of us, and Black Mo, Hadouch's black shadowman, and Simon the Berber, his red shadowman, the lords of the three-card trick from Belleville to the Goutte d'Or, and not entirely respectable, what did they all make of it? What had been their first reaction when told that Clara was marrying a top screw?

Answer: amused consternation.

"Things like that only ever happen to you, Benjamin my brother . . ."

"Your mother pisses off with that copper Pastor, and then Saint-Hiver weds your sister!"

"You're now a pig's son-in-law and a screw's brother-in-law. You're in it up to here, Benjamin!"

"What about you, Benjamin, who are you going to wed?"

"Here, have a drink . . ."

My Belleville friends poured me another drink.

Sincerely sorry to hear . . .

Until the day Clara gave me the chance to hit back. I'd told them there was an emergency and everyone was to meet at Amar's. They were already at table when I arrived. Hadouch kissed me and asked: "Feeling better now, Benjamin my brother?" (since hearing about Clara's marriage, Hadouch had stopped asking me if I was well and started asking if I felt "better", the little bugger found that highly amusing . . .), and Simon's grin spread all over his features:

"What's the big news this time? Your mother and Pastor have got another little brother on the way for you?"

Then, not to be left out, Black Mo added:

"Or maybe you've decided to join the force. Is that it, Benjamin?"

But I just slumped down like a death at a birthday party.

"It's far worse than that, lads . . ."

I took a deep breath then asked:

"Hadouch, you were there when Clara was born, remember?"

And it was Hadouch who first twigged on that things were getting serious.

"Yeah, that's right, I was there with you when she was born."

"When she was little, you changed her nappies, you wiped her behind . . ."

"Yeah."

"And, later, you taught her all about Belleville, you were her street godfather, so to speak. In fact, it's thanks to you that she takes such great photos of the neighbourhood . . ."

"Yeah, I suppose so . . ."

"And you, Simon, you protected her like a brother as soon as she was old enough for little hooligans to start fancying her, isn't that right?"

"Hadouch asked me to watch out for her, that's right, but for Thérèse as well, and Jeremy, and now Half Pint. They're all like members of the family, Ben. We didn't want them getting up to any mischief."

At that, one of those grins formed on my face which are the fruit of having a lovely little secret stashed away in your brains. So, without taking my eyes off the Berber, I slowly repeated:

"You said it, Simon, Clara's like one of your family . . ."

Then I turned towards Black Mo:

"And when Ramon tried to get her chasing the dragon, you were the one who bounced his head off a lamp-post, weren't you Mo?"

"What would you have done in my place?"

My grin widened.

"The same as you, Mo. Which means that you're her brother, just like I am . . . or nearly."

I let the silence do the talking for a while, before adding:

"There's just one snag, lads."

I let them stew for another couple of seconds.

"Clara wants you to be at her wedding."

Silence.

"All three of you."

Silence.

"She wants Mo and Simon to be her witnesses."

Silence.

"She wants to walk into the chapel on your father's arm, Hadouch, and on Yasmina's too, and she wants Nourdine to be a page boy and Leila to be a bridesmaid."

Silence.

"She wants you and me to follow behind her. Right behind her."

Hadouch then tried to slither out of it.

24

"What the fucking hell would a load of Muslims like us be doing at a roumis' wedding?"

I had my answer ready.

"These days, Hadouch, you can choose your religion, but not your tribe. And you're Clara's tribe."

No escape. It was Hadouch who ran up the white flag.

"All right. Where's the church? Saint-Joseph's on Rue Saint-Maur?"

Upon which, I calmly finished them off.

"No, Hadouch. She wants to get married in the prison chapel. Inside, if you see what I mean . . ."

Chapter 4

YES, BECAUSE THE cherry on the cake was that I got treated to a religious awakening. Up until then, Clara had been raised with the idea that loving Humanity meant also being against God and other mortal beliefs. But then, lo and behold, she and Clarence decided that their meeting was down to the agency of some All-Powerful Being. And Clarence, our criminal creativity guru, laid his oh-so delicate hands on my shoulders and murmured with a winged smile (angels, after all, are nothing if not winged):

"Benjamin, why do you refuse to admit that our meeting came about by the grace of God?"

So the result was: an entire upbringing up the spout, a white wedding in a prison chapel, the couple to be blessed by the official lock-house chaplain, and all this explained in detail on the invitations. Which, Saint-Hiver being who he was, were printed in embossed letters. Twice married in registry offices and twice divorced, a confirmed rationalist, a militant behaviourist, and then a third marriage to a bright white adolescent, in a church! Oh, Clarence de Saint-Hiver . . .

I rolled over in bed, I sought out Julie's breasts. Clarence de Saint-Hiver . . . "Why do you refuse to admit that our meeting came about by the grace of God?" . . . fucking wanker.

"Calm down and go to sleep, Benjamin. Or you'll be totally knackered tomorrow."

Never has there been anything so humanly warm as Julie's breasts.

"Maybe it won't last that long, maybe it's just Clara's rough draft of real love . . . eh, Julie . . . what do you reckon?"

We could hear Paris sleeping. Julie's index finger dreamily curled up a lock of my hair.

"Love doesn't come in rough drafts, Benjamin, as you well know. Each time, it's final copy, written straight off."

(Or written off, perhaps . . .)

"Anyway, why don't you want her to love the man she's marrying?"

26

(Because he's sixty years old, for Christ's sake, because he's a head screw, a God botherer, because he's fucked and dumped others before her!) As none of these answers was admissible, I kept them to myself.

"You realise that if you keep carrying on like this you're going to end up making me jealous?"

That wasn't really a threat. Julie was half-asleep when she said it.

"No, I'll love you always," I said.

She just turned her back to the wall and said:

"Just try and love me all the ways."

*

Julie's breathing became smooth and streamlined. I was the only person left awake in the former hardware store where we live. Except for Clara, perhaps. I got up. I went downstairs to check . . . but of course she was sleeping as she always slept, wrapped up out of harm's way. In their bunk-beds, the others were spark out, too. Old Thian had narrated an episode from *The Fairy Gunmother* to them. Jeremy dozed off with his mouth agape and Half Pint forgot to take off his glasses. Thérèse, as usual, was sleeping so stiffly in her bed that she looked as though she'd walked straight into her slumbers and then someone had tucked her in, while being very careful not to fold her up. Julius the Dog was snoozing in the midst of them, his jowls making the noise of the pages of a dictionary being flicked over. Above Julius was Verdun's cot. Verdun, the latest arrival, had been born angry. She slept like a grenade with its pin pulled out. Only Thian managed to make her accept her existence. So it was that when she woke up it was always to find old Thian's face peering down at her. That way, the grenade agreed not to go off.

Laid across a chair, floating like the ghost of happiness in that dark room, was the white dress. Yasmina, Hadouch's mother and Amar's wife, had come by that evening for a final fitting session with Clara. Another tale hangs on that one . . . typical of the Malaussène tribe! I'd phoned Mum to tell her the glad tidings. "Really?" Mum replied from way out yonder in Venice. "Clara's getting married? Hand me over to her, then, number one son." "She isn't here, Mum, she's gone shopping . . . " "Well, then just tell her from me that I hope she'll be as happy as I am" . . . then she hung up. Hadn't called back since or even dropped us a line, wasn't coming to the wedding, zero . . . our Mum.

So Yasmina thereupon adopted her role. As far back as I could remember, Yasmina's skirts have been our real mother. I went to fetch a chair from the kitchen, I positioned it right in the middle of them all, my sleeping darlings, all products of maternal love affairs. I straddled it, with my arms folded on top of the back-rest, my head on my arms and fell fast asleep.

*

That's right . . . I fell fast asleep. Too fast. I shot straight past it and ended up submerged in memories. Saint-Hiver's one and only family visit. You know, the presentation of the dearly intended. About a fortnight back. A lovely little dinner party. A blushing Clara doing her Cordon bleu bit. "Guess who's coming to dinner this evening?" Jeremy and Half Pint played at that game all day. "Our Clawa's pwisoner," Half Pint answered. And the two little idiots started screaming with laughter, which Thérèse considered "vulgar" and which made Clara turn beetroot. But, that evening, when confronted with a real flesh and feathers archangel, our double act went all sheepish. Because our Saint-Hiver had a genuine *presence*. He was no scout leader you could playfully punch in the guts, or who gets all pally with you right from the word go. He had an other-wordly dignity, a distracted gentleness which kept the kids at a more than just respectful distance. Even Jeremy! What's more, our brother-in-law to be was no bundle of laughs. He definitely did not enjoy a good joke as much as the next man. If he had agreed to leave his prison to have a quick gander at his fiancée's family, then he had also brought along his topic of conversation like others turn up with a bottle of wine. Our man was a man with a mission. At Julie's first question, he was off:

"Yes, I deal with a particular brand of criminal: those who have always felt from their childhood on, since their school days, or even since kindergarten, that Society sets up a block between them and their true selves."

The look on the girls' faces . . . Jesus help me, the look on the girls' faces!

"They have a powerful sense of their own existence and do not kill, as others do, in order to destroy themselves, but rather to *affirm their existence*, just as one would knock down a wall which was keeping one prisoner."

Even Verdun, in Thian's arms, looked like she was listening to him, with her Semtex stare, still glowing, like she was constantly on the point of blasting her own wall to smithereens.

"That, Mademoiselle Corrençon, is the sort of person whom I lodge at Champrond. Many of them are parricides, or killed a teacher, a psychoanalyst, or a drill sergeant . . ."

"So as to be 'noticed'," my journalistic Corrençon concluded, already feeling the first kicks of a wonderful new article in her professional womb. (When I stop and think about it, how lonely I felt at that frigging dinner party!)

"Yes . . . " Saint-Hiver muttered pensively. "The strange thing is that no-one has ever wondered what it was that they so desperately wanted us to *notice*."

"No-one until you," Clara added going ever redder.

Our mouths were all agog and seemed to be saying "more! more!", and Clara was listening to Clarence like a wife whose female passion feeds off her man's passion. Yes, that evening, in Clara's saucer-like eyes, I saw a regiment of devoted wives, Martha Freud and Sofia Andreievna Tolstoya, dusting down the images of their brilliant hubbies. Our little genius, after flicking back his white mane, served us up the following axiom:

"Murderers are often people whom no-one believed."

"Dictators too," Julie added.

(This wasn't the chattering classes, this was classy chattering.)

"Quite. Some of my lodgers would probably have had brilliant careers in Latin America."

"Instead of which, you have turned them into artists."

"Rather than mould others' existences, they mould their own."

(Stop, please! So much wisdom in so few words. I just can't take it any more!)

Upon which, our highly serious Saint-Hiver treated himself to a wicked grin:

"Among our various artists, we even boast a few architects who are now drawing up plans to extend our prison."

Never had our flabber been so gasted.

"You mean your prisoners are busy building their own cells?" Julie exclaimed.

"Isn't that just what all of us do?"

That lock of white hair again . . .

"Except that the rest of us are bad architects. Our conjugal cells smother us, our business complexes devour us, our family prisons push our children into taking drugs, and that tiny little televisual window, through which we pathetically stare at the outside world, inevitably drives us back onto ourselves."

Jeremy then proudly butted in:

"We haven't got a telly!"

"Which is part of the reason why Clara is Clara," Saint-Hiver replied, as po-faced as ever.

As for me, our archangel was starting to get seriously on my tits. Apart from the fact that he kept flicking at his white lock, like a barrister fiddles with his sleeves, his carry-on reminded me of the good old days when, while I was changing my mother's kids' nappies, my mates used to come round to see me in the attempt to convert me to Real Life. Even then, the refrain about the smothering nuclear family, the sharks in business, the boa-constricting couple and the telly mirror had already been done to death. It was enough to make you drop the whole dropping-out bit! And just dream of spending the rest of your life with your family, in front of the idiot box, eating past their smell-by date TV dinners, and only venturing out once a week, with the kids firmly in tow, to take on board a good old Latin Mass. No, cut the Mass. Saint-Hiver would only approve. That man had a vicary voice, all sweetness and light, sounding like it was coming down from an observation platform positioned way above his head. Christ, was he pissing me off! I just felt like telling him: "Get off your cloud, Saint-Hiver, you're twenty years late!" But I was immediately struck by the following disturbing question: *"Late compared with what?"*

After all, he had shown me round his wonderful prison! And it was true that it had left me speechless! When I think back, it was amazing: you reckon you're opening the door to a cell and you come across a state-of-the-art auditorium, or a painting studio flooded with natural light, or a monastic library in which scholars sitting bent over their labours, waste-paper bins overflowing with rejected drafts, hardly had time to turn round and say "hello" to their visitors. Who were, in fact, a rarity. No sooner were Saint-Hiver's prisoners locked up, than they refused to have visitors. Saint-Hiver claimed that he had nothing to do with this. (Flick of the lock.) It was that these men soon started to experience a freedom within the walls which they had to preserve from exterior disturbances. If they had killed in the outside world, then, according to them, it was because this freedom had been denied to them.

"And their refusal to have visitors has now extended to an outright rejection of the media in all of its forms, Mademoiselle Corrençon," Saint-Hiver emphasised pointedly. "No newspapers, no radios, nor any other inlet for the *zeitgeist*. Our television is home-produced."

Then, with a truly archangelic smile:

"Indeed, the sole element from the outside world which my lodgers accept within our walls is Clara."

Yeah . . . Yeah . . . Yeah . . . that was, in fact, the crux of the problem. Our inspired lags had adopted my Clara and her ever-present camera, which she had at once put to use for propagating their image. She'd snapped them at work, she'd snapped the walls, the doors, the locks, she'd snapped the waste-paper bin overflowing with rejected drafts, two profiles leaning over the blueprints of the new cells, their in-house television studio, the grand piano gleaming like a killer whale which had been beached in the central courtyard, she'd snapped the reflection of a pensive brow in a computer screen, a sculptor's wrist at the moment when the hammer strikes the chisel, then she'd developed them all, and the lags had seen themselves brought to life, all along the corridors, hung up on the lines Clara's photos were drying on, they'd discovered an extraordinarily vibrant existence in which each and every gesture had a meaning that had been captured and magnified by Clara's lens. They had become their own exterior images. Thanks to her, they were now both inside and outside. They adored Clara!

*

And I, Benjamin Malaussène, brother of a large family, trying to nod off on a chair stuck right there in the middle of my charges, solemnly asked myself the following question: was this really a life for Clara? Didn't a girl, who'd spent her childhood looking after her mother's offspring, now deserve something better than coddling this blue-eyed archangel's lost souls?

Chapter 5

"IT'S TIME, BENJAMIN."

Clara was in her wedding dress. Angels are white, I can testify to that, totally immaculate, sculpted with whipped cream. Rivers of airy whiteness stream down from the tops of their heads then bubble all around them. Angels are made of vapour and froth. They have no hands. They have no feet. All they have is an uncertain smile with whiteness all around. And everyone takes great care so as not to tread on all that whiteness, or else we'd have an angel stripped bare.

"Benjamin, it's time . . ."

The place had silently readied itself around me. Clara was handing me a cup of coffee. So be it. I drank it, still straddling my chair, like one of those old-world traitors who were shot with their backs to the firing squad. Total silence. Into which Hadouch arrived. Dressed up like the lord of the concrete jungle, crammed into his suit, he had the expressionless face of a guest who's just deposited his wreath in the hallway. All of which perked me up a bit.

"Hi there, Hadouch my brother, feeling better?"

He nodded back at me with a grin that presaged revenge. "You not dressed yet, Ben? You don't want to keep the bridegroom waiting, now, do you?"

Behind him, Mo and Simon looked like bodyguards done up in their Sunday best. The Black was togged out in brown. His slightly unbuttoned jacket revealed a waistcoat of pure gold which made a perfect match with a whole set of tomfoolery I'd never seen him wear before. With a carnation in his buttonhole and his two-tone shoes, he totally looked the part. All that was missing was the Borsalino hat and the pair of cream braces. He smelt of cinnamon. As for the Berber, he'd perfumed himself with fresh mint and married the natural flames of his mop of red hair with a day-glo green suit consisting of a slim-fit jacket and bell-bottom kegs. Despite his stack heels, he was still broader than he was tall. Something like a giant cockroach with its head on fire.

"Mo! Simon! You look wonderful!"

Angels can fly, I can testify to that as well, and when they fly from the arms of

32

a Berber into those of a third-generation Belleville Black, angels turn pink with delight. A round of applause from Julie, Thian and the kids. Mind you, when Inspector Van Thian saw the Berber and the Black come in, he did feel a tad taken aback. At the time when he'd been investigating the murders of Belleville's old dears he'd disguised himself as a widow from his homeland and, with his scrawny body squeezed into a Thai dress, Mo and Simon had been the first to rumble him as a cross-dressing copper. Thian's pride had been hurt so deeply that it'd taken a long time to heal. As for our two Mafia henchmen over there, finding themselves all done up to the nines in front of a copper, who knew them like the back of his hand, didn't exactly make them feel at home either. But, thanks to the dissolving power of love, the Malaussène household became the UN of the beat and the street. Plus everyone's attention was attracted by what Thian was carrying clasped to his chest in a leather harness. It was tiny, livid with rage and done up in a dress almost as white and as massive as Clara's. It was Verdun, with her six months of life and fury, Verdun and her little fists clenched against the world. Thian always represented a genuine threat when he had Verdun in his arms. If he let go, then she'd explode. Everyone there present knew that. When carrying, Thian could hold up any bank he fancied.

All the same, someone still said:

"Isn't she cute?"

But I asked:

"What's she doing in that dress? Is Verdun getting wed as well? Who to then? You, Simon?"

Not at all a bad idea, in fact. I could offload my three sisters all in one go: Clara to a priest, Verdun to an ayatollah and Thérèse to Thian, so long as she agreed to take on his native Buddhism. Altogether highly ecumenical, and so guaranteeing my ticket to heaven no matter who was really in charge.

"Benjamin, really! You haven't forgotten that she's getting baptised today?"

Oh right. Yes, that little detail had slipped my mind. So as to get a religious ceremony, Clara had to get herself baptised and so had decided on dragging Verdun into the halo chase. When he heard that, Half Pint's peepers turned into greedy saucers behind his specs. He begged:

"Me too, I want to get popetised."

But, there, I did put my foot down:

"You can get popetised when you're old enough to think for yourself. Like Verdun!"

For one thing I was sure about was that Verdun, in her primal fury, had been thinking for herself from the word go. And if I had agreed to her being baptised, it was only because I was certain we'd never manage to go through with it unless she agreed as well. Boiling with rage, she'd steam all the water from out of the font! In fact, that day it was the only event I was actively looking forward to: the drop of holy water which would make Verdun explode and the entire Roman and Apostolic church with her.

Behind Thian, Jeremy and Half Pint were looking pretty good, too. Royal-blue blazers and mouse-grey kegs, hair slicked back into looking glasses and partings as straight as a communicant's conscience. It was Thérèse who'd taken care of their uniforms. She'd even chosen the same togs for herself, except that instead of trousers she squeezed herself into a pleated skirt, which made her look just the same as ever. Thérèse is Thérèse. Even if she did herself up in sequins for a night out on the samba, she'd still have that stainless-steel rigidity which her close relationship with the stars gives her. Yesterday evening, during dinner, I leant over and whispered into her ear: "Death is an on-coming process. What do you make of that, Thérèse?" She didn't even look round at me. She replied: "That's right, Ben. And the length of a life depends on the speed of the projectile." Then, ever the professional, she added: "But all that doesn't concern you. You're going to die in your bed on the day of your ninety-third birthday." (She thought she was being reassuring, but I'd done my sums. My ninety-third year was still one hell of a long way off! I was going to have to die a little on the way, otherwise I'd never make it.)

Jeremy had just crossed the room with a terrible shriek from his polished shoes.

"Mo! Simon! I've got a present for you!"

Once he'd piped this out, Mo and Simon found themselves unwrapping a long thin parcel, with everyone's attention riveted on them. Then, there they were, each of them standing there holding a file – small sharp files with points, made of the finest steel.

"As Clara's getting wed in the clanger," Jeremy calmly explained, "I thought these might come in handy. Just in case they decided to hang onto both of you."

The double whack he immediately received left him pink for the rest of the day. After which, Mo and Simon managed to grin weakly.

"Benjamin, aren't you going to get dressed?"

Julie was standing next to me. Julie, in that crisscross dress, which is my own special favourite because it frees her breasts as soon as I get thirsty. She smiled at my striped pyjamas. Why should I get dressed? I was already in the right uniform, wasn't I? . . . A wave of fatigue swept over me, plunging me straight into such deep despair, such total darkness, that my legs started to give way and my hand instinctively groped for Julie's shoulder. And I heard myself say, in a voice that used to be mine and which sounded like Half Pint's now is:

"I want Yasmina to give me a bath."

34

Then:

"I want Yasmina to dress me."

*

So Yasmina gave me a bath. Just as she'd given all the kids a bath the night before, Thérèse included. Just as she used to do when I was kid, each time Mum took her love someplace else and left Louna and me on our own.

I don't want Clara to get married. I don't want her to spend even one week of her life playing the muse to Saint-Hiver's jail birds. I don't want them wearing my Clara out. I don't want her to be in the arms of a man who'll snuff it thirty years before her. I don't want her to act out the tragedy of happiness. I don't want her to be locked up in that prison.

So Yasmina gave me a bath, her fingers yellowed from henna, soaping down what had to be soaped down:

"You're a big boy now, Benjamin my son."

I don't want that fanatic with his archangel's hair and salamander's fingers to fuck my Clarinette. I don't want to play the goat at the Vendetta Press any more. I'm up to here with it, right up to here with it . . .

"You're tired, Benjamin my son, you shouldn't sleep on a chair."

Eighteen years back, when Clara was born, Hadouch and I had rushed Mum round to the local clinic. She'd become full of light and translucent which, in Mum's case, always means there's an imminent arrival. Hadouch nicked a car and off we went. "Don't panic, kids, she's only just gone into labour." The midwife's eyes were like oysters and her voice slurred. We left again for a spin round the ring road but, feeling decidedly uneasy, headed back early. Flat out among the test-tubes, the midwife was snoring her head off. She'd been snorting ether, and my little Clara had been left to deliver herself. Her head had emerged and she was already gazing at the world with that look of dreamy assent which Julie, many years later, would identify as being the eye of a photographer. "She focuses on things, then absorbs them." I delivered Clara while Hadouch was dashing through the corridors looking for a medic.

"Now come here and get dried."

I didn't want Clara to get married. And yet, Yasmina was dressing me. I wanted Clara to get her photographer's eye back. I couldn't stand her looking like an enamoured nun. I wanted Clara to see what there was to be seen. And yet, there I was, dressed.

Chapter 6

THE WORST OF the worst is waiting for the worst to happen. The worst thing about French weddings is the motorcade of horns blaring to announce to the entire world the coming consumption of the bride. I had hoped that we'd be spared all that, but the kids weren't to be robbed of their bit of fun. As Champrond Prison was sixty kilometres from Paris, we thus had to lap up sixty kilometres of hooting. Any observant motorist who'd passed us would surely have found it rather amusing that such a noisy wedding parade, with its cars done up in ribbons, included so many people who looked like they were off to a funeral. The exception being the last car, which contained the kids (Jeremy, Half Pint, Leila the bridesmaid and Nourdine the page boy) and which was being driven by Theo, a great pal who'd met while playing the Scapegoat at the Store, on Rue du Temple. When I asked Theo if he wouldn't mind joining us, he answered: "I love weddings. I never miss the chance to see what I've escaped from. What's more, a wedding in the clanger . . ."

The most beautiful motor was obviously the bride's, a spotlessly white Chambord which Hadouch had finally settled on after almost making the car-hire rep top himself. "No, not a BMW," Hadouch went, "they're for pimps. And not a Merc either, they're for gippos, and we can't take that Traction there, we're not shooting a film about the Gestapo, and not that Buick either, it looks like a hearse, this is a wedding, for fuck's sake, not a funeral . . . well, not exactly, anyway . . ." It went on for hours, until at last he said: "What about that Chambord over there, is it for hire?" Then, going all serious: "See what I mean, Benjamin? That white Chambord there, that's Clara to a tee, that is."

The white Chambord, with Clara in it, was the car behind me. She'd put her hand into old Amar's and it didn't look like she was going to let go again till she laid it in Clarence's. (Clara and Clarence! . . . Jesus Christ!) Yasmina was sitting on the other side and, alone in the front, Hadouch was driving with his elbow jutting out the window, like a genuine white Chambord chauffeur. Julie and I were out in front in her yellow 4 CV, which was purring along merrily, happy to be out of the pound, like a lag on special day release. Apart from Julius the Dog, lording it on the back

36

seat with the pink ribbon which Half Pint had tied round his massive neck, we hadn't taken anyone on board. I wanted to be alone with Julie. As a mark of respect for my fraternal mourning, Julie wasn't hooting her horn. She was driving with that brand of dynamic nonchalance which emancipated ladies used to put on at the wheels of their long 1920s convertibles. She looked beautiful and I slid a hand into the opening of her dress. One of her breasts immediately nestled into it.

"Did I ever tell you that I once interviewed A. S. Neill at Summerhill?"

No, she never had. She doesn't talk shop much, does Julie. Which is just as well, because she spends so much time globetrotting after her articles that if she started telling me all about them, then life would really be elsewhere.

"Well, I've just remembered that he mentioned Saint-Hiver to me."

"No kidding? Saint-Hiver went to see A. S. Neill at Summerhill?"

"Yes, a French judge who was thinking about applying Neill's methods with kids to adult delinquents."

Black Mo and Simon the Berber were following Clara in a van containing seven sheep, skewered and ready for the final *méchoui*. The artistic lags had, of course, been invited as well, plus their turnkeys and maybe even the coppers who'd nailed them, the judges who'd sent them down and the briefs who'd so gamely defended them. Half a ton of couscous was to accompany the *méchoui*.

"And what did A. S. Neill make of our loverboy, then?"

"He was wondering whether his project would work. I think he had his doubts. In his opinion, the success of institutions like that depended more on the person in charge than on the methods used."

"That's right, my dear, educational theory doesn't exist. There are only educators."

Julie smiled round at me. But the cogs inside her head had started to whirr. I'd seen it all before. The journalist was taking over. And not just any old journalist! Julie is to society at large what Queen Zabo is to the world of paper: an insatiably curious delver who makes foolproof diagnoses.

"All the same, there is something I'd like to know . . ."

"What's that, Julie?"

"It's how Saint-Hiver managed to get Chabotte to agree to his new model prison. You do remember Chabotte, don't you? At the time, he was permanent under-secretary at the Ministry of Justice. And nothing was done without his say so."

Of course I remembered Chabotte . . . the inventor of the two-pig motorbike, the rear one being armed with a long stick. In the 1970s most of the bruised heads which used to come round to my place for medical treatment owed their bumps to Chabotte's motorised truncheons.

"It can't have been easy to convince Chabotte that, with a bit of nous, you could turn a Landru into a Rembrandt."

But I objected:

"Someone who, at the age of sixty, can seduce Clara then turn her into a font-diver in five minutes flat can talk anybody into anything."

Then I sneakily added:

"For instance, talk Julie Corrençon out of writing an article about his paradise penitentiary, even though she's dying to."

Julie opened her mouth to answer, but the wail of a siren cut her short. A motorcyclist had just overtaken us, with his arse in the air and stomach on the ground, gesturing at the wedding party to dump itself in the ditch so as to let the quality past: in this case, an official limo with mysterious smoked-glass windows, which crossed over the horizon the second it passed us, followed by a second outrider no less strident than the first. "A VIP guest," I murmured with a smirk.

*

"No!" Saint-Hiver replied after Julie had asked him straight out. "No! You must not write an article about us!"

His voice had snapped down like a guillotine. He pulled himself back together at once:

"But our press is a free one, Mademoiselle Corrençon, and it is not in my nature to forbid anything."

(A bit tempting though, all the same?)

"Now, let us just imagine that you wrote that article . . . "

His voice was begging her not to.

"Imagine that it has been published: 'A Centre For Artists and Artisans Inside the French Penitentiary System', or something along those lines, I am afraid that I am not very good at titles (you're telling me!). It would be what you call a 'scoop', would it not? And, what is more, the sort of 'trendy-experimental' scoop which so titillates the modern mind, don't you think?"

She did. Julie honestly couldn't disagree with that.

"Very well. Then what would happen during the week after your paper had been published?"

Silence from Julie.

"Then I shall tell you! We would be on the receiving end of every sort of nonsense, that's what. Well-intentioned journalists would rain down on our heads, singing our praises, while others would cry out at such a waste of public money!

The result? A competition between ideologies! A legion of critics would besiege my painters, my authors and my composers in order to compare their work with what is being produced in the outside world. The result? Artistic competition! Someone would certainly want to put our products on the market. Economic competition! Some of my lodgers would be sucked into this whirlpool of publicity. Narcissistic competition! Now, I must remind you that . . ."

Then, very slowly, with his finger trembling . . .

"I must remind you that if these men once became murderers, then it is because they were incapable of tolerating such an atmosphere of universal competition . . ."

Silence over the dinner table.

"Do not put temptation their way, Mademoiselle Corrençon, do not write that article, do not throw my lodgers into the lions' den."

. . .

"They would slaughter the lions."

Chapter 7

THERE WERE so many police cars clustered round Champrond Prison . . . it was as if the building was rising up from a sheet-metal shell, reflecting the image of its old walls like in stagnant water.

"I can't help wondering if there's going to be enough mutton to go round," I said. Silence from Julie.

"Look, they've already lit the fire for the *méchoui* in the main courtyard."

Sure enough, a thin ribbon of smoke was rising up from the heart of the prison then gliding up into the bright blue sky.

"I rather think the wedding's off," Julie said at last.

"What do you mean?"

The whirring of a chopper broke the silence above us. A red chopper from the security forces, with its blades slicing through the pencil of smoke over the prison. Then it vanished, somewhere behind the walls.

"Something must have happened."

Julie pointed out the gendarmerie road-block. Barriers, motorcyclists, gendarmes on foot brandishing machine guns and an officer with four silver stripes who was conducting this little orchestra. And who was walking over towards us.

"It's a major," said Julie, switching off her engine.

Silence.

Over yonder, the ribbon of smoke had recovered from its emotions. It streamed straight up into the heavens again. At its summit, it produced a few wisps. The gendarmerie major came up to us and leant down. His eyebrows were as silvery as his stripes.

"Are you the bride?"

Put like that, to Julie, his question sounded rather funny. She's my bride, hands off! But, below his brows, his eyes were brimming with condolences. This was no time to laugh. I leapt out of the car to intercept Clara. Too late.

"I'm the bride, officer."

She was there in front of him, like she'd just dropped down from the heavens in her white dress, her hand still in Amar's. The major started weighing his words.

"Has something happened?"

A vague, terribly polite smile hovered on Clara's lips. Hadouch, Mo and Simon joined in:

"What's the problem?"

From them, this wasn't really a question. More like a cultural tic. Uniforms rarely meant anything other than problems, as far as they were concerned.

"Officer," said Clara. "Would you please answer my question."

There was more authority in that bride-to-be's voice than in all those uniforms, road-blocks, machine guns and motorbikes, in all of that force which had been deployed.

"Monsieur de Saint-Hiver has passed away," the major said. Then he repeated it three times over. He got caught up in his words. He hadn't wanted to delegate this sad duty to one of his underlings. But now he'd rather have been a private. Or a motorbike.

*

Clara let go of Amar's hand.

"I want to see him."

"That's out of the question."

"I want to see him."

Even though it must have seemed genetically unlikely to him, the major asked old Amar:

"Are you her father?"

To which Amar replied in his Amar way:

"She's my daughter, but I'm not her father."

"Can you make her understand . . ." said the major.

"Clara . . ."

That was me speaking. I called her name as softly as I could, like I was waking up a sleepwalker.

"Clara . . ."

She looked at me with exactly the same expression she'd shot at the silvery-browed military policeman. She repeated:

"I want to see him."

And I, who'd delivered her into this world, knew that that was all she would say until she'd seen Clarence.

Along the sunlit road, the kids were running towards us.

"Simon, get the kids back into the car and tell everyone else to stay put!"

Simon obeyed Hadouch's order as he always did, without a moment's hesitation.

"Apart from you, who's in command here?"

Pinned to his uniform, the major's parachutist ribbon was looking put out.

"I'm her brother," I said. "Her elder brother."

The major's head nodded to show that it was following.

"May I have a word with you?" he said curtly.

He slid a hand under my arm and led me away.

"Now listen carefully, elder brother . . ."

He was speaking rapidly:

"Saint-Hiver has been murdered, he was tortured, mutilated, if you must know, he's just not fit to be seen. If your sister goes there, it'll be the death of her."

The police road-block opened up in front of us. A press car brushed past us on the way. It then bombed back towards Paris. The eternal speeding messenger bearing ill tidings.

"And when she sees the photo in the papers, won't that be the death of her? You mean to show him to the entire world, except for her?"

Silence. We looked at Clara. Hadouch and Mo had moved back. Amar was sitting in the white Chambord once again. Clara had stopped the sun in its tracks over our heads.

"The only way you'll get rid of her is to run her in."

All this in whispers. Motionless words. A motionless wedding party, frozen into the pack-ice of the wheat fields, motionless uniforms, motionless prison which, for the first time, looked massive to me, motionless air with that vertical stroke sketched in by the ribbon of smoke. The artist must have had a steady hand. It was absolutely straight. *Death is an on-coming process.*

"There's been a riot," said the major. "No-one can go into the prison."

But there was such total silence around us that, if there was a riot going on, then someone must have stuffed one hell of a handkerchief into its mouth.

"There isn't the slightest sound of a riot," I said. Then, even nearer the uniform, if that was possible:

"What happened? Did the prisoners cut up Saint-Hiver?"

A quick shake of the decorated head.

"Not exactly."

"What do you mean, 'not exactly'? They didn't cut him up exactly?"

The major's patience was in the same mould as that of the bride's, standing there all alone under the sun's disk. He'd probably got a fair-haired daughter

42

the same age as Clara, or something like that, who was getting married tomorrow, to an investigating magistrate . . .

"Please, I beg of you, you really have to convince your sister to go home."

From behind the windscreen of her 4 CV, Julie was watching me parley. Julie hadn't got out of her car. Julie hadn't gone to Clara. Julie knew Clara as well as I did. "Don't fool yourself, Benjamin, whatever Clara decides to do, she decides on her own."

"My sister has decided to see Saint-Hiver's body."

*

A car door slammed behind the major. And slammed loudly. A character built like a daddy-long-legs strode over towards us. The awaited person who unjams the gridlock always turns up in the end . . . This particular one headed straight past the major and me without even glancing at us, brushed by Clara as though he was walking through her, and came to a halt in front of Hadouch:

"Well, well, well. If it isn't Ben Tayeb! You one of the wedding guests, Ben Tayeb?"

Without waiting for an answer, the daddy-long-legs pointed a thumb at Mo and Simon.

"And your Black and your Berber have gone Christian on us, have they?"

At this, Simon grinned beatifically. There was a gap between his incisors. According to legend, it is through this gap that the wind of the prophet blows. And history tells how this wind has overturned many a citadel. Hadouch knew Simon's smile.

"We don't move, do we Simon, we stay where we are and say 'good morning, inspector."

Simon didn't move. He said:

"Good morning, inspector."

His smile, too, didn't budge an inch.

"Berthier! Clamard!" the inspector yelled.

Two more car doors slammed. Berthier and Clamard. A good head shorter than their boss, but with the same manner. Wise monkeys from the force's menagerie.

"With your permission, major?" the daddy-long-legs called over to us. "It's Belleville come to visit me. My patch. My bread and butter. My existence. So let's make the most of it and get some work done!"

The major didn't answer. He silently disapproved. The eternal conflict between the city coppers and country gendarmes. The daddy-long-legs walked up the line of cars. One car per stride. A slap of his palm on the roof of each. Boom!

"Everybody out! This is an ID check!"

"We might even lay our hands on a hot motor," one of the wise monkeys sniggered as he passed by the major.

All that humanity emerging slowly from those cars stuck in the wheat fields, that lanky geezer going up the line and banging on their roofs (boom! boom!) in a planetary silence, the earth sliced into two yellow horizons by a brutally straight road, and that bride standing there under a brutally round sun . . . All we needed now was the voice of God . . .

And, lo and behold, the voice of God suddenly roared forth from above the whole carry-on.

And the wheat fields shimmered.

"Inspector Bertholet! Leave these people alone and get back into your car!"

The voice gripped the daddy-long-legs just as he had his hand raised over the kids' car ("I thought he'd just been frazzled by lightning," Jeremy said a little later).

God had the crackly voice of police megaphones.

"You've already sparked off a prison riot. Isn't that enough for one day?"

Inspector Bertholet knew that voice well.

"Are you determined to cause a disturbance outside as well?"

It was a public announcement of the end of his career.

While Inspector Bertholet was slinking back into his motor, God emerged from his official car, the very same one that had overtaken the wedding party earlier, with an angel in front and an angel behind.

"Good morning, Monsieur Malaussène. Who else but you gets himself into such situations?"

An oily comma on a pale white forehead, a bottle-green suit over a waistcoat embroidered with bees, hands crossed behind his back, stomach thrust out, it was Chief Superintendent Coudrier, old Thian's boss, someone I'd met on numerous past occasions during my existence and who, being the celestial copper he is, knows more about me than I do myself.

"This is your sister Clara, I presume."

Clara, still there under the sun.

"Poor lass."

And Chief Superintendent Coudrier really did look as if he considered that bride, abandoned in the road by life's little horrors, to be a "poor lass".

"She's absolutely insisting on seeing Saint-Hiver, Chief Superintendent," the major intervened.

"Naturally . . ."

The Chief Superintendent sadly shook his head.

"Nothing is stopping her, Monsieur Malaussène, except for the state of the victim. Monsieur de Saint-Hiver is scarcely presentable."

Another glance at Clara:

"But I suppose there will be no talking her out of it."

Then, after taking a deep breath:

"Shall we go?"

*

Two gendarmes pulled aside the barricades, scratching a hole in the silence.

I took Clara's arm. She pulled herself away from me. She wanted to walk on her own. On her own and in front. She knew the way to Saint-Hiver's rooms. Coudrier and I only had to follow her. We followed. It was as if a young bride was inspecting the *gendarmerie nationale.* The men straightened themselves and lowered their heads. They wept for the mourning bride. It was snowing on France's gendarmerie. Then it was the turn of the *Compagnons Républicains de Sécurité,* muskets at ease, to see the bride break through their ranks. They, who had just been merrily beating up rioting prisoners, now felt their hearts beating in their helmets. The bride ignored the lot of them. The bride was staring at the tall grey gate. The gate opened all by itself onto the prison's main courtyard. In the middle of it, a grand piano was quietly smouldering away among the overturned chairs. A straight column of smoke was ferrying it up to the heavens. The warders' caps fell to the ground as the bride passed by. Moustaches quivered. The back of a hand chased away a tear. The bride was now gliding down the prison corridors, so silent that it was as if the whole place was deserted. Alone and white, the bride was floating like the memory of those ancient walls, around her the furniture looked as if it had always been overturned, and those torn-up photos scattered across the floor (a flautist with his head at an angle, a sculptor's fist clutching his iron chisel . . . a wastepaper bin overflowing with incredibly neatly written rough drafts, in a cramped hand, with crossings-out done with a ruler) as if they were ancient snaps. And so, floating in silence, the bride went along the corridors, up the spiral staircases, haunted the galleries until at last the door she'd been looking for was there in front of her and an old warder with red eyes and trembling hands tried to stop her:

"Don't, Mademoiselle Clara, you mustn't . . . "

But she pushed the warder aside and went into the room. Inside, men in leather jackets were taking measurements, while others, with small brushes between the tips of their gloved fingers, were dusting every inch of it. There was a doctor with a deathly wan face, and a priest in prayer, who suddenly got to his feet, his alb dazzling bright, his chasuble taking wing and his stole flapping, to stand between the bride and what she had decided to see.

45

She pushed the priest aside with more force than she had used on the old warder and then found herself alone, utterly alone now, in front of a mutilated form. It was twisted, frozen. Bones emerged from its flesh. It no longer had a face. But it still seemed to be screaming.

The bride looked long and hard at what she had come to see. None of the men there even dared to breathe. Then the bride did something which all of them, doctor and priest included, must have wondered about for the rest of their days. She put to her eye a small black camera, which had emerged from God knows where in all that whiteness, she stared once more for a moment at that mutilated corpse, then came the crackling of a flash bulb and the gleam of eternity.

III

COMFORTING CLARA

"What are you going to do now?"
"Comfort Clara."

Chapter 8

O H REALLY? AND how are you going to go about comforting Clara, my little lad? You who were so set against this marriage, what on earth can you come up with? How about . . . that deep sense of relief you are feeling despite yourself (because you do feel relieved, somewhere deep down, don't you Benjamin? you do feel just a tinsy bit relieved). How are you going to hide that from her? This time it's not a simple question of dreaming up a nice little porky to calm down an unpublished and unpublishable colossus . . . this time it's something else, it's pain, real pain, the uncut version, unnameable pain, laid on with all the skilful refinement that Sod Almighty is capable of. If Saint-Hiver had died of a heart-attack on his wedding day, happiness overflowing from his coronaries, his soul bursting, like some people die of indigestion, with a blissful smile on his face, then the job wouldn't have been that hard . . . But like this? What now? What to do? What to say? Because my brother-in-law to be's death was a slow and horrible one, a slow roasting on the spit. Tortured according to all the rule books of horror, tortured to the full, to the bitter end. There wasn't even any consolation in the idea that his last thought must have been for Clara . . . No, his last thought must have been if only it would stop, and his penultimate one as well, if only it would end, if only they would finish him off. Whoever did that to him didn't pull any punches . . . And you're going to comfort Clara, are you? Clara, who locked herself up in her dark room as soon as she got home from her lovely wedding, all alone under her red bulb, developing the martyr in real time, the entire household already in bed for ages but holding back from sleep, her way of accompanying her man I suppose, of understanding what they did to him, of uniting herself with him who had been so alone during that time, so abandoned, so utterly *cast off*, as they used to say when talking of the loneliness of a pebble . . . because that's the true nature of torture, it's not just a matter of hurting somebody, it's a matter of casting him off far enough that he loses touch with humanity, no longer has any connection with it, just a screaming solitude, and perhaps Saint-Hiver was in such agony that he didn't even think that death could relieve him . . . And you, you're going to comfort Clara even

49

though she's understood all of that, drop by drop, during her long red night . . .
after the departure of Amar.

"Will you be all right, my son?"

"I'll be all right, Amar."

"Can Yasmina do anything?"

"She can take the dress away, give it to someone else, do what she likes with it . . ."

"Very well, my son. Can Hadouch do anything?"

"Take back the Chambord, and tell him I'm sorry about our little drive."

"Yes, my son. And I, can I do anything?"

"Amar . . ."

"Yes, my son?"

"Thank you, Amar."

"Forget it, my son, *in niz beguzared*, that too will pass away."

Okay, okay, but some things do pass away more quickly than this photo development session . . . Children tucked in, lights out, the sweltering covers on my bed, and the red bulb in the dark room . . . How much of Clara will there be left to comfort when she at last returns to the light of day? Do you reckon you'll be able to plant something new in that desolation, Malaussène? You're so sublimely optimistic it's enough to make anybody puke . . . Pour a little brotherly love over it all and everything will be hunky-dory. Is that it? As a matter of fact, you're just loving the idea of comforting Clara, aren't you? And the more difficult it will be, the better. Come on, cough it up! You so wanted to keep your little sis all to yourself that, now you've got her, it would be a pity not to make the most of it . . .

*

And so on and so forth all night. Until that fatal phone call.

"HELLO!" (A rusty screech. Queen Zabo.)

She yelled so loudly that it sat me up.

"Half a decibel lower, your Majesty, I have a large family sleeping here."

"At this time?"

True. It was ten in the morning already, and Julie had gone.

"Didn't have a wink all night, your Majesty. I thought it was just daybreak."

"Insomnia is an illusion idlers have, Malaussène. During our lives we always sleep far more than we imagine."

Here we go . . . the unchanging technique to get the conversation started: a service with top spin. But I was in no mood to play ping-pong that morning.

"I thought that we had a sufficiently full and frank discussion last time, didn't we?"

"Frank but not full, Malaussène. I have something to add."

"What's that?"

"My condolences."

Jesus, her condolences . . . True enough, we were now going to have to swallow our way through platefuls of condolences.

But, hang on a sec, how did she know?

"Death travels quickly, Malaussène, on the wings of the press! They flutter down every morning onto my desk."

Definitely in no mood for a chat.

"And apart from this deeply moving expression of your heart-felt sympathy, to what else do I owe this phone call, your Majesty?"

"Apologies, Malaussène."

(What?)

"Please accept my apologies."

It must have been the first time in her life that she'd said those words. Hence my suspicious astonishment.

"I fired you in the heat of the moment, and I'm sorry I did. Loussa told me when he got back. About your sister, I mean. And this marriage that was bugging you . . ."

("That was bugging you"?)

"You were depressed, Malaussène. And I never sack anyone for nervous depression."

"You didn't sack me. I resigned."

"That's right, just as if you were committing suicide."

"It was a decision that had been maturing for some time."

"Never talk about maturing and you in the same breath, my lad, you couldn't even mature camembert, let alone a decision . . ."

(Here we go again . . .)

"At your age you ought to know that people don't just resign, they leave with massive golden handshakes. That's what maturity's all about, Malaussène."

"Okay, your Majesty, how about giving me two years' salary, then. Will that do for you?"

"No way. You won't get a red cent out of me. I just want to offer you something else."

Never accept one of Queen Zabo's offers.

"Listen . . ."

"No, you listen to me, Malaussène. We're halfway through the morning already. And, first of all, listen to this: each and every time you try to get away from me – last year during your fake sick leave and the day before yesterday with your so-called resignation – you wind up firmly planted in the shit, swimming in a sea of it, aren't I right?"

(Put like that, I had to admit there was an element of truth in it . . .)

"Pure coincidence, your Majesty."

"Coincidence? Don't make me laugh. By dumping the Vendetta Press, you emerge from your nest and the world gobbles you up at the first flutter of your little wings."

Funnily enough, I'd never thought of a publishing house as a nest before. It seemed to me to be more a matter of corridors, angles, levels, basements and cupboards under the stairs, the inextricable chemical still of creation: an author enters stage left from the veranda, all bursting with new ideas, and exits stage right through the street door, all sliced up into volumes, straight into a disinfected cathedral of a warehouse.

"Are you listening to me, Malaussène? Good. On to the next point, then. You don't want to play at being a Scapegoat any more. That I can accept. It took me all night, but I can finally accept that. You couldn't spend your entire life being bollocked for everyone else's balls-ups. You're not a Christian, nor a masochist, nor even sufficiently mercenary. So I've decided to offer you something else."

I then heard myself ask:

"So, what have you decided to offer me, your Majesty?"

Oh! Of course I said it with suitable sarcasm, with a hint of ironic distance in my voice. But she wasn't taken in. She uttered her victory cry:

"Love, my lad! I'm offering you love!"

(Love? I've got Julie. I've got the kids. I've got Julius . . .)

"Let's get this one straight from the word go, sonny Jim. It's not a crush I'm talking about, nor even that run-of-the-mill affection which your peculiar charm may occasionally arouse in other people. What I'm offering you is love with a capital 'L', all the love in the world!"

She was having a good giggle between the lines, I could hear it in her voice. But the lines themselves were serious. There was a bee in Queen Zabo's bonnet, and it was buzzing in my direction. (Love with a capital "L": suspicion with a capital "S".)

"So, what do you reckon? Going directly from hatred to love is one hell of a promotion, don't you think?"

"Right now, what I need is a cup of coffee, your Majesty, a nice cup of Turkish coffee, with a nice lower-case 'c'."

"Come and have one here!"

That invitation was the flick of the angler's wrist, when he reckons he's hooked his prey.

"Sorry, your Majesty, but my first cup of high-society coffee this morning will be with Chief Superintendent Coudrier, at eleven o'clock sharp, at police headquarters."

*

The honest truth. But before going to see Chief Superintendent Coudrier I went downstairs to the kids' flat to make myself a cup of my own coffee, in my own Turkish coffee pot, with its long spout, which, long ago, Stojilkovicz had brought me from Imotsky, his native village. Was Uncle Stojil still quietly translating Virgil in Saint-Hiver's can? I reckoned that the prison riot must have blown one hell of a blast through his old Graffiot dictionary. Let the foam rise, go down again, then rise again, a golden velvet, and go down again, three times: Turkish coffee. Drink it unhurriedly, sip after sip, once the grounds have settled into a murky pool at the bottom of the cup. Hand the cup when drunk to Thérèse, who turns it over into a saucer and, in that brown sludge, reads what the day has in store.

"You will be offered two things today, Benjamin. You must accept one of them and refuse the other."

Jeremy and Half Pint were at school. Julie was off Julie alone knew where. Old Thian was walking Verdun in Père-Lachaise cemetery. But Thérèse was still there, faithful to her stars, and so was Clara . . .

"Thérèse, and Clara?"

"In the bedroom, Benjamin. Yasmina's come back."

Who says that Arabic is a guttural language? A dry desert voice, a gasping of sand and thorns? Arabic is also the language of the doves, the promise of faraway fountains. Yasmina was cooing: "*Wa eladzina amanu wa amilu essalahat* . . .". Yasmina was sitting on Thian's story-telling stool: "*Lanubawanahum min eljanat ghurafan* . . .". Yasmina's buttocks were spilling over the edges and, from Yasmina's bill, a song of consolation poured forth, Clarence the dead prince's elegy, and the young widow's first slumbers. For, sure enough, Clara had fallen asleep. No smile on her face. Peace hadn't yet returned, but she was still sleeping, her drooping hand in Yasmina's hand . . . "*Tajri min tahtiha ellanhar halijin fiha* . . .".

"You coming, Julius?"

Julius the Dog had sat up in vigil all night outside the dark-room door. But it was over. Clara was asleep. Julius the Dog got up and followed me.

*

His lower jaw had been torn away. It flopped down onto his chest. His mouth, with its crown of teeth, was screaming from the front pages of all the morning papers.

His right eye was hanging like a pendulum at the entrance of the pit. GOVERNOR OF MODEL PRISON BRUTALLY MURDERED BY HIS PRISONERS. His entire body was scratching at the air. VICTIM OF HIS OWN LAXITY? His legs were folded backwards: a dead heron. AMNESTY? WHO MENTIONED AMNESTY? His fine lock of white hair had gone; his scalp with it. WORSE THAN MURDER-ERS! And that colour ... what progress the four-colour process had made! PRISON OF BLISS WAS HOME OF HATRED. The Métro nodded, of course, nodded away with its countless heads. And had its doubts. How could such a thing happen? HOW COULD IT HAPPEN? On mornings like that, the people in the Métro have heads like headlines.

> *As for those who believed,*
> (Yasmina's voice sang)
> *and who have accomplished good works*
> *we shall make them dwell*
> *in the gardens forever ...*
> (So sang Yasmina, her voice evoking
> clear streams
> running below spacious rooms ...)

Chapter 9

"COFFEE?"

Chief Superintendent Coudrier's office was an old memory in which the furniture hadn't changed. Napoleonic from floor to ceiling, including the bookcase and the entire collection of commemorative knick-knacks to the little Corsican. Napoleonic to the tips of my fingers, which were holding a coffee cup stamped with an imperially capital "N".

"I seem to remember that you are a connoisseur of coffee."

Quite. And I seemed to remember the coffee made by Elisabeth, Chief Superintendent Coudrier's till-death-do-them-part secretary: far from Turkish, not at all velvety, a mixture of nitroglycerine and gunpowder which Elisabeth dumps into your cup, without the slightest precaution, from her great spindly height.

"Thank you, Elisabeth."

Then, as ever, off with Elisabeth, without a word, through the antique air-cushioned door which protected the Chief Superintendent from the rest of the Republic. She'd left the coffee pot behind her, on its silver tray, just by the leather blotter – chats with Chief Superintendent Coudrier could last a very long time.

"Good. Now, let's sum up the situation, shall we, Monsieur Malaussène?"

With a push of his foot, he lowered the intensity of his rheostat like he was turning the volume down. The curtains, which stayed drawn until nightfall, made even the half-light in Chief Superintendent Coudrier's office Empire green.

"Two years ago, stop me if I'm wrong, you were employed as a Scapegoat in a department store, in which bombs started to go off wherever you happened to be. Everything seemed to point to you, and yet you were innocent. Isn't that right?"

(It is. It is.)

"Fine. Then, last year, one of our police officers was killed in Belleville, the old women in the neighbourhood were having their throats cut, the old men of Paris were being drugged up to their eyeballs, your friend Julie Corrençon was the victim of attempted murder aggravated by particularly vicious torture and, for each of these crimes, you became an increasingly probable suspect.

You were turning into a walking anthology of presumptions, and yet . . . "

(Here, he stared at me as the dots dot dotted . . .)

"Not only were you innocent, but you were, so to speak, innocence made flesh."

(In a sense.)

"And then, yesterday, I was told of the particularly brutal murder of a prison governor. I sent along one of my subordinates, who immediately sparked off a riot by accusing the prisoners. So, to reestablish law and order, I went there myself and, as I was about to return to my office, whom should I find in my path?"

(Me.)

"You, Monsieur Malaussène."

(What did I tell you . . . ?)

A pensive sip of coffee and a change of tone:

"We have known each other for some time, and I seem to have noticed that you are very much attached to your sister Clara."

(Quite an attachment, that's right . . .)

The Chief Superintendent slowly nodded his head.

"I suppose that you were not very keen about her marrying Saint-Hiver?"

(Ah, so that's it!) I felt my nerves go taut.

"Not really, no."

"That I can understand . . . "

The light dimmed another semitone.

"A prison governor . . . "

His voice had indeed gone all understanding.

"Who was almost sixty years of age . . . "

He gave me a wistful smile.

"It would almost be like handing a schoolgirl over to a Chief Superintendent on the verge of retirement."

(What to do at moments like that? Laugh politely or tell him there's life in the old pig yet?)

"Forgive me. I was teasing you. Another drop of coffee?"

(Yes, a nice drop of pure black coffee to cast some light on the situation.)

"Why didn't you try to stop this marriage?"

(Because the person who will successfully stop one of the Malaussène offspring from doing what they want hasn't been born yet. Those kids were their mother's children, passion fruit!)

"Clara was in love."

"Indeed."

(That was obviously not going to do the trick.)

"And of age."

"Legally, yes. But of all your brothers and sisters, she is the one whom you most consider to be your own child. Isn't that right?"

That took the words out of me. How the hell did Coudrier know that? So I immediately spilled the beans:

"I was the one who delivered her."

Then added:

"Me and my friend Ben Tayeb."

No reaction. He was still following his train of thought.

"And yet, isn't Clara also the one who adopts the role of mother in your household when your own mother is away?"

(My own mother had done a bunk with Inspector Pastor, one of his very own coppers, his favourite, even! In fact, this was family business we were talking about. Specially since I'd just twigged that it could only be old Thian who was keeping him informed!)

"Am I wrong?"

(No, you're right. Even before Louna got married, it was Clara who'd helped Yasmina fill in as a mother.)

"And so, if she had married Saint-Hiver, you would have simultaneously lost both your child and your mother."

(Which gave me two motives in one for getting rid of old Saint-Hiver.)

"You mean I . . ."

He cut me off at once.

"What I mean is that you have an extraordinary knack of dropping yourself in the shit, young man."

At that point, I thought I'd better intervene:

"Saint-Hiver was murdered the day before yesterday during the night. And, that night, I was asleep at home, downstairs, with the children."

(On a chair.)

"I know. Inspector Van Thian told me. On a chair."

(What did I tell you? . . . It was old Thian, of course.)

"But do you know where Ben Tayeb was that night? Or Black Mo? Or the Berber?"

(Shit no, not that!)

"Those people are your firm friends, Monsieur Malaussène. They knew that you disapproved of this marriage and, if they are excellent friends, they are certainly not angels. It is just what they would have done if they had decided to do you a good turn. And I do not suppose that the death of a head jailer weighs very heavily on the consciences of Belleville."

"They'd never do that to Clara!"

I was so sure of that, that I bawled it out. He let the echoes die down before agreeing with me:

"I don't think so, either. But a run-of-the-mill investigator might."

(Long live investigators that don't run on mills!)

"You do realise that you're one in a million?"

(There was a sudden tone of admiration in his voice.)

"Never seen anything like it in all my years on the force! We could use you to train entire generations of investigators . . ."

(Sorry?)

"Wherever you happen to be, whatever you happen to be doing, people get murdered, it rains corpses, most of them in horribly mutilated states, blown to pieces by bombs, heads splintered by exploding bullets, tortured in indescribable ways, and everything points to you: motive, acquaintance, opportunity, daily round, family life . . ."

(A flurry of professional enthusiasm.)

"You are a first-class exercise for any apprentice police officer! When you protest your innocence, you are merely denying the obvious. It is impossible to imagine that such a network of presumptions, such an incredible convergence of suspicions could lead to the arrest of an innocent man . . ."

His palms were flat on his desk, elbows akimbo, arse in the air and head lit up by a cone of Napoleonic light. He looked like a historian driven gaga by the suspense of the battle he was narrating.

"You expect to meet a monster, the most Machiavellian of murderers and, at the end of your inquiries, what you find is a model of virtue!"

(In fact, maybe it was me he wanted to marry.)

"An irreproachable son, such a devoted brother that he's willing to sacrifice himself, a loyal friend, a faithful lover . . ."

(I look after my dog pretty well, too . . .)

"The investigator's heart slumps down into his boots!"

(Stop, I beg of you . . .)

He stopped. Just like that. His butt sank back onto his leather chair with the speed of an air-cushioned door.

"And so, Monsieur Malaussène, I have something of importance to tell you."

Silence. Coffee. More silence. Then, as calm as you like:

"You are starting to be a serious pain in the arse."

(I beg your pardon?)

"You cast such an impenetrable shadow over our inquiries that, thanks to your virtuous little existence, you make us waste one hell of a lot of time!"

Things were starting to look serious on the other side of the desk.

"Are you really suggesting that the police force exists with the sole aim of proving your innocence once a year?"

(I don't imagine anything of the sort, I don't ... Don't even have any imagination.)

"Listen to me carefully."

I listened. He talked with such controlled fury that, as listeners go, I was all ears!

"I shall endeavour to find out who murdered Saint-Hiver, Monsieur Malaussène. I have half a dozen prominent politicians on my back – left, right and centre – who are all being highly insistent. Meanwhile, you will keep yourself as far as possible away from this business. I shall give my orders accordingly. My men will question neither you nor your friends in Belleville. The newspapers will leave you absolutely alone. In return, once you have answered my questions, you will wipe from your mind the slightest recollection of that prison and its prisoners. If you take the slightest step outside Paris in the direction of Champrond, if, willy nilly, you cast the slightest shadow over my investigations, if you put the tiniest suspicion in the heads of any of my men, I shall then have you locked up as a preventative measure until the end of our inquiries. Is that clear? And perhaps even for the rest of your natural life . . . "

(Just keep innocent . . .)

"Be under no illusions, Malaussène. I am a copper. I uphold law and order against whatever tries to undermine them. And innocent people, when they are like you . . . "

(Okay, I get the picture.)

He suddenly calmed down, but his smile didn't come back. He poured me another cup of coffee without asking if I wanted any.

"Very well. Now, tell me about Saint-Hiver."

*

And, God help me, tell him I did. I told him everything I knew, that is to say, not a lot: how he met Clara, his enthusiasm for his mission, his unwillingness to reveal Champrond to the eyes of the modern world, his visits to Summerhill, to the University of Stanford at Palo Alto, his lectures on behaviourism, his knowledge of the work of Makarenko, in fact everything he'd told me . . .

And, as the atmosphere had grown less tense, I asked him if he had any idea of what really had happened. No. It wasn't the prisoners, was it? He didn't know. When the local gendarmerie arrived on the scene, they witnessed an incredible sight: the prisoners dressed in tail coats in the main courtyard where Joseph, the old head warden, had told them to congregate while he went off to see Saint-Hiver for his final instructions regarding the ceremony. They were all deeply affected. According to the statement of the gendarmerie major, most of them were quietly crying, while others were sobbing . . . men who'd been locked up for life for the murder of one or more persons! Of course, they could have been putting it on . . . of course, it could have been a mass put-on . . .

Whatever, things only began to turn nasty when Inspector Bertholet arrived. The idiot had started questioning the prisoners right there, in the yard, in the open air, all left standing there like a load of boarding-school boys after a fight in the dorm. Bertholet had narrowly escaped being lynched and the gendarmerie had to call in a squad of riot police, based in Etampes. The riot police had obviously barged straight in firing tear gas, one of the canisters landed inside the grand piano, the prisoners took shelter in the buildings, where they were hunted down, their work destroyed, the photos celebrating their creative lives in the prison torn from the walls, as if, in fact, Saint-Hiver was being murdered all over again . . .

At that point, Coudrier became pensive:

"Stupidity, Malaussène, stupidity . . . in the end there are only two things wrong with this world: your kind of innocence and the police's stupidity."

And so, when he arrived on the scene of the crime, it had become an encircled battlefield. He calmed down the situation then, on leaving, came across that stationary wedding party which Bertholet was in the process of winding up as well.

"Well then, do you have nothing more to tell me about Saint-Hiver?"

No, I had nothing more to tell him.

"One last question."

(Oh yes?)

"That photograph which your sister Clara took . . ."

(Ah . . .)

"Why do you think she took it?"

A hard question to answer, that. I would have had to go all the way back to when Clara first set eyes on the world. Her strange attentiveness. As if Clara had always refused to have things revealed to her, as if, right from the start, she'd always insisted on discovering them for herself. My Clara . . . Staring at the worst in order to accept it. As always.

"You mean the only way she could make her grief bearable was to photograph that mutilated body?"

"Thanks to your men, that 'mutilated body' as you put it, has been hanging on every newsagent's meat hooks since first thing this morning."

He took the blow. It was fair enough. Among the other cock-ups, Inspector Bertholet had given the vultures of the press free access to Saint-Hiver's corpse.

"Given that the news-stands were going to ram it down her throat for at least a week, Clara preferred to see the entire horror with her own eyes. Is there anything wrong in that, Chief Superintendent?"

*

After Clara's photo, we left the prison quickly. Clara was back down to earth again. Her heels clicked audibly along the corridors. The chaplain had trouble keeping up with us. Outside, everyone had got out of the cars. The family took in Clara. Belleville closed in around Clara. Clara cried at last. She cried in Amar's arms.

Reassured by this expression of grief, the chaplain put his oar in:

"Divine mercy, my child . . ."

Clara turned round towards him:

"Divine mercy, father?"

He had been about to launch into an inspired sermon, but he fell as silent as the holy of holies. Then he noticed little Verdun, hidden away in Thian's arms, and murmured:

"As for the baptism of this child . . ."

There, too, he was politely cut off.

"Don't even think about it, father. Just look at her."

Old Thian brandished Verdun in front of him, as though presenting arms during an inspection. Verdun's stare shot out, pinning down the priest. He instinctively took a step backwards.

"You see," Clara said, "our little Verdun doesn't think your God's altogether . . ."

She looked for the right word for a second. Then, smiling with true divine mercy:

"That your God's altogether reasonable."

*

"Whatever happens, do not forget what I have told you, Monsieur Malaussène. I shall get the people who did this, but on one condition and one condition alone, that you get out of my hair."

Coudrier opened the door. He showed me out.

"If either you or your friend Corrençon puts even the tips of your noses in this business, then I'll have you locked up."

Then, as I was passing in front of him:

"What are you going to do now?"

"Comfort Clara."

61

Chapter 10

A ND WHAT IF publishing houses really were like nests? Not comfy ones,
of course, with beaks and claws, natch, and places you can fall out of
(but who ever passed his entire life in a nest?), but a nest all the same, a nest
made of printed leaves, constantly being revamped by the long-beaked Zaboes
of this world to follow the latest fads, an age-old nest woven out of sentences,
with a gluttonous hatch of new hopes cheeping in it, ever tempted to go off and
nestle elsewhere, but in the meantime opening wide their beaks and going: Do I
have talent, Madame? Do I have genius?

"Quite a feather in your cap, my dear Joinville, I must admit. If you follow
my advice, you'll turn into a high flier . . . Ah, Malaussène, there you are!"

Queen Zabo packed the young writer off to do another six months' work on
his manuscript, then led me into her office, or should I say into her parlour?

"Take a seat, my lad . . . Have you ever read any of young Joinville's stuff?
What do you make of it?"

"If I had a good nose, I'd probably be able to identify his after-shave."

"He's a young writer who's typically French. At present, all he has are ideas,
which he mistakes for emotions, but I haven't given up hope of one day making
him tell a story. I've got one hell of a project for you, Malaussène."

Julius the Dog sat his fat arse down next to mine. Like me, Julius the Dog found
Queen Zabo amazing. With his twisted neck and lolling tongue, Julius the Dog
seemed to be wondering just how many seconds this woman had agreed to
squander on the process of being born.

"But first of all, do tell me. Are the police bothering you about this unpleasant
business?"

"No, it's more me that's bothering them."

"Really? Then you should stop doing that at once, Malaussène. It's an essential
part of our plans. No dallying with the police. I'm going to need you full-time."

Then she segued rapidly into the intercom:

"Calignac? Malaussène's here. We'll join you in the conference room. Tell

Gauthier and Loussa, too, if he's here."

She moved to switch it off, then:

"And Calignac? Lay on some coffee."

And to me:

"I did invite you round for a cup of coffee this morning, didn't I?"

*

Then, in the corridor:

"One more thing, Malaussène. You may accept this offer, or you may tell me where to put it, we may even end up at each other's throats again, but whatever happens, not a word to anyone, agreed? This is a company secret."

*

Different premises, different shakes. Vendetta Press coffee is office coffee. One franc twenty in the slot, a scalding plastic cup in your fingers, which is totally weightless when empty . . . a writer-cup, in fact, which should be drained very slowly – the bin was just to hand.

Loussa, Calignac and Gauthier were waiting for us. At the sight of Julius the Dog, Gauthier blanched and, sure enough Julius's muzzle was firmly implanted between the young man's buttocks before I'd had time to call my dog to heel. It never failed. What sort of stench could this highly educated *Normalien* who was devoted to the book trade possibly give off? Calignac, the sales manager, laughed his rugby player's laugh then went to open the window so as to give Julius's odours an escape route. When he'd finishing checking Gauthier's ID, Julius the Dog loped off to give Loussa de Casamance a good lick on the hand, as though approving my choice of friends.

"Right, let's be seated, then."

Thus spake Zabo. A council of her ministers always began with this ritual invitation: "Right, let's be seated, then." Not: "Sit down", nor even: "Hi, there lads, how you all doing?" No, always with precisely the same words: "Right, let's be seated, then."

Which, with a few discreet scrapings of chair legs, is what we did.

"Malaussène, if I said 'Babel' to you, what would spring to mind?"

The session had opened.

"Babel? I see a tower, your Majesty, mankind's first block of council flats, the multitudes of the Almighty Paranoid flooding in from the four corners of the earth to the hell hole of Dien Bien Phu then, tired of wandering, putting up the Empire State Building so that they can live in it like sardines."

63

She smiled. She smiled, did our Queen. Then she said:

"Not bad, Malaussène. Now, if I said 'Babel', but first added two initials: J. L. Babel. J. L. B., what springs to mind then?"

"J. L. B.? Our very own J. L. B.? Our best-seller factory? Our goose who lays the golden inkwells? He puts me in mind of my sisters."

"Sorry?"

"Of Clara and Thérèse. Two of my sisters."

And of Louna, too, the third one, the nurse. J. L. B. was my sisters' favourite writer. A few years ago, when Louna met Laurent, her medic husband, I lent them my bedroom. They got into bed and only got out of it again a year and a day later. A whole year of full-time love. Of love and reading. Every morning, I used to take them up their supply of food and books. Then, every evening, Clara and Thérèse used to take down the dirty plates and finished books. Sometimes, they would hang around. As they both had homework to do, I'd clamber up after them and would find the two little girls in bed between the lovebirds, with Louna serving them up huge slices of J. L. B.:

Scarcely had Sophia the nanny departed with little Axel-Jules than Tania and Serguei were deliciously rediscovering each other's bodies. It was 6.12 pm. In three minutes' time, Serguei would have a controlling interest in the National Ballistics Company.

That's J. L. Babel for you (or J. L. B. to his fans), a writer who's buttered on both sides, whom lovers dunk into their breakfast-time hot chocolate each morning, and who lulls Madame Bovary to sleep each evening. And he represented the Vendetta Press's largest print-runs. He paid our salaries.

"Fourteen million readers per title, Malaussène!"

"Who don't give a toss what you think . . ."

"Which gives us a figure of fifty-six million readers if we multiply by the x4 book-lending coefficient," Calignac added, all his lights suddenly switching on.

"In twenty-seven countries and in fourteen languages," Gauthier emphasised.

"Not to mention the Soviet market, which is now opening up thanks to *perestroika* . . ."

"I've started translating him into Chinese," my mate Loussa chipped in, before adding fatalistically: "There's more to life than literature, shit-for-brains, *you shangye*, there's also business."

All in all, one hell of a business. Thanks, in large measure, to one of Queen Zabo's little strokes of genius: the author's anonymity. For none of us, seated around that table, with the sole exception of Her Majesty, knew who J. L. B. really was. The Vendetta Press's name didn't even appear on those huge glossy dust jackets. Just three upper-case italic initials at the top of each tome, *J. L. B.*; then three lower-case italic initials at the bottom, *j. l. b.* Which naturally gave the impression that J. L. B. published J. L. B. and that his genius owed nothing to anybody . . . a self-made man, like all his heroes, the lord of all he surveyed, distribution circuits included, who had constructed his own tower and who, from way up there, cocked a snook at God Almighty. Better than a surname, more than a first name, J. L. B. had turned himself into a set of initials, three letters which could be read in any language. And the boss bridled up her triple crop above her wasted body:

"A secret, my children, is what powers a myth. Those businessmen described in J. L. B.'s novels all ask themselves the same question: who is he? Who knows them so well that he can depict them so faithfully? This emulation bred on curiosity percolates down into the world of small businesses as well and this, believe you me, goes some way to explain our turnover!"

The figure was unfurled, like a standard:

"Almost two hundred million copies sold since 1972. Coffee, Malaussène?"

"Yes please."

"Gauthier, a coffee for Malaussène. Have you got the right change?"

A little shower of coins into the machine's innards. Steam, glugging, castor sugar.

"Now, Malaussène. We've decided to pull a big publicity stunt for the publication of J. L. B.'s next novel."

"A stunt, your Majesty?"

"We're going to reveal his identity."

Never interrupt the boss when the inspiration's flowing.

"Great idea. So, who is J. L. B. then?"

A pause.

"Drink your coffee, Malaussène. This is going to come as a shock."

Would life really be worth living if there wasn't a good director working on it? And, ladies and gentlemen, isn't it the brilliance of the direction which distinguishes us, apart from a host of minor details, from the beasts of the field? So, I was going to fall flat on my arse when I heard who our prolific J. L. B. really was, then, was I? All right. I put on a suitable dying-with-curiosity expression. But careful not to scald your throat, all the same. Sip the coffee. Gently does it . . . Around the table, they all sat quietly waiting. They were observing me, but all I could see was my poor little Clara, two or three years back, reading a J. L. B. door-stopper on the sly while I was trying to turn her on to Gogol, Clara jumping out of her skin and stashing the book away, and me all ashamed of having barged in on her, feeling like a shit for having bawled out Laurent and Louna, for playing the smart aleck, the bright spark . . . Just read whatever you want, my Clarinette, read whatever comes to hand, don't worry about big brother, it isn't up to him to pick your pleasures for you, your own life will do the choosing, your own desires will be the selector.

There. The coffee was finished.

"Right then, so who is J. L. B.?"

They glanced at each other one last time:

"It's you, Malaussène."

Chapter 11

WHEN I GOT home, Clara was still asleep, Yasmina was still singing and Julie was cooking. This last point was worthy of note: it was the first time I'd seen Julie in front of a stove. Journalists of her kind rarely cook. Their beef is corned, not roasted. Julie spent her life snacking so as to keep tabs on the world. If she hadn't been horribly injured last year (drugged to death, one leg broken in three places, plus double pneumonia) at that very moment she would certainly have been chewing on a chickpea in some subtropical swamp, while trying to figure who was diddling who, for how much and for how long . . . Luckily enough, the hoods who'd given her the third degree had handed me back a Julie who was now spending her time convalescing, while making a happy man of me.

Julie, then, was cooking. She was leaning over a small copper saucepan in which a reddish liquid was popping into sugary craters. She was busy stirring it to stop it from sticking. That simple wrist movement, via her curved shoulder, bent arm and supple spine was enough to make her hips dance. The last few months' enforced rest had beautifully rounded her out. More than ever, the dress which enveloped her was a promise of hidden fullness. When naked, the ochre marks left by the burns turned her into a leopard woman. When dressed, she was still my Julie of three years back, the one I'd awarded myself without a moment's thought, so much did her flowing mane (as J. L. B. would have put it), the autumnal sparkle in her eyes, the graciousness of her shoplifting fingers, the purr of her voice, her hips and her mammaries whisper to me that, if there was one woman made for me, then she was definitely it. One hundred per cent physical, in fact. The woman I love is an all-round creature, a wonderfully superior vertebrate, my ideal mammal, totally female. And, as I'm jammy in love, her interior lived up to her exterior promise: Julie has a beautiful soul. The entire world beats in her heart. Not just the world, but each and every one of the sprogs that make up her world. Julie loves Clara, Julie loves Jeremy and Half Pint, Julie loves Thérèse, Julie loves Louna, Julie loves Verdun – yes, even Verdun – and Julie loves Julius. All in all, Julie loves me.

And, lo and behold, Julie could even cook. An ancillary detail? Bollocks it was. Every woman's magazine confirms the fact: happiness is a recipe book.

"A hollyhock tart, Benjamin."

"Hollyhock?" gasped Jeremy, a young shoot from the concrete jungle.

"One of my father's recipes. Our house in the Vercors was swamped over with hollyhocks. Until the day when my father, the Governor, decided to eat them."

Julius the Dog's mouth watered with a connoisseur's saliva, greed steamed over Half Pint's glasses, the entire house was a hollyhock simmering in its own sugar.

"All the same, Julie, a tart, with Clara in mourning and everything? . . . Do you really think . . . ?"

(Malaussène and the decent thing . . .) Yes, that's right, I really did just half-ask that question. Julie answered without even turning round.

"Haven't you noticed anything, Benjamin? Just listen to Yasmina's singing."

In the children's bedroom, Yasmina was still singing, with Clara's sleeping hand still in hers. But the sorrow had gone out of the song. The trace of a smile was easing out Clara's face.

"Anyway, Yasmina's brought us round some couscous."

*

We ate Yasmina's couscous and Julie's tart while old Thian was giving Verdun her baby food. Since Verdun's birth, old Thian had lost one of his arms. He had to do everything that needed to be done using the hand that wasn't holding Verdun. Now into his sixties, old Thian had found out, as soon as we entrusted him with Verdun, what younger men learn, that being a father means lopping off a limb.

We ate through Yasmina's chanting, which was keeping the ghost of Saint-Hiver at bay.

A little slice of peace. Concentrated chewing. All the same, something was bugging Jeremy. It was written all over his face. And when Jeremy's face can be read, then the worst is often on its way.

"What's up, Jeremy?"

I asked him, although I knew he'd just answer "oh, nothing".

"Oh, nothing."

There. A few more digs with our forks, then Thérèse had a go:

"Jeremy, don't you think you ought to tell us what's bothering you?"

In that stiff, clumsy voice which, from the moment she uttered her first word, had cut Thérèse off from the rest of humanity, making her easily irritated and as sensitive as a naked wire.

"Do I ask you for your horoscope?"

Thérèse and Jeremy are a model of sibling devotion. They can't stand each other, yet stand up for each other whenever they can. The day Jeremy was deep-fried in the fire at his alma mater was the only time I ever saw Thérèse have a fit of professional guilt: "How could I not have foreseen it, Benjamin?" She was literally tearing her hair out, fistfuls of it, like in a Russian novel. Her scrawny arms were flaying around like fishing reels. "What's the point of it all?" She gestured at her books, her tarot packs, her amulets and lucky charms. Her one and only moment of doubt. And, one day, on the way out of the cinema (we'd been to see *Monsoon*, the story of a man who starts out by drinking a lot of whisky and ends up drinking a lot of water), Jeremy turned round and said to me: "If I was a bloke, I mean, if I wasn't her brother, Thérèse is the one I'd go for." There must have been a question mark all over my face, because he immediately added: "She's brilliant, that bird." Then, a little further home: "Hey, Benjamin, do you reckon all the other blokes are too thick to see what a great bird she is?"

Anyway, right there and then, something was up with Jeremy.

It was right in the middle of the hollyhock tart that Half Pint quietly took off his glasses and, while wiping them, said:

"I know."

I asked:

"What do you know, Half Pint?"

"I know what's up with Jeremy."

"Shut it, you!"

Nothing doing. Apart from his own dreams, Half Pint wasn't scared of anything.

"He's wondering if Thian's going to tell us a bit of *The Fairy Gunmother* this evening."

We all raised our heads and turned them towards Thian.

Never underestimate fiction. Especially when it's liberally laced with facts, like old Thian's *Fairy Gunmother*. It's shit that even life's worst disasters can't make you kick. The idea that Saint-Hiver's sad demise might rob him of his slice of myth for one more evening was making Jeremy hurt so much he almost passed out. Old Thian glanced at me, doubled with Verdun's stare which was always aimed in the same direction as his, and I gave a discreet nod.

"I am," Thian answered. "But this evening, it's going to be the last episode."

"Shit! It isn't? Already?"

Relief and panic zigzagged over Jeremy's gob.

"And a short one, at that." Thian went on relentlessly. "It won't even take all evening."

"And then? What are you going to tell us next?"

Jeremy wasn't the only one worried, everyone's face was asking the same question.

69

When it comes down to it, I reckon it was then, in that silence, sitting at the dinner table, that I made up my mind. I suppose I said to myself that if I didn't come up with something sharpish, if Thian was incapable of being a fit successor to himself, then that terrible thing would happen which the responsible educator in me (oh yes!) had always struggled against: group paralysis, blue-neon hypnotism, the idiot box for life.

And so, looking at Jeremy's face falling to pieces, Half Pint's eyes about to brim over, Thérèse's silent anxiety, and thinking about Clara waking up as well, I suddenly took the only way out. I said:

"After *The Fairy Gunmother*, Thian's got seven more fat novels in store for you. Six or seven thousand pages at the very least!"

"Six or seven thousand pages!"

Enthusiasm from Half Pint. Distrust from Jeremy:

"As neat as *The Fairy*?"

"No comparison. Streets ahead."

Jeremy looked long and hard at me. One of those stares which tries to figure out how the conjuror's just managed to turn a cello into a grand piano.

"Oh really? And who wrote these little gems, then?"

I answered:

"I did."

Chapter 12

"IT'S ME, YOUR Majesty?"

"It will be you, Malaussène, if you agree."

"If I agree to what?"

She looked at Gauthier. She said:

"Gauthier . . ."

Little Gauthier opened his old student's briefcase, laid out his little papers and, just when he was about to open his little mouth, was curtly summarised:

"The long and short of it is, Malaussène, that J. L. B. is flourishing, but we have noticed that his foreign sales have started to stagnate."

"And have peaked at between three and four hundred thousand in France."

As for Calignac, he didn't have an old briefcase, nor a pocket calculator, just a large head with a Gascon's elephant-like memory crammed into it.

"We could let things go for another few years, Malaussène, but that isn't how we operate here."

"What is more," Gauthier tried to wheedle his way back in, "a united Europe means a potentially massive market for us."

The Queen nodded charitably:

"So we need to pull off a big stunt for his next book. We're planning one hell of a launch, Malaussène."

As for me, I obviously went back to my initial question:

"So, will you tell me then? Who is J. L. B.? A ghost committee?"

At that, Queen Zabo used her favourite weapon. She leant her scrawny bust over towards Loussa and said:

"Explain it to him, Loussa."

Loussa was the only one of her employees that she was on first-name terms with. Not because he was black, but because they were very old, childhood friends. Their respective fathers, one as black as the other was white, had been rag-and-bone men. "We learnt to read in the same dustbin."

"Okay. Sit still, shit-for-brains, and listen good."

And off Loussa de Casamance went, explaining how J. L. B. was someone who, for the moment, didn't want to become Someone. He wasn't caught up in the "absurd obsession with his own name". Not even Loussa knew who he was. The only person there present who knew him personally was Queen Zabo. A genuine anonymous author, in fact, like a teetotal alkie. I rather liked the idea. The corridors of the Vendetta Press were swarming with obscure first-person singulars whose only aim in writing was to become publicly acclaimed third-person singulars. Their pens wilted and their ink dried up with all the time they wasted courting critics and make-up girls. They were men o' letters from the first flash of the camera and developed hunchbacks from posing at a three-quarter angle for posterity. They didn't write for writing's sake, but for the sake of *having written* – and to give the chattering classes something to chatter about. So, J. L. B.'s anonymity did seem highly worthy to me, never mind what he came out with. But the snag was that today's world is a world of images and market studies had all clearly revealed that the readers wanted J. L. B.'s head. On the dust jackets, on the billboards in their towns, on the pages of their magazines and in the frame of their TVs. They wanted it inside them, pinned to their hearts. They wanted J. L. B.'s head, J. L. B.'s voice, J. L. B.'s signature, they wanted to queue up for fifteen hours to get J. L. B. to dedicate a book to them, to whisper a word in their ears, and to confirm their readerly love with a smile. Countless simple souls, Clara, Louna, Thérèse and a few million more, not posy well-read readers who love saying "I've read so-and-so . . .", but naively solid readers who'd give their eye teeth to be able to say "I've seen him". And, if they didn't get to see J. L. B., to hear him talk, if J. L. B. didn't give them his televised opinion of the state of the planet and the destiny of mankind, then they would quite simply buy fewer and fewer of his books until, little by little, by refusing to become an image, J. L. B. would no longer be good business. Our good business.

I reckoned I was starting to cop on. All the same, my slow methodical wits had me ask:

"And so?"

"And so," Queen Zabo took over again, "there's a snag. J. L. B. *absolutely* refuses to be talked round. There's no way he's going to show himself."

Ah! . . .

"But he's not averse to someone representing him."

"Representing him?"

"Acting his part, if you prefer."

Silence. The round table had suddenly shrunk. Oh well, here we go:

"Me, your Majesty?"

"What do you reckon?"

*

"And you accepted?"

Julie asked, catapulting up from the tangle of our bedclothes.

"I said I'd think about it."

"You're going to accept?"

Her fingers had abandoned my hair and the tone of her voice was new to me.

"I'm going to think about it."

"You'd accept to be that shit-merchant's puppet?"

She was definitely getting stroppy.

"What's eating you, Julie?"

She got to her feet. She looked down at me from a great height. A lingering rivulet of our sweat gleamed between her breasts.

"What do you mean, what's eating me? Do you realise what you've just told me?"

"I haven't said anything yet."

"Listen . . ."

To think how much warmth we'd just given each other, and now she was freezing me out. I didn't like that. It was like opening the front door to find a burglar at home. You feel hemmed in. You get legitimately defensive . . . the most dangerous thing of all.

"What am I supposed to be listening to?"

My voice had changed, too. It wasn't mine any more.

"Haven't you had enough playing silly buggers? Can't you be yourself for once in your life?"

That was, in fact, one of the objections I'd raised to Queen Zabo. But she'd just launched into a fit of Zaboesque hysterics: "'Be yourself', Malaussène, 'be yourself'! 'Identity'? Whatever will you come out with next? Do you think that we, sitting here round this table, are 'being ourselves'? Being oneself, my man, means being the right knight on the right square of the chessboard at the right moment! Or the queen, or the bishop, or even the meanest little pawn!" But I could already hear myself answering Julie, with a venomous streak in my voice, which wasn't like me at all:

"Oh yes? Because I'm not myself, then, am I?"

"No! Not for a second! Never have been! You aren't the father of your children,

73

you aren't responsible for all the fuck-ups you get slapped around for, and now you're going to play at being some shit-head writer who isn't you! Your mother exploits you, your bosses exploit you, and now that bastard as well . . ."

Then I put my oar in:

"Because this beautiful journalist with her lion's mane and heifer's udders is really herself?"

Yes, I said that . . . I can't cross it out, I said it. But Julie being Julie, it wasn't the lion's mane or heifer's udders that got her goat, it was the bit about the journalist.

"At least the journalist is *real*, for Christ's sake, and even more real than that, because she's *at the call of reality*! She doesn't slither her way into J. L. B.'s skin, that public cretiniser, that churner-out of lousy stereotypes, that speculator on the stupidity of the poor!"

What got me, Benjamin Malaussène, howling with rage wasn't the reference to my chameleon nature, but her arrogant denunciation of "the stupidity of the poor".

"And what does our real-world journalist speculate on, then? Have you been out in the street today, Julie? Have you seen Saint-Hiver's smashed gob hanging from all the newsagents' hooks, his broken teeth, his eye out of its socket? Have you seen it or haven't you?"

(Journalism was the only thing we rowed about . . . but really rowed about. On a very short fuse.)

"Nothing to do with it! I've never done stories like that!"

"No, you've done worse!"

"What was that?"

She was so white with fury now and I was so white with rage, that our sheets were looking decidedly in the pink.

"No, not shock-horror pieces like that, Julie, you go in for highly selective horror, the misery at the other end of the world, massacres of freedom fighters, the poor bastard interviewed in his cell the night before his execution, shock horror in an exotic setting with a clean conscience thrown in: focus on the boat people, a tearful lens snaps a little drowned Mexican girl, we have to keep you informed, irreproachable shit, a nice trickle of blood, as pure as molten gold . . ."

She got dressed.

She left.

On the threshold of the door all she said was:

"Tonight's tart wasn't hollyhock, it was rhubarb. Hollyhocks are like you, Malaussène, smothering and inedible."

74

There we were, then. Three years of happiness out the window. I hadn't even managed to tell her why I might be accepting Queen Zabo's offer. Might or might not. Definitely not, in fact. Not at that price, in any case. Consider what a job will earn you, but also what it will cost you. And Julie's going was too high a price to pay. What on earth had made me come out with all of that? As if I didn't already know that Julie's journalistic eye on the world was the only thing saving us from having others make it spin backwards . . . All right, Julie, all right. Tomorrow I'll go to the Vendetta Press and pack Queen Zabo off to play at being J. L. B. in my place. Come to think of it, maybe she was J. L. B. Which would explain why she was the only person who knew him and why he refused to be photographed: with her cauldron of a head on her broomstick body, she'd make even his blind readers run a mile. Right. So I wasn't going to do this job, then. I'd find something else. Definitely. No turning back.

That calmed me down a bit.

I got up. I remade the bed. I got back into it. I stared at the ceiling. Someone knocked on my door. Three short timid knocks. Julie. The three knocks of making it up. I leapt to my feet. I opened it. It was Clara. She looked up at me. She smiled. She came in. She said:

"Julie isn't here?"

I lied.

"No, she had an appointment."

Clara nodded.

"She's been off work for too long."

And I:

"Yes, it's a miracle she held out during even half her convalescence."

One of those conversations between people talking about what's not on their minds.

"She'll be back in a fortnight with a new article," said Clara.

"Or in three months."

Silence.

Silence.

"Sit down, my Clarinette, sit down."

Her two hands in mine, she sat down on the edge of the bed.

"I've got something to tell you, Benjamin."

And then, of course, said nothing.

I asked:

"Has Yasmina gone home?"

"No, she's downstairs listening to Thian's story. She wants to sleep next to me tonight."

Then:

"Benjamin?"

"Yes, sweetheart?"

"I'm pregnant."

And, just in case I needed further explanation:

"I'm expecting a baby."

Chapter 13

"**I** ACCEPT, YOUR Majesty."

"Wonderful, my lad! With your gifts as an actor, your ability to improvise, your greatness as a storyteller and your love of the public, you'll go down a storm, a legend in your own life time!"

"I accept, but only on one or two conditions."

"Go on."

"The first condition is financial. I want one per cent of each copy sold back-dated to include all of the books I'm supposed to have fathered. I want five per cent of the foreign rights, I want to be paid for each interview, to have my sister Clara as my exclusive photographer and, of course, I want to keep my usual salary."

"That's just money talk, Malaussène, which is Calignac's department, not mine."

"I thought giving orders *was* your department."

"Anything else?"

"Yes. I want to meet the real J. L. B. There's no way I'm going to be packed off to the front if I don't know who's sending me."

"That goes without saying. You shall meet J. L. B. this afternoon, at half past four precisely."

"This afternoon?"

"Yes, the appointment has already been made. Knowing you as I do, I was just sure you couldn't say no."

*

So Clara was carrying? Clara had a little lodger? Saint-Hiver was stealing back in through the window? Another passion fruit? Another Malaussène sprog, deserted by his father right from the word go? It was going to be born? Assault and battery without intent to give life? It was going to take the dive? It was going to wander off into the streets one fine day? It was going to stroll in front of news-stands? It was going to drink in the four-colour drama of its existence? Loving optimism had fooled around again with the void? It was going to tumble down from nothingness into the fire? A peeled slice of fruit between the world's jaws? In the name of love! True love? And, meanwhile, it was going to try and understand? Build itself up? A castle of illusions on foundations of doubt, with metaphysical walls, the fixtures and fittings of convictions, the flying carpet of feelings? It was going to take root on a desert island, pathetically waving at passing ships? Yes . . . and it was also going to glide alongside other islands. It was going to eat, drink, smoke, think, love, and then it was going to decide to eat better, drink less, give up smoking, avoid ideas and downgrade feelings. It was going to become a realist. It was going to advise its own children. But it was also going to believe in them, a little. Then stop believing. Listen only to its own engine ticking over, tighten its bolts, get its oil changed more often . . . but without counting too much on it . . .

Something, at least, was sure. Something which depended on me. If Clara really had a lodger, if it was true that my little Clara was going to have a baby, then, God help me help myself, that baby was going to be born *rich*! Not rich with expectations, no, not rich with feelings, nor even necessarily having a thruppence worth of brains – who knows? – but money rich, for Christ's sake, loaded, stinking, rolling in it, overflowing with cash, dosh, spondulicks, folding stuff, ackers! I was going to put a dowry together for it which would make all of Rothschild's savings look like a student grant. Oh yes! I knew all that wouldn't buy it love, but at least it would save it from thinking that money was buying other people love, and from having to work, and believe in the sanctity of labour! Clara's little one could spend its whole life twiddling its thumbs and, given J. L. B.'s cosmopolitan streak, it could twiddle its thumbs with US or Canadian dollars, marks, rubles, piastres, yen, lira, florins, francs and even euros. Yes, if it wanted to, it could even be a federal European thumb-twiddler! What it did with its jackpot didn't interest me in the least. Invest it, share it, squander it, spend it on worthy causes, use it to erect a platinum statue to itself, who cared! And if it packed me off to a hospice with my teeth in a glass, then I'd go away happy with the final reassurance that there really was a meaning to life!

*

But right then, while Queen Zabo and I were in the car heading off towards our mysterious J. L. B.'s mysterious residence, all I could see in my mind's dazzled eye was a pink, naked baby, giggling and bouncing up and down on a huge mattress of banknotes which a friendly breeze had blown together under its innocent behind.

"Stop here!"

"Where do you mean, 'here'?" the taxi driver grumbled.

"There, just by that branch of the Crédit Lyonnais!"

"What do you want the Crédit Lyonnais for, Malaussène?"

"To open an account in my sister's name. It's urgent."

"We're going to be late."

"Give us a break, your Majesty."

*

J. L. B. dwelt in the 16th *arrondissement.* Rue de la Pompe. And his dwelling-place looked more like Herod's palace than the Bethlehem crib. It was one of those wonderful old city mansions, of which the Lord surely cannot have that many.

The flunky who opened the door was just like what you'd expect the flunky behind such a door to be like. Telling us that sir was expecting us, he showed us in, but we still had to sit in expectation for quite some time – in a wood-panelled library in which alphabetic chance had lined up Saint-Simon, Solzhenitsyn, Suetonius and Han Suyin. When life runs out of surprises, this is what it looks like. I was so disgusted I was incapable of describing the rest.

"Good afternoon, my dear!"

Thus our man, with his delightfully tinkling voice, made his entry. Queen Zabo and I stared round towards a door which had been flung open to reveal a bouncy, svelte sixty-year-old, gliding across the library floor with a charming smile held out in front of him.

"Good afternoon, my dear minister."

Not the slightest hint that Queen Zabo was putting it on. Her voice sounded genuinely friendly, the sort of urbane familiarity which makes it sound as if calling a man by his title, decoration or rank is a form of intimacy. They were off the same shelf. Must have played bridge together on frequent occasions, while quipping away like old pals.

"Monsieur Malaussène, I presume?"

The bugger presumed right. And I said to myself that I'd already seen him before somewhere. But where? I wasn't in the habit of hanging out with ministers.

"If you're wondering, young man, then stop. I'm Chabotte. Ex-minister Chabotte, the bogeyman of your turbulent youth, the inventor of the two-seater motorbike, with the rear rider armed with a big stick for putting little boys and girls to beddy-byes."

All that spoken in a weirdly juvenile way, while shaking me vigorously by the hand and with me saying to myself: "Chabotte, Jesus Christ, if Julie could see me now, she'd hit the frigging roof." A fleeting thought of my loved one, which clouded over my eyes and made Chabotte feign alarm.

"Do not fret yourself, young fellow, all that is ancient history now, and I am the first to admit that my motorbike was not the happiest of my inventions. I have one sole passion and that is writing. And I am sure you would agree with me when I say that a man with such novel experiences cannot be all bad."

(Who the hell is this comedian?)

"Shall we step into my study?"

We stepped. With Chabotte gliding across the library in front of us, like a toddler with a hoop. He was just scrumptious. Like a silver spoon fallen out of his own mouth.

"Here we are, then, this way, do take a seat. Tea? Coffee? Whisky? Name your poison. I suppose you will be having your inevitable Vichy water, my dear. Good heavens, how could anybody drink such muck?"

Was Queen Zabo up against someone faster than she was? If so, it didn't seem to bother her. She just sat down on the hardest thing she could find – a small, altogether monkish Louis XIII chair – while I was being swallowed up by an English leather armchair with a pair of massive ears.

"He looks perfect. An indistinct, malleable appearance. Just what is required."

Who, me? Was he talking about me?

"Do please forgive me, Monsieur Malaussène, I have just been speaking about you as if you were not here. It is a hangover from my days as a politician. In politics, one spends most of one's time talking about people who are absent; sometimes even their presence makes little difference."

"Coffee."

"I beg your pardon?"

"You just read out the menu. And I've chosen coffee."

"Ah, yes, coffee! An espresso!"

A graceful twist of his frame towards the parlophone: "Olivier, be so good as to bring us a large glass of Vichy water and a coffee, would you?"

Then, with a twinkle in his eye:

"So, Monsieur Malaussène, tell me everything. What did you imagine the mysterious J. L. B. was like?"

"Like that."

My bent thumb indicated Queen Zabo, sitting quietly on her chair but lapping it all up. A jolly peel of ministerial laughter:

"I do not know if that is the highest compliment you could have paid your boss, but I feel rather flattered myself."

Upon which, Olivier arrived. He wasn't the same as the flunky at the door, just another one who could easily have been the same.

Vichy water.

Coffee.

"No, seriously, how do you see J. L. B.? What, in your opinion, *should* he look like?"

Ah, so that was the question, was it? We were obviously already hard at it . . . I thought for a couple of seconds (Christ, wasn't the coffee good!) and then went:

"Like Concorde."

That got Chabotte going. He opened wide his peepers in amazement, turned straight round towards Zabo and exclaimed:

"Extraordinary! This young fellow is quite extra-ordin-ary!"

Then, to me:

"Bull's-eye, Monsieur Malaussène. You have a perfect understanding of what I mean to do. Concorde! That is exactly it. A flying attaché case! J. L. B. must look like Concorde! Well, young fellow my lad, be ready to be disguised as Concorde! Have you read me?"

"Sorry?"

"Have you read J. L. B.'s novels? My books . . ."

(Well, as a matter of fact . . .)

"You haven't, have you? Rather look down your nose at them, eh? Which is all to your credit, in fact. I want you brand new. Now, let me explain my theory to you. Are you sitting comfortably? Shall I begin? More coffee? No? A cigarette? You don't smoke . . . Very good. Now, attend carefully and keep any questions for the end. The title of my lecture is:

J. L. B., OR FREE-MARKET REALISM

"J. L. B. is a new sort of writer, Monsieur Malaussène. He is more of a man of business than a man of letters. But letters are, in the end, his business. If I cannot claim to have invented a literary genre, then I have certainly set off a *current*. An absolutely original current. From my earliest novels on, *Last Kiss on Wall Street, Gold Mine, The Dollar* and *The Child Who Could Count,* I dug the foundations of a new literary school which we shall, if you have no objections, call Capitalist Realism. Smile, Monsieur Malaussène. Now, *Capitalist Realism,* or, to bring the term up to date, *Free-Market Realism* is in fact the diametric opposite of our sadly missed *Socialist Realism.* While our cousins in the East wrote novels telling the story of a heroic girl from a collective farm who falls in love with a deserving tractor driver and how their mutual passion had to be sacrificed for the good of the Five-Year Plan, my novels are the epic tales of individual fortunes and how nothing, not other fortunes, not the State, not even love, can stop their rising. In my work, man, *the businessman,* is always the winner! Our world is a world of shopkeepers, Monsieur Malaussène, and my aim is to give the shopkeepers of the world their reading matter! If the aristocrats, workers and peasants have all been provided with their literary heroes down the ages, tradesmen never have! 'What about Balzac?' you may object. But, when dealing with business, Balzac produced the very antithesis of heroes. He had already caught the analysis bug! And I do not do analysis, Monsieur Malaussène, I do *the books.* The public I aim at are not book-readers, but book-keepers. Everyone who keeps a shop can also keep his books and no novelist has ever turned this into a point of novelistic excellence. Apart from me! I am the first. And the result? To date, two hundred and twenty-five million copies sold worldwide. I have raised book-keeping to an epic height, Monsieur Malaussène. My novels contain reams of figures, avalanches of stock-market quotes which are as beautiful as cavalry charges. The sort of poetry that appeals to every tradesman. J. L. B.'s success resides in the fact that I have at last given that multitude of merchants their mythical status. Thanks to me, tradesmen now have their gods in the novelistic pantheon. What, today, they are crying out for is a vision of their demiurge. And that is where you come in, Monsieur Malaussène . . ."

Chapter 14

*T*HE MONEY VOCATION *appears early. At four o'clock in the morning. When the binmen are doing their rounds. And any binman's son can be touched by it.*

Knowing that he was one of the dregs of society, sixteen-year-old Philippe Ahoueltène followed his father, enveloped in a rubbish collector's green overalls with their day-glo hems, in order to earn a little pocket money.

In the early light of dawn, as they were driving through Place de la Concorde, Philippe was hanging onto the back of the van when he suddenly saw a tidal wave of people beating against the front of Hôtel Crillon, eager for an unlikely glimpse of Michael Jackson. And Philippe had his first idea: Jackson's trash must be worth a fortune!

With a map of Paris in one hand and a high-society guidebook in the other, Philippe sought out and located stars' dustbins, thus mapping out his first fortune.

After one morning's hunt, he'd acquired Jane Birkin's recently nibbled apple core, Catherine Deneuve's bottle of Dior nail varnish, Richard Bohringer's bottle of Jack Daniels . . .

"Fucking brilliant! So he's going to flog them off, is he? Ace idea, that!"

"Shut up, Jeremy."

"What? Don't you reckon going through stars' dustbins is a really ace idea?"

"Let Uncle Thian read on!"

Three months later, Philippe had twelve enthusiastic bincombers working for him, plus thirty informers who were concierges or concierges' children and all keen to share in the profits of what was soon to be a highly lucrative business.

"What's 'lugrative' mean?"

"Lucrative, Half Pint, with a '*cra*'. It means something that makes loads of money."

"Loadsamoney?"

"Yeah, tons."

"And 'awkin', what does that mean?"

"What?"

"Awkin."

"Ah! 'all keen'! Well . . ."

"You tell him, Thérèse. That way, Uncle Thian will be able to continue!"

Meanwhile, he had graduated out of high school with top grades and bought himself a penthouse in Ivry.

The following year, he opened subsidiaries in London, Barcelona, Hamburg, Lausanne and Copenhagen. His headquarters were situated in a huge office on the Champs Elysées. He won first place in the entrance examination to the Hautes Etudes Commerciales.

"Jesus, what a hero!"

"Jeremy . . ."

"Sorry."

On his eighteenth birthday, he left the H. E. C., slamming the door behind him. When he returned two years later, it was as a teacher.

During those two years, he learnt Danish, Spanish, Dutch, and perfected his knowledge of German and English, the latter of which he spoke with a very slight Yorkshire accent.

He played saxophone at the Petit Journal and had a dazzling career as a stand-off half in the P. U. C. rugby team . . .

There. It was called *Lord of the Currencies* and it was the latest brainchild of ex-minister Chabotte, alias J. L. B. It was as rapid as lightning and as vapid as anything, but the kids were lapping it up so much that even little Verdun started following the text with her eyes as Thian read it out. Thian, who'd never read a single novel for his own pleasure, was a marvellous reader. His voice fleshed out the fiction. It was a perfect gravelly film cop's voice, which heightened whatever he read out. The only reason why Jeremy and Half Pint had dared interrupt the beginning of the reading was because they were so excited. But they were soon caught up in the stream, carried by its current over the depths which Thian's voice dug out, word by word, line by line, in whatever text he read.

Philippe made the acquaintance of Tania while he was setting up a subsidiary in

New York. Their eyes met in the very heart of Greenwich Village.

She, too, had risen from nowhere and she it was who introduced him to Goethe, Proust, Tolstoy, Thomas Mann, André Breton, architechtonic art and serial music. They mixed in high society. Madonna, Boris Becker, Platini, George Bush, Schnabel, Mathias Rust and Laurent Fignon were among their closest friends.

*

I left them, Verdun in old Thian's arms, Thérèse starched into her night dress, Clara in her bed (with her hands already crossed over her belly), Jeremy and Half Pint in the upper bunks with solid gold futures gleaming in their eyes, Yasmina sitting at Clara's feet with an expression of pious seriousness on her face, as if Thian was reading out a *sura* specially concocted by the Prophet in memory of Saint-Hiver.

I got to my feet.

Julius the Dog got to his feet.

We slipped out, as so often we do at that time of night.

*

The Dog and I were off to plead for Benjamin Malaussène before Julie Corrençon. While I rehearsed my speech, Belleville continued to crumble around us: "I agreed to play in this farce to comfort Clara, Julie my love. I agreed because there are times when horror strikes us so hard and true that we absolutely have to abandon 'reality', as you put it, and play somewhere else. I agreed so that the children could play else-where and stop thinking about Saint-Hiver. Jeremy and Half Pint will help me rehearse my lines, Clara will take the photos and Thérèse can act all disapproving. It'll take their minds off things. I also agreed in order to obey Coudrier and steer the family raft as far as possible away from his investigations. I agreed because, all things considered, I think we've had more than our fair share of major fuck-ups recently, don't you? So, I said to myself, right, let's be superficial for once, a bit daft, a tad dishonest. Let's stop being irreproachable, because that's what Coudrier is reproaching us for. Let's just for a moment abandon the inhospitable shores of sublime devotion. You see what I mean, don't you Julie? Let's play. Let's play for a while. And let's play at being J. L. B. since that's the game which is up for grabs."

*

She wasn't in, of course. Knock, knock, knock, Julie? Julius the Dog sat himself down and waited for the door to open. But it didn't. So with pencil, paper and Julius's back as a desk I summarised what I'd just said to myself. I added "I love you", and conjugated it in every tense, mood and voice, said that I would still be her

85

aircraft-carrier, that she could land or take off as often as she wanted . . . It was what we'd said when we first met: "Will you be my aircraft-carrier, Benjamin? I'll come and land on you from time to time so that you can fill me up." Delighted, I answered: "Touch down, my lovely, then take off as often as you want. From now on I'll be sailing in your coastal waters."

I apologised for my nastiness about her journalism and her "highly selective horror", forgive me Julie, I was only trying to hurt you . . . sorry, sorry, and I signed.

Then I stopped for thought.

Something was missing. A truth that I mustn't hide.

Chabotte.

In a post-script I told her that J. L. B. was really Chabotte, ex-minister Chabotte, him and none other. Amazing, isn't it, Julie?

Then I slid it under her door.

*

After his Free-Market Realism lecture, Chabotte led the Queen and me into his private cinema.

"Follow me, Monsieur Malaussène, I am going to show you what a real flesh-and-blood Concorde looks like."

A dozen seats, each with an ashtray. A sloping ceiling and chamfered walls converging around an immaculate screen. Behind us, Antoine, a third flunky identical to the other two, was manoeuvring the eye of the projector. Our visit had turned from being an urbane smiles and chatter session to a top-secret briefing, like James Bond before a mission.

"I am going to turn you into a truer than life J. L. B. You'll see, this is going to be rather fun . . ."

Darkness, a splash of white, then an image on the screen: a forehead. Two wings of black hair greased backwards from a perfect central point. (Jesus, not a single one of them was out of place!)

"As you can see for yourself, Monsieur Malaussène, a Concorde is immaculately groomed."

(He wasn't wrong about that. This customer really did look as if he had a black Concorde parked on his bonce.)

"Do you know whose forehead this is, my dear?"

Queen Zabo hesitated.

"The young Chirac?"

"No. Copnick, Wall Street's éminence grise, at the age of twenty-eight. Notice the height of his forehead, Monsieur Malaussène, the transverse and not perpendicular double lines. There is no room for doubt in that expression, just one hundred per cent energy! J. L. B. must have this forehead and the same haircut. Very well, let us move on. Antoine!"

Click-clack, a sideways movement, and two eyes appeared on the screen. Steely blue, of course, and staring straight ahead. The sort of character who's cooked up a fixed gaze for himself. When he wants to look round, his entire head has to turn like a tank turret.

"Wolbrooth, the tungsten king," Chabotte announced. "Complete personal control over the space industry. What matters, Monsieur Malaussène, is not the colour of his eyes, but the intensity of his stare. See how it shoots out from below his eyebrows. With such a malleable face as yours, you should be able to mimic it perfectly."

And so on and so forth: the weighty jowls of a Flour King, the fleshy chin of an Emperor of Chips (of the silicone variety), the half-smile of a Belgian tinned-food magnate, etc. . . . All in all, the King of Plonkers, in my opinion.

An opinion which Chabotte didn't share:

"And thus we obtain J. L. B.: a fine balance between authority and determination, irony and healthy pleasure. For one thing I would like to emphasise is that J. L. B. is no ascetic. He loves money and luxury in all its forms, good food included, Monsieur Malaussène. You're going to have to put on some weight, flesh yourself out a little."

Chapter 15

"Eat up, eat up, Benjamin my son."

"I can't take any more, Amar. Thanks a lot, but really . . ."

"What do you mean 'but really'? . . . Do you want to become a big writer or don't you, Ben?"

"Leave it out, Hadouch."

"Yeah, all the big names in your roumis literature were podges, just look at Dumas, Balzac, Claudel."

"Leave it out, Simon."

"I reckon they all stuffed themselves with couscous, just like Ben."

"You know what? Mo's right. When you stop and think about it, everything comes from Islam."

"I wonder if Flaubert would have come up with Madame Bovary if it hadn't been for couscous . . ."

"Look, just give us a break, will you?"

"Another helping, Ben."

"Come on, J. L. B., work away . . ."

*

Months of it! Months of forced feeding! Months of J. L. B. special high-calorie couscous! Morning, evening and night! As light as the witticisms of Hadouch and his two henchmen. Of course, my cheeks didn't put on a single gramme. All I got was a pot belly and a flabby arse. With my hollow cheeks, it made me look like an ex-romantic who'd hit the beer barrel.

Chabotte didn't agree with me.

"You are deluding yourself, Monsieur Malaussène. You are filling out and find that surprising. It is simply that, for the first time in your existence, you are weighing in as a real man on the scales of life. I can now call in the tailor."

The tailor had a wop name, fingers like dragonflies and the smile of Danny La Rue. Chabotte merrily gambolled around us, suggesting a pin here and a fold there, considering such-and-such a pinstripe too eye-catching and such-and-such a dark grey too clerical.

"Socks, Monsieur Malaussène. Socks . . . Never neglect one's underclothes. They must meld in perfectly with the suit. Isn't that right, my dear?"

I can now make the following assertion: if you've never stood stark naked in front of your publisher, being smiled at by Danny La Rue, while an ex-Minister of the Interior hops and chatters around you, then you know nothing about complete and utter humiliation.

The result was that they bespoke me three three-piece suits made of one of those ultra-fine exotic fibres which would have bankrupted Gatsby. (Benjamin Malaussène, or the cash-mere kashmir.)

"Now you must wear them, Monsieur Malaussène. Break them in until you feel at home in them. I do not want you to look as if you had just tumbled into your writer's clothes by chance. A best-seller has to be worn in!"

*

"Who's got a lovely new whistle, then, Benjamin my brother?"

"You going to buy up all of Belleville and all?'

"Keep clear of the gutters, Ben. If a pigeon shits on you, it'll cost you a grand per dropping!"

"At the very least."

And, pushed on by Mo and Simon, Nourdine, the little sod, started following me everywhere with an open umbrella to protect me from pigeons.

*

The teaser campaign was in full flight.

As soon as you left Belleville, as soon as you'd crossed Boulevard Richard-Lenoir, Paris was smothered with cryptic posters. FREE-MARKET REALISM, in huge capitals. FREE-MARKET REALISM, without a word of explanation. All this was supposed to be titivating the general public. The artillery softening them up before I launched the final offensive. "Concept Awareness", "Percolation through the Urban Fabric" . . . there were twice-weekly briefings about all this carry-on at the Vendetta Press. Half a dozen ad. men would show up, all tanned like they were just back from a safari, with knitted brows and jabbering mouths, laying out their schemes on the conference table, playing with pointed pointers and swift felt pens, as though they were Sioux war chiefs getting ready for the longest day. They displayed Clara's first photos of the J. L. B. stare, beaming out from beneath my brows and fixing the target of a billion copies sold. They said:

"What we are doing here is offering a totally incisive rhythmic dichotomy between the concept and the stare, don't you see? FREE-MARKET REALISM . . . then the stare. Rather satisfying, isn't it?"

"What I'd give to have that stare . . ."

The brat pack looked over at me and, just to make me understand what worthless crap I was, smiled politely. Because when I took part in these briefings, it was in my Malaussène hide and not my J. L. B. glad rags. Not one of them recognised me, which thrilled Loussa.

"You have to know what you want to have a stare like J. L. B.'s. You can't be a doubting Thomas like you, shit-for-brains."

I smiled back at Loussa. There are times when you really know who your mates are. Period.

*

Clara went everywhere with her camera. The photos she took were excellent: the J. L. B. publicity photos, which I talked up to record prices (her little one's piggy bank was filling up nicely), and family snaps which we kept to ourselves. It was the metamorphosis that fascinated her most of all, the transformation of her Benjamin into his J. L. B.

"You could have been a brilliant actor, Benjamin!"

She was enjoying herself. My Clarinette was enjoying herself. All the same, she still kept thinking about Saint-Hiver (I sometimes heard her crying in the evening, while I was learning my lines in the dining-room, just beside the sleeping children). Chief Superintendent Coudrier had insisted that she go to Saint-Hiver's funeral alone. He came to pick her up in his official car, the same one that had overtaken us on the way to the wedding, then he brought her back home. He was "nice" to her, as Clara put it. And Coudrier was nice to me, too, when on his way out he pinned me against the door and whispered in my ear:

"Don't forget now, Malaussène. Steer well clear of my inquiries. Keep yourself and your family occupied, otherwise . . ."

When the door had closed, Clara said:

"They've appointed a new prison governor. He's young and he's going to continue where Clarence left off."

I butted in:

"The ad. men just loved your photos. They say they've never seen anything like them."

*

During this entire saga, Thérèse only intervened once: on the day that the Concorde touched down on my head.

"I don't like that haircut, Benjamin. It makes you look like Lucifer. It isn't you, and it isn't wholesome."

*

On the walls of Paris, the photos and the slogans were now alternating. ONE MAN: my Wall Street forehead. ONE CONVICTION: my platinum smile. ONE CREATION: my tungsten stare. And FREE-MARKET REALISM all over the place. The photos and the slogans were not apparently connected, but the posters were insidiously drawing together, giving the impression that they all might be pieces of the same jigsaw puzzle, that a face was slowly being formed, that a truth was step by step being announced.

The public was supposedly on tenterhooks.

*

"If I ask 'What is your main strength, J. L. B.?', what do you answer?"

"Enterprise!"

"Spot on. 'And your main weakness?'"

"No weakness."

"No, no, Benjamin, you're supposed to answer 'that I don't always succeed'."

"Oh right, 'that I don't always succeed'."

"So, you sometimes fail?"

"I have lost battles, but this has always taught me what I needed to know to win the war."

"Great stuff, Benjamin. You see, it's starting to sink in!"

Jeremy was getting me to rehearse my coming interviews. Fifty pages of questions and answers, concocted by Chabotte, which I had to learn by heart and then parrot spontaneously. "Above all, Monsieur Malaussène, do not look as though you are thinking. J. L. B. must spout convictions, as if he were a Texan oil well."

Jeremy would shoot straight home from school and, instead of showing me his exercise books as usual, hunt me out even if I was in the bog.

"It's no good hiding, Ben. I know you're in there."

And off we went again.

"Now, age. What do you think about age?"

"Some people are old at twenty and others still young at eighty."

"And at forty?"

"When you're forty, you're rich or you're nothing."

"Right. 'How about money?'"

"What do you mean, 'How about money?'"

"I mean, what does J. L. B. think about money?"

"He loves it."

"Come on, Ben, give us the *right answer*, will you? 'What is your position regarding money problems?'"

"Just beside the mint with the hole."

"Stop it, Ben. What's the real answer?"

"I don't know."

"The French have always found money suspect. What seems suspect to me is wanting money and not earning any."

I was saved by the bell. The sacrosanct time for the book at bedtime.

*

One January, he was on Concorde flight number AF 516 and, as soon as he set eyes on her, he knew that she was the one. In the seat next to his, she immediately seemed to him to be as alluring and inaccessible as an edelweiss growing on a sable summit. One thing was certain: she was going to be the mother of his children.

His heart started to leap against his chest and he got to his feet several times without any reason. He was not particularly tall. He still moved like an adolescent, something which gave him his charm and which had cost many an enemy his fortune. Anybody who knew him well (but very few people did know him well) would have seen from the quivering of the dimple which punctuated his chin that Philippe Ahoueltène, the sole victor of the Battle of the Yen, he who had laid low Hariett the Texan and Toshuro the Japanese, was moved.

*

That's right, the kids were enjoying themselves. That was the whole idea. But I wasn't much. No, to be quite honest, not very much. Even felt a bit ashamed. (A cameo from Julie: "Can't you be yourself for once in your life?") I even used to have a good moan at the one behind it all. I'd go into the sleeping children's bedroom. I'd lean over Clara's mound, gently unhook her laced-up fingers and have it out with our little money-grabber there:

"Pleased with yourself, are you? Cos all of this is down to you . . . you do realise that, I hope? Course you don't. I'm selling my soul to make a millionaire of you and you couldn't give a toss, ungrateful from the start, just like all the others . . . Honestly, do you really think it's a man's job to earn an angel's bread?"

"You are not going to crack up on us, now are you, Monsieur Malaussène?" Chabotte's concern went straight to my heart.

"You are standing up to the task manfully, isn't that right?"

We'd now reached the point of no return. The posters and the slogans had joined together. FREE-MARKET REALISM: ONE MAN, ONE CONVICTION, ONE CREATION! My huge gob and my initials all over the place. In all the Métro stations. In all the railway stations. In the airports. On the backsides of the buses: J. L. B.'s tense stare, winning smile, dominant chin and planetary cheeks. All the same, it had taken two cheek pads to plump out those planets. And the imminent publication of *The Lord of the Currencies*, billed as the surprise of the century!

"Please, do take a seat. Olivier, a cup of coffee for Monsieur Malaussène! Whatever is troubling you, old chap? Haven't we done a marvellous job?"

"Nothing, everything's dandy, just dandy . . . "

"Ah, that is music to my ears. Do you have the interviews off by heart? The interviews are absolutely capital!"

"Everything off by heart."

"Your sister's photographs are magnificent. I should like another set to illustrate the first article about you. Between you and me, you are not going to be disappointed . . . "

*

That batch of photos was taken in Saint-Tropez, the backdrop was the Mediterranean, which is used to this sort of thing. J. L. B. stepping out of his personal Mystère 20, J. L. B. at the wheel of his spanking new Jaguar XJS V12, 5.3 litres, 241 kph, Colonny leather upholstery and burr walnut, not unadjacent to 385,000 francs, his little Saint-Tropez runaround. J. L. B. in top-secret discussion in the midst of his villa with a turbaned Arab (*"he is a personal advisor to the oil sheiks"*). This particular Arab was none other than old Amar and, through the shrubbery, you could just make out his "bodyguards", Hadouch, Mo and Simon – equipped with walky-talkies and looking every inch the part.

"There's never a dull moment with you, Benjamin my brother. One minute it's a roumis wedding in the slammer, the next it's the Côte d'Azure. When are you taking us to the moon?"

And then, at last, J. L. B. alone in his marble study, putting the finishing touches to his last novel, *The Lord of the Currencies*.

"Yes, you heard me correctly, Monsieur Malaussène, his *last novel.*"

This harmless-sounding observation from Chabotte was the one and only ray of sunshine during the entire stay.

"You mean you're giving up writing?"

"Of course I am not. But I am giving up this sort of nonsense. Thank heavens."

"This nonsense?"

"You surely do not imagine that I am going to spend the rest of my life producing airport novels? I may have made a fortune in this line, I may have invented a literary *genre*, I may have rammed stereotypes down imbeciles' throats but, while so doing, I have also concealed myself behind the anonymity which my code of honour as a politician demanded. But, in nine months' time, I shall be retiring, Monsieur Malaussène, and then I shall throw off my anonymous hack's rags in order to start really writing, producing books one signs with one's own name, which are bound in green leather, the sort of things which fill up the shelves of this library!"

His voice had gone shrill. He was in the grips of adolescent fervour.

"All of this! All of this! I shall add to all of this!"

He pointed at the shelves, which disappeared up into the panelled half-light of the ceiling. His library had taken the dimensions of a cathedral.

"And do you know what I am going to write about next?"

His eyes sparkled, whites whiter than white. He looked like something out of a J. L. B. novel. The spitting image of a twelve-year-old about to bite his first chunk out of the world.

"You are what I am going to write about next, Monsieur Malaussène!"

(Are you, now . . . ?)

"Or the whole J. L. B. saga, if you prefer. I shall show all of those jumped-up literary critics who did not even deign to write a single article about me . . ."

(Ah, so that's the score . . .)

"I shall show them what the J. L. B. universe contains. How deep a knowledge of the modern world such books require!"

Queen Zabo sat po-faced on her chair, while I was the mouse being toyed at by an affectionate tomcat. He was purring now:

"Writing, Monsieur Malaussène, 'writing' above all entails forward planning. And, in this field, I have planned everything. To begin with, what my contemporaries wanted to read. Shall I tell you why J. L. B.'s novels sell so well?"

(Please do . . .)

"Because they are a universal caesarean! I didn't invent a single stereotype, I simply extracted them all from my public! All of my characters are my readers' recurrent dreams . . . That is why my books multiply like biblical hot cakes and fishes!"

In one leap, he was in the middle of the library. He pointed at me, like Julius Caesar showing something of capital importance to his adopted son Brutus:

"And my greatest stereotype is you, Monsieur Malaussène! The time has now come to test its efficiency. You have an appointment at the Hôtel Crillon tomorrow afternoon at four o'clock precisely. Don't be late, Benjamin, we are going to introduce the world to the world!"

Chapter 16

NOTHING LOOKS MORE like a Hôtel Crillon suite than another Hôtel Crillon suite – particularly if you haven't got a suite tooth. All the same, no sooner had I stepped into my very own specially reserved suite than I insisted on changing it.

"Why?" the gilded porter asked, as he held open the door, and immediately wished he hadn't.

"I'm only following orders, Jim lad," is what I almost replied. ("A writer of J. L. B.'s stature has to be capricious," Chabotte had explained. "You shall demand a different suite.")

"The orientation," I said.

The gilded porter's head nodded in understanding, and His Obsequiousness guided me to another one. It would do. A tad smaller than Place de la Concorde, but it would do.

"Will this do for you, my Clarinette?"

Clara's eyes were as saucer-like as her lens, pupils dilated in undetermined exposure time. I answered for her:

"It will do."

I slipped the gilded one a Texan tip. Enough to spend the night in that other hotel over the way, across the bridge, the one with the tricolour flag and columns.

Upon which, Gauthier arrived with the equipment. He, too, was all in a tizzy from the Crillon's razzmatazz. He even seemed, all of a sudden, to be treating me with due consideration.

"Place the lectern by the window then plug the computer into that socket will you, Gauthier? There's a good chap," I instructed from a great height.

He laughed, then whispered to me:

"Loussa is dealing with the telephones, sir."

And, sure enough, Loussa de Casamance made a triumphant entrance, with three telephones in each hand, like the Saint Nicholas of telecommunications. He nearly broke out into a Fred Astaire shimmy.

"There are times when I'm proud to be your mate, shit-for-brains. Who's the babe?"

He'd just noticed Clara.

"My sister Clara."

He immediately twigged the Saint-Hiver connection, but didn't let it show. He just said:

"In that case, now I've met her, I even plouda to be you mate. You plobably don't even deserve her."

He then peppered the suite with phones. When Calignac arrived, everything was in order. Chabotte's idea was that J. L. B.'s office should be stuffed full of tele-apparatus, phones, faxes and company, giving the impression that he was plugged into the entire world. Meanwhile, at several centuries' remove from his era, the writer would be taken unawares by a photographer near the window as he stood writing at his lectern. White leaves of immaculately spun, carefully weighed paper which, the hired hackette would say, were specially made for him by the Moulin de La Ferté – the last remaining producer of pulped linen paper, sold by the sheet, following the most ancient traditions of Samarkand. On these sheets, J. L. B. did not write with a Mont Blanc, nor of course with a biro, and certainly not with a felt-tip pen, but quite simply with a pencil – a habit he'd never lost since scribbling away his schoolboy essays. These pencils, made by the extremely ancient Östersund workshops, were normally set aside for the Swedish royal family and were personally sent to him by the Queen. As for the meerschaum pipes he smoked while working (he smoked *only* while working), each one was several centuries old, with its own history, and used for only one sort of tobacco: the most rustic of shags which was no longer commercially available, but which SEITA had specially agreed to make for him each month.

"Okay?" Calignac asked. "Everything in place? You haven't forgotten the pencils?"

"The pencils are there, on the lectern."

"What about the penknife?"

"What penknife?" Gauthier asked, going pale.

"His father's penknife! He's supposed to sharpen his pencils with his father's penknife, an ancient Laguiole. Didn't you know that, Gauthier?"

"I'd completely forgotten . . ."

"So run off and buy a Laguiole at the nearest tobacconist's. Then sand it down a bit so that it looks a good century old."

In fact, Calignac, Gauthier and Loussa were enjoying themselves just as much as the kids.

"And are you all right?"

"So-so."

Calignac gripped my shoulders in his scrum-half's fists.

"This is no time to panic, my little lad. Do you know how many first-edition copies of *The Lord of the Currencies* are being printed?"

"Three?"

"Stop taking the piss, Malaussène. Eight hundred thousand! We've printed eight hundred thousand in one run."

*

SHE: If I asked you what your main strength is, J. L. B., what would you answer?

ME: Enterprise!

SHE: And your main weakness?

ME: That I don't always succeed.

SHE: Have you sometimes failed, then? When I look at you, it seems barely credible.

ME: I have lost battles, but this has always taught me what I needed to know to win the war.

SHE: What advice would you give to a young person today who wanted to succeed?

ME: To know what he really wants, to get up early, to rely on no-one but himself.

SHE: How are the characters in your novels conceived?

ME: From my will to overcome.

SHE: The women in your novels are always beautiful, young, intelligent, sensual . . .

ME: They owe that entirely to themselves. Each person moulds his own appearance and creates his own truth.

SHE: Are you saying that anyone can become good-looking, intelligent and rich?

ME: It is a question of will power.

SHE: Beauty is a question of will power?

ME: Beauty is basically interior. Will power exteriorises it.

SHE: You frequently mention will power. Do you despise the weak?

ME: The weak do not exist. There are only people who do not really want what they really want.

SHE: What about you, did you always want to be rich?

ME: From the age of four. As soon as I realised that I was poor.

SHE: To get your own back on life?

ME: No, to conquer life.

SHE: Does money really buy happiness?

ME: It is the prerequisite.

SHE: Your heroes become rich very young and age is a recurrent theme in your books. What do you think about age?

*

So far, so good. She'd learnt her questions in the right order and I replied in the right order. We were like two worshippers religiously reeling off a litany of bullshit. She was nervous when she arrived, not knowing where to park her bum or direct her stare. Her editor must have laid it on a bit thick, and she was obviously shit-scared that I wouldn't pop back with the right answer to her first question: "J. L. B., you are a prolific writer, your books have been translated into numerous languages, you have millions of readers, so why is it that you have never been interviewed or photographed before?" To her intense relief, I trotted out the right answer. Answer No. 1: "I was busy. By answering your questions today, I am giving myself my first break in seventeen years." The rest followed on naturally, questions and answers that were numbered like the dishes in a Chinese restaurant.

And then we got to the age question.

My mind went blank.

Or, rather, was illumined.

I suddenly saw myself back at Chabotte's place. Chabotte was giving me and Queen Zabo his impersonation of Charlie Chaplin with the globe, the Great Dictator of Art and Literature, prancing about all on his own in the half-light of his library; Chabotte giving me the appointment for the kick-off at the Crillon; but most of all Chabotte taking my hand as I was leaving, just as if he was my playmate.

"Come with me. I want to show you something."

And, as I glanced round in panic at the boss:

"No, no. Wait for us here, my dear. We shan't be long."

Running like a crazed schoolboy down the corridor, he dragged me after him, under the glazed stare of the flunkies, who'd obviously seen it all before, bounding up the stairs four at a time (with me following on like a rag doll), hitting a ton for the sprint down the final corridor, over a parquet as immaculate as a bowling alley, slithering across the last ten metres and banging into a massive door which looked as though it stood at the end of the known world. A couple of seconds to get our breath back, then he opened the door and screamed in a high-pitched voice:

"Look!"

It took some time for my eyes to get accustomed to the gloom and make out what there was to be looked at. It was a room of Swiftian dimensions with a four-poster bed large enough to accommodate a Gulliver. But for all my peering about, there didn't seem to be anything particular to be seen.

"There! Over there!"

Screeching, he pointed towards the most distant of the windows:

"Over there! There! There!"

And I saw.

I saw, perched on a wheelchair above a mound of blankets, a woman's head staring at us with hatred burning in her eyes. A *horribly ancient* head. I first thought that she was dead and that Chabotte was doing a Hitchcock remake, complete with embalmed mother. But I was wrong. White-hot life was glowing in those eyes, the last glimmers of a malevolent existence now reduced to bed-ridden incapacity. Chabotte yelled:

"My mother! Madame Nazaré Quissapaolo Chabotte!"

Then he added, with the smugness of a gloating brat which was perhaps even more terrifying than his mummy's stare:

"She always tried to stop me from writing!"

*

SHE: What do you think about age?

ME: Age is a bitch, young lady.

SHE (*jumping*): Sorry?

ME: I say that, at whatever age, age is an utter bitch: childhood, the age of tonsils and total dependence; adolescence, the age of onanism and pointless questioning; maturity, the age of cancer and rampant bullshit; old age, the age of arthritis and vain regret.

SHE (*brandishing pencil*): Do you really want me to write that?

ME: It's your interview. Write whatever you want.

She skipped a couple of pages and, hoping that things would improve, picked up the thread further on.

SHE: What is your position regarding money problems?

But things only got worse.

ME: If I saw myself reflected in a pauper's empty bowl, then my position would be at the trigger end of a gun.

Chapter 17

O KAY, SO I cracked up.

I cracked up. These things happen, don't they? There was that old woman's stare, like an electric shock, and I cracked up. Memories don't give warnings, they're tricky, they leap out on you when least expected. And that old woman's stare throttled me, just as little Verdun's stare had done with the baptising chaplain at Saint-Hiver's prison! Verdun and that old lady . . . both extremes of age in one stare that was as tense as a scream . . . meanwhile I was supposed to keep on dishing up the crap: "*Some people are old at twenty and others still young at eighty.*" So bloody what?

The girl hurriedly packed up her bits and bobs, then scurried off. I half wanted to call her back and start all over again, but I just couldn't. That crone's wheelchair was parked in my memory. All my answers had melted under her blowtorch gaze. In my confusion, I also said to myself that Julie had been right. You'd have to be completely off your trolley to get caught up in an act like this one. So, instead of calming down my hackette, I piled it on even thicker. A gush of lyricism. She'd come along to map out J. L. B. and had been hit by a coked-up Palestinian bomber.

*

The worst of it was that my mates were all waiting for me at the Vendetta Press, already celebrating the final victory. With Queen Zabo in the role of Marshal Kutuzov.

"Your performance at the Bercy Palais Omnisport is going to be quite something, Malaussène! A one-off event! Never before has a writer given a showbiz première to his new book!"

(Forget it, your Majesty, I've just ballsed the whole thing up.)

"Behind you, your interpreters will be sitting fanned out in a semicircle. One hundred and twenty-seven interpreters from the four corners of the earth. An impressive sight, believe you me! In front of you, three to four hundred seats reserved for the French and foreign media. And, all around you, row after row full of your readers!"

(Stop it, your Majesty, stop it! There won't be any Palais Omnisport. In a week's time, when our little hackette publishes her interview, there won't even be a J. L. B. any more! Chabotte will have packed up his bags and started talking with our competitors . . .)

"The journalists will ask you a fresh set of questions, the ones printed in italics on the questionnaire which J. L. B. gave you to learn. So, my lad, off you go and rehearse one more time and everything will go swimmingly, you'll see."

"Then after that, I suppose he can have a short break, can't he?"

The Queen glanced round in astonishment at Gauthier, who immediately blushed. (Please, Gauthier, stop liking me, I've just signed your ticket for the dole queue, you're protecting your own murderer. I've betrayed you, for Christ's sake, can't you see betrayal written all over my face?)

"There will then be ten book-signing sessions, spread out over one week. We can't let your provincial readers go home empty-handed, Malaussène. 'Then after that', as Gauthier put it, 'after that' a full month off, wherever you like, with whoever you like, your entire family if you want, and your Belleville friends who took part in the advertising campaign. One month. And the princess is paying. Does that seem reasonable, Gauthier?"

Gauthier was over the moon. I was six feet under.

"Meanwhile, we will have our work cut out for us. Has Calignac told you? We've printed eight hundred thousand copies of *The Lord of the Currencies*. They now have to be placed. Calignac will tour round the provinces with three-quarters of our sales staff. Loussa will take care of Paris with the rest. But it's going to be tight, Malaussène. We could do with an extra pair of hands. It would be wonderful if you could help out Loussa and his team."

*

"Something's bugging you, shit-for-brains."

Loussa's red van was touring round the bookstores, dicing with death at every junction.

"What makes you say that?"

"You're not frightened of my driving, which means you must be in one hell of a state."

"No, it's all right, Loussa. I'm frightened."

So that was all right then. It was all right just as it is with a kid who's made the cock-up of the century and is sitting, with his little butt perched on the school pew, waiting for the century to notice.

"I can quite understand it if this dodgy business is starting to do your head in, you know. As for me, I'd rather get back to my Chinese literature . . . "

"Please, Loussa, don't talk when you're driving."

He'd just narrowly missed a mother wheeling a pram.

"All things considered, you must be feeling the same way I was at your age."

Kids coming out of school this time . . . The red van made a detour along the pavement opposite.

"I don't want to tell you about my war experiences, but in 1944, before Monte Cassino, the British often used to send me behind the German lines, near Medjez-el-Bab, in the mountains of Tunisia. I was already black at the time, I faded into the night and, with my pouch stuffed full of gelignite, I felt what you're feeling now: an unpleasant sensation of being underground."

"What you were doing was at least honourable, Loussa . . . "

"I don't see what's so honourable about shitting yourself while listening to the shrubbery talk in German . . . Anyway, let me tell you, honour is a matter of historical perspective."

The van screeched to a halt. *Lords of the Currencies* rained down onto our heads. We went in and dropped a copy off with the local fags 'n' mags man. Loussa was all out to convince me that I was on the right path to being historically honourable.

"All right, shit-for-brains, so J. L. B. is a pile of crap. Of course he is! But he's our one and only pile of crap. And the Vendetta Press survives *all thanks to* J. L. B. By temporarily wearing that turd's colours, you are in fact defending the glory of Literature, all the best stuff we publish, stuff worthy of the most honourable of bookstores!"

As he spoke, he pointed at the Terrasse de Gutenberg with one hand, while having a swig with the other.

"Come on, be brave, shit-for-brains, *hao bu li ji*, as the Chinese say, 'total self-denial', and *zhuan men li ren*, 'commitment to others' . . . "

*

In other words, Malaussène or the Death of Literature. Thanks a lot, Loussa.

Julie wasn't there. The bed was cold. The children were plunged into the idiotic sleep of the just. Chief Superintendent Coudrier was calmly conducting his inquiries. Mum was getting laid by Inspector Pastor. Stojilkovicz was translating Virgil. And Saint-Hiver was chatting about rehabilitation with his good old mate the Almighty.

That's life for you.

When it comes to a stop.

If I could at least sleep? No, I couldn't. No rest for traitors. As my eyes closed, old mummy Chabotte, Madame Nazaré Quissapaolo Chabotte (Portuguese? Brazilian?), fluttered down onto the roof of my slumbers. That face mummified by hatred and the childish squeals of her elderly son: "She always tried to stop me from writing!" Then, Queen Zabo's bereaved face filled up my screen. Not a word of reproach. Not a single tear. She was just content to occupy my nights. With that fatal magazine in her hand.

A week.

A week of insomnia.

*

Then, of course, the magazine came out.

I was even one of the first to be informed.

Ring, ring! Eight in the morning. I answered. Queen Zabo.

"Malaussène?"

Yes, it was her all right.

"Your Majesty?"

"Your interview is in all the newsagents."

Alas, interviews and newsagents inevitably end up converging!

"Pleased with yourself?"

. . .

"Chabotte's just called me."

. . .

"He's delighted."

"What?"

"He's delighted. As happy as a sandboy. He kept me on the phone for a good half an hour."

"Chabotte?"

"Chabotte! The politician! J. L. B.! Who do you imagine I'm talking about? Aren't you awake yet, my lad? I'll give you ten minutes to make yourself some coffee, then call you back."

"Don't bother. How about you?"

"What do you mean, how about me?"

"Have you read it?"

"I have it right here in front of me."

"And?"

"And it's perfect. It's just what I expected of you. And the Saint-Tropez photos are excellent. Whatever's the matter, my lad?"

I must still have been starkers when I hit Yussuf's, our local newsagent, because he asked me:

"What's up, Ben? Your bed's on fire?"

"*Playboy*, give me *Playboy*!"

"So that's it. Julie's still not back yet. You missing it that much?"

I couldn't find the right page. I was trembling like I was in detox. I didn't dare believe it. I didn't dare hope that mankind was that wonderful. That even Chabotte, the inventor of the combined-bludgeoner, could really appreciate this turnabout from J. L. B . . . Everything was possible, sweet Jesus! Everything could be hoped for from humanity!

"Don't look any further," said Yussuf. "The one on page 63 is a bit of all right. Dorothy from Glasgow. You can use my stockroom if you like."

Some mornings, I loathe my pessimism. Smile, Third World! Start hoping again! Exult! Even the Chabottes can admit that the starving should be at the trigger end of a gun! Lay down your arms, Third World, the share-out's coming!

Not a bit of it.

The hackette had stitched the whole lot back together again.

After all, she had the questions, she had the answers, she had a chief editor, they'd done it all as it was supposed to be done.

No doubt about it. The interview there in front of me was precisely the same as the one Jeremy and the kids had got me to rehearse for weeks on end. Down to the last comma.

*

My Vendetta pals greeted me champagne glasses in hand. The bubbly was flowing and joy lit up their faces.

The day flew by on the wings of relief. That evening, Thian read out Chapter 14 of *The Lord of the Currencies*, the one in which Philippe Ahoueltène's young Swedish wife gives birth to their first child. The delivery takes place in the heart of Amazonia, in the eye of a cyclone which is sending trees into orbit. I listened to it nearly through to the end.

*

Then Julius and I went out for our stroll. I had the light aimless step of someone who has simultaneously lost both his fears and his illusions . . . Belleville looked less wrecked than usual . . . Quite something, that! Yes, it seemed to me that the new architects were making a point of respecting the neighbourhood's "character" a little. Take that big pink building on the corner of Rue de Belleville and Boulevard de la Villette for instance. Well, if you look carefully, way, way up there, above the last row of windows there is a sort of Hispanic-Moorish dome. No kidding! Of course, while this marvel was under construction, the ground-floor had become Chinese . . . But that didn't matter. When all of Belleville had become Chinese then, way, way up there, they could add on some jagged pagoda-like wavelets . . . Architecture is the art of suggestion.

I suddenly felt sleepy. I had some catching up to do in that line. I left Julius the Dog in Amar's kitchen ("Have you seen how handsome you are in that magazine, my son?") and I took myself off home like a big boy.

They jumped me twenty yards from my door. Three of them. A tall thin one with a knobbly knee which crushed my balls, a second one who was wider than he was high and who picked me up by the throat, while a third one laid into my guts with a volley of highly professional punches. Since the hulk's fist was pinning me against the wall I couldn't even double up in agony. So my legs shot up instinctively and kicked the boxer in the chest. He coughed up his oxygen and I stuck out my tongue. The second one's fist started to squeeze my throat so tightly that I almost popped.

"So, Malaussène, we wanted to have our own little say in the press, did we?"

The tall thin one was handling his stick like it was a flail. Tibias, knees and thighs. He was quite literally flaying me right there on the public highway. I wanted to scream, but my tongue was taking up all the available space.

"It was very foolish of you not to act out your part properly, Malaussène."

The hulk spoke slowly, with a Russian accent, and a sort of tenderness in his voice.

"Specially if you have a family to protect."

He stopped the boxer's supersonic fist just two millimetres from my nose.

"Not the face, Selim. He's still got a job to do."

So the boxer went back to my ribs.

"You're going to have to be a good boy at Bercy, Malaussène. Just answer what you're supposed to answer. That's all."

With a simple twist of his wrist, he turned me round, flattening my gob into the wall while the tall thin one's stick dealt with my kidneys.

"We'll be there in the crowd. Just beside you. We can read, we can. We love J. L. B."

Old Belleville, my beloved old Belleville, tasted of saltpetre.

"You wouldn't like anything to happen to Clara, would you?"

His two fists were now ploughing into my deltoids. Once again, I wanted to scream, but this time I had a mouth full of Belleville.

"Or to Jeremy. Kids that age can so easily have accidents . . ."

Chapter 18

L ITERATURE IS A feast, as all the world's book fairs will tell you. Literature can even look like a Democratic Convention in good old Atlanta. Literature can have its groupies, its streamers, its majorettes, its brass bands, just like the candidates to any of Paris's town halls. Two outriders can open up the way before Literature's limo and two rows of Republican Guards can present their sabres to it. Literature is honourable, and so must be honoured. Even if, a fortnight after getting the beating of a lifetime, the King of Literature was still counting his ribs and bricking it for his brothers and sisters, he was nevertheless the Godfather of that feast!

That evening, Paris opened out before me, Paris became a sea in front of my hired limo's prow, all of which certainly didn't leave me indifferent. You understand how once someone has tasted this, then it gets hard to give it up. You're ensconced in your seat, you lift a world-weary nose towards the outside world and what is it that glides past your bullet-proof windows? Your posters, screaming your name, with your gob blossoming out, a whole multicoloured wall reciting your thoughts, expressing your position. J. L. B. OR FREE-MARKET REALISM – ONE MAN, ONE CONVICTION, ONE CREATION! – J. L. B. AT BERCY! – 225 MILLION COPIES SOLD!

To start out with, they had to give the truncheons a bit of an airing to open up a path in front of the Crillon's doors, then air them quite considerably on arrival in order to force our way into Bercy. But, when it comes to glory, a truncheon is the proof of love. Hands stretched out pinning photos of adoration against the car windows. Lovingly dishevelled girls, with come-hither eyes and serious mouths, addresses, phone numbers, books opened on the windscreen for an autograph, a split-second glimpse of beautiful breasts (truncheon), chattering mouths running alongside the car, tumblings, streamers, the false note of a bottle of ink exploding on the rear window (truncheon), three-piece suits and nodding complicity, mothers and daughters, fathers and sons, red lights driven through with the Prefecture's blessing, two whistle-blowers in front, and two behind, little Gauthier, my "personal assistant", beside me, experiencing all the stages of terror and delight, Gauthier in the firing line of glory for the first and last time in his life, and the armada of coaches around Bercy, all come up from the provinces to reach the 29 and 06 bus lines, all day and all night, even the drivers with books under their arms, *Last Kiss on Wall Street, Gold Mine, The Dollar, The Child Who Could Count, The Yen's Daughter, Having* and, of course, *The Lord of the Currencies*, all being brandished about in the vain hope of a dedication.

*

The stage was an emerald-green shimmer in the half-light of that packed-out Palais Omnisport. Above the stage, an endless screen had been suspended, enough to make the one in the Grand Rex look like a postage stamp. "This way", "this way", Calignac's natural body-armour welcomed me as I arrived. He'd alerted his rugger pals: Chaize the concrete prop-forward, Lamaison the least standoffish of halves, Rist the back-breaking back, Bonnot the wing of a storm, and ten other oval-ball specialists whose pack swallowed up J. L. B., closing round him, keeping the enthusiastic crowd at bay ... Detour, corridors and at last the refuge of the dressing room. The dressing room! It was like diving head-first into a shell hole.

"Didn't I promise you all the love in the world, my lad?"

Queen Zabo's chuckling voice in the silence of the dressing room. My ribs were in ribbons, my guts gutted, my legs folding rulers . . . my eardrums were sticking out my nostrils, my recklessness was making wreck of me, but I was all right, I guess. Right as rain . . . as usual.

"It's incredible," Gauthier stammered. "It's incredible . . ."

"I must admit that things are going even better than expected, but this is still no reason to get into a state like that, Gauthier."

Queen Zabo . . . as much mistress of herself as she was of my little universe. All the same, she stood up, walked over to me and did something that nobody had ever seen her do before. She touched me. She laid her enormous hand on my head. She gently stroked the nape of my neck. Then she said:

"This is the final sprint home, Benjamin. After this, you'll be at your very own pleasure. Her Majesty's word on it!"

"Don't take your hand away, your Majesty."

*

Question: Could you explain to us exactly what is meant by the literature of "Free-Market Realism"?

(If there hadn't been three hoods waiting for me in the wings, then I would have been only too pleased to explain what crap like that means.)

Answer: Literature to the glory of businessmen.

(As literary as stock-market prices, as free as a jail bird and as realistic as a starving man's dreams.)

Question: And do you consider yourself to be a businessman?

(I consider myself to be a poor little fucker who's up to his ears in a sting with no safety exit and who is here and now the shame of the literary world.)

Answer: My business is literature.

The questions were asked in all the world's languages, each of them being translated by one of the one hundred and twenty-seven interpreters splayed out in a massive semicircle behind me. And my answers, multi-translated in turn, were broadcast out to raise cheers in even the darkest corners of the Palais Omnisport. A literary Pentecost. The whole thing had been rehearsed to death. If an unexpected question burst into that galaxy of agreement, then it was immediately quashed by the next one from the catalogue, one that I was allowed to answer.

Somewhere in the tidal wave of my admirers, three bastards were watching to see that I obeyed orders: a tall thin one with an efficient stick, a professional boxer and a Hercules with a Russian accent, whose fingerprints were still on my neck.

Question: After the press conference, the film version of your first novel, *Last Kiss on Wall Street*, will be screened. Could you remind us of the conditions in which this novel was written?

Of course I could. No problem. And, while I was spreading out J. L. B.'s bull-shit, I could hear once again Chabotte's sugary voice congratulating me on "that magnificent *Playboy* interview". "You are a natural born actor, Monsieur Malaussène. Even though your answers were all scripted, they ring extraordinarily true. If you do likewise at the Palais Omnisport, then we shall have succeeded in pulling off the greatest hoax in literary history. In comparison with us, the wildest of the surrealists will now look like altar boys." No doubt about it. I'd fallen into the clutches of a pen-and-ink Doctor Mabuse, and if I didn't do exactly as I was told, then he'd have my children minced into sausage meat. Not the slightest allusion to the beating I'd got from his boys, of course. "You are looking very well this morning." Yes, Chabotte had even piled it on thicker than usual, handing me a cup of coffee, with a smile thrown in.

Queen Zabo and my mates at the Vendetta Press were obviously above suspicion and, seeing how the launch arrangements were making them all so excited, I didn't have the heart to talk to them about what had happened. As ever in life's crises, I looked for help in Belleville.

"A tall one with a stick, one of our own little featherweights and a big lad who talks Eastern? If they're the ones I think they are, then it looks like you've hit the jackpot, Benjamin my brother!"

There are police records and then, of course, there are street records. In the end everyone winds up knowing just about everyone else.

"Did they hurt you?"

Hadouch had just sat down between Simon the Berber and Black Mo. He put a glass of mint tea in front of me.

"It's all over now, Ben. We're here. Drink."

I drank. Then Simon said:

"There, see, you're not scared any more."

Question: Will power is a recurrent theme in your books. Could you give us your definition of will power?

In my mind's eye I could see the catalogue answer: "*Will power is having the power to will what you want*", and I was just about to trot it out, like the good cassette recorder I'd become, when suddenly, in front of me, I saw Simon's mop of flaming hair. A beautiful red flare in the darkness surrounding me. The Berber's star in the Palais Omnisport's heavens! Simon was there, right in front of me, behind my throttler's massive form. The throttler was being held in a half-nelson and the expression on his face made me understand what Dresden china feels like when being trodden on by a bull. With the index finger and thumb of his free hand, Simon made the letter "o", signalling to me that everything had been taken care of. This meant that Hadouch and Mo must have collared my other two guardian angels and that my mouth was now as free to speak as the poet's quill in the land of honey. And since they wanted me to define will power, then define it I would. Oh, friends at the Vendetta, this is now going to be flagrant high treason in public, but when you find out, you'll forgive me, because you're not like Chabotte, you don't go in for truncheon literature, your business, all of you, Zabo Queen of Books, Loussa the beautifully facetious salesman, Calignac the quiet arranger of utopias, and Gauthier the page boy of pages, your business is the business of eternity!

So I opened my mouth to spill the beans, to grass up Chabotte and, while I was at it, speak up for Justice and Literature, both with big beautiful capitals . . . then I shut it again.

Because two rows behind Simon the Berber was Julie! Yes, Julie, my Julie! Sticking out in the midst of a circle of admirers, she was staring straight at me. With a smile on her face. And her hand on Clara's shoulder.

So, stuff vengeance, stuff justice, stuff literature. I changed targets again. I was going to speak about love! J. L. B. had become Benjamin Malaussène once more and was going to improvise a public declaration of love which would blow your smouldering affections to the moon and back! Because, to be perfectly truthful, Julie's love is something that could make even the oldest, dampest flotsam burst into flames! Yes, when I'd spoken of Julie's kisses, Julie's breasts, Julie's hips, Julie's warmth, her fingers and her breath, not one of you, man or woman, could look at the man or woman next to you with eyes other than I have for Julie, and then this feast would be a real love feast for once, and that verdant erection of Bercy's Palais Omnisport would at last be justified!

Question: Shall I repeat my question, sir?

I smiled at Julie. I opened wide my arms, words of love welled up inside me . . . then the bullet entered my field of vision.

It was a .22 calibre high-penetration bullet. State-of-the-art stuff. Apparently some people's lives flash in front of their eyes. What I saw was a bullet.

My reader's vision took it in when it was a foot away from me.

It was spinning.

"*Death is an on-coming process . . .*" where the hell had I read that?

And that copper shell, whose point gleamed under the light of the projectors, entered my skull, digging out a perfect round hole, churning up the acres of my thoughts, throwing me backwards onto my occiput, and I knew it was all over as clearly as, according to Bergson, you know that it has all begun.

IV
JULIE

COUDRIER: *Tell me, Thian, just how far will a woman go when she has decided to avenge the man she loves?*

VAN THIAN: . . .

COUDRIER: . . .

VAN THIAN: *Yup, at the very least.*

Chapter 19

JULIE HAD BEEN born beautiful. First as a lovely baby, then as a radiant child, after that as an exceptional adolescent and finally as a beautiful woman. This created a vacuum around her: admiration from a distance. Whenever people saw her, they always stood back from her. But this distance became elastic from the tugging desire to approach her, to smell the scent of her body, to enter the aura of her warmth, to touch her. They were attracted and held at bay. Julie had long been used to this sensation of living in the centre of a constantly taut and dangerously elastic space. Few had dared enter that circle. But she was no haughty woman. From a young age she had quite simply acquired the stare of the extremely beautiful: eyes that express no preferences.

"There are only two races on this earth," Julie's father, Colonial Governor Corrençon, used to say. "The very beautiful and the very ugly. As for skin colour and the rest of that nonsense, it is a mere question of geographical fluke."

The very beautiful and the very ugly was one of Governor Corrençon's favourite subjects . . . "and, then, there are the rest of us," he would add, pointing to himself as though he were the only genuine aesthetic yardstick for average mortals.

"No-one dares look at the very ugly for fear of hurting them and such universal nicety means that the very ugly die of loneliness."

Much of Julie's childhood had been spent listening to her father talk. She couldn't have imagined a more thrilling game.

"As for the very beautiful, everyone looks at them, but they dare not look at anyone, for fear that they will be jumped on. And such universal admiration means that the very beautiful die of loneliness."

He acted out everything he said. He played up the pathos. She laughed.

"I am going to graft a potato nose onto you, my lass, and cauliflower ears. You will then live out a common-or-garden vegetable love and fill my nursery with tender young shoots."

*

Even in the tightly packed crowd at the Bercy Palais Omnisport, an empty space formed itself around Julie. They all kept their distance as though she had sprung up from the ground right in the midst of them. Everyone had one eye on the stage and the other on her, fascinated by that writer answering questions in the magic circle of his interpreters and that woman who seemed to have walked straight out of one of his books. So literature wasn't mere lies. Some of them then imagined meeting that woman, way up yonder, between two continents, in one of those planes that stitch the world's wealth together. Reality had confirmed their readerly dreams: beauty existed and everything was possible.

And so it came to pass that, in the fervour of the Palais Omnisport, in reflected limelight, enthralled by the writer's cool, snappy answers, they started to feel better-looking and stronger themselves. They looked at the beautiful woman more openly. She no longer seemed inaccessible to them. Or less so, in any case. Yet the circle didn't close around her. She still stood there, alone, at its centre. They smiled knowingly at her: that J. L. B.! what a guy, eh?

Then Clara nestled in Julie's arms.

"You're here?"

That empty circle around Julie did have its practical side. Her friends had no trouble picking her out in a crowd.

"I'm here, Clara."

There was a mixture of excitement and sorrow in Clara's embrace. She was totally wrapped up in that absurd farce, wrapped up in her pregnancy and wrapped up in Saint-Hiver's death. "What a family of loonies," Julie said to herself, putting her arm round the girl. And she smiled. Up there, on stage, Benjamin was looking for the answer to that thorny question about "will power".

Question: Will power is a recurrent theme in your books. Could you give us your definition of will power?

Julie smiled. "It looks like will power is beyond you, Benjamin."

*

All the same, she was in no smiling mood. He was playing with fire up there, and she knew it. She was acquainted with Laure Kneppel, the journalist who had put her name to the *Playboy* interview. A free-lance specialising in artistic gossip, but also a former war correspondent who'd come to the end of her tether in the middle of the Lebanon conflict. "Car bombs, lumps of flesh hanging off balconies, children killed and children killing . . . I can't take any more of it, Julie. I'm now going to stick to the chattering classes."

Julie had taken refuge for the last few weeks in her birthplace in the Vercors and so hadn't seen the copy of *Playboy*. But the copyright had gone into metastasis throughout the entire press and Julie had read large extracts of the J. L. B. interview in *Le Dauphin Libéré*. She felt as if Benjamin was calling out to her. She was far from being superstitious, but it did seem to her that if Benjamin had found her out here, in her most secret hiding place, then it had to be a sign. Julie decided to go back to Paris. There was nothing particularly striking about that interview, however. It was a perfect example of its kind: a mechanical roll-over of totally cretinous questions and answers which produced a totally cretinous piece.

Julie locked up the old *Rochas* farmhouse.

The yard was smothered with Malaussenian hollyhocks, which she hadn't cut down.

Julie drove all night. All night, Julie said to herself: "No, Benjamin could never have given such a smooth interview." "But whyever not? He's capable of doing anything for a laugh . . . even when the joke isn't funny, just to get the biggest laugh of all."

As soon as she reached Paris, Julie took in the sheer scale of the J. L. B. advertising campaign. Benjamin was everywhere. The only thing she recognised of him in that gangster's face was how the photos had been taken: with Clara's loving eye.

Julie had problems getting into her flat. Love was blocking the door. A good forty letters from Benjamin for the two months she'd been away. Another invasion of hollyhocks . . . Benjamin told her in writing what he had told her to her face, with a few extra flourishes, some amusing images, clever turns of phrase to camouflage any gushes of lyricism. He really was a sly dog. He told her everything about J. L. B. The fitting sessions at Chabotte's place, the diet of couscous, Jeremy, Thérèse's unspoken disapproval, everything.

But not a word about the interview.

She thus deduced that he was hiding something from her.

Her instinct told her not to go and see Benjamin. They'd only end up in bed and she needed to keep her wits about her.

She decided to grill Laure Kneppel. She found her at the *Maison des Ecrivains*, on Rue de Verneuil, busy noting down the dying words of wisdom of an ancient poet who had just, *in extremis*, been decorated by the Ministry of Culture – "It's what they stick on your back during your last lap round the literary treadmill," Laure laughed in the nearby café. "So, Julie, to what do I owe the honour?"

Julie told her. Laure blanched.

"Don't stick your nose into this J. L. B. business, Julie. It's a bomb waiting to go off. And there I was, thinking I was as safe as houses with my dearies . . ."

Then she went on to explain how, right in the middle of their prearranged ping-pong match (she had been supplied with both the questions and the answers by a certain Gauthier, J. L. B.'s personal assistant), lo and behold J. L. B. had suddenly gone off the rails and started spouting inflammatory rhetoric in praise of the Third World and the Seven Ages of Man. Laure had tried to put him back onto the rails, but there was nothing doing.

"He'd blown a gasket, Julie. An outburst from his guilty conscience, like a dying soldier, see what I mean?"

Julie saw.

On her way out of the Crillon, Laure had said to herself that this had really been her lucky day and that she had witnessed a precious moment of truth. Which, in her profession, was rare enough. And since chummy had been so insistent, then she'd publish everything chummy had said. But then . . .

"But then, what?"

Laure had been accosted by three lads who insisted on listening to her tape and reading her notes.

"What did they look like?"

"One was massive, with a Russian accent, the second was tall and skinny, and the third was a small wiry Arab."

At first, Laure had told them where to get off, but the massive one had a soft, persuasive voice.

"They knew everything about me, Julie, down to my mother's address, my bra size and my credit card number . . ."

The tall skinny one had given her a gentle little tap with his stick in the small of the back. On one of the final vertebrae. She felt as if she had been electrocuted. She published the interview as previously agreed.

"J. L. B. will be eternally grateful to you, Mademoiselle."

Sure enough, when the piece came out, Laure received a huge bouquet of flowers.

"It was so bulky that it wouldn't fit into the dustbin."

*

So, Julie smiled. Even though this was no smiling matter. With her arm around Clara, she smiled. "What a family of loonies . . ."

Benjamin saw her.

And lit up. As clearly as if Julie had turned on a switch.

She saw Benjamin light up. She saw him open his arms. Caught up in a wave of emotion, she just had time to say to herself: "Jesus, just pray he isn't going to make a public declaration of his love to me!"

Then she saw Benjamin's head explode and Benjamin's body being thrown backwards off the dais by the force of the impact, then landing on the nearest of the interpreters, who collapsed under him.

Chapter 20

AND THAT BEAUTIFUL woman threw her guts up. Of all the things that her admirers saw that evening: the assassination of J. L. B., the moment of stupor, the succeeding panic, the young pregnant girl who tore herself away from the beautiful woman's arms to rush screaming onto the stage, the blood-stained interpreters getting to their feet, the body being hastily carried away into the darkness of the wings, the little boy with rose-tinted glasses hanging onto the body while another boy (how old could he be? thirteen, fourteen maybe?) turned back towards the crowd and yelled: "Who did that?" of all the things they saw, the sight that they carried away with them as they rushed towards the exits (more shots were feared, a shower of grenades, perhaps a bomb) was the fleeting glimpse of that beautiful woman standing alone, immobile amidst the general panic, busily throwing her guts up, motionlessly spewing out geysers over the crowds, pouring out boiling torrents, her fine legs stained with brown streams, an image which they would vainly try to chase away, which they would mention to nobody, even though they could already vaguely sense, as they elbowed and shoved their way out, that the event itself would make for one hell of a conversation piece: J. L. B., the writer, had just been shot down in front of their very eyes . . . Yes, old fellow, I was there! He was blown into midair! I never thought that one single bullet could send a man flying like that. He was blown right off his feet!

*

Some women rush towards the fallen, some faint, some hide, some try to get out of the car fast enough to save their own skins . . . but I, thought Julie, am a woman who stands still and throws her guts up. It was a savage thought, strangely ecstatic, and murderous. Some of those who barged into her in their flight learnt that to their cost. She deliberately spewed over them. She didn't hold herself back. She knew that she wasn't going to hold anything down. She vomited like a volcano. She spewed like a dragon. She was already in mourning and already at war.

She didn't go up onto the stage. She didn't follow Benjamin's body into the wings. She went out with the others. But calmly. She was one of the last to leave the Palais Omnisport. She didn't get her car. She dived down into the Métro. The vacuum opened up around her. As usual. But not quite for the usual reasons. Grim delight seized her.

*

Back home, she cut the electricity, unplugged the phone, sat cross-legged right in the middle of her flat, let her arms droop, with the backs of her hands on the floor, and stayed still. She hadn't got undressed, she hadn't washed, she let the mess dry on her, become brittle, she'd sit there as long as it would take, until it all crumbled away on its own if need be. Long enough to understand. Who? Why? She thought through it. Which was far from easy. She had to hold back the waves of sorrow, upsurges of memory, reminiscences. For instance, Benjamin waking up in her arms in the middle of the night after Saint-Hiver's murder and screaming out that it was "treason". His choice of words had surprised her. An exclamation in a kid's comic strip: "treason!" What do you mean by "treason", Benjamin? And he'd given her a long explanation of why murder was so horrible: "It's treason against the species. There can't be anything worse in the world than the solitude of the victim at that moment . . . It's not so much that you are dying, Julie, it's the fact of being killed by someone who's as mortal as you are . . . like a fish drowning itself . . . see what I mean?" All that while Clara had been developing the photo of her mutilated Clarence . . . Clara under the red lamp in her dark-room, accompanying the slaughter of Clarence, "family of loonies" . . .

The next morning, Julie had gone out early and looked through all the papers: GOVERNOR OF MODEL PRISON BRUTALLY MURDERED BY HIS PRISON-ERS. . . VICTIM OF HIS OWN LAXITY? . . . PRISON OF BLISS WAS HOME OF HATRED . . . and she'd immediately decided to add nothing of her own, to leave this corpse to her colleagues – in any case, it had been Saint-Hiver's wish that she wrote nothing about the prisoners of Champrond – and then she was still too tired to carry out an investigation, her leg hurt and, what was more, she couldn't breathe properly, every breath she took left her feeling unfulfilled, she wasn't being pumped up fully, as Benjamin put it. It was the first time in her life that she had given up on the idea of writing an article. Hence her fury that evening when Benjamin had started spouting on about irreproachable hackery and "highly selective horror".

She didn't cool down during the six hundred kilometres that separated her from her native Vercors. It was only when she saw the hollyhocks around *Les Rochas* that she realised how much she'd over-reacted. After all, she'd never meant to ditch the bloke! Yes, as she pushed her way through the hollyhocks, Julie was astonished to discover that she'd just played at splitting up, like a little girl who was so sure of herself that she had pretended to give her lover boy the big E, and then she said out loud: "Well, well, well, that really does take the biscuit!" No, she didn't have the slightest desire to leave Benjamin but she had, for some time, been vaguely considering the idea of coming here, to *Les Rochas*, for a rest cure, a breath of pure air, to drink unpasteurised milk and eat freshly laid ducks' eggs, with their huge yolks . . . And lo and behold she had transformed her desire for recovery into a stormy slamming of doors . . . "Well, well, well, that really does take the biscuit!"

It was this discovery that saved the hollyhocks from the slaughter. Anyway, as her father, the Governor, used to say: "Of all the struggles I have undertaken, the vainest is the one against hollyhocks." One summer evening, her father had asked her to photograph him amid the relentless anarchy of these plants, which were taller than he was, and which he described as being: "the vegetable world's version of the Myth of Sisyphus". The Governor could hold forth for hours about holly-hocks: "the Mister Hyde of just plain holly". Julie had taken that photo a few days before he died. He was so thin in his white uniform that, if you had painted his hands green and dyed his hair red, you could have mistaken him for a hollyhock, "though rather less hardy, my girl" . . .

*

It got later. Julie glided from one man to the other, from one place to another, from one time to another, from one event to another. She couldn't think. Who? Why? The question was to find out who had killed Benjamin, this question needed answering but it set off a whole litany of deliciously pointless questions which she had constantly been wondering about during her two months' stay in the Vercors: "Why does that man mean so much to me?" "Don't mince your words, why do I *love him* so much?" Objectively speaking, Malaussène was certainly not her type, he didn't give a damn about anything, never listened to music, hated television, would witter on like a senile idiot about the evils of the media, sneered at psychoanalysis, and if he had ever had a political conscience, then it must have been like a "passing watermark", admittedly "passing watermark" had no meaning, but it said what it wanted to say loud and clear in Malaussène-speak. Benjamin was, in every respect, the exact opposite of ex-Colonial Governor Corrençon, Julie's father, who had devoted his life to decolonisation, had made History his daily bread and Geography his secret garden, and who would have died of thirst if cut off from world news. Malaussène was as much a slippered family man as her father had been a foot-loose travelling man (the Governor had chucked his daughter into boarding school and the only memories she had of him from that time came from cruelly brief holidays) and, to round off the list of comparisons, the Governor had started taking opium and wound up on heroin, just like a youngster, while the mere sight of a joint turned Malaussène into a raving Spanish inquisitor.

Malaussène, who had ended up with a bullet in his brains.

*

The sun was now rising and Julie understood what she'd always known deep down. The only reason why she had loved those two men, and those two alone, was that they were *commentaries on the world*. The expression was absurd, but Julie couldn't find another way of putting it. Her father, Charles-Emile Corrençon, the former Colonial Governor, and her man, Benjamin Malaussène, the Scapegoat, had that much in common: they were *commentaries on the world*. Benjamin was his own music, radio, press and telly. Benjamin who never went out, Benjamin who was so "un with-it", Benjamin exuded the *zeitgeist*. During the months of her convalescence in Benjamin's bedroom, Julie had breathed in the *zeitgeist* just as surely as if she had been wading over some terrible battlefield. It could be expressed differently, you could say, for instance, that the Governor and the Goat had been the active consciences of their respective eras and that, in his way, the Goat had been the living memory of the Governor: "*I dream of a society in which mankind's sole concern will be his neighbour's happiness*," the Governor had proclaimed.

Benjamin was that dream come true.

*

I'm losing it, Julie said to herself. I'm losing it. This is no time for a remembrance service, the only questions I have to answer are "who?" and "why?"

Because, when it came down to it, whatever the Governor and Benjamin had once been, they were now no more.

*

"Julie!"

A child's voice outside her door.

"Julie!"

Julie stayed mum.

"Julie, it's Jeremy . . ."

(Oh! Jeremy standing there on the dais, Jeremy looking round the dimly-lit pandemonium of the Palais Omnisport, Jeremy yelling: "Who did that?")

"Julie, I know you're in there!"

123

He was hammering on the door.

"Let me in!"

Then there were also the Malaussène children, the mother's children . . . "family of loonies" . . .

"Julie!"

But Julie sat motionlessly wrapped up around her heart. (Sorry, Jeremy, I can't move. I'm deep-baked in shit.)

"Julie, I need your help!"

He was shouting now. He was kicking at the door.

"Julie!"

Then he started to tire.

"Julie, I want to help you, you won't be able to do this on your own . . ."

He'd guessed what she meant to do.

"Listen to me, I've got one or two ideas."

Julie didn't doubt that.

"I know who did it and I know why . . ."

Lucky you, Jeremy. I don't. Not yet . . .

There was a redoubled hammering at the door. Feet and fists together. Then silence.

"Too bad," said Jeremy. "Then I'll do it all on my own."

You won't do anything at all, Jeremy, thought Julie. Someone will be waiting for you outside the main entrance, Hadouch, or Simon, or old Thian, or Mo, or the whole lot of them. They must have sworn in Benjamin's memory not to let you burn down two schools in one lifetime. You won't do anything, Jeremy. Belleville's watching out for you.

Chapter 21

"IT WAS THE Vendetta Press which sent you here, I imagine?"

Ex-minister Chabotte was eying Chief Superintendent Coudrier up and down. Or, rather, down and up.

"The fact is that one of my inspectors was informed by the head of the Vendetta Press that you are the real J. L. B., sir."

"And you thought it more appropriate to come and see me yourself, rather than submitting me to the questions of one of your inspectors. My sincere thanks to you, Coudrier."

"The least I could do . . ."

"We are now in one of those situations in which the least that can be done may take on the greatest of importance. Do take a seat. Can I offer you anything? Whisky? Port? Tea?"

"No, nothing. I shan't be staying long."

"Neither shall I, as a matter of fact. My flight leaves in an hour."

. . .

"Yes, well, I've taken to scribbling in my idle moments and would rather all this remained hush-hush. It is incompatible with my position, at least until I retire. We shall then see if it would be appropriate for me to reveal myself. Meanwhile, we sent off this young man to impersonate J. L. B. in the limelight. It was publishing strategy, nothing more."

("Apart from a bullet in Malaussène's head" . . . Chief Superintendent Coudrier thought to himself, but didn't share his observation. He preferred to stick to routine questioning.)

"Do you have any idea why Malaussène was shot?"

"No, not the slightest."

("I'd have been amazed if you had.")

"Unless . . ."

. . .

"Unless someone wanted to gun down an image."

125

"I beg your pardon?"

Always keep your head down in front of a minister. Never give him the impression that you might cop on more quickly than him, could even replace him.

"You are not unaware of the extent of the advertising campaign which preceded the launch of my new novel at Bercy. The Vendetta Press has, I suppose, also informed you of my sales figures . . . all of which is quite sufficient for some lunatic or other to decide to make a name for himself by shooting down a myth. This leaves us with a large choice: some international revolutionary treating himself to Free-Market Realism's star author, a crazed fan consuming his god in public, just as someone gobbled up poor old John Lennon, who knows? . . . We are spoilt for choice, which is rather a pity for you, my dear chap . . ."

All of which was spoken in a detached voice, in a library so large and full of volumes that it created an impression of profound wisdom.

"How long have you been writing?"

"For sixteen years. Seven titles in sixteen years and two hundred and twenty-five million readers. The oddest part of it all is that I never had the slightest intention to publish."

"Didn't you?"

"No. I am a state servant, Coudrier, not a public entertainer. I had always imagined that, if I ever did write a book, then it would be my memoirs. Something to occupy one's retirement from politics so as to remain unretired from one's battles. But destiny was to decide otherwise."

("How can anybody come out with such sentences?")

"Destiny was it, sir?"

A moment's hesitation. Then, rather brusquely:

"I have a mother. Upstairs. Madame Nazaré Quissapaolo Chabotte."

Chabotte indicated the library ceiling with his thumb. His old mother's bedroom, no doubt.

"Deaf and dumb for the last sixteen years. And all of the world's sorrows written across her face. Would you like to see her?"

"That won't be necessary."

"Indeed not. In fact, you have just saved yourself from a rather trying experience. Excuse me one moment, will you? Olivier! Olivier!"

Since the above-mentioned Olivier did not put in an instantaneous appearance, ex-minister Chabotte bounded over towards the library door, his fists clenched. He, who had just alluded to his old mother, now looked like a capricious child. The door, of course, opened before he reached it. Olivier had arrived.

"What about the car, for heaven's sake? Is it ready?"

"The Mercedes? It's ready, sir. Antoine has just called me up from the garage. He'll be here any minute now."

"Thank you. Take the bags down to the hall."

The door closed again.

"Where was I?"

"Your mother, sir."

"Oh yes! The strange thing is that she always wanted me to write. Women! They do get ideas into their heads about their offspring . . . but I digress . . . So, I started scribbling when she fell ill. Every evening, I read her what I had written. Lord knows why, but it used to cheer her up. Despite her deafness, I continued . . . sixteen years of reading, with her not understanding a blessed word . . . but it is the only smile we get out of her all day. Can you understand that sort of thing, Coudrier?"

("You are pissing me off, Chabotte . . . You are probably lying, but you are certainly pissing me off, for that matter, you always have pissed me off, especially when you were in charge of the police force . . . ")

"Of course I can, sir. May I ask what made you decide to publish?"

"A bridge evening with the head of the Vendetta Press. She wanted to read me, she did so, and . . . "

"Could you show me one of your manuscripts?"

That question, slipped in among the others, did not have the same effect. Surprise, stiffness, then at last scorn. Yes, a slight, but extremely scornful grin.

"A manuscript? Whatever are you talking about, Coudrier? Have you gone mad? Are you the only person who still writes with a pen in this country? Follow me."

Little detour into the adjoining study.

"Here, this is my 'manuscript'."

And the ex-minister handed the Chief Superintendent a floppy disk, which he gratefully pocketed.

"And this is the finished product. You can read it when you have nothing better to do."

It was a brand-new copy of *The Lord of the Currencies*. Royal-blue dust jacket and huge title. Author's name J. L. B. in capitals right at the top, and publisher's name j. l. b. in tiny lower-case letters at the bottom.

"Would you like me to sign it for you?"

Too much irony in the question to require an answer.

"May I ask you the terms of the contract which you have with the Vendetta Press, whose name, I notice, does not appear on the cover?"

"A solid gold contract, old chap. 70/30. 70% of the rights for me. But this leaves them ample to keep their little co-operative time-piece ticking over. Will that be all?"

("That will be all.")

"Yes, thank you, that will be all."

"Don't thank me, Coudrier. One more question and you would have made me miss my plane. I'm scarpering off because this whole business puts the willies up me, believe it or not. If we live in a country in which a killer can quite simply shoot down a man in public, I do not see what will stop him from finding out J. L. B.'s real identity and coming round here to bump me off."

"You are under police protection, sir. My men are watching over you."

The ministerial hand on the Chief Superintendent's elbow. The waltzing ministerial step as the Chief Superintendent was ushered out.

"Do tell me. That murder at Champrond Prison, our Monsieur de Saint-Hiver who was tortured to death, you are the one leading the investigation, are you not, Coudrier?"

"I am indeed, sir."

"Have you arrested the guilty party?"

"No."

"Do you have a lead?"

"No, nothing conclusive."

"Well, that is precisely why I am flying out of here, my dear Coudrier. I am not satisfied with a police force that merely protects future possible corpses. I shall return only when you have arrested Malaussène's murderer. And not before. Good luck, Coudrier. And wish me God's speed."

"God's speed, sir."

Chapter 22

SEVERINA BOCCALDI, AN Italian, appeared in Rue de la Pompe at about 6.00 pm. Thanks to her horse's head and ox's eyes she was able to spot both the mechanical and human cameras. Ex-minister Chabotte was being well protected. His mansion had been wired up (swivelling camera, interphone with closed-circuit television) and was also being eyed up (a plain-clothes copper idling on the pavement, who looked too much like Joe Soap to be true, and an undercover van at the entrance of the street – an old sausage-and-chip vendor's Tube Citroën, as inconspicuous in Rue de la Pompe as huskies in the Sahara). But the Force is a public body, Severina Boccaldi told herself charitably. It must have been the only vehicle available for Chabotte's protection that day.

She parked her BMW about a hundred yards from the ex-minister's mansion, on the other side of the road, and strode away from it. Outside the ministerial gate, Severina Boccaldi asked the cop in mufti for directions, and confirmed that it really was a cop in mufti: he couldn't help her, wasn't from round there, hardly knew Paris, knew Rome even less, no, he apologised nervously, practically telling her to move on. Severina Boccaldi made use of this minute of non-explanations by taking a good look at the black four-door saloon with its tricolour badge, neatly parked there on an immaculate white gravel drive, in front of a delta of marble steps. She calculated the time it took the exterior camera to rotate. She also analysed its sweep and noted, with satisfaction, that her car was out of shot.

While walking past the sausage-and-chip van, which looked as if it had been abandoned there, with its flap down and its bodywork rusting up from the bottom, she distinctly heard the following exclamation:

"You wanna see what I'm holding? Then I'll show it to you!"

Severina Boccaldi said to herself that this was either an illegal gambling den or a lover's hidey-hole, depending on what exactly the gentleman was holding. After that, she got back into her car, thus freeing a parking space which was soon to be taken by a Giulietta which Miranda Skoulatou, a Greek citizen, had hired that very morning from a certain Padovani.

"Greek, are you?" Padovani had cooed over her brand-new European ID card. "That means we're just about cousins."

And he gave a friendly wink, which got him precisely nowhere.

*

When the limo with its official badge pulled out of Chabotte's gate, Miranda Skoulatou's hand reached out towards her ignition. Then fell back again. It wasn't Chabotte's car, it was Chief Superintendent Coudrier's. With his window down, the Chief Superintendent drove past her without noticing her. He was at the wheel himself. She thought she could see an expression of fury on his pale Napoleonic profile.

Miranda Skoulatou slid down once more under her steering wheel, her legs folded beneath the seat, her eye riveted on the rear-view mirror, which gave her a good view of the entire street, as far as the undercover sausagemen. The service automatic weighed heavily in her coat pocket. Had it ever fired a single shot? Miranda doubted it. She'd greased it down with some oil from her car, had turned over the mechanism several times and had then put the cartridges back into the cylinder. It wasn't really a lady's weapon.

Just as for Severina Boccaldi, it wouldn't be prudent for Miranda Skoulatou to stay in the same place for too long.

She waited for the plain-clothes cop to be relieved by a fellow officer, then drove off at once. Twelve minutes later, an Audi 80, hired by Almut Bernhardt, a vaguely hysterical Austrian teacher of history, found a different parking space on Rue de la Pompe, nearer Chabotte's mansion, within the sweep of the rotating camera.

Aware that she was being filmed, Almut calmly got out. She entered the building which was immediately adjacent to her car door, reemerged at once, then sat back down in her car while the camera continued on its sweep. Lying down on the front seats, she started to wait. Each turn of the camera filmed an apparently empty car, whose rear-view mirror gave a perfect reflection of ex-minister Chabotte's mansion.

Then, suddenly, the police were everywhere in Rue de la Pompe. Sirens wailing from one direction, sirens wailing from the other. Almut instinctively threw her revolver under the back seat. "Blown it," she said to herself. Bent double below the dashboard, her head shrinking into her shoulders, she wondered where she'd slipped up, if a pair of eyes had spotted her and been following her since early that morning and why, if that were the case, the uniforms had taken so long arriving. Meanwhile, the sirens from the top of the street screamed past her to meet up with the sirens from the bottom of the street. "It's not me they're after," Almut Bernhardt thought. A rapid glance in her rear-view mirror confirmed that they were after the Citroën sausage van, parked further down the street. One of the cars glided to an immaculate halt, blocking the road diagonally. Four inspectors leapt out of it, revolvers aimed at the van. The rest had already formed a gun battery behind their own vehicle, at the junction with Rue Paul-Doumer.

The officer who was now approaching the van stood out from his fellows by his coolness and total lack of style. He was a big lad, with a bull neck and glowering eyes, wearing one of those jackets with fur-lined collars which had been made eternally fashionable by the allied airforces during World War II. He wasn't carrying a gun. He was walking towards the van so calmly that it really did look as though he just wanted to buy himself some chips. He politely knocked at the window of the door to the left. The door didn't open. He said something. The door opened. And Almut Bernhardt saw a Berber with a flaming red mop of hair get out of the van, soon followed by a big Black who unfolded himself through the flap at the back. Eight coppers leapt on them. The Berber's red hair disappeared into a car whose light then started flashing. The plain-clothes cop who'd been on the beat outside Chabotte's residence took the wheel of the sausage van. Sirens, starters, the two police cars drove off escorting their exhibit.

Apparently, the Black and the Berber had had the same idea as the Austrian woman.

"But the sausage-selling bit really was not a good idea, my lads."

Almut Bernhardt would have sympathised with their lot a while longer if a black Mercedes hadn't just parked in front of Chabotte's gate. At that very moment, a valet loaded two suitcases into it, while the chauffeur held the door open to a bouncy Chabotte, who threw himself into the car, as if it was a double bed. The valet returned to his hearth and the chauffeur to his wheel. Almut Bernhardt got her gun back and turned on her ignition.

The collision wasn't a violent one, but it was enough to stop the Mercedes and make the Austrian woman leap out of her Audi and shout:

"*Mein Gott! Mein Gott! Schauen Sie doch mal!*" (My God! My God! Look what you've done!)

She pointed at her dented wing, but the chauffeur who was rushing towards her was holding a big revolver, pointedly aimed at her.

"*Hilfe!*" the history teacher screamed. "*Hilfe!*" (Help! Help!)

Until Chabotte turned up.

"Put that gun away, Antoine. You're being ridiculous."

Then, to the lady:

"*Entschuldigen Sie, Madame.*" (My apologies, Madame.)

131

And, back to his chauffeur:

"Park her car for her, will you, Antoine? The plane will not wait for me all day."

The chauffeur got behind the wheel of the Audi 80. While he was reversing it with a scream of tortured bodywork, Chabotte offered his card to the unfortunate Austrian lady.

"*Ich habe es eilig, Madame.*" (I am in a hurry, Madame.)

"*Ich auch,*" said Almut Bernhardt. (So am I, said Almut Bernhardt.)

But what she had to offer in exchange for the card was a hefty service automatic. A truly massive piece. Then, without the trace of a smile:

"*Steigen Sie hinein, oder Sie sind tot.*" (Get in, or you're a dead man.)

*

When Antoine got out of the Audi 80 and saw the Mercedes driving away, his only thought was what a fast worker Chabotte had been once again. Antoine the chauffeur felt very proud about that. When it came to scoring, no-one worked faster than his boss Chabotte.

Chapter 23

THE MOTHER WHINED:

"But it's *unheard of*. For goodness sake, something should be *done about it*!"

The younger of the two coppers looked at the little girl. Her eyes were staring in horror. At their feet, the stiff was stiff. Never mind what the mother said, there wasn't much they could do about it now.

"These days, people are being murdered *absolutely everywhere*."

In the early-morning air, steam was coming out of the mother's mouth.

"And this isn't the sort of place where you're *supposed* to murder people!"

Even though he was a recent recruit, the younger of the two coppers had already just about seen it all when it came to murders. But he hadn't heard it all. He had only been transferred to the leafy suburb of Passy three weeks before.

"It is *quite* unacceptable," the mother went on. "One goes for one's morning run and one's nine-year-old daughter stumbles over a corpse!"

"Whatever is the world *coming to*?"

The mother was very pretty and the little girl charming, despite the look of horror in her eyes. They were wearing matching tracksuits. With day-glo stripes. Jogging fire-flies. Or, in this context, will-o'-the-wisps. But the younger of the two coppers was no cynic. He just found the mother pretty, that was all. Around them, the wood smelt of dawn.

"It is three generations now that we have been living in the neighbourhood, and we have *never* seen anything like this before."

I've only been in the force for three years, thought the younger of the two coppers, and I've already seen fifty-four "things like this".

The trees went on growing. The grass glistened. The young copper's team-mate went through the dead man's pockets. Wallet, credit cards, papers.

Oh shit!

He leapt to his feet, brandishing the deceased's ID.

"Oh shit!"

It was as if all the hassles he'd carefully avoided during his long career as a uniformed officer had made a date with him in that lovely wood.

"Whatever is the matter *now*?" the mother asked.

The old copper looked at her blankly, or as if he'd just noticed her, or as if he was going to ask her advice, or as if he'd just woken from a dream. He finally said:

"No-one move, don't touch anything, I have to contact HQ!"

That was his name for the Quai des Orfèvres. He was a very old copper, one of the old school, with retirement just around the corner. He could easily have done without this *corpse*. Slowly, he trudged back towards the van.

"You don't imagine that you are going to make me spend the *entire day* here! Come along dawling..."

But dawling didn't budge. Dawling couldn't take her eyes off the corpse. Dawling was fascinated by that small purplish hole in the back of his neck – his hair, reddened by the gun blast, had turned into a crown of curls.

The young copper wondered which was more *traumatising* (a word the mother had used), for a child to discover a dead adult, or for an adult to discover a dead child. The answer slipped away from him, so the young copper stared down again at the small purplish hole and the tiny halo of singed hair and said out loud, though it was meant for himself:

"An execution."

Then added:

"And no messing."

"*Would you mind...?*" said the mother.

She spoke in italics, in a laboured voice, as though translating her own words.

*

When the telephone rang in Chief Superintendent Coudrier's office, he was turning over page 320 of *The Lord of the Currencies*. It was the tale of Philippe Ahoueltène, a third-generation immigrant, sociologically condemned to being a dustbin man, but who had the idea of collecting and selling Paris's gilded garbage, then that of the entire world's capitals. Philippe Ahoueltène had started out hanging onto the rear end of a rubbish van but, by halfway through the novel, he was already the undisputed master of the currency markets, lording it imperiously over the world's exchange rates – hence the title of the book. Meanwhile, he had wed a galactically beautiful, incredibly cultured Swedish girl (she was already married, he ruthlessly ruined her husband), making her pregnant with a child that was born at night, in the middle of Amazonia, during a typhoon which the local Indians saw as presaging the arrival of a demigod...

Chief Superintendent Coudrier was filled with consternation.

The previous evening, Elisabeth had prepared three thermos flasks of coffee for him before she went home – "Thank you, Elisabeth my dear. I am going to need it" – then Chief Superintendent Coudrier, laying aside his current reading matter with a twinge of regret (the Bossuet-Fénelon quarrel, brought about by Madame Guyon's quietism), had plunged into *The Lord of the Currencies* with all the enthusiasm of an illuminator of manuscripts who'd been sent off to repaint the Forth Bridge.

But the Chief Superintendent was a methodical man, who knew how to make sacrifices, and now he was also an extremely angry policeman.

Chief Superintendent Coudrier blamed himself personally for the bullet that had dug a path through Malaussène's head. A high-penetration .22-calibre job, fired with the intention of killing him outright. Hadn't he been the one who had packed Malaussène off to receive that bullet, so that he himself might have his hands free to investigate Saint-Hiver's death? And his inquiries hadn't progressed one inch, just as he had admitted to Chabotte last night. They had even regressed: under the new governor, the prisoners were wreaking havoc, another murder had been committed among the inmates, and the killer had escaped. An utter fiasco. It could hardly have been any worse if Malaussène *had* become involved. The image of Malaussène's death haunted J. L. B.'s ill-written pages. Coudrier had had a soft spot for him. He remembered every word of their first conversation. Three years ago now. The evening when Inspector Caregga, in his inevitable pilot's jacket, had rescued Malaussène from being lynched by his work mates, then laid him out on his boss's divan. When the lad woke up, his first question had been about the divan:

"Why are Récamier divans so hard?"

"Because victors lose their empires when they fall asleep on sofas, Monsieur Malaussène," Chief Superintendent Coudrier had replied.

"They lose them anyway," had been Malaussène's riposte.

Before adding, with a grimace from his entire body:

"On the sofa of time."

And Coudrier had taken a liking to him. He had a fleeting image of his son-in-law, a scrupulous fast-laner who spent their Sunday lunchtimes quietly drafting answers to even the slightest question . . . Not that Chief Superintendent Coudrier would have liked to have Malaussène as his son-in-law . . . although . . . no, honestly not, but he would still have liked his son-in-law to be more like Malaussène from time to time . . .

Oh well! A dedicated son-in-law is . . . a dull son-in-law.

With Malaussène there was never a dull moment, hence that bullet between his eyes.

That was the point which Chief Superintendent Coudrier had reached with his reading of *The Lord of the Currencies* when the telephone rang. A sergeant in the Passy Commissariat informed him of Chabotte's demise.

"An execution, Chief Superintendent."

("Here we go," Chief Superintendent Coudrier thought.)

"In the Bois de Boulogne, on the path around the *lac inférieur*, sir."

("Just near his house," Chief Superintendent Coudrier thought.)

"A little girl discovered the body while she was having an early-morning run with her mother."

("Making little girls go for early-morning runs?" the Chief Superintendent thought, chalking up a black mark against the mother.)

"We've left everything as it was and closed the area off," the sergeant recited.

("Inform my lords and masters . . ." the Chief Superintendent thought as he hung up. "Terrible people, lords and masters. Bossuet broke Fénelon's back and Madame La Maintenon sent Madame Guyon off to the Bastille . . .")

"Quietism is not for tomorrow," the Chief Superintendent murmured.

Then he dialled the number of the Minister of the Interior.

*

The four inspectors were among the strongest and the most patient men that Headquarters had to offer. The sun had set long ago, their wives were asleep. There were just two suspects, a big Black known as Mo and a Berber, broader than he was tall, with a flaming head of red hair, the blazing colour of which fully justified the sunglasses the four inspectors were wearing. He went by the name of Simon. A fifth copper stood back from the others, not saying a word. He was a tiny Vietnamese. The spitting image of Ho Chi Minh. In a leather harness, he was carrying a baby which had intense staring eyes. Both the coppers and the delinquents avoided looking at the Vietnamese and the child.

"Okay, lads, let's take it from the top again," the first inspector said.

"We've got all the time in the world," pointed out the second one, whose shirt now looked like a used Kleenex.

"It's all the same to us," the third one halfheartedly agreed.

"Let's go," said the fourth one, throwing away an empty paper cup, which landed beside an overflowing bin.

For the eighth time, Mo and Simon trotted out their names and those of their fathers and of their fathers' fathers unto an extremely remote generation. The Berber was smiling as he answered. A mere illusion, perhaps, caused by that gap between his incisors. The big Black was more serious-looking.

"So, what were you doing in that Citroën van?"

"Merguez," said the Black.

"You were going to sell merguez. On Rue de la Pompe? In the sixteenth *arrondissement*?"

"People sell spring rolls on Rue de Belleville," the Berber remarked.

"Without a permit, you don't sell anything anywhere," one of the coppers butted in.

"So why hadn't you opened the flap of your van?"

"It wasn't opening time yet," said the Berber.

"Rich bastards work late," the Black explained.

"Not as late as us," one of the inspectors couldn't help adding.

"That's our fault," said the Berber. "We're really sorry."

"Shut it, you."

"So, merguez on Rue de la Pompe, that's it, is it?"

"Yup," the Black confirmed.

"And do you know Selim the Sting?"

"Nope."

It was a quick-fire conversation. A nice little chat about this and that.

"A little Moroccan boxer. A featherweight. You sure you don't know him?"

"Yup."

Selim the Sting had been discovered dead after the stampede at the Bercy Palais Omnisport. Horribly dead. Curled up like a squashed spider on the dry floor of a shower.

"And you don't know the Gibbon either?"

"Nope."

"A tall skinny lad, who could swat flies out of the air with his stick."

"We don't mix with blokes like that."

"What about the Russian?"

"What Russian?"

"The other two's mate. The muscleman."

"We stick to our own mates."

"Were you there, at Bercy?"

"Not half we were! There was our mate Malaussène up on the stage . . . the poor bastard."

"The Gibbon, the Sting and the Russian were there too."

And had died there. Of the same squashed-spider death.

"We dunno what you're talking about."

The ambulance men's first thought was that they had been killed in the panic.

Trampled to death. But . . . the way they were curled up in agony, their faces blue, almost black . . . it just wasn't possible.

"Look," one of the inspectors calmly said. "You and Ben Tayeb snuffed our three little villains there. What we want to know is why."

"We never snuffed no-one, inspector."

The forensic scientist had been thrown for a while. Until he discovered a tiny needle prick at the bottom of their necks. Then the autopsy told the story: an injection of caustic soda into their brains.

"Mo and Simon . . ."

Everyone turned round. It was the little Vietnamese. He hadn't budged. He was still leaning his back against the wall. The baby was nestling his service automatic. Two pairs of eyes and that gravelly voice.

"What did those three bastards do to Benjamin which made you go out and top them?"

"Malaussène never mixed with blokes like that," the Black said.

Was it because of the baby's stare? The Black had spoken too hastily. Just a tad too hastily. Thian was the only one to notice. The others started up with their questions again.

"Why were you hiding out in that van on Rue de la Pompe?"

"Sausages," said the Berber.

"I'll tell you what you were doing," said one of the coppers. "You were causing a diversion in your shit-heap of a van. While we were collaring you, someone else kidnapped Chabotte and whacked him."

"Who's Chabotte?" Simon asked.

"You're going down for a very long time."

"That's life for you, innit?" the Black sadly said to the Berber. "You run a three-card trick for donkeys, then the day you try and go straight, you wind up in the shit . . . What did I tell you, Simon?"

"Let's take it from the top again," someone said.

Chapter 24

I LEFT HIM *after making a scene!* Julie woke up in a cold sweat. She'd just seen herself again, straddling Benjamin, berating him for being what he was, ordering him to become himself ... A mother superior crouching over the possessed!

And him, locked between her thighs, an incredulous fury in his eyes, unrecognisable, like a trusting animal caught in a trap. They'd just made love.

She stuck in the dagger: "You have *never* been yourself!"

Identity ...

She was part of that generation ... the Credo of Identity, the sacrosanct duty to remain clear-headed. And never to be taken in! Above all, never to be taken in! That was the greatest crime: to be taken in! "Always at the call of reality!" ... "A right royal pain in the arse, more like it." ... "And a liar, too." ...

She'd wrapped herself up in her professional dogma. In *reality*, when getting at Benjamin for his Scapegoat's existence, his mother's children, his lending his face to another, she was really yelling out something quite different to him: that she wanted him to herself, all for herself, with children who'd be theirs, that was what that explosion of anger had really been all about, the abscess of marriage had popped. "Realistic journalism, bullshit ..." She'd set off like an eternal adventurer, fire bursting from her eyes and from her pen and now she found herself, at thirty-something, in the grip of uncontrollable panic ... the loneliness of the explorer who returns to his village too late and tries to buy up all the houses. That was the long and short of it. She had demanded that aircraft-carrier Malaussène turn itself into a houseboat, a family home for her, period.

Now that Benjamin had been taken away from her, there was no room left for doubt.

*

Fine. Sleep was now out of the question. Panting for breath, Julie got up. The wash

139

basin in her tiny bedsit, one of her five Parisian hideouts, spat out icy-cold rusty water.

Julie dowsed herself. She stood for a moment, head down, her tense arms leaning on the enamel of the basin. She felt the weight of her breasts. She lifted her head. She looked at herself in the mirror. The day before yesterday, she'd cut off her hair. She'd stuffed it into a bin liner, before scattering it into the Seine. There had been another knock at her door after Jeremy's. She'd heard: "Police!" She'd continued to cut her hair in silence. There had been a second knock, but it had lacked conviction. She'd heard the sound of a note being pushed under the door. A summons to the police station, which she was not going to obey. From her professional life (journalist at the call of reality), she had unearthed a revamped Italian passport and two fake identity cards. Wigs. Make-up. She would be successively Italian, Austrian and Greek. This fancy-dress stuff used to amuse her. She'd raised the female prerogative of transformation to the highest degree of perfection. She knew how to make herself ugly, just plain Jane. (No, no-one's condemned to being beautiful . . .) At the age when well-intentioned mothers teach their daughters how to smile without giving themselves wrinkles, her father the Governor had shown Julie how to make the most unimaginable grimaces. Thanks to his universal sympathies, he was a clown, a human chameleon. When imitating Ben Barka making a speech, he became Ben Barka. And if Ben Barka had to hold a discussion with Norodom Sihanouk, then he became both Ben Barka and Norodom Sihanouk. Outside, he acted out street scenes for her. With astonishing rapidity, he mimed a dog, its mistress, then the tomato plant it had just pissed on. Yes, her father the Governor had even been able to mime vegetation. Or objects. He stuck his spindly frame in front of her, his bent arms forming a perfect circle above his head then, like a ballerina, he hiked himself up onto the tips of his toes, his left leg at a right angle with his foot perpendicular to his leg.

"What am I, Julie?"

"A key!"

"Well done, sweetheart. Now, can you be a key for me?"

*

The motor of the Giulietta turned over silently. Miranda Skoulatou, the Greek, had spotted Gauthier, the personal assistant. The one who appeared in the background of the shots of J. L. B. Malaussène. The one who'd given Laure Kneppel the copy of the model interview. The one who'd made certain that the text was returned to its original state. The one who'd decided that Benjamin needed to be taught a lesson.

"Yes, it was Gauthier," Chabotte had admitted, the barrel of the automatic in the nape of his neck.

Then he'd added:

"A head-strong chap, even though he scarcely looks it."

Gauthier lived on Rue Henri-Barbusse, in the fifth *arrondissement*, just opposite Lycée Lavoisier. He had a fixed routine. He left home then returned, like clockwork. The face of a student in a woolly duffel-coat.

Miranda the Greek checked the cylinder of her automatic one last time.

In her rear-view mirror, she saw Gauthier approaching.

He had a chubby face.

He was carrying a schoolboy's briefcase.

Miranda Skoulatou released the safety catch on her automatic. The car's motor was as silent as a morning breeze.

Chapter 25

"SEVERINA BOCCALDI. AN Italian."

"Was she wearing a wig?"

"Sorry?"

"Do you think it was her real hair, or a wig?"

"All I saw was her teeth."

"Can you tell me what colour her hair was?"

"No, all I could see was her teeth. Even in her passport photo she was all teeth."

Boussier, the car-hire man, was a bit of a joker. Caregga, the police inspector, patience made flesh. Tenacious, with it.

"Fair or dark?"

"Sorry, I honestly couldn't tell you. There's something I do remember, though. She made the clutch screech when she pulled off."

"Neither particularly fair, nor particularly dark, then."

"Don't reckon so, no . . . You should never hire a car out to a woman. And specially not to an Italian woman."

"Red?"

"Definitely not. I can sniff them out with my eyes closed."

"Very long?"

"No."

"Very short?"

"Not that either. She had this sort of hairdo, I reckon. See what I mean? You know, a hairdo, like women have . . . "

"A wig," Inspector Caregga presumed.

*

The second customer was Austrian. She'd gone to an agency on Place Gambetta, way up in the twentieth *arrondissement*.

"Her name?"

"Almut Bernhardt."

"Helmut?"

"Almut."

"Almut?"

"Almut, with an 'a'. A girl's name, apparently."

Inspector Caregga noted it all down. He was the silent type. Maybe a bit shy. Come rain or shine, he wore a pilot's jacket with a fur-lined collar.

"Was she tall?"

"Hard to say."

"What do you mean?"

"She seemed creased up. The same goes for her face . . ."

"Her face?"

"According to her ID card, she was born in 1954, which isn't that old, but her face was marked."

"With scars?"

"No, by life. Marked by life . . . life's scars."

("This character is never going to make his fortune hiring out cars," Inspector Caregga thought to himself.)

"Profession?"

"Teacher. A history teacher. You see, Austrians have a lot of history to deal with," the car-hire man explained. "To start out with, the break-up of their empire, then the Nazis, and now the risk of Balkanisation . . ."

("Ought to change jobs," Inspector Caregga said to himself.)

*

"Yeah, what's the problem?" the third car-hire man asked at once.

He was a little bloke who always got aggressive when faced with big blokes, but Caregga was a big bloke who was always patient with little blokes – which made them all the more aggressive.

"An Audi, registration number 246 FM 75. Apparently it's one of yours."

"Maybe it is. So what?"

"Could you please check?"

"Why, what's happened to it?"

"We'd like to know who you hired it out to."

"That's none of the old bill's business, that isn't. I'm bound by an oath of secrecy."

"It was found on the scene of a murder."

"Is she all right?"

"I beg your pardon?"

"The motor. She's not a write-off, is she?"

"No, not a mark on her."

"So, can I have her back?"

"Yes, when the lab's through with her."

"And how long's all this bullshit going to take?"

"Who did you hire the car out to?"

"You know how much a day this is going to cost me?"

"It's a murder case, so it'll be quick."

"Quick, eh?"

"Who did you hire the car out to?"

"The only thing you lot are quick about is shit-stirring."

Inspector Caregga changed the subject.

"Alexandre Padovani, illegal selling of number plates and stolen cars, possession of firearms, three years in Fresnes Prison, two years' expulsion from France."

It was the car-hire man's CV.

"Youthful errors. I've gone straight."

"Maybe you have, Padovani, but if you keep on pissing me about, I'll straighten you out even more."

Inspector Caregga occasionally had a way with words.

"Skoulatou," the car-hire man said. "Miranda Skoulatou. A Greek."

*

COUDRIER: If my calculations are correct, we now have five corpses on our hands since the shooting of Malaussène.

VAN THIAN: Malaussène had loads of friends . . .

COUDRIER: It seems quite probable that the three bodies in Bercy were the work of Belleville.

VAN THIAN: Caustic soda . . . yeah, that's pretty likely.

COUDRIER: But what about Chabotte and young Gauthier?

VAN THIAN: . . . .

COUDRIER: Could I ask you a favour, Thian?

VAN THIAN: . . . .

COUDRIER: Be so good as to point that baby somewhere else.

VAN THIAN: It's a girl, Chief Superintendent. Her name's Verdun.

COUDRIER: All the more reason.

(Old Thian turned Verdun round on his lap. The child's eyes released Chief Superintendent Coudrier from their grip, then seized on the bronze Napoleon in exile on the mantelpiece behind Thian instead.)

COUDRIER: Thank you.

VAN THIAN: . . .

COUDRIER: . . .

VAN THIAN: . . .

COUDRIER: Are you still not a coffee drinker?

VAN THIAN: Since I started looking after Verdun I don't drink anything any more.

COUDRIER: . . .

VAN THIAN: . . .

COUDRIER: All the same . . . she does seem very good.

VAN THIAN: She's perfect.

COUDRIER: No illusions from the outset . . . That is probably an advantage in life.

VAN THIAN: The only one.

COUDRIER: But I didn't call you in to discuss the raising of children . . . Tell me, Thian, just how far will a woman go when she has decided to avenge the man she loves?

VAN THIAN: . . .

COUDRIER: . . .

VAN THIAN: Yup, at the very least.

COUDRIER: She hired out three cars in three names under three different nationalities. She didn't leave a single fingerprint on the vehicles, but she did on the rental agreements because she took her gloves off to sign them. To be on the safe side, I have had all three handwritings analysed, and they are one and the same. Heavily disguised, but still the same. As for her physical appearance, each time she becomes utterly unrecognisable. An Italian with horsy teeth, an hysterical Austrian and a flamboyantly beautiful Greek.

VAN THIAN: A real pro . . .

COUDRIER: I suppose that she hasn't exhausted her stock of disguises.

VAN THIAN: Nor her hideouts . . .

COUDRIER: . . .

VAN THIAN: . . .

COUDRIER: So, logically, what do you think her next move will be?

VAN THIAN: She'll wipe out the rest of the staff at the Vendetta Press.

COUDRIER: That is just what I am frightened of.

*

"I loved him."

Julie had changed hideouts once again. A bedsit on Rue Saint-Honoré.

145

"I loved him."

Lying on a rotten mattress, Julie repeated it out loud.

"I loved him."

She let her tears flow. She wasn't crying, she was letting her tears flow. The plain truth was emptying her out:

"I loved him."

That was her conclusion. It had nothing to do with the Governor, nor with the fact that Benjamin had been a "commentary on the world", nor with how old she was, her supposed fear of loneliness . . . All just excuses, just bullshit.

"I loved him."

She'd now been though every excuse in the book. To begin with, he'd just been the subject of one of her articles. His amazing job as a Scapegoat. Something she just couldn't miss. She'd written her article. But when the subject was all over, Benjamin had remained. Still there. Her own special subject: Benjamin Malaussène.

"I loved him."

She'd used him as a stop-over. She'd disappear for months then come and rest up on him. Until the day when she found that she was at home with him. He wasn't her aircraft-carrier. He was her houseboat. He was her.

"I loved him."

Now Benjamin had been reduced to this: her missing subject and the plain truth which was emptying her out.

"I loved him!"

There was a knock on the wall.

"Who did you love, for crying out loud?"

Chapter 26

G AUTHIER HAD LIVED a good Catholic life. And had died a good Catholic. With a bullet in the back of his neck, but still as a good Catholic – despite his years of study and being around so many books. The priest considered such faith worth a mention. And mention it he did, in his nasal voice, to the friends gathered in Saint Roch church around a coffin pointed towards the high altar. The family wept. The friends lowered their heads. Chief Superintendent Coudrier wondered why priests' voices always went up an octave as soon as they started preaching. Did the Holy Ghost speak through its nose? But, that aside, Chief Superintendent Coudrier was also resolutely against the entire staff of the Vendetta Press being wiped out. True enough, they were J. L. B.'s undercover publishers, but they were also reissuing the Bossuet-Fénelon polemic concerning the fundamental question of Madame Guyon's view of Pure Love. Such a publisher didn't deserve annihilation. But Chief Superintendent Coudrier feared that Julie Corrençon saw things otherwise. Saint Roch church had filled up with relatives, friends, publishers and coppers. Some hearts were breaking, while others were weighed down under their service automatics. Despite the circumstances, the men were eying up the women. And the women were blushing. They didn't realise that the men's fingers were on their triggers. Julie Corrençon could easily be among the mourners, or disguised as a choirboy, or lying in ambush in a confessional. She may even fly down from a stained-glass window, on an immaculate pair of wings, holding a pump-action shotgun to carry out her divine mission. The inspectors had itchy fingers and eyes sprouting from the backs of their heads. Some of them had already encountered women in love during their careers, and these ones were wearing bullet-proof vests. That girl wouldn't stop until she'd shot her way through to the end of her vengeance. There would be no quarter. She would go the whole hog. A high-penetration .22 bullet had blown her man away. When something like that happens, the woman is either grateful, or else finds it hard to forgive. The boss had ordered that the staff of the Vendetta Press be kept under close protection. And that anything remotely resembling a woman be scrutinised.

Other bodyguards had spontaneously joined the boys in blue: Calignac the rugby player's fourteen mates had formed a walking fortress around him. A scrum which a Celtic sorcerer had welded together for all eternity. The fifteen of them shuffled around like a wary crab. This bugged Calignac. His prayers had trouble taking wing. He needed someone to break through the pack so that his last farewells could rise up to Gauthier. Feelings that were as fraternal as an oval ball. Calignac had nurtured Gauthier under his protective love. Calignac had also loved Malaussène. Everything that was alien to rugby seemed unnervingly vulnerable to him. Neither Malaussène nor Gauthier had ever played rugby . . . and now look. But Calignac was no fool. He knew perfectly well that that wouldn't have made any difference . . . but all the same . . . all the same.

They were burying young Gauthier. They'd laid out this paper child in his coffin. Aspergillum. It was raining holy water. Aspergillum. In the name of the Trinity. Aspergillum. Loussa de Casamance, meanwhile, was not carrying the gun which his record in the Resistance allowed him to wear like a poisoned medal. He was a negro who'd survived Monte Cassino. Being shot down by a woman in love, however unjustly, seemed to him to be a wonderful way to go. Loussa de Casamance refused to be a national hero. The Nation, with Marshal Juin as its mouthpiece, had packed him off to get shot to ribbons on a lovely little Italian hillside, overlooked by impregnable fortifications. The negroes first. Then the A-rab skirmishers, who were later to offend the Nation when, at the end of hostilities, they demanded their independence. Those who had come back alive from that hill were laid low by the Nation, one fine morning, in the dust of Sétif – by machine guns. That very morning, the children of Monte Cassino had been playing with the skulls which they kept on unearthing in the still-warm ruins of the fortifications: a place of prayer before war nestled on it. Loussa didn't want to be a national hero. All Loussa wanted was to be a woman's hero. He'd been in love a few times. Always passionately. They had all been wonderful. Taking one of Julie Corrençon's bullets seemed like the least he could do in return. And Malaussène would have found it funny. Loussa and Malaussène had had lots of fun together. The lad had come into Loussa's life twenty years too late, and now he had left it too early. But the time they had worked together had really been fun. All the same, Loussa had never pushed their friendship. He'd never gone to see Malaussène at home. They'd met only in the corridors of the Vendetta Press. But that had been fun enough. So what had been the basis of Loussa and Malaussène's intimate laughter? Their common love of books, perhaps, a particular sort of love, their sort, a delinquent's love. They had a delinquent's love of books. They'd never imagined that a book could improve a bastard. And they'd been amused to watch how books fooled others into believing they were human. But they had really loved books. And this illusion was part of the work that they loved. It was certainly more of a laugh than slaving away on behalf of .22 high-penetration bullets . . . And, when feeling down, they had always been able to console themselves with the thought that the best arms merchants also have the best libraries. Loussa and Malaussène had often talked over that point, between shots of 13.5°-calibre Sidi-Brahim red.

Young Gauthier had started to levitate. His wooden coffin had sprouted four pairs of legs. He passed back up the aisle with a horizontal dignity which made heads bow. He pulled the crowd after him like a pied piper. Relatives first, then friends, everyone was in on the act, following little Gauthier, who'd been no leader while still alive. Loussa had carefully placed himself in front of Isabelle. He didn't want La Corrençon to kill his Isabelle. Isabelle, whom the Vendetta staff called Queen Zabo (and Malaussène had done to her face), but who, for Loussa, her gopher de Casamance, had always been just plain Isabelle, that little prose-merchant who had, from their earliest childhood on, always considered books to be the soul's true resting place. One afternoon in June 1954, just after the fall of Dien Bien Phu (one of the anecdotes that Loussa had told Malaussène), Isabelle called him into her office and said: "Loussa, we've just lost Indochina and I would-n't give the Chinese twenty years before they leave South-East Asia and set up home here in Paris. So learn Chinese for me as fast as you can, then translate everything of importance in their literature. When they arrive, their books will already be here. We'll have their bed made for them." (And Loussa had concluded by raising his glass to Benjamin: "And that's why you hear me jabbering away in Chinese, shit-for-brains. *Ganbei!* Cheers!")

No, no matter how much he had liked Malaussène, Loussa was not going to let his friend's Julie blow away his Isabelle. Loussa hadn't touched a shot of the Sidi-Brahim since the beginning of the slaughter. With all his reflexes back in working order, he was now ready, if necessary, to throw himself between Isabelle and the ladykiller . . . to perish as he had always wanted to: for a woman . . . and, what bliss, by a woman's hand!

*

The attack took the lot of them by surprise. It didn't come from a woman, it came from the skies. At the moment when they were loading Gauthier into his last ever taxi, Calignac felt an explosion in his left shoulder. Everyone else heard the blast. Calignac was hedged off. He couldn't be hit from the ground, so he had been hit from a perch. The scrum immediately flattened him.

"Let me go, for Christ's sake. I want to see where it's coming from."

149

"Move, and we'll ruggerbugger you."

Before being completely carpeted, a second bullet ripped into his calf. Lamaison, the stand-off half, at once leapt down onto the bloodied leg.

"That bitch is a fucking good shot!"

No more Calignac. Nor anyone else left standing on the steps of Saint Roch. Everyone was lying on everyone else. Loussa on Isabelle.

"Admit it . . . you've been dying to do this for the last fifty years."

"Don't move."

The crowd was flat out. Except for the corpse. Now abandoned, little Gauthier had slid out of his hearse. He bravely stuck up his coffined head right in the middle of the laid-out living.

The skies hesitated for a moment.

That hesitation was fatal.

A double being leapt up from that human mosaic. It had the inscrutable face of Ho Chi Minh, plus the face of a furious baby. Crouched solidly on his splayed legs, he was brandishing a huge Manhurin, which he was methodically emptying towards the window of a bedsit in the building over the road, sixth floor, third window to the right. The stare of the baby, who was strapped onto his back, seemed to guide his aim. On its ears, the baby wore the felt muffs which protect professionals' eardrums from gun blasts. The panes of glass in the bedsit window exploded, the frame fell away in splinters. Thian was firing like a battalion of Mexicans at a single target.

"Sorry, Julie."

Thian was speaking to Julie as he fired.

"You'll feel better afterwards."

Thian knew about the sorrow of being a widower. In his day, he'd lost his wife, Big Janine, and Gervaise, Janine's daughter, who Thian had carried around in a leather harness like Verdun, had left him for God. A nun. At the time, Thian would have liked a battalion of Mexicans to cut short his suffering.

"Life is a long agony after the death of love."

Thian was shooting kindly at Julie. One by one, the other coppers joined in. But they left their feelings out of it. Thian would have liked to have gunned down the lot of them. But his clip was empty.

A big lad was now running calmly across the street. He was wearing a pilot's jacket with a fur-lined collar. He pushed open the door. He leapt up the back staircase. Outside, just as the young Napoleon Bonaparte did on 13 *vendémiaire* 1795 on the steps of that very same church, Chief Superintendent Coudrier ordered the cease-fire.

V

THE PRICE OF THREAD

When life is hanging on a thread, doesn't thread get expensive!

Chapter 27

"**H**E SAID IT! I heard him!"

Jeremy was holding a scalpel to Doctor Berthold's throat.

"Put that down, Jeremy."

But, this time, Clara's soft voice proved ineffective.

"My arse I will. He said he was going to unplug Benjamin!"

Back against the wall, Doctor Berthold looked as if he was sorry he had done so.

"He wouldn't do that."

"Not if I slit his throat he won't!"

"Stop it, Jeremy."

"He said: 'We'll unplug him as soon as that jerk Marty's gone off on his lecture tour of Japan.'"

True enough. Doctor Berthold was waiting for Doctor Marty to go before unplugging the ventilator on Benjamin, Jeremy's eldest brother. Doctor Berthold's motives were simple: he didn't like Doctor Marty.

"Jeremy, please . . ."

"He said it to her over there, and to that big fat bastard."

Jeremy nodded towards a nurse, who was whiter than her uniform, then at the big fat bastard, who was whiter than the nurse.

"If anyone moves, if you try and call someone, I'll operate!"

They were Berthold's assistants. They didn't move. They were desperately trying to think of a new career where they wouldn't have to assist anyone.

"Jeremy . . ."

Clara had taken a tentative half-step forwards.

"And don't you move, either."

She hung suspended.

"Shut the door."

They were alone now.

*

The Malaussène case had sparked off one hell of a slanging match between Berthold and Marty.

"The bloke's dead. Brain dead!" Berthold yelled.

Marty wouldn't budge.

"I'll unplug him when he's as brain dead as you are, Berthold, not a second before."

Marty didn't like Berthold either, but his dislike hadn't become passionate.

"I mean, for crying out loud, Marty: irreversible lesions to the central nervous system, artificial respiration at a hundred per cent, complete loss of reflexes, not the slightest signal on the electroencephalograph, what more do you want?"

("Nothing," thought Marty. That said it all. Malaussène was dead.)

"Silence, Berthold, what I want is silence."

"Don't count too much on my silence, Marty. If you start using our beds to cultivate vegetables, tongues will wag, old chap, tongues will definitely wag!"

That was the bee in Berthold's bonnet.

"This really will be the first time that you've taught somebody anything."

Berthold was a brilliant surgeon. But as a teacher, he emptied lecture halls as fast as a dose of typhus.

"I hate you, Marty."

They were standing face to face. The large furious one and the little calm one.

"And I love you, Berthold."

As for Marty, he could fill even the most hermetic skulls. Crowded lecture halls, tours, emergency calls from the four corners of the earth. People listened to him, and were turned into doctors. He was a patient's dream.

"Brain death, Marty!"

Berthold's waggling finger pointed at Malaussène in his ventilator.

"Irreversible coma."

Berthold indicated the encephalogram. An unbroken horizon.

"Trotsky and Kennedy were in better shape!"

Inwardly, Marty agreed. But still he wouldn't give way.

"Prolonged coma, Berthold. A chronic vegetative condition. But he's still very much alive."

"Oh really? And how are you going to prove that?"

That was the snag. All the clinical data pointed towards the same conclusion: irreversible lesions. Malaussène had had it. Disproving that would be like resurrecting Lazarus all over again.

"You realise what you're doing here, don't you, Marty?"

"Catching your coryza, that's what I'm doing. Blow your nose and speak to me from the regulation three steps away."

"Striving officiously to keep alive! Your megalomania is making you ventilate this lump of dead meat in a bed which could be needed by another patient, who may be dying some place, and all thanks to you!"

"Berthold, if you keep getting on my tits like this, then you'll be the one needing this bed."

"What's that? A threat? A physical threat? From you? To me!"

"No, just my diagnosis. So, hands off my patient. Get me?"

*

That's where things stood. For now. A rain check. But it couldn't last. After all, Berthold was quite capable of unplugging Marty's Malaussène. And Marty wouldn't have a leg to stand on if he did. He'd just have to keep his eyes peeled. Once more, he'd have to be more than just a doctor. Professor Marty glided off on his scooter between the Parisian traffic. Perhaps Berthold wouldn't dare. They were like two entangled wrestlers. Marty had him by the right testicle, but his own left testicle was between Berthold's teeth. As usual, Berthold's complex was playing up and, as usual, Marty was putting himself out for a patient. The patient was fucked, but this wasn't just any old patient. It was Malaussène. Red light. Green light. All right, no patient was ever just any old patient, but Malaussène was Malaussène. Even though he was on a scooter, the traffic jammed up around Marty. Two years before, he'd saved Jeremy Malaussène, grilled like a piece of bacon by the fire in his school. A year later, he'd saved Julie Corrençon, stuffed like a gefüllte fish. And now they'd brought him along Malaussène in person, with a tunnel through his brains. No matter how hard you try, you always end up getting personally attached to certain patients. Marty certainly could not complain that this family bothered him with sties or indigestion. When they got appendicitis, they operated on themselves. So, they'd brought him along Malaussène. With Jeremy up front.

"Doctor, you have to save my brother."

The entire family. Apart from the mother, of course. With a large Arab woman instead, whom they called Yasmina. And old Ben Tayeb with his fleece of white hair.

"It's my son, Benjamin."

They'd invaded the hospital, after being announced by a wave of police sirens.

"Is there anything you can do?"

The first to ask that question had been a young Arab, with the profile of a falcon, dressed in a skin-tight suit.

"My son Hadouch," the old man had explained.

All this while they were rushing through the corridors towards the emergency operation unit.

Luckily enough, Berthold had been there.

Without saying a word, he and Marty had set to work.

Berthold was a right prick, but also the best scalpel in Paris. A pure genius of human plumbing. Surgery wasn't Marty's speciality, but he never missed out on the chance to assist Berthold. He stood calmly by his side. He passed him the instruments. He couldn't believe his eyes. That man's fingers were like human intelligence in motion. The two of them operated alone. In their masks, they looked as if they were a couple of true gourmets who couldn't abide having anyone else at their table. They'd apparently just smoked the peace pipe. But there was nothing peaceful about what was really going through their minds at special moments such as this. "I'm buggering him over a barrel," Berthold said to himself when he saw Marty's astonished gaze. Berthold mistook Marty's admiration for envy, which lent wings to his scalpel. He was a simple soul. But Marty's admiration was based on pure curiosity, as were most of his emotions when it came to the world of medicine. Berthold's case fascinated him. What plunged Marty into profound scientific observation was how such a complete cretin, on the verge of being a basket case, could be such a wonderfully dexterous surgeon and have such unfailing intuition of how the organs he was operating on would react. How was it *possible*? Here was one of the secrets of the species. And it was a secret that Marty had been pursuing for some time. From his earliest youth he had collected cretinous geniuses, just as others rummage through junk shops in the hope of finding particularly ghastly specimens. He'd unearthed a leader of the Berlin Philharmonic, a chess grandmaster who had twice been a world-championship finalist, and a Nobel laureate nuclear physicist; three indisputable geniuses who all made the most mindless of molluscs look like a highly complex intelligence. And now Berthold! These encounters thrilled Marty. Nature clearly had plenty more surprises in store in her bag of neurons. It was a defence against herself. Everything could be hoped for. In moments of depression, Marty would use this certainty to recharge the batteries of his professional optimism. Berthold was Marty's wild card.

So, Berthold and Marty had opened up Malaussène's head. They'd taken a look inside. They'd looked at each other. They'd closed him up again. Berthold had motioned to unplug the machine. Marty had stopped him.

*

"So?"

Packed into the waiting room, the whole tribe had asked that one question with Jeremy as their mouthpiece.

"I think you should know at once, Jeremy. There is absolutely no hope."

Marty had decided to be frank.

You're going to unplug him?

The eternal question.

"Not without your agreement."

Louna, Malaussène's nursing sister, had insisted on dotting the i's.

"Is there *really* no hope?"

Marty had glanced across at Clara then, despite her wanness, dropped the bombshell.

"Brain death."

"Which means?" someone had asked.

"He'll die if they unplug the ventilator," Louna translated.

"Ridiculous!"

Thérèse. Thérèse's icy carcass. She was standing back from the others. She hadn't moved. She'd simply said:

"Ridiculous!"

Without the slightest trace of emotion.

She then added:

"Benjamin is going to die in his bed at the age of ninety-three."

*

Red light – green light. Professor Marty changed into first. His scooter leapt forward. If it hadn't been for Thérèse's tuppenny-worth, everything would have been so simple. Marty was not exactly a fan of the occult sciences. Rotating tables, the permanent revolution (of heavenly bodies), the meaning of life in the palm of your hand, all that claptrap made his rationalistic hairs stand on end. The only crystal ball which he could put up with were the ones that were firmly screwed into banister rails. They stopped children from sliding down onto their arses, and that was an end to it. That said, when he'd told Berthold that Malaussène was in a prolonged coma, a vegetative condition, and was to be classed among "the very much alive", he had been thinking about Thérèse. "Oh really? And how are you going to prove that?" Marty's only proof was Thérèse. The only answer he had: Thérèse. He'd played dumb and Berthold had scored a point.

Now, Marty had seen Thérèse in action. On three occasions. Three years before, he had heard her predict a bomb explosion, which had indeed happened on the very day and at the precise second she'd said. Then, the following year, he'd seen her help an old man slip away into death as though his future were still in front of him. Red light. And Thérèse had also resurrected old Thian, even though he'd been stuffed full of lead and only too anxious to die. Gridlock again. When faced with Thérèse, Marty felt as though he was Don Giovanni confronted by the Commander. "Something escapes me about all this, but I remain more than ever a doctor."

The scooter suddenly dived to its left and raced away from the traffic jam. Marty was heading for Belleville, Marty was going to see the Malaussènes, Marty was going to grab hold of that girl and explain to her that, this time, there was no way, her brother had had it, completely and utterly had it, that the stars could all go to blazes, and that ice-cold Thérèse would do better to invest in this world and sow what could be reaped. When a bullet had scooped its way through a brain, like a spoon in a hard-boiled egg, then Thérèse Malaussène she might be, but there was still no chance, absolutely none, that the mince would turn itself back into steak again.

"Hello there, doctor. Come round for dinner, have you?"

It was Jeremy who'd opened the door. The kid was beaming and the ex-hardware store was smelling of a generous couscous. It only took Marty a split second to understand that, thanks to Thérèse, the whole family was carrying on as though their brother Benjamin was in Saint-Louis Hospital for mild bronchitis.

"What's more, Julius hasn't had an epileptic fit."

"And I haven't had any nightmares," the little kid in rose-tinted glasses added.

They were clutching onto omens. Even Clara smiled at Marty. "No worries about her pregnancy, then," he thought.

Marty abandoned the idea of confronting Thérèse, swallowed his couscous, with the dog's dribbling jowls on his lap, and decided to bring forward his lecture tour of Japan.

*

The next day, he did still try to patch things up with old Berthold. He invited him to *La Closerie des Lilas* in the attempt to convince him not to unplug Malaussène. They sat at the table of Lenin, who had succeeded against similarly difficult odds.

"Look, Berthold, don't unplug Malaussène. He could still pull through."

There was a Gascon *foie gras* on their plates and the luxurious amber of a Sauternes in their glasses.

"Your proof?" Berthold asked, with his mouth full.

"You're my proof, Berthold."

"Oh yeah?"

Berthold was knocking back the Sauternes as if it was lager.

"You're a brilliant surgeon, Berthold."

"True enough. Give us a bit more of that pâté."

("*Pâté!*" thought Marty. "Jesus Christ, a pure *foie gras de Gascogne!*")

"You are the greatest."

Berthold emptied his glass with a nod of approval, then brandished the empty bottle at a passing waiter.

"If you lobotomised a telegraph pole," Marty went on, "then it could still end up as bright as Edison."

"What's all that got to do with Malaussène?"

"Simple, Berthold. If such a complete plonker as you can achieve such feats, then nature makes everything possible and Malaussène can recover."

The contents of a glass of Sauternes shot just over Marty's head to land on a retired surrealist, who made the scene of the century.

*

Marty's case was packed. All his latest research findings concerning haematology neatly filed away in his head. He didn't have that much time to spare, but he still decided to drop in on the hospital. There, he found Berthold pinned against the wall by Jeremy, who was threatening him with a scalpel. He strode across the room, snatched the scalpel and gave Jeremy two thunderous clips round the ear. Then, to Berthold:

"In the end, I suppose this is the sort of argument you needed."

He left for Japan, reassured that Berthold would not unplug Malaussène.

Chapter 28

INSPECTOR CAREGGA HAD reached the sixth-floor landing and was standing in front of the right door just at the very moment that Chief Superintendent Coudrier ordered the cease-fire on the steps of Saint Roch church. Inspector Caregga nodded in admiration. The boss had timed it according to the pace he ran at. Caregga had crossed Rue Saint-Honoré and gone up the six flights of stairs at a steady speed. The heavy artillery stopped firing precisely as he reached the door. You had to hand it to him. Caregga wouldn't have liked to work under anyone else. With his back to the wall, gun in hand, he now waited for the door to open. Caregga didn't want to kill Julie Corrençon . . . In the first place, she was a woman. And then she was also Malaussène's woman. Caregga shared his boss's liking for Malaussène. Three years before, he'd saved him from a lynching. The following year, he'd helped Inspector Pastor prove his innocence. Malaussène was a good reason to remain a good copper. No, Caregga wasn't going to blow his woman away. After all, La Corrençon was quite simply revenging her man. Caregga was in love with Carole, a young beautician. If someone shot down her Caregga, would Carole be capable of letting all hell break loose in Paris like this? (Maybe, but not before eleven in the morning. Carole was no early riser.) Caregga listened for sounds from the bedsit. In theory, if La Corrençon wasn't dead, then she'd take advantage of the break in firing to open the door and make her getaway. That was the whole point of concentrated fire. You forced the sniper down onto his belly in his hideout. He could neither show himself at the window nor move towards the door because of all the bullets ricocheting off the ceiling. Meanwhile, a team was closing off his escape route. Caregga liked being a one-man team. So the team was him. He was blocking off the escape route. If La Corrençon made a move, then he'd do his best not to shoot her down. He'd rugby-tackle her, perhaps, or get her into a half-nelson. It all depended on the height at which she was holding her gun. But Inspector Van Thian had probably killed her. Caregga had seen Thian in action. And he had recently gone back into training. He was the station's crowd-puller. Thanks to that baby, of course, which he carried slung round him like a monkey fallen from its tree, but also because of the way he shot. Even without the kid, Thian still emptied all the offices in the station when he was practising. No-one shot like he did. After Thian had been at it, a target was a single hole surrounded by cardboard. He was the marksman, weapon, bullet and target all rolled into one. He sent shivers down your spine. Not to mention how quick he was. His hands were empty then, in a flash, he was armed, then, in another flash, his clip was empty. What was more, he used the big artillery. 350s, bigger than he was. His arm remained motionless. A mysterious force absorbed the recoil for him. It was, of course, all the more impressive with that baby girl clutching onto him like a crab. Thian had had ear muffs made for her, which made her look like a giant fly. He carried her around in a leather harness, which went over his shoulder holster. It seemed as if that sprog with its furious gaze was sitting on his gun, waiting for it to hatch. When he drew, he pushed the child aside with a flick of his left hand. As his other hand pulled out the gun and aimed at the target, the little girl spun round behind him, her head popping up over his right shoulder with her eyes staring down his firing line. Every copper that saw them reckoned that the social workers would have had a field day. But they kept their thoughts to themselves. They watched Thian shoot. Even though most of them were too young to have been there, they figured that Dien Bien Phu must have been one hell of a nightmare.

Not the slightest sound from the room. Caregga pulled away from the wall and stood in front of the door for a moment. "At the count of three, I'm in there." When he reached three, a sharp kick snapped the lock and Caregga was in the middle of the room before the door had swung to behind him.

The bedsit was empty. Peppered like a Beirut block of flats, but empty. Empty and bloodied. Drops of blood glistened on the shards of the window pane. Two fingers were sticking out of the wall. Yes, one of Thian's bullets had ripped into the hand and pinned two of its fingers to the wall. They seemed to be trying to tell him something. But the important thing was that the bedsit was empty. Apart from three woman's wigs lying on the floor ("Wigs," Inspector Caregga thought. "I wasn't wrong about that.") and the remains of a rifle with a telescopic sight. A high-precision piece with its barrel sawn off. A Swinley .22. The fingers must have belonged to the hand that was holding the stock.

*

"*Ni hao*, shit-for-brains." (Hello, shit-for-brains.)

Loussa de Casamance was keeping up his regular visits to Malaussène.

"*Wo shi.*" (It's me.)

Every day at 7.30 pm precisely.

"*Zhenre! haore!* in your gaff . . . " (Isn't it hot in your gaff!)

He sat down like sponge.

"*Tianqui hen men* outside as well." (It's sultry outside as well.)

A twinge of conscience made him ask:

"*Nin shenti hao ma* today?" (How are you feeling today?)

The brain machine replied with a green trace without beginning or end, the true depressing definition of a straight line.

"Never mind," Loussa said. "*Wo hen gaoxing jiandao nin.*" (I'm pleased to see you.)

In fact, he wouldn't have liked to have found an empty bed.

"*Wo toutong*, too. (I've got a headache, too.) One hell of a migraine, actually."

He spoke to him in Chinese, but scrupulously translated everything. He'd got it into his head that he was going to teach him Chinese. ("Belleville is becoming Chinese, shit-for-brains, and apparently we learn better when we're asleep . . . If you ever do wake up from your nap, then this way you'll have learnt something from it.")

"What do you know but your sweetheart has decided to blow us all away. She reckons we're responsible for your death."

He spoke to him as though he was brain alive, but never doubting for a moment that he was addressing a dead man.

"Mind you, she's not completely wrong about that. But I think you'd agree that our responsibility is, at the most, indirect."

Loussa wasn't squeamish. He didn't mind the dead. Like Hugo (Victor) he was certain that the deceased were extremely well-informed conversational partners.

"A woman's revenging you, just think about it! Such an honour would never fall to me."

Malaussène was a mere green line.

"I'm more the sort who drives them to suicide. Not someone to avenge, more someone to punish. See what I mean?"

Medical science was doing Malaussène's breathing.

"Your Julie has already done in Chabotte, Gauthier and, this morning, Calignac. Well, Calignac's shoulder, at least, and his leg. The rest of him will keep for later. Your friend Thian fired at her, but all she lost was two fingers."

Medical science was feeding Malaussène, stingily, in drips and drabs.

"I'm not afraid for my own hide, you know me. Well, just reasonably afraid. But I don't want her to kill Isabelle."

Medical science was plugged into Malaussène's immensely empty head. It was canvassing for messages.

"You couldn't intercede for Isabelle, now, could you? You couldn't take a little trip into your Julie's mind for me?"

The fact is that, reduced to silence, the dead look as though they are capable of anything.

"Because, you see, shit-for-brains, Isabelle is . . . God knows the slanging matches the two of you had . . ."

Loussa was struggling to find his words. Chinese words and their French cousins.

"Isabelle . . . Isabelle is innocence . . . I swear to you . . . Innocence, *wawa, yng'er*, a baby, a tiny little girl threatening us with a waggle of her finger."

Loussa spoke, his heart awash, his words trembling.

"That's right, the only crime she's ever committed, and I swear it to you on her very own head, is to threaten the huge world with the waggling tip of her finger. She's a baby, I tell you . . ."

And, that evening, at a few minutes past 7.30 pm, Loussa de Casamance set about pleading the case for Queen Zabo before a Malaussène who seemed to be the one in the firing squad best placed to see that the report got into the right hands.

"Shall I tell you her life story? Our life story?"

(. . .)

"Well?"

(. . .)

"Right, then listen good. *The Story of Queen Zabo*, by her gopher de Casamance."

Chapter 29

THE LITTLE PROSE-MERCHANT

The Story of Queen Zabo
by her gopher de Casamance

(Digression)

Queen Zabo is a legendary princess which, shit-for-brains, is the only genuine variety. She rose up from the gutter to reign over a kingdom of paper. She didn't inherit her passionate love for books, but picked it up from a dustbin. It didn't come from libraries, but from rags. She is the only publisher in Paris to have raised herself onto her throne by means of the raw material itself and not the words that are printed on it. You should have seen her close her eyes, flare her nostrils, then breathe in an entire library, sniffing out the five named copies on pure Japanese vellum among the shelves crammed with Vergers, Van Gelders and the humble legion of Alfas. She never slipped up. She could classify the whole lot just by smell: paper made of rags, linen, jute, cotton fibre, Manilla hemp . . . Loussa used to play at this with her. It was their secret game. When they were alone in Isabelle's home, Loussa would blindfold her, put gloves on her hands, then give her a book to hold. Isabelle's senses of sight and touch couldn't tell her anything. So her nose did the talking:

"What you've just handed me is beautiful, Loussa. This is no mortal paper, but a finely woven Holland . . . as for the glue, it's Excellence-Tessier . . . and the ink, if I'm not mistaken, the ink is . . . just a second, now . . ."

She picked out the airy scent of the ink from the powerful animal odour of the glue, then reeled off its ingredients one by one, finally naming the dead artisan who had long ago produced this marvellous ink and giving the date of its vintage. She would sometimes break into cackling laughter.

"You're trying to pull a fast one on me, aren't you, you little swine. The binding

164

doesn't date from the same period . . . the hide is twenty years older. Good try, Loussa, but you won't get me that way."

After which, she'd come out with the name of the mill where the paper had been produced, the name of the only printer to use that combination of ingredients, the title of the book, the author's name and its publication date.

Sometimes, Loussa would let Isabelle's fingers have their say. He'd take off her gloves, block her nostrils with little lumps of cotton wool, then watch Isabelle's hands stroke the paper:

"This paper is harsh to the touch, too bibulous, will go yellow in eighty years' time, just see if it doesn't. For the grandchildren of the children we haven't had, this book will be as yellow as a quince. Hepatitis has already set in."

All the same, she was no enemy of perishable, wood-fibre paper. She may have been a connoisseur, but she wasn't a snob. She found the fact that books, too, were mortal profoundly moving. She aged at the same rate that they did. She never pulped one, never threw a single copy away. If it was alive, she let it die.

*

At Malaussène's bedside, Loussa was trembling with conviction.

"So how can you think that a woman who's incapable of junking a paperback could have sent you off to be killed? That's what you're going to have to explain to your Julie."

But Julie was going to have to be told much more besides, if she was going to understand Isabelle. It was necessary to go back to the night when Loussa had first met her. It was necessary to dive back into the crisis years of the 1930s, a time when the whole of Europe was starving to death, but when the cloth kings and paper fanatics, the tycoons of high fashion and the princes of bibliophilia still blithely went about satisfying their passions at opposing ends of a chain, whose most disreputable links were to be found in the dark night of dustbins.

Now, dustbins were rarely full in that time of famine. People threw little into them, and salvaged a great deal from them, they fought to the death over them. All wars arise from the same axiom: *dustbins abhor a vacuum.* If a dustbin was taken by storm in a Paris suburb, the whole of Europe caught fire. And people still want wars to be a clean fight . . .

The first armies of the Second World War were the battalions of ragmen, wallowing in sludge, with determined stares and meat hooks in their hands. ("You've no idea of the scars those hooks left, shit-for-brains . . . ") Squadrons of binmen surged up from the paving stones, and the light of dawn revealed the

165

ragmen of the surface, meat hooks in their skulls, piled up in the empty bins. Such skirmishes were nothing in comparison with the set battles fought in the sewage farms of Saint-Denis, Bicêtre or Aubervilliers. These motionless struggles were a true foreshadowing of Stalingrad. Statues of shit grappling with one another for the conquest of a cesspool, the control of a sullage pit, the entrance to a treatment plant, thirty yards of rail where the skips were unloaded.

This prewar war had its armies, its strategies, its generals, its intelligence services, its quartermasters, its organisation. And its mavericks.

The Coot was one such.

The Coot was a Pole who'd been spat back up to the surface by a flatulent mine shaft. The Coot was Isabelle's father. Unemployed and Polish, he resolved never to go down a pit again. In the abyss where he'd worked, the Coot had lost the finest head of hair ever seen in Poland. Now he walked the streets without a single strand left on his bonce. Because of his professional hatred of the colour black, he always wore a white suit. The Coot was the only one who knew that he'd emerged from a coal pit. Everyone else took him for a ruined Polish prince, one of those men from the East who'd come to take over our taxis. But the Coot didn't want to be a cabby either . . . cab-driving was a horizontal mine shaft. No, the Coot lived off other people's wallets. He didn't beg. He mugged. He mugged, pocketed, spent, then mugged again. He knew that this couldn't go on forever. But he kept on mugging while waiting for a better idea. He believed in this "idea" as firmly as a gambler believes in his martingale. His wife had come up with her idea, so there was no reason why he shouldn't have his idea, too. The Coot and his wife had separated by mutual disagreement. She'd taken to the knitting needle, that was her "idea", a back-street abortionist. The Coot was Catholic, so they separated. He left her their three sons and went off with their daughter. Isabelle made her father feel miserable. She ate as though she mistrusted life, like a sparrow. This meant spending a lot of money, trying everything, the finest possible foods. The Coot would tip the caviar into the bin and go back down onto the streets. He thought that Isabelle didn't eat well because she read too much. Each time he went out to mug for her, he promised himself that he'd sort the situation out. But he always ended up giving way, and returning home with the little girl's favourite magazines. He loved seeing Isabelle's huge head, so like his own, leaning over *Modes et Travaux*, *La Femme Chic*, *Formes et Couleurs*, *Silhouettes*, *Vogue* . . . Would Isabelle become a fashion designer, another Claude Saint-Cyr or Jeanne Blanchot? Then she'd have to eat. But what Isabelle devoured was magazines, paper . . . and, in particular, the novels in those magazines. Serials paraded themselves endlessly through Isabelle's mind. She cut out the pages, sewed them together, and turned them into books. Between the ages of five and ten, Isabelle had read everything she could lay her hands on, without distinction. And she still wanted more.

The Coot came up with his "idea" one night while on the prowl in Faubourg Saint-Honoré. He was tailing a big, jaunty sixty-year-old wearing a tweed suit. He got his fist ready. But then, just under the arches of the Tuileries, the competition beat him to his prey. Two shadows leapt out of the shadows. Quite unexpectedly, the man in the tweed suit didn't want to give them his wallet. So they pulverised him. One of them kicked his face in, while the other laid into his kidneys. Smothered by pain, the man couldn't cry out. The Coot reckoned that they were overdoing it a bit. He became a life-saver. He flattened the two thugs one against the other. Two youngsters were as light as empty billy-cans. Then he helped the man to his feet. He was a fountain of blood. The Coot staunched the flow, dabbed at his wounds, but all the victim said was:

"My Loti, my Loti . . ."

Gobbets of blood spewed up from his guts and, among them, these two words:

"My Loti, my Loti . . ."

Another sort of pain was bringing tears to his eyes.

"A first edition, sir . . ."

The Coot didn't understand a word. The suit had lost his glasses. He dived back down onto the pavement. Whatever was the bloke up to, wallowing around in his own blood like that? He was groping about like a blindman.

"On Imperial Japanese vellum . . ."

A pure product of mine shafts, now transferred to nocturnal muggings, the Coot was nyctalopic. He found what the suit was looking for. A little book which had come to rest a few yards away from them.

"Oh, thank you sir, thank you . . . If you only knew . . ."

The suit clutched the little book convulsively against his heart.

"Here, please . . . please . . ."

He'd opened his wallet. He was offering the Coot half a king's ransom. The Coot hesitated. For a mugger, this was money dishonestly come by. But the suit pushed the wad of notes into the Coot's pocket.

When he recounted his little adventure to Isabelle, she gave him one of her special smiles:

"He was a bibliophile."

"A bibliophile?" the Coot asked.

"Someone who prefers books to literature," the little girl explained.

The Coot was all at sea.

"For people like that, all that matters is the paper," Isabelle said.

"Even if there's nothing written on it?"

"Even if it's a load of old rubbish. They protect their books from the sunlight, they don't cut their pages, they stroke them with thin gloves on their fingers, they don't read them, they *look at them*."

Then the little girl had a fit of the giggles. For a long time, the Coot had thought that her giggling fits were asthma attacks, brought on by the dust of the mining town. But they weren't. That air seeping out from between Isabelle's cheeks was long, endless laughter. This time, the little girl explained:

"I've just had a very 'chic' idea."

The Coot was all ears.

"Wouldn't it be funny if we made rare books with cloth from Hermès, Jeanne Lafaurie, Worth or O'Rossen . . ."

She hiccuped out the names of all their local fashion designers.

"How chic can you get?"

Isabelle's idea became the Coot's idea. The lass was right. The Coot had just made a discovery: *aesthetes never let up*. Whatever is happening in the world, *haute couture* will go on stitching ever higher, *haute cuisine* will keep on feeding princes, concert-goers will continue tuning their violins and, during the worst planetary crisis, there will always be a fat man in a tweed suit ready to die to save a first edition.

The Coot went round the designers. They, too, found the idea "chic". The Coot picked up their off-cuts. Isabelle went through the dustbins, sorted out the different cloths, throwing away the wool and early synthetics, keeping the linen, the cotton, the hemp and the thread. The Coot supplied the most reputable paper mills and soon the best publishers were bringing out Barrès in Balenciaga, Paul Bourget bound in Hermès, Anouilh dressed by Chanel, or the young de Gaulle's *Le Fil de l'Epée* in Worth threads. A few numbered editions per author, but with prices so high that there was always food on the table for Isabelle.

The Coot should have stayed put. His "idea" was far more "Christian" than his wife's had been, his suits were now impeccably white, and his little girl could eat her fill, having at last found the world to her taste.

Alas, the Coot was an expansionist. He now had a nice little earner in the rare-book trade, but he wanted to become the bibliophiles' Godfather, lording it over the rags which produced paper for immortal books. *Haute couture*'s off-cuts were no longer enough for him. What he wanted was a complete monopoly of the entire capital's rag trade. But the Coot was an extremely Christian Pole. He didn't want to do business with the Jews of Sentier or Le Marais. And that was where the cloth was. And animal hide, too, for the bindings. The Coot recruited an army of scavengers, which he let loose on the Jews' dustbins. His troops came back beaten, bruised and empty-handed. The Coot was taken aback. It was the first time that someone had resisted him. He armed his ragmen with poisoned meat hooks. Two of them came back dead. The survivors were so terrified that they were incapable of saying what had happened. No, they just couldn't explain it. No, they hadn't seen a thing. It was as if the night had suddenly become compact, as if they'd hurtled into a wall of night. They'd been routed by haunted dustbins. They didn't want to go back to the Jewish quarters. Despite his promises of easy money, despite his fists, the Coot's armies disbanded themselves. This gave him terrible nightmares. Isabelle heard him scream in his sleep: "The night is Jewish!" His terror echoed throughout the Faubourg Saint-Honoré: "THE NIGHT IS JEWISH!" Nightmarish bedtime stories swam up to him from his Polish childhood. Grandma Polska was leaning down once more over the Coot's cot. Grandma Polska made him say his prayers. Grandma Polska told him stories. She told him of the shtetl on the banks of the Vistula, where sacrificers of foreskins spent all Friday night slicing up little boys. And, said Grandma Polska, the wails of those martyrs floated back up the river, from Gdansk to Warsaw, on the frozen winds of the Baltic to torment the souls of sleeping Christian children. "Sleep well, little one." The Coot sat up and awoke. That race was even worse than his wife. They didn't rip children from the womb, they ripped them to pieces after they'd been born.

One night, the Coot decided not to go to bed. He put on his most immaculate alpaca suit, did up his white tie, stuck a white carnation in his buttonhole, took Isabelle by the hand and set off on a pogrom. He needed his little girl to sniff out the cloth. For the rest, all he needed was his faith, his fists and his Latil tractor with its three trailers and four-wheel drive.

Isabelle could smell out the best off-cuts from a distance. The Coot grabbed hold of the bins and emptied them into his trailers. It was only at the fifth bin that he sensed danger. But, in Rue du Pont-aux-Choux, there was no-one to be seen. However, his grandma used to say: "The Jews believe in ghosts so much that they become invisible. They are everywhere and yet you can't see them." The Coot punched the danger area. His fist met a face and the Coot heard a body hit the deck, far away from the impact. He didn't waste time wondering about what he'd hit, he simply emptied the bin into the trailer then moved on, like an avenging archangel.

*

"That fucking anti-Semite had just killed my big brother."

About fifty years later, Loussa de Casamance was shaking his head at the bedside of his friend Malaussène.

"Of course, you're in no mood to sympathise. But all the same, whenever I think about it, it really does my head in."

Malaussène was horizontal.

"One single punch, and my brother's face was as flat as a hedgehog on a motorway."

Malaussène could hear it all.

"But that was the night I first met Isabelle."

Loussa's voice had melted.

"While my brothers were scavenging, I usually hid. I'd find myself some nice quiet place, somewhere cosy, near a lamp-post, and I'd take a book out of my pocket."

*

That night, when the little girl's huge face had leant over Loussa's bin, his first thought was that there had been an eclipse of the moon. Or that someone had pinched his lamp-post. But he heard a voice:

"What are you reading?"

It was a breathless, hoarse voice of an asthmatic little girl. Loussa answered:

"Dostoievsky. *The Devils.*"

An incredibly chubby hand shot into his dustbin.

"Lend it to me."

Loussa tried to defend himself.

"You wouldn't understand a word of it."

"Quick! I'll give it you back."

There were two prayers in that voice: he had to lend it and he had to do it quickly. Isabelle was the first woman that Loussa gave way to. And the only one never to make him regret it.

"Whatever you do, don't move."

She covered the bin with a convenient sheet of cardboard, shook her head at the approaching Coot and went on to the next one.

*

When Loussa's brothers took the body of the first-born back home, they were no more capable of explaining to their father what had happened than the ragmen had to the Coot.

"We were attacked by a ghost."

"A big white ghost on a Latil tractor."

"Ghosts don't drive tractors," their father said. "That's plain nigger superstition."

"We're not going back there again," the sons replied.

As for the Coot, he didn't yet realise who he'd declared war against. He quite simply went home, having vanquished the Jewish night, that was all. And back he would go the next night. But when he returned from his second expedition, his warehouses were in flames. The fire had been started by a colossal African, as curly-haired as he himself was bald, as black as he was white, and who others of his race also mistook for a prince, a prince of the Casamance, king of Zinguapor, who'd come to take over our taxis, whereas he had really been a butler to a peanut merchant, whose head he'd staved in one day when the merchant had called him a giant baboon once too often. The prince of Casamance looked down on taxis. He lorded it over the dustbins of the Marais quarter, but this was in order to clothe his own people, and not to share with the Coot.

*

"Well, shit-for-brains, to cut a long story short, the two of them were on a collision course. All the ingredients for a mythical duel were present. This duel took place one night under a full moon and it marked the end of my childhood. They were both found dead, in the pure tradition of the rag trade, blood and guts everywhere, torn to ribbons by each other's meat hooks."

Malaussène's breathing was so artificial that he no longer looked completely real either.

"And what about Isabelle, you may ask?"

Which was, indeed, the question that Malaussène would have asked.

"Well, while our two giants were packing each other off to the bone orchard, Isabelle came and found me in my favourite bin. She'd read the Dostoievsky and, as promised, gave it back to me. 'So, did you understand anything?' I asked. 'No, not a word.' 'Told you so . . . ' 'But that's not because the book's complicated.' 'Oh, isn't it?' 'No, there's something else.' (Don't forget, shit-for-brains, our fathers were hacking each other to pieces just two streets away.) 'What's that, then?' 'It's Stavrogin,' Isabelle answered. She looked just the same as she does now. Impossible to guess her age. 'Stavrogin?' 'Yes, Stavrogin, the main character, he's hiding something. He doesn't tell the truth, and that's what makes the book so complicated.' 'What's your name?' 'Isabelle' 'Mine's Loussa.' 'Loussa?' 'Loussa de Casamance.' (We could hear our colossal fathers' breathing and the clicking of their meat hooks.) 'Loussa, we must see each other again, when all this is over.' 'Yes, we must see each other again.' 'We must see each other again for always.' That's what made it clear that it was little girl speaking. But, if you stop and think about it, 'always' and 'never' are still parts of today's vocabulary.

"After the two funerals, they put us both away into homes. Two different homes, of course, but we stuck it out. We saw each other as often as we could. Walls are made to be climbed over.

"Now listen carefully, shit-for-brains. On July 9 1931, Isabelle and I visited the *Palais des Colonies*. The colonies were part of my make-up, if you see what I mean. So off we went to the *Palais des Colonies* and, lo and behold, we came across the first mobile library. Two thousand five hundred books on a ten-horsepower engine. Culture on wheels. Perhaps to send the Three Musketeers to the Casamance . . . Just imagine how thrilled we were!

"We drove all round Paris with a bunch of street urchins with books open on their laps.

"Don't forget that date, July 9 1931, it's Isabelle's true birthday. She picked out a slim volume from the shelves and said: 'Look.' It was *Stavrogin's Confession*, the last part of Dostoievsky's *The Devils*, in a separate edition printed by Plon, I think it was. Isabelle started to read it, as if it was a letter personally addressed to her. Then suddenly she started to cry. And weren't the mobile librarians touched! 'How beautiful it is to see a little girl crying over a novel . . .' She cried all the way through to the end and there was nothing at all beautiful about it. Total dehydration. I thought that she was going to wilt on the spot, drop like a dead branch. They had to get rid of us on the way. It wouldn't do to have a little girl drown on her own tears during their first day out. Standing below the Lion on Place Denfert, Isabelle said to me: 'Now I know why Stavrogin acts like a madman in *The Devils*.'

"Her eyes were now as dry as flints. All I was thinking about was that we had to fill her up with water again so that she'd be able to cry once more sometime in her life. 'He raped a little girl.' What could I answer to that? 'And do you know what the little girl did, Loussa?' 'No.' 'She waggled her finger at him.' 'Is that all?' 'What else could a little girl do?' 'I don't know.' 'She hanged herself.'

"Then came another burst of dry sobs. It was terrible, because what with her head, which was already so soft, and her bony body, I was worried that she was going to impale herself on her own skeleton. 'When I grow up . . . ' She was choking. 'When I grow up, I'll be unrapeable.' Then suddenly she burst forth with her victory laugh, you know, her hissing chuckle . . . In the air, her hands sketched out the figure of her enormous head planted on the stake of her body and, still chuckling, she repeated: 'Like I am now, unrapeable!'"

*

Loussa now had one foot in the corridor, his hand on the door handle, and the vague desire to be shot down on his way out. He turned back towards his comatose friend:

"That's what you're going to have to explain to your Julie, shit-for-brains. You don't shoot a woman who's got a dead little girl hanging in her mind."

Chapter 30

HAT'S RIGHT, JULIE. Stop the massacre, for crying out loud, cease firing, put down your guns, pack it in! What's with all this vengeance bit? Have you started carrying on like everyone else and set out to find who's *to blame*? Chabotte had me killed, Gauthier worked for Chabotte, Calignac paid Gauthier, Zabo employed Calignac, Loussa loves Zabo . . . So they're all to blame, are they? Where will it end, Julie? Where are you going to draw the borderlines of innocence across the vast continent of guilt? Just think about it for a second, damn you, and you'll see that there will never be an end to it! Put a gag on your woman's bleeding heart! Chabotte was at the top of the pyramid, so are you now going to gun down everybody beneath him? You're going to blow away Coudrier, Caregga, Thian, the entire police force? And when you're through cleaning up that lot, will there be any bullets left in your chamber to deal with the rest? Vengeance is an ever-expanding territory. Didn't your father the Governor explain that to you often enough? The Treaty of Versailles created victimised Germans, who created wandering Jews, who created wandering Palestinians, who created wandering widows pregnant with tomorrow's avengers . . . Are you really going to wipe out the entire staff of the Vendetta Press, Julie? Then why not the Ben Tayeb tribe, while you're at it, or my little family? Clara, for instance, who took those lovely photos of J. L. B., Jeremy and Half Pint, who did such a good job making me revise my J. L. B. interviews. They're all to blame, too, aren't they? Not to the same *degree*? But there are no *degrees* in Vengeance Land, Julie! A country with no climate! A mental landscape! Not the slightest atmospheric variation! A humourless planet, a macro-climate of certainties! Nothing to disturb the succession of chain reactions: shoot the one to blame and, as he falls, he'll point out the next one to blame, the guilty party passes the buck and Lady Vengeance cleans up, as blind as the Grim Reaper. Stop it, Julie! Put your gun away! You'll end up getting blisters on the fingers which Thian hasn't shot off yet and, when you've massacred the lot of them, then, like the good logical avenger that you are, you'll come along and finish me off! You remember the scene you made before leaving me? Do you? Or don't you? I was to blame, you said, guilty of not being my good self, the worst crime of the lot, according to you!

It's true, Julie. That's what you'll end up doing, I swear to you. You'll wind up unplugging that other in me who has deprived you of my real self. It'll be on a winter's evening – no, more like at dawn, executions always happen at dawn so that they can rob you of a life plus a day – a winter's dawn, and there I'll be, laid out, my skin conscious, all my vibratiles extended, pricked up waiting for Berthold, that loony who wants to switch me off. And then my papillae will register the vibration of your tread, for the air palpitates around us, did you know that, Julie? And our skin spends its life decoding these signals, did you know that? "It isn't Berthold," my skin will tell me. "Relax, Malaussène, it's Julie." And, sure enough, it will be you, I'll recognise you as easily as I capture Jeremy's outbursts, Clara's peaceful voice, the two-fold beating of her pregnant woman's heart, Thérèse's brief volleys, the trilling of Half Pint, who still speaks the astonished language of the birds, delighted at the mere sound of words . . . From the first step you take in the corridor I'll recognise you, Julie, I won't be able to hear you, no, but the air which your powerful hell-raising stride pushes in front of you will beat against my skin and I'll recognise you, because nobody else walks like you do in this vale of tears, driven on by such a strong certainty that you're going somewhere.

*

So cogitated Malaussène in his irreversible coma. If ever he managed to get out of that tunnel, which the bullet had dug out inside him, then he wouldn't add to those light-filled tales which those who have returned from the dead tell to the TV cameras (divine surprises with all the colours of the rainbow, spirit at peace, heart at rest, orgasm of the soul) no, he would tell of his fear of Berthold the unplugger, his every-day concerns which greatly resembled the concerns of the living. He didn't really think that Julie would finish him off. It was a way to avoid thinking about Berthold. A ploy. He summoned up Julie. He laughed at their love. Arms open, he glided towards her along the green line which crossed the screen. He fled Berthold's image to take refuge in Julie's image. Jeremy had saved him once, but bastards only mend their ways so long as they stay frightened. And Berthold was not going to stay frightened of Jeremy's scalpel indefinitely. The only person he really feared was Marty. And now Marty had gone off on a lecture tour of Japan, for the good of Nippon health. Marty, Marty, why hast thou forsaken me? When life is hanging on a thread, doesn't thread get expensive! But was Malaussène really alive? Irreversible coma . . . brain dead . . . the void . . . How could he disagree with that diagnosis? "The bloke's dead. Brain dead!" Berthold hammered his point home . . . "Irreversible lesions to the central nervous system!" . . . "Trotsky and Kennedy were in better shape!" Marty's voice replied firmly, but lacked conviction: "*Prolonged* coma, Berthold. But he's still very much alive!" It didn't ring true. It sounded affectionate, sad, but, for once, unscientific. Marty was answering despite himself. Against Berthold's science what he needed was science. Then Thérèse had put her oar in: "Ridiculous!" Thérèse's exclamation marks were something else. Even if you took a chainsaw to them, you still couldn't hack them down. "Benjamin is going to die in his bed at the age of ninety-three!" Very comforting, that . . . All that time spent on this mattress . . . Years of immobility then, under you, things start cracking up, oozing, running, and you wind up with an air-pressurised bed like in some specialised motel . . . Malaussène also had images of sticky figs on trays, their juices sizzling in the sun . . . Ninety-three years . . . Thanks a lot, Thérèse! "If you start using our beds to cultivate vegetables, tongues will wag, old chap, tongues will definitely wag!" . . . But how the hell did I *hear* that? – he who medical science says can no longer hear – and how do I *think*? – he whose brain was endlessly unravelling woolly ideas into one straight aimless thread, a flat encephalogram, a piece of uncooked spaghetti – how do I know all this, and who is being informed, given the fact that I'm no longer with us . . . ?

But there was no doubt about it. He did know all this, understood it all, remembered it all, from the very moment when that bullet had sent him flying, everything, the stampede into emergency, the two rival quacks opening his dream box, the continuing visits of his family to the hospital (they rarely came in a gang, they shared out the visiting times so that he was never alone and never over-burdened, they spoke to him as though he really was still very much alive, following Thérèse's excellent advice – while she was the only one that never said a word to him) . . . How was it that he recognised them, his loved ones, Jeremy bragging about getting twenty out of twenty in chemistry (careful, everyone's in danger when that kid starts getting full marks in chemistry), Clara announcing her little portable Clarence's achievements: "He's moving, Ben. I can feel him kick." (Good start, that . . .) Julius the Dog's mighty love affairs, as told by Half Pint, Loussa's Chinese lessons, Loussa's fears for Zabo, Loussa reading to him for what must have been much of the night: "This is what we're publishing this week, shit-for-brains. A cut above your J. L. B. stuff, don't you think?" Was he really still alive, so that Loussa felt he could still make fun of him? Or was that what death really meant, floating deliciously in the affections of the people you cared about, without taking any active part yourself, relieved of the right to answer and of gravity, too, just the perpetual pleasure of your loved ones' presence, then long live death, if it was to be lived out like that! . . . No . . . too beautiful . . . the loved ones would end up deserting his room, all of them, even down to Loussa, the last addition to the list, and Malaussène's thoughts would no longer follow them, still trapped by the attraction of the earth, crushed down onto that bed by the weight of his body, and Malaussène would remain alone, with a hospital all around him.

Then the fear of Berthold the Unplugger surged back. And, with it, the proof that he was definitely alive, pinned there as he was by the fear of death. Perhaps that fear was the only explanation for his mute encephalograph. His brain, gagged by terror, had planed out. Resigned, it was spinning out its thread under Berthold's scissor eyes. As expressionless as a man in front of the firing squad. It was, of course, not what his brain should have been doing, it should, of course, have bridled up, traced out the jagged points of its panic, swamped the screen with its peaks and chasms, but who ever saw a condemned man fight back when the guns were aimed at him? It's always a sack of potatoes that gets shot, annihilated before the volley, scarcely less dead before than after the *coup de grâce*. The apprentice corpse's docility was the ultimate expression of respect for authority, a final tug of the forelock at Mother Justice: "After all, they did condemn me . . ." After all, that was perhaps what his brain was telling itself: "Brain dead? If they say so . . ."

So, what was still kicking in this body that was so scientifically dead? . . . What was waiting for Berthold? If his brain had been definitely knocked flat, where did this vigilance come from? An independence movement had started up in his organism, there was no getting away from that any more. Against his brain which was passively playing the role of the deceased third person, ("*he*" is dead, "*he*" will be greatly missed, "*he*" was a wonderful guy), a passionately resolute first person now stood up: "*I*" am here, alive and kicking! "*I*" say fuck you, you fat bastard, with your two cretinous hemispheres and your nine thousand million pyramidal cells! "*I*" won't let Berthold bugger me up by cutting the thread! "*I, too, exist!*" and, what is more, "*I want to exist!*"

It was like a voice from a soap box, haranguing the countless multitudes of non-encephalic cells. A protest for life which was now taking terrifying proportions. He, who had never been a protester, now felt that he was the focal point of an unprecedented mobilisation, the amphitheatre of a gathering where what was being expressed in his first person was being spoken in the name of all his cells. And he sensed these cells' attentiveness even in the least mentionable confines of his body. It was one of those atmospheres of totally shared consciousness which give rise to historic words, magic formulas which rock the established order, a sentence that transforms humanity, words that mark an epoch. He felt a truth maturing within him. It was swelling. Any moment now it was going to hatch. All of his cells, receptive to the point of self-awareness, made a cathedral of silence for that truth to erupt into, and then be inscribed for all eternity . . . for eternity at the very least!

It finally burst out.

It erupted in the form of a slogan to mobilise them all instantly: ALL CELLS ARE LIVING INDIVIDUALS! DOWN WITH CEREBRAL-CENTRISM!

"DOWN WITH CEREBRAL-CENTRISM!" his cells all chorused back.

"DOWN WITH CEREBRAL-CENTRISM!" his organism cried out unanimously.

"DOWN WITH CEREBRAL-CENTRISM!" Benjamin Malaussène's supine form yelled out silently in the shadows cast by his room's flashing lights.

*

Green and unbroken on the pale screen, the encephalogram's trace made not the slightest judder to celebrate this revolution. And, when Berthold's angular form glided into the room, he didn't even glance at what was lying there under the ventilator.

"Come on," he said to the nurse he'd brought with him. "We've wasted enough time as it is."

Chapter 31

NEITHER CLARA, THÉRÈSE, nor Jeremy was sure what woke them up first that night, Half Pint's screams, or the Dog's deep plaintive wail. Old Thian's first instinct was to rush over to Verdun. With her fists clenched and eyes open, the child was staring at the darkness. Her cot was trembling around her fit to bust. Thian knew that she'd explode any second.

Half Pint was having a dream.

The Dog was having a fit.

While Thian dived onto Verdun's cot, Thérèse gave out a series of short, crisp orders, like a captain thrust out onto the bridge by an unexpected attack.

"Jeremy, give Half Pint his glasses! Clara, Julius's tongue! Stop him from swallowing his tongue!"

"What the bleeding hell's he done with his glasses?"

"On the dining-room table, beside his book."

"Help me, Thérèse, I can't get his jaws open!"

"Let me do it, you call Louna, and tell her to send round Laurent. How's Verdun, Uncle Thian?"

"She's calming down."

"His glasses aren't on the fucking table!"

"Try the pocket of his dungarees, then."

"Louna? Hello, Louna? It's Clara. Julius is having an epileptic fit."

To which was added the awakening of the building, the first blows rained down on the ceiling of the ex-hardware store, insults echoed in the courtyard, demands for sleep, protests from early-birds, reminders of office hours, the Dignity of Labour besmirched, indignation, threats of complaints to the agency, the fire brigade, the police, lunatic asylums, a litany of previous causes for complaint, forecasts of coming misdemeanours, saturation, total saturation! A formidable block of noise, but with Half Pint's screams cutting through it, a chorus of universal hatred, drowned out only by Julius the Dog's lamentations which sounded like a crazy woman wailing, at the beginning of the century, when hysteria was still worth its weight in terror.

Then sudden silence.

Silence from Half Pint, who'd just had his glasses put on his nose by Jeremy, which woke him up at once, as ever.

Silence from Julius, whose tongue Thérèse had just hiked up from the pit of horror in his throat.

Silence from the building, vaguely ashamed at being the only ones making a din. Lights going out one by one. Shutters being closed.

Then, crescendo, Jeremy questioning Half Pint:

"You were dreaming, Half Pint, now what were you dreaming about?"

"There was this man . . ."

"Yes . . ."

"There was this man."

"What sort of man? What was he like?"

"A white man."

"Come on, try and remember for once. What was this white man doing?"

"There was this white man."

"Okay, Okay, you've already said that. So what was this white man in your dream doing?"

"He was white all over, a white coat, a white hat, a white mask."

"He was wearing a mask?"

"Yes, a mask over his nose and his mouth."

Jeremy to Thérèse:

"Did you hear that, Thérèse?"

Thérèse had.

"What was his hat like? Can you tell us that?"

"It didn't have any edges. It was like a bonnet."

"A white bonnet, Thérèse. Go on, Half Pint, don't stop now . . ."

"He was holding a sword."

The sword was still in Half Pint's mind and perhaps in the Dog's crazed stare, too, as he lay there stiff and bloated, like desert carrion, his four paws pointing up to the heavens.

"And then?"

"Then he went into Benjamin's room."

Half Pint rolled up into a ball.

"He went into the room, Thérèse, did you hear that? Berthold has gone into Benjamin's room!"

"'*Benjamin is going to die in his bed at the age of ninety-three!*' That's what you said, isn't it, you silly bitch! '*Benjamin is going to die in·his bed at the age of ninety-three!*' Fat chance! With a bloke like Berthold to tuck him in, I suppose. Why did you and Clara stop me from sleeping in his room, from staying in the hospital, from watching out for him? Why, Thérèse? Answer me, for fuck's sake! Because Thérèse is a know-all! Because Thérèse is always right! Because Thérèse is even smarter than Sod Almighty! Ain't that right? Course it is. Listen up, Thérèse, I'm going to get that bastard Berthold, I'm going to scalpel him and bleed him dry, like that you'll have one unplugged brother and another one a ripper. You'll have won the jackpot and Clara'll be able to take some great photos! You're a pair of silly bitches, you're all a load of fuckheads, and when it's all over, I'll burn down the Vendetta Press, I'll leave home, I'll hook up with Julie, and the two of us will whack the lot of them. Julie's the only one who's got it right, and that's why Benjamin loved her! What are you lot doing while she's revenging your darling bro? Just tell me that! You left him in Berthold's clutches, that's what! You went off back to your nice quiet little lives and left him with Berthold. Mother Clara with her belly and you, Thérèse, with your fucking stars, the ones that told you Benjamin was *going to die in his bed at the age of ninety-three*! What's even dafter than a star? Thérèse is! She's dafter than all the stars in the sky! And the only thing the stars write up there is: praise to Thérèse's thick-as-shitness! How pleased the stars are to find someone thicker than they are, after millions of light years of looking! And it's on planet earth that they finally discovered her, the one that's crawling with thickoes, the one that stinks the worst, the most god-forsaken one of the lot, the one that produces Thérèses, Bertholds and Chabottes! I'll tell you what, Thérèse, it's lucky you're my sister, because otherwise I wouldn't see much difference between you, Berthold and Chabotte! You listening to me? You're not, are you? I'm speaking for the stars, I am! Well, you just go and ask them, ask the stars what officially I, Jeremy, your brother, mean to do about it, what's in my mind and what's in my pocket, and, while you're at it, ask them how long Berthold's still got, that might help him to sort out a few last details . . . "

*

So said Jeremy as they were heading towards the hospital in Thian's car, with its siren blaring, so he said (and more besides) while clutching a carpet cutter with a short triangular blade in his pocket (they'd decided to do up the hardware store for Benjamin's return, but hadn't yet got past the preliminary stage of bickering), so he said in the gleaming corridors that led to Benjamin's room and, if they hadn't known where his room was, they'd still have found it with their eyes closed.

But now they were in front of his door.

After so much haste, their immobility surprised them. As did their silence.

They were in front of the door. The truth lay behind it. Which always gives us pause.

The two-fold body of Thian and Verdun stood between the door and Jeremy.

"Open it, Uncle Thian."

His voice lacked conviction. It needed Thérèse, who'd been so silent up till then, to say:

"Uncle Thian, open that door."

*

No, Benjamin was there. Laid out among the flashing lights of his machines. A sort of alternative Benjamin, like a neon dream. But it was definitely him. Perfectly plugged in. A little more motionless, perhaps, in that intermittent light. And in that slumbering hospital. And with that city, all around, suddenly so drowsy. It was enough to make them wonder what the hell the four of them were doing there, the only vertical beings on that half of the planet. Thian, Jeremy and Verdun held their breath. Only Thérèse, putting the palm of her hand on Benjamin's chest – respiration okay – lifting Benjamin's eyelids – same eyes, same irises, same void – taking his pulse – no faster, no slower – quizzing the machines with her stare, even though she was so totally unsuited to things technical she was still one hell of a lie detector! The machines weren't lying. They were still maintaining Benjamin in his interior life with all the comfort that this turn of the century could provide for him. They ate for him, breathed for him, defecated for him. Benjamin was resting. Technology had taken over. The turn of the century was living instead of Benjamin. The poor soul needed it, after wearing himself so thin in this world. He deserved a rest. That was Thérèse's opinion.

"Let's go home," she said.

Chapter 32

WHAT DO YOU mean, "Let's go home"?

How is it possible? Billions of non-encephalic cells were screaming into the night, and the beings that were closest to them went back home without hearing them! An entire body was emptying itself out in distress, and those at the foot of the bed didn't notice a thing! But what high hopes when they'd come in! How they'd put the word round to one another! What a welcome! "It's Jeremy, it's Thérèse, it's old Thian and Verdun!" The tactile corpuscles played their role of dermic watchdogs to the hilt, transmitting the information to the hypoderm, preaching to the fatty tissue: "Wake up! Transmit directly, do not pass by the brain, it's betrayed us!" And the whole body, tipped off thanks to lateral transmission, all the cells informed of the loved ones' presence, all those nuclei in fusion screaming out in the first person: "Save me! Take me away! Don't leave me in Berthold's clutches! You don't know what the bloke's capable of!"

But Thérèse just checked the breathing, the pulse, pondered . . . Then said:

"Let's go home."

VI
DEATH IS AN ON-COMING PROCESS

Where the hell had I read that?

Chapter 33

WHEN HE HEARD the news from the lab, Chief Superintendent Coudrier didn't believe his ears, nor did he believe his eyes when the lab messenger laid out the evidence in front of him. All the same, Chief Superintendent Coudrier didn't die of astonishment. He quite simply changed ears and screwed in his copper's eyes. But the truth did still seem astonishing as it lay there on his blotter in a shiny little surgical tray. Astonishing, but now, quite suddenly, professionally acceptable. They had all got it wrong, that was all, and he more than any of them. Self-inflicted blindness.

"Elisabeth, would you be so good as to make me a nice cup of coffee?"

Such negligence, after so many years in the force . . . You never learn. With a slight push of his foot, Chief Superintendent Coudrier dimmed his rheostat.

"And would you also ask Inspector Van Thian to come and see me . . . without the baby in the harness, if possible."

*

But it wasn't possible. When Inspector Van Thian sat down in front of his boss, Verdun's stare leapt out at the Chief Superintendent.

Silence.

Silence until Inspector Van Thian obligingly pointed the baby's eyes towards the bronze Napoleon.

"Thank you."

Silence again. But this time it was pregnant with vital questions.

"Tell me, Thian, why did you join the force?"

"Because of my school cert and post-war France," is what Inspector Van Thian would have replied if his boss had really wanted an answer. But the Chief Superintendent was soliloquising. The Chief Superintendent had undertaken an interior voyage. Thian was well used to this.

"As for me, do you know why I joined the force?"

("The sort of question youngsters ask at the beginning of their career," Thian

187

or Coudrier said to himself, "and oldsters ask, too, whenever the shit hits the fan.")

"I joined the force to avoid surprises, Thian, because I loathe the unexpected."

("Just why Clara takes photos," Inspector Van Thian thought and, while he was at it, set off on his own voyage round himself. There was the school cert and post-war France, true enough, but he'd also joined the force so that his cape would give him an exterior identity and his bike trace out the borders of his territory. In his youth, he'd suffered from a lack of definition, half-white, half-yellow, a Tonkin Parisian, Ho Chi Minh with a Parisian accent, Louise, his French mother, in the plonk trade and Mong Kai Thian, his Annamite father, in the poppy trade. Why not become a copper? Then, under his cape, his heart would finally become as hexagonal as France.)

"I could easily have ended up behind a microscope tracking new viruses, my dear Thian. And that was, in fact, how I started out. In medical research."

As for Inspector Van Thian, he'd started out as a newspaper vendor, a true surprise merchant, in fact: "Buy *Ce Soir*! Ramadier excludes the Communists from government!" "An epic in *L'Equipe*! Robic wins the first post-war Tour!" "Read *Combat*! Independence for India!" "Stop press! Stop press! *Le Figaro*! Leclerc's plane crashes in Algeria!"

A little yellow lad, throwing the world's confetti . . .

"But what is even worse than the unexpected, Thian . . . is certainty!"

Chief Superintendent Coudrier's monologue went on, in the depths of his green light. Thian took the opportunity to Malaussènise a bit. After Benjamin had been shot, it was obviously out of the question to read the children a single word of J. L. B. Everyone had been at sixes and sevens. What to do when the sun went down? The kids were hurting. So Clara made a suggestion: "What if you told us your life story, Uncle Thian?" My life? He felt stripped to the bone. As if he'd just been informed that he'd had a life. "That's a good idea," Thérèse chipped in. "Yeah, your investigations . . . " Jeremy leapt into bed. "And what you were like when you were little!" They pulled on their pyjamas. My life? They sat him down on his stool and waited for him to come alive.

"That's right," Chief Superintendent Coudrier soliloquised on. "It is our certainties that create the worst surprises!"

And it's certainly true that there's no surprise without certainty, Inspector Van Thian had to admit. My life? He'd felt as lost as if Thérèse had asked him to predict the future. "Your first love . . . " Clara had murmured. "Yes, tell us about your first love, Uncle Thian!" "First love! First love!" The slogan was caught on. Thian hadn't had a first love. All he'd ever had was Janine. He'd gone straight from his teenage scraps to Janine the Giantess whose business had been just that, selling love in a

Toulon whorehouse. Just Janine, right from the start and until the end of Janine, as though Thian had granted himself a monopoly of love. How many widowers had he created when he carried off Janine? Every sailor in the port. But was it something he could tell the children? He was still wondering about that when he'd already been telling them about Janine for the last two hours . . .

"A wretched job, Thian . . ."

Chief Superintendent Coudrier was slowly surfacing. Any minute now, his lamp would beam out again and Inspector Van Thian would find out why he'd been sent for.

Thian had told the children about the set-to when he'd eloped with Janine. Even worse than if he'd been caught red-handed in a convent. A hoard of Corsican cousins had got onto his case. They didn't mind their cousin earning their pocket money for them (a question of tradition) but couldn't stomach her choosing a yellow lover (a question of principle). A hell-for-leather chase. A real Tour de France of the kinship vendetta. The big guns out to turn their love affair into a sieve. It'd been to carry Gervaise, Janine's daughter, that Thian had come up with the leather harness he now used to cart round Verdun. When ambushed, Thian shielded Gervaise with his own body by spinning her behind his back. Bullets whistled past Gervaise's curls. Thian was the only man who'd learnt to shoot because of love. But he was also naturally gifted. Big Janine didn't do so badly for herself, either. Quite a few of the cousins were left laid out on the paving stones. "And after all that you say you haven't lived!" "Shut up, Jeremy, let Uncle Thian tell what happened next."

"What are, in your opinion, Thian, a policeman's strongest and weakest points?"

"The fact of being a copper, sir."

"Doubt, my old chap, *doubt*!"

Chief Superintendent Coudrier was back with us. With the light full on his face, he looked more imperial than ever, ringed with a furious halo of lucidity.

"Tell me, Thian, what exactly did you shoot at the other day, on Rue Saint-Honoré?"

*

COUDRIER: Tell me, Thian, what exactly did you shoot at the other day, on Rue Saint-Honoré?

VAN THIAN: At Julie Corrençon.

COUDRIER: I didn't say "who", I said "what".

VAN THIAN: At a glint from a telescopic sight, at a woman's hair, and at a hand holding the stock of a high-precision rifle.

COUDRIER: What came first? The sight, the hair, or the hand?

VAN THIAN: I dunno. The hand, I think.

COUDRIER: The hand? Why not the hair?

VAN THIAN: . . .

COUDRIER: Shall I tell you why? Because you didn't really want to kill La Corrençon.

VAN THIAN: I don't agree. Anyway, at that distance . . .

COUDRIER: Distance does not exist for marksmen such as you. That is something you have already demonstrated any number of times.

VAN THIAN: . . .

COUDRIER: . . .

VAN THIAN: . . .

COUDRIER: The truth is that, willy nilly, you fired before your fellow officers in order to save La Corrençon's life.

VAN THIAN: That isn't the way I remember it.

COUDRIER: What colour was the hair?

VAN THIAN: Red, I reckon.

COUDRIER: Really red, or vaguely red?

VAN THIAN: Really red.

COUDRIER: Auburn, Thian . . . an auburn wig. So much for your memory . . .

VAN THIAN: . . .

COUDRIER: Now, let's get this straight. I am not for a moment doubting your good faith. We have known each other too long for that. Let us suppose that you did decide to finish off La Corrençon, maybe with a view to saving her from the consequences of her actions. That would be just like you. Let us just suppose. Well, something in you saved that young lady. The fact that she is Malaussène's woman, perhaps . . .

VAN THIAN: . . .

COUDRIER: . . .

VAN THIAN: . . .

COUDRIER: Which is all to your credit, Thian . . .

VAN THIAN: . . .

COUDRIER: But which has dropped us in deep shit.

VAN THIAN: Sorry?

COUDRIER: Just take a look at this.

*

"This" was one of those small surgical trays, whose metallic brightness inevitably

190

reminded Thian of penicillin, that intense burning pain they injected into the buttocks of TB sufferers in the 1950s, instead of packing them off to scatter what was left of their lungs over a mountain resort. A fleeting image crossed Thian's mind of his mother, Louise, and his wife, Big Janine, the former pinning him down onto the floor, the latter taking aim at his arse, which had frozen with terror. The penicillin laughter of his two favourite women: "These days, Thianie, no-one goes to sanatoriums, they come to you in needles." Why not tell the kids about his TB that evening? The only thing that had ever made him shit-scared: syringes . . .

"Pull yourself together Thian, I'm not going to give you a jab in the behind. Please open it."

It was slippery. He couldn't get a grip.

"Here, let me."

Chief Superintendent Coudrier snapped it open, then handed the tray back to Thian, as if he was offering him a cigar. Except that, what Thian could see, snug in a cotton-wool nest, weren't cigars, but two fingers. Two sectioned fingers. Absolutely unreal-looking, but altogether there. Two fingers. A matt yellow which had once been a flesh pink.

"Your target, Thian."

Two fingers linked by a strip of skin and with a small halo of torn flesh at their base. Two ghost fingers. So why was Chief Superintendent Coudrier, quite out of the blue, making Inspector Van Thian look at the two fingers he'd shot off Julie Corrençon?

"Because they're not La Corrençon's fingers, Thian."

(Ah!)

"No. These fingers belong to a man."

(A pianist, then . . . some arty-farty type . . .)

"A trainee in the forensic lab noticed this quite by chance. We were so certain that it was La Corrençon that nobody had even bothered to examine these fingers. Not bad, eh, for big boys our age . . . "

Then, as though the i's really still needed dotting:

"Therefore, the person who shot at us from that window was a man."

And, as though the nails still needed driving home:

"A man whose life you spared, Thian."

Final blow:

"A killer."

191

Chapter 34

IN CIRCUMSTANCES LIKE this, Julie was pretty much the same as the rest of the human race. Same instincts. Same reflexes. When the firing started from her very own window, Julie hit the deck like everyone else, hoping that the tarmac would swallow her up. She didn't even have time to see the bullet rip into Calignac's shoulder. Before the shot, Julie's eyes had been all for Queen Zabo. And the little Black who was acting as her bodyguard with such touching determination. Loussa de Casamance, presumably, Benjamin had often spoken to her about him. Friend Loussa was puffing up his scrawny chest in front of his friend Zabo's bones. ("The farce of resolution," thought Julie, citing one of her father the Governor's expressions.) Loussa was quite right to be covering his Queen. Julie knew that the killer was after her. And get her he would, if the coppers didn't keep their eyes open. Julie moved nearer the Queen. Julie was counting on her reflexes to get the first shot in at the killer. Her father's governmental service automatic was making a noticeable bulge in her jacket. Julie was a copper among the coppers looking for Julie. Not a uniformed officer – operettas left Julie cold – but a modern-day copper, bomber jacket, identity bracelet, trainers, wedding tackle clearly discernible under the skin-tight jeans. Julie was a young copper with designer stubble, hips a tad wide, for sure, but with a natural swagger. One of the coppers at Gauthier's funeral, directing their peepers at everything that wasn't a copper. There were men from the local brigade and inspectors from Headquarters. Julie was banking on this being a mixed bag, on them not all knowing one another, but recognising that they were all members of the same body. To one of her neighbours (the same hunk in a pilot's jacket who'd hauled Mo and Simon out of their chip van) Julie'd even whispered:

"There's nothing more dangerous that a bird avenging her geezer."

A hint of ruggedness in her naturally husky voice, her "Savannah growl" as Benjamin used to put it, and the other one had nodded. Julie was clearly in search of an enigma. She had no more idea than her fellow officers what the lurking killer might look like.

When Julie heard the first gun blast, she just had time to see Loussa pin his Queen to the ground, before hitting the concrete herself. Stuck under her left breast, her father's service automatic was now of no use to her. (While flattening her chest so as to disguise herself as a man, Julie had remembered something Thérèse had icily said when first they'd met: "With such big bosoms, how do you manage to sleep on your stomach?" Since they'd all been deprived of a mother, the Malaussène tribe was obsessed with breasts. "Obsessed? My arse!" Benjamin sniggered. "Leave out your trick-cyclist routine, Julie, and give us a lend of your mammaries." Benjamin fed entirely on Julie's breasts.) There was a second shot, followed by an exclamation which Julie supposed was meant for her:

"That bitch is a fucking good shot!"

Then, a brief silence, and suddenly, just beside Julie, repeated fire from a single weapon, a large-calibre hand gun.

Julie was the first to her feet, standing beside Thian, firing at the same target, her own window, which was being shot to splinters. Then the rest joined in. Julie fired with an anger that astonished her, her body braced to take the shooter's powerful recoil. In that mood, Julie could have taken the recoil from a bazooka. She would have blown the building's head off. Her fellow officers felt the same way, wiping out the fear that had pinned them to the ground. But Julie's reasons were more serious. She had realised right from the word go that her life would begin again only when she had that character firmly in her sights. Julie realised how furious she was looking when she felt the weight of old Thian's stare on her. While firing at that window, Thian had stammered out some inaudible words. He was now staring at Julie with glistening eyes, but without recognising her. Julie felt certain that Thian would have gunned her straight down, her and a few other coppers, if his clip hadn't been empty. Instead of which, the old policeman had rapidly slid his gun back into his holster and left the firing ground, with Verdun's eyes opening up a pathway in front of him.

*

"She's not in her bedsit any more."

"You're kidding!"

"She's wounded. She's split leaving two fingers stuck in the wall."

"What?"

"The Viet shot two of her fingers off."

"She went off with two of her fingers missing?"

"The Viet didn't shoot her legs off!"

"All the same . . ."

"Tough cookie, eh?"

"I can think of better places to have her than on the end of a shooter."

"Alone against the world. Miss Rambo . . ."

The crowd chattered and drifted apart. Julie slipped out of the hermetically sealed neighbourhood, each building being fine-toothcombed, police reinforcements, a concert of sirens, all the local Japanese regretting the fact that they'd acquired a slice of Saint-Honoré-Pyramides-Saint-Roch, an area they'd reckoned to be sheltered from violent death.

Julie headed off towards Rue de Rivoli, where her car was parked, a police card stuck up behind its smoked-glass windscreen. Julie had hired a young copper's car, a 205 GTI, with a double red stripe, to match her trainers. She felt like lapping the ring road with her foot down, until the penny finally dropped. Until she managed to get into chummy's head. Julie had kept one bullet in her cylinder, just in case. For chummy's head. But she didn't know what he looked like. All the same, she did know far more about him than all those boys in blue who'd been staking her out. What did Julie know? Julie was carefully going through it.

Firstly, Julie knew that he'd executed Chabotte after she'd grilled him – because all she'd done was to grill Chabotte.

Secondly, Julie knew that he'd executed Gauthier after she'd grilled him – because all she'd done was to grill Gauthier.

Thirdly, Julie knew that he'd left a lovely little clue on the scene of each murder pointing to her: the BMW she'd hired, abandoned on the edge of the Bois de Boulogne where they'd found Chabotte, and the Audi she'd hired, abandoned just by Parc Montsouris where they'd found Gauthier's body, on Rue Gazan.

Julie knew that he'd been dogging her every step, her every turn of the wheel, stealing one of the cars which she wasn't then using for each of his murders. Julie knew that he knew all of her identities: the Italian, the Greek, the Austrian and now her brand-new vocation as a plain-clothes inspector. He knew her hideouts, her disguises, her ploys, her movements and her cars. He knew her, Julie, personally. There was no getting away from that. He knew her and was out to frame her for a massacre which she didn't even understand. Was he killing the people she grilled to stop her from learning something? Absurd, since he always killed them *after* she'd grilled them.

So pondered Julie as she headed off towards her macho copper's car. Who is he? What does he want? Where will it all end?

At that moment was she still a widow, or had she become an investigative reporter once more? Julie reckoned that this question would have fascinated Benjamin. Why didn't she just explain the whole business to the first copper she came across? She had the police force after her for murders she hadn't committed. All she'd have to do to prove her innocence would be to lay her full set of ten fingers on Chief Superintendent Coudrier's desk. Two irrefutable fingers. Instead of which, Julie preferred to play the moving target in a city swarming with officers out to gun her down. Even worse, by stubbornly trying to unmask the killer, she was throwing Coudrier's bloodhounds off the scent. The real murderer was relaxing with his feet up, covered by Corrençon the Red Herring.

Widow, then, or journalist? Julie, is your heart beating fast because of the tears you're swallowing or from the thrill of the chase? Leave it out, Benjamin, can't you? Let me get on with my job . . . Your job? My job, Benjamin: getting there first! "A journalist, getting there first? Don't make me laugh. Personal investigations? Bullshit!" Benjamin sneered. "All you hacks do nowadays is take your notepads along for police dictation! They're your sources! No wonder you don't want to reveal their names! You're just police auxiliaries, Julie, you scribble out early versions of the prosecutor's report in the name of freedom of the press!" Benjamin and Julie . . . the only subject they rowed about. But rowed fit to burst.

Completely wrapped up in her row with Benjamin, Julie was livid with rage when she hit Rue de Rivoli. She now understood why she was pursuing this killer. One sole reason: to prove to Benjamin that if there was still anything honourable about journalism, then Julie was it! To have the last word, once and for all. It was one way of being a widow. No, she wouldn't go and see Coudrier. No, she wasn't a police auxiliary. She'd finger this character, all on her own. She'd uncover the truth, all on her own. She'd blow his brains out with her last bullet. All on her own.

*

She now had to find her car.

But, on Rue de Rivoli, no car.

The parking space was empty.

Right, thought Julie.

I see.

Especially because what she could see, in the exact spot where she'd parked her 205, was a puddle of blood, dripping down discreetly from the pavement into the gutter.

Chapter 35

COUDRIER: YOUR CONCLUSION, Thian?

VAN THIAN: If it isn't Julie Corrençon, then it's someone else.

COUDRIER: You've been in the force too long to stick to a conclusion like that, Thian.

VAN THIAN: . . .

COUDRIER: What would you do if you had the entire French police force on your arse and you could prove your innocence?

VAN THIAN: I'd go straight along to the nearest police station.

COUDRIER: Of course you would. But Julie Corrençon has done nothing of the kind.

VAN THIAN: . . .

COUDRIER: . . .

VAN THIAN: Maybe she's dead?

COUDRIER: From the Lebanon to Afghanistan, that young lady has covered our worst wars, she brought about the downfall of a Turkish Interior Minister for drug-smuggling, she escaped alive from a Thai prison that was infected with typhus, she removed her own appendix on a raft in the China Sea, last year she was thrown into the Seine with lead bracelets round her ankles . . . You know all that as well as I do, Thian. That woman is about as mortal as a hero in a Belgian comic book.

VAN THIAN: Belgian?

COUDRIER: Belgian. According to my grandsons, they do the best line in that sort of thing.

VAN THIAN: . . .

COUDRIER: . . .

VAN THIAN: . . .

COUDRIER: How is your Malaussène family?

VAN THIAN: Half Pint's had a nightmare, the dog's had an epileptic fit, Clara's into her eighth month, Thérèse wants to open a psychic consultancy, Jeremy's cooking up a fire bomb and Verdun's growing a pretty painful molar.

COUDRIER: A fire bomb?

VAN THIAN: He's just perfecting the fuse.

COUDRIER: The target?

VAN THIAN: The Vendetta Press's warehouses in Villejuif, going by what he's told me.

COUDRIER: He told you that?

VAN THIAN: Only when I promised not to tell anyone else.

COUDRIER: . . .

VAN THIAN: . . .

COUDRIER: Books burn badly. Particularly in a warehouse. Too compact.

VAN THIAN: . . .

COUDRIER: What about Malaussène?

VAN THIAN: Kidney problems. They've put him on dialysis. But Thérèse's still certain he'll pull through.

COUDRIER: . . .

VAN THIAN: . . .

COUDRIER: Why on earth hasn't La Corrençon given herself up, her and her ten fingers?

VAN THIAN: Maybe she doesn't know I shot two of chummy's off.

COUDRIER: I don't believe that.

VAN THIAN: Me neither.

COUDRIER: It is incredible how useful your deductions are to me, Thian my dear chap.

VAN THIAN: We're both missing Pastor. He was the one with the deductions.

COUDRIER: Pastor . . . Any news of him?

VAN THIAN: No.

COUDRIER: Nor I.

VAN THIAN: . . .

COUDRIER: . . .

VAN THIAN: . . .

COUDRIER: There is one possible explanation, Thian.

VAN THIAN: There is?

COUDRIER: She's covering someone.

VAN THIAN: An accomplice?

COUDRIER: Obviously an accomplice! Who else do you think she'd cover. Buck your ideas up, for heaven's sake.

VAN THIAN: My ideas are perfectly bucked up, Chief Superintendent. It's just that someone who pins three murders on you doesn't sound like much of an accomplice to me.

COUDRIER: . . .

VAN THIAN: . . .

COUDRIER: . . .

VAN THIAN: . . .

COUDRIER: Unless they are simply giving us the run-around. Making us follow a false lead, while he quietly gets on with the business.

VAN THIAN: Possible.

COUDRIER: Who among Malaussène's friends do you know who would be crafty enough to set up such a scheme?

VAN THIAN: Black Mo and Simon the Berber are inside, Hadouch Ben Tayeb has more men on his tail than the rest of Belleville put together . . .

COUDRIER: So?

VAN THIAN: Me excepted, I don't know.

COUDRIER: I do.

VAN THIAN: . . .

COUDRIER: A killer, Thian. A real killer. One of our friends. A killer with ethics.

VAN THIAN: . . .

COUDRIER: . . .

VAN THIAN: Pastor?

COUDRIER: Pastor.

VAN THIAN: Pastor's in Venice. In perfect bliss with old Ma Malaussène.

COUDRIER: I'm going to check up on that, Thian. And at this very second.

(The Chief Superintendent's figure bent over the intercom.)

COUDRIER: Elisabeth? Be so good as to telephone the Hotel Danieli in Venice for me. Very good. And ask for Inspector Pastor.

*

Pastor . . . that was the conclusion Julie had reached, as well. There was no other possible explanation. Pastor was in true love with Benjamin's mother, in Venice. One way or another, Pastor had heard the news. Pastor now had sufficiently strong family ties to go after Benjamin's murderer. Pastor was here. Pastor was cleaning up. In his usual, rather unscrupulous way. Pastor was killing the baddies. Pastor knew Julie. Pastor knew that she was the sort of woman who'd revenge her man. Pastor had followed her, had taken advantage of her own investigations, grilled Chabotte and got him to confess what she had been unable to get out of him. Exit Chabotte. Then Pastor had grilled Gauthier. Good-bye Gauthier. Pastor had sheltered behind her, that much was true. No-one must suspect for a second that it was him. A phone call to Venice is easily made. He had to act incognito. And now this business had cost Pastor two of his fingers. Pastor had nicked her car once again. Somewhere in Paris, Pastor was pissing blood while calmly waiting for Julie to turn up.

Julie knew where to find him. Quite simply, he had to be in one of her flats, one of the hideouts she'd used and he'd identified.

Pastor . . .

She obviously didn't have the intention to shoot his brains out any more.

Julie went round her bedsits. No Pastor on Rue de Mauberge in the tenth *arrondissement*. No-one on Rue Georges-de-Porto-Riche in the fourteenth. But, at number 49, Rue du Four, amid the passageways on the sixth floor, last door on the left, at the end of the corridor . . .

In her adventurous existence, Julie had heard enough wounded men breathing to know that the person who was there in her room wasn't in the best of shape.

The door wasn't locked.

She opened it.

Even though his hand was wrapped up in a blood-stained rag, the tall wan stiff lad who was standing there in front of Julie, holding a revolver, was not Jean-Baptiste Pastor. Julie had never seen him before. Which didn't stop a bloodless grin from flickering over his face.

"You're here at last."

And him from fainting as though he'd known her for ages.

*

VAN THIAN: There's no point phoning Venice, sir, because there's no way it's Pastor.

COUDRIER: Why is that?

VAN THIAN: Pastor can't shoot to save his life. If he'd taken aim at Calignac from way up in that window, then he'd either have hit you, or God Almighty in person.

Chapter 36

"WANSHANG HAO, SHIT-for-brains." (Good evening, shit-for-brains.) There's no getting away from it, thought Loussa de Casamance, visiting a brain-dead friend really does end up getting tiresome.

"*Duibuqi, wo lai wan le.*" (Sorry, I'm late.)

It's not so much because he never answers, but because you despair at making yourself heard.

"*Wo leile . . .*" (I'm tired.)

Loussa had never imagined that a friendship could wind up being so like a marriage. Absorbed in his thoughts, it took him a few seconds to notice the new machine which seemed to have sprouted from Malaussène's body.

"*Ta men gei ni fang de zhe ge xin ji qi henpiao liang!*" (What a nice new machine they've given you there!)

It was a sort of hanging motorway above Benjamin's bed, full of valves, intersections, delicate membranes, a spaghetti junction through which his friend's blood was tracing an enigmatic arabesque.

"*Zhe shi shenme,* in fact? (What is that, in fact?) A new way to exteriorise yourself?"

Loussa glanced round at the encephalograph just in case. No, Benjamin still wasn't responding.

"Oh well, never mind. I've got some good news for you, shit-for-brains. Just for a change."

*

The good news was quickly said: Loussa had just translated one of J. L. B.'s novels into Chinese – *The Child Who Could Count.* (*Hen hui suan de xiao haizi,* shit-for-brains.)

"I know that you couldn't care less, and that it's one you didn't even bother to read, but don't forget that, no matter how comatose you are, you're still earning one per cent on it. The Vendetta Press has just published it for the Chinese over here, and also for the Chinese over there, who are pretty numerous, as you know. Shall I tell you the story? No? A quick précis, then? . . . Let's go: it tells the story of a little soup-seller in Hong Kong who can calculate more quickly on her abacus than all the other children in the world put together, more quickly than adults as well, and even more quickly than her father. She's the apple of his eye, and he brings her up like a boy and calls her Xiao Bao ("Little Treasure"). Can you guess the rest? No? Well, the father gets himself bumped off in the first few pages by the local mafia who want to have a monopoly over Chinese soup, the little girl then makes a fortune during the next five hundred pages and revenges her father in the last thirty, having taken over all the multinationals present in Hong Kong – all this without using any other instrument than her childhood abacus. There we are. Pure J. L. B., as you can see. Free-Market Realism put at the disposal of the awakening Dragon."

Malaussène was circulating around himself. Impossible to tell what he thought about all that. Loussa took the opportunity to lick his lips and say:

"Would it amuse you to see how I translated the first, say, fifty pages? What do you reckon?"

Without waiting for a word of reply, Loussa de Casamance produced a set of proofs from his coat and dived in:

"*Si wang shi zhe xian de xin cheng . . .*"

A sigh.

"The first sentence was a real pain in the arse to translate. You see, Chabotte decided to start by describing the father's death, his throat pierced by a Moi crossbow bolt – one of those tiny poisoned arrows the Mois use for tiger-hunting, follow me? And to suggest at the same time the idea of destiny and the tension of the shot, Chabotte wrote: *Death is an on-coming process.*"

Loussa gave two or three doubtful shakes of his head.

"Death is an on-coming process . . . Hmm . . . so I went for a literal translation: '*Si wang shi zhe xian de xin cheng.*' . . . Yes, but a Chinese would have turned it a different way . . . On the other hand, it really is a direct sentence, isn't it? Apart from the fact that the word 'process' slows it down, fatally slows it in fact, just like destiny, for we're all headed the same way, even those who run the fastest, but this slowness is propelled by the preceding 'on-coming', which gives the sentence its rapidity . . . its slow rapidity . . . there's a truly Chinese idea for you . . . So I wonder if I was right to translate it literally. What do you think?"

Chapter 37

W HAT I THINK, Loussa, what I think is that if you'd read that sentence to me a few months ago, I'd never have adopted J. L. B.'s identity, and that lousy .22 high-penetration bullet would have lodged itself in someone else's brains, what I think, Loussa, is that if you'd read me that sentence on the day when, for example, that prehistoric giant was demolishing my office – remember him? – then Chabotte would still be alive, Gauthier too, Calignac in one piece, and my Julie in my bed. Loussa, oh Loussa, why is it that the worst blows must always come from our dearest friends? Why read me that today, this particular evening, when I had almost peacefully decided to leave my cells behind me and pack my bags? If you'd come to see me right at the beginning with your translator's scruples, which are all highly to your honour, no doubt about it, if you'd sat yourself down in my office and asked me: "*Life is an on-coming process,* shit-for-brains. How should I translate that into Chinese, literally, or with a bit of leeway?", if you'd mentioned the title of the book, *The Child Who Could Count,* the author's pseudonym, J. L. B., and that Chabotte was the one hiding behind it, I'd have answered: "Put away your paintbrushes, Loussa, stash your ideograms into the Chinese pigeon-holes in your brainbox, and don't translate that book." Cut to the quick, as they say in novels, you'd have asked me: "Whyever not, shit-for-brains?" And I'd have replied: "Because if you translate that book, you'll be an accomplice to the most disgusting literary scam imaginable." "Oh yeah?" that's how you would have reacted, with one of your "oh yeah?"s, with your green eyes wrinkled up in amusement. (Have I ever told you that you have wonderful eyes, green on black, the most expressive stare in this multi-coloured world?) "Oh yeah?" "Yeah, Loussa, a lousy scam, or rather a squeaky-clean one, a classy set-up, if you see what I mean, premeditated in high places, thoroughly well thought through, scruples carefully shelved, legal protection at every stage, a copper-plated fiddle, the scam of the century, and we're all up to our necks in it, drowning in our ignorance, Zabo, Calignac, you, me, the Vendetta Press . . . "

Calmly you'd have listened, then calmly taken me to Amar's, calmly sat us down in front of our glasses of Sidi-Brahim and then, heart to heart, you'd have calmly asked me:

"Cut the crap, shit-for-brains, what's all this about a scam?"

And I'd have given you the real truth:

"Chabotte isn't J. L. B."

"He isn't?"

"He isn't."

Here, of course, you'd have marked your usual pause.

"Chabotte isn't J. L. B.?"

You'd have given expression to your thoughts:

"You mean Chabotte didn't write *The Child Who Could Count*?"

"Right, Loussa, nor *The Lord of the Currencies, Last Kiss on Wall Street, Gold Mine, Dollar, The Yen's Daughter, Having . . .* "

"Chabotte didn't write a single one of those books?"

"Not a word of them."

"They were ghosted?"

"No."

Then the emergence of truth would have blossomed over your face, Loussa, like a sun rising over an unknown world.

"He nicked all those books from someone else?"

"Yes."

"A dead someone?"

"No, still very much alive."

And I would finally have heard you ask the inevitable question:

"Do you know who it is, shit-for-brains?"

"Yes."

"Who is it then?"

*

It's the bloke who plugged me between the eyes, Loussa. A tall, fair-haired lad, extraordinarily good-looking, of an unguessable age, a sort of Dorian Grey, a character straight out of one of J. L. B.'s novels with that precociousness that seems to give them eternal youth. They look their age until they're ten, at thirty they're at the summit of their glory and look fifteen, at sixty they could be mistaken for their daughter's boyfriend, and their beauty at eighty is of the sort that still hasn't given up the fight. A J. L. B. hero, I'm telling you. An eternally youthful, eternally handsome fighter. A slice of Free-Market Realism. That's what the bloke who murdered me looks like. And the poor sod wasn't wrong to do so, given that he's the real author of all those books I was pretending I'd written, while giving myself the airs and graces of a cock on the dung-heap. Yes, Loussa, he shot me instead of Chabotte, and *Chabotte had set me up on purpose for that very reason*. He assumed that I was the one who'd pinched his life's work, he got my head focused in his telescopic sight, he pressed the trigger. There we are. I'd done my job.

Now, as to why that sentence "death is an on-coming process" suddenly struck gold with me, as to why I immediately glimpsed its author's face in my mind's eye when you read it out to me – me, who had been vainly fumbling after it that day when the giant made matchsticks out of office furniture – I'm sorry, Loussa, but it'd take too long to explain. It'd be too tiring.

You see, right now, I really am too busy dying. I know that, put like this, in the first person singular, it sounds a bit incredible. But, if you stop and think, when people die, it's always in the first person singular. Which is hard to accept, I'll grant you that. The kids that go fearlessly off to war send only their third persons out onto the battlefield. To Berlin! Nach Paris! Allah Akhbar! It's their enthusiasm, not their real selves, which packs them off to die, a third party stuffed full of blood and guts which they don't even realise are their own. They die in ignorance of themselves, their first persons confiscated by twisted, Chabotte-like ideas.

I'm dying, Loussa, I'm telling you this straight, I'm dying. That machine you were so excited about is quite simply a state-of-the-art dialyser, an innovation which I'm testing out, so to speak, which is replacing my kidneys, my two kidneys which Berthold ripped out. (A motorbike accident, apparently, a young man and a young girl, the small of the boy's back bounced off the edge of the pavement. His kidneys popped. Emergency. He needed a pair of kidneys and Berthold took mine.) Like many others, I'm dying from having fallen into the hands of one of humanity's benefactors: Berthold! And if all he'd ripped out were my kidneys . . . Loussa, you've no idea what can be whisked away from out a body during a period of a few weeks without anybody noticing! Your kith and kin keep visiting you, even ultra-lucid examples like Thérèse and Half Pint, and they're completely hood-winked. They stand there in front of a bag which is being emptied before their very eyes, but that bag continues to be their brother. "Benjamin is going to live until he's ninety-three . . ." At the rate Berthold's ripping me off, I wonder what will be left of me at the age of ninety-three. A fingernail, perhaps? Then Clara, Thérèse, Jeremy and Louna, Verdun and Half Pint will carry on visiting that fingernail. I'm not kidding, Loussa, you'll see that I'm right. You, too, will persist in visiting the fingernail and teaching it Chinese, you'll tell it about your Isabelle, you'll read beautiful things to it, because what you'll then be visiting, you and my family, will no longer be a brother, but brotherhood, will no longer be a friend (*pengyou* in

Chinese), but friendship (*youyi*), and it will no longer be a physical person who will be attracting you to the hospital but the remembrance of an emotion. Then, your vigilance will inevitably wane, you won't ask yourself medical questions any more, you'll swallow the quacks' explanations ("yes, he's having a wee kidney problem, we've had to put him on peritoneal dialysis"), and the friend will go into ecstasy before the new machine: "Well, well, well, what a nice new machine they've given you there!" And the way my kidneys screamed out when Berthold tore them from my body was nice, too, I suppose?

Here we go. I had promised to myself that I'd die peacefully, only too pleased about being scattered to the four winds for the good of my species, but now I'm starting to get worked up. I mean, for Christ's sake, do you reckon it's fair for them to nick my kidneys so that some fucking richkid, who was trying to impress his girlfriend by doing a ton, can carry on pissing nice and comfortably? Is there any *justice* in that? I never even took my driving test, I hate bikers, they're a load of peabrains on wheels, suicidal maniacs the lot of them, who endanger the lives of my little ones. And do you reckon it's fair for them to cut my lungs out, yes, my lungs, they're next on Berthold's shopping list, and graft them onto some two-bit city slicker who's given himself the cancer of the century by chainsmoking while he was diddling the pants off us all? I don't even smoke! The only person I've ever diddled is my good self! . . . If, at least, they transplanted my prick onto a perfect lover who'd lost his own between a set of over-amorous teeth, then I wouldn't argue. Or the skin off my arse to restore a Botticelli, then, why not. But the trouble is, Loussa, I'm being stolen to pay robbers . . . I'm being stolen, Loussa, stolen piece by piece as I lie here, I'm being turned into machines which are taking my place, which are being visited instead of me, I'm dying, Loussa, because even though each of my cells has several billion years' evolution behind it, they're all dying, too, they've given up hope and are dying and, each time, it's a tiny individual death, a first person passing on, a scrap of poetry fading away . . .

Chapter 38

"**I** DON'T BELIEVE women who don't say anything," Inspector Van Thian said to himself, after sitting for a good hour in front of a woman who wasn't saying anything.

"Madame hasn't said a word for sixteen years, sir. Madame has been deaf and dumb for the last sixteen years."

"I don't believe women who don't say anything," Inspector Van Thian had replied to Antoine, ex-minister Chabotte's highly discreet butler. "I've come to see Madame Nazaré Quissapaolo Chabotte."

"Madame receives nobody, sir. Madame has been deaf and dumb for the last sixteen years."

"I didn't say I'd come to listen to her."

Inspector Van Thian had adopted the following simple reasoning. If Julie hadn't executed Chabotte, then someone else had. If it was someone else, then their inquiries had to be started again from scratch. Which meant, in inquiries such as this, quizzing the victim's friends and relations. And the family first of all, which was almost invariably the starting point and the finishing line. Eighty per cent of bloody murders are family gifts. That's right, the family kills four times more often than the Family. That's the way it is.

"I didn't say I'd come to speak to her."

Now, all the extant family which Chabotte, the deceased ex-minister, now had was his mother, a deaf mute ninety-year-old, who hadn't been seen outside the house for the last twenty years.

"I've come to see her."

*

He'd come to see her, and she was quite a sight! At first, she had looked like a big heap of dust which had accumulated over several decades in the corner of a huge bedroom. The spick-and-span half-light of the death chamber and then, over there, in that corner by the window, a heap of dust which had once been a woman. If Thian had slammed the door, he would have blown her all over the shop. He tiptoed across the floor. From closer-up, she was no longer a heap of dust, but a mound of completely threadbare blankets, of the sort used for protecting lacquerware or the family furnishings. But the overall impression remained the same. She was something that had been forgotten there during a move. Especially since the room was empty, or practically. A four-poster bed, a spindly chair at its foot, and that heap of blankets by the window.

Thian grabbed the chair – its black back-rest picked out with gold leafing – and quietly positioned it between the window and what was left of Madame Nazaré Quissapaolo Chabotte. When the woman's stare fell on him, it seemed to confirm the most pessimistic statistics regarding family killings. There was enough hatred accumulated in those eyes to wipe out the largest of families. A stare capable of piercing a pregnant belly and frying a grandson in his egg. Thian knew he was onto something. The fossil's stare suddenly left him to cross swords with little Verdun. And Thian, who'd never hidden anything from the child, who shaved naked in front of her, who took her for her daily walk through the tombstones of Père-Lachaise (marble fingers reaching up from the graves, faces half-swallowed up by granite . . .), Thian, who'd exposed the child to a killer's bullets, now felt his first scruples as a child-raiser. He went to get up, but felt Verdun stiffen against him, he heard her cry a brief "no!" and found himself sitting down again as though he'd never had the intention to leave. He just took a moment to celebrate the arrival of language in the child's mouth. "No . . . " Verdun's first word. (Nothing particularly surprising about that, in fact.) No? Right, then. Thian played a waiting game. A stake-out which could easily last an eternity. It was now up to the two women: the extremely ancient one, who was out to wither up the brand-new one; and the brand-new one, who was weighing up the advantages of being an orphan. One hour.

"You are a lucky man, sir."

When it happened, Thian almost felt as if he'd spoken the words himself. What do you mean "lucky", for crying out loud? He prepared himself for an interior debate.

"To be loved that much . . . "

No, it wasn't him speaking. It was the heap of blankets over there in the armchair. A crackly voice was emerging from those blankets.

" . . . but it won't last."

A crackly, evil voice. The eyes were staring at him again.

"It never does."

What was this woman who never spoke talking about?

"I'm talking about the little girl, there, whom you carry around on your stomach."

Lips like the parched plaster of a tombstone.

"That is just how I used to carry mine."

Hers? Chabotte? She carried old Chabotte round on her stomach?

"Until the day I set him down on his feet."

Each word opened another crack.

"You set them down on their feet then, when they come back, they lie to you."

Each crack was widening out into a crevice.

"They are all the same."

Until they bled.

"Forgive me, I am not used to speaking any more."

A tortoise's tongue lapped up the drop of blood.

*

She fell silent again. But Thian was now sitting comfortably. "I don't believe women who don't say anything." The idea wasn't Thian's, but Pastor's. Inspector Pastor liked questioning the deaf, the dumb, the unconscious. "The truth isn't usually got at by the answers you receive, Thian, but in the logical sequencing of the questions you ask." Thian felt a sort of saddened jubilation. "I've just improved your approach, Pastor, I turn up, I put my chair down in front of an old biddy who's as dumb as a nightmare, I shut up, then she starts speaking."

*

And speak she did. She told him everything about the life of ex-minister Chabotte, and about his death. The life and death of a lie.

The fact that she'd given birth to a Chabotte who was such a little liar didn't bother her at first. She'd put this tendency down as an hereditary trait. Something to be proud of. Her maiden name had been Quissapaolo, her country of origin that highly inventive land of Brazil, and she'd been the daughter of Paolo Pereira Quissapaolo, the most truly Brazilian writer ever to have put pen to paper. Her child's lies could be seen as being a part of the honourable qualities of his race. As a storyteller's grandson, little Chabotte wasn't a liar, he was a story made flesh. This is what she haughtily explained to the teachers who called her in, to the headmasters who expelled her child and to the new ones that replaced them. And little Chabotte was, indeed, a brilliant pupil. Gifted with an insatiable memory and extraordinary powers of synthesis, he raced ahead of the others. He was the apple of her eye. No matter how brief his stays were in the schools which expelled him, he always received top marks and departed leaving his teachers astonished. If he did spark off a war wherever he went, that didn't worry her. He was quite simply a misunderstood child prodigy, who was revenging himself on the rest of this mediocre world. She was delighted when he simultaneously passed the entrance exams to *L'Ecole Normale* and *La Polytechnique*, coming out top in both cases, and she was furious when he was expelled from the latter after only three months. But the war which had just broken out wiped clean this slate of injustices. One of Pétain's aides, young Chabotte was also one of de Gaulle's main informers. A principal private secretary under Vichy, and a hero in London, he emerged from the war having achieved the impossible: maintaining the continuity of the Republic but without dishonouring France. He'd squared a circle into which most of his detractors were to vanish. From 1945 onwards, Chabotte was in every government. But politics was not his vocation. Or so he said. Just a tribute which his intelligence paid to the privilege of living in a democracy. Or so he said. His vocation lay elsewhere. His vocation reached up through his mother's roots. "Through your roots, mother dear." Or so he said. He was a born storyteller. He wanted to write. But writing, so he said, was not a way to live. "Writing is a way of life." That's what he said. And now, at last, it was time for him to adopt that way of life. That's what he told her. And she believed him.

*

A life story was being told, and night fell. Outside, the lights were coming on. Thian could no longer see that woman's face, nor even the fire in her eyes. All that was left was her voice. She was no longer a heap of blankets, but a tree-trunk abandoned there by a river long ago. Sixteen years of silence poured out in a clear stream with turbulent depths. Don't butt in, thought Thian, don't stick your oar in, or you'll be swept away.

"Half a century of lies!"

She was getting her breath back. The story rumbled on beneath her. Its words were pushing her on.

"For almost fifty years I was taken in by a liar. Me! And all because he was my son."

Thian fleetingly wondering if the succeeding sixteen years of silence had been the unspoken expression of that enormous surprise.

"If I hadn't been a widow, then things would certainly have turned out differently."

But Chabotte, her husband, the young French ambassador to Brazil, who had taken her affections away from her father, had had the stupid idea of dying while she was pregnant. A silly death. From a bad case of flu.

"If he had lived, then he would have opened my eyes. Truth is a man's business. Police officers, lawyers, judges, bailiffs, they are all male careers. Winning a trial is but a travesty of the truth. And losing a trial but the triumph of a lie."

("Keep to the point, Madame, keep to the point," Thian inwardly begged her.)

*

She would certainly have returned to Brazil if that same year – the year of her pregnancy, the year of her husband's death – had not also killed off her father.

"Hounded to suicide by an intelligentsia of liars. I shall explain."

She had estranged herself from Brazil. She had consecrated herself to bringing up her little Chabotte. Here. Then, one evening, sixteen years ago, that son of hers had burst into this very room, with his jaunty stride, so jolly, so tirelessly elastic, a bundle of energy which had bounced through half a century going from prizes to honours, from the backbenches to ministries, just as if he were playing tag, no more, no less, what incredible lightness of being! What a delightful child he still was! He had come into her room, grabbed a chair between two fingers – the same chair Thian was now sitting on – had positioned it in front of her – just as Thian had done – at the evening hour when he used to confide in her, the awaited time when he would tell her that day's achievements, the time when, for the last fifty years, he would lie to her punctually, but she did not know that yet. So, he sat down in front of her, a large manuscript on his lap, and looked at her without saying a word, his eyes beaming, waiting for her to catch on. She held back the joy she felt rising inside her. She did not want to catch on too quickly. She let the seconds tick by, as if she were taking the time to watch a chick hatch out. Then, unable to control herself any longer, she murmured:

"You have written a book?"

"I have done even better than that, mother."

"What can be better than writing a book?"

"I have invented a literary *genre*!"

He yelled that out: "I have invented a literary *genre*!" Then he launched into a breath-taking explanation of the extraordinary originality of what he called his Free-Market Realism. He was the first to give Business its place of honour in the world of books, the first to raise the businessman up to the status of a founding hero, the first to praise this era of commerce openly . . . She interrupted him and said:

"Read it to me."

He opened the manuscript. He read out the title. It was called *Last Kiss on Wall*

Street. There was nothing especially wonderful about the title but, if she had understood his theory of Free-Market Realism correctly, then her son's ambitions had nothing to do with any aesthetic preconceptions. When providing reading matter for half the world's population, cryptic titles are out of the question.

"Read it to me."

She was trembling with impatience.

She had been waiting for that moment ever since that far-off winter when a telegram from Brazil had informed a young pregnant widow that her father, Paolo Pereira Quissapaolo, had committed suicide.

"I must explain to you who my father was."

("No, lady," thought Thian. "Please don't. Get on with it! Just get on with it!")

"He was the founder of 'identitarism', does that mean anything to you?"

Zilch. It meant nothing whatsoever to Inspector Van Thian.

"No, it wouldn't."

But she still explained. An incredibly confused tale. A writers' squabble in Brazil during the years 1923–1928.

"Not a single writer was authentically Brazilian in those days, except for my father, Paolo Pereira Quissapaolo!"

("Good, but it's your son I'm interested in, Chabotte, the minister . . .")

"Brazilian literature? What a farce! Romanticism, symbolism, parnassianism, *fin-de-siècle*-ism, impressionism, surrealism, our writers were set on producing a waxworks of French literature! A race of apes! Parrots! Brazilian writers possessed nothing that they had not stolen. Then turned to stone!"

("Cha-botte! Cha-botte!" Thian silently chanted.)

"My father alone stood up against this francomania."

("But I digress . . ." Thian said to himself.)

"He declared out-and-out war against that cultural alienation in which he saw his country eagerly losing its very soul."

("Digressions are the poison ivy of interrogations, their inflation, their eczema . . . there's no getting away from them . . .")

"And since, in those days, there was no literary life without a school, my father founded his own: identitarism."

("Identitarism . . ." thought Inspector Van Thian.)

"A school of which he was the only member, unreproducible, untransplantable, untransmissible, inimitable!"

("All right, all right.")

"His poetry spoke only of himself and of his identity . . . and his identity was Brazil!"

("A loony, in other words. A harmless loony. A crackpot poet. Fine.")

"Three lines sum up his poetic art. Just three lines."

Which she nevertheless recited:

> *Era da hera a errar*
> *Cobra cobrando a obra . . .*
> *Mondemos este mundo!*

("Which means?")

> "Era of errant hedera
> Cobra covering constructs . . .
> Prune this planet!"

("Which means?" Inspector Van Thian mutely repeated.)

*

Whatever . . .

The hour was now late. The night was chill. Paris was a halo. Thian was walking, with little Verdun on his automatic and his automatic on his heart.

Whatever . . . Inspector Van Thian summed up. This character, this Brazilian poet, the late Chabotte's maternal grandfather, was never published. Not a single word. Neither in his lifetime, nor after it. He spent a fortune having his books privately printed, then showered them on anyone and everyone who could read in his country, free gratis and for nothing. A loony. Unreadable. The laughing stock of his social class and of his era. Even his daughter had a good giggle. Then, lo and behold, she marries the French ambassador in Rio! The least acceptable match she could have found.

And then, exile. And then, pregnancy. And then, widowhood. And then, remorse. She wanted to go home. Too late. The *poète maudit* had blown his brains out. She gave birth to a son: Chabotte. She reread her father's works: brilliant! She thought they were brilliant. "Unique." "Authenticity is always a century ahead of its time." She swore to avenge her father. She'd return to her country, but only on the back of her son's works!

An old story . . .

It's a long way from Rue de la Pompe to the hills of Belleville, but it goes quickly when you've just spent hours listening to a life passing by. Verdun had gone to sleep. Thian was walking through the streets of Paris.

An old story . . .

Old ma Chabotte had always thought that, one day, little Chabotte would start writing. She'd never tried to influence him at all ("I'm not that sort of mother . . . ") but she had wanted him to be a writer so badly that, when gazing at himself reflected in his mother's eyes, poor little Chabotte must have seen a bloke done up in the regalia of the *Académie Française*. Or something like that . . .

And then, one evening, her Chabotte had made one too many visits to her mausoleum of a bedroom. He read out the first lines of his book, his long-awaited "work", and his mother said:

"Stop!"

And Chabotte the son asked:

"Don't you like it?"

And the mother said:

"Get out of here!"

The son opened his mouth, but the mother cut him off:

"And never come back!"

Then repeated it, in Portuguese:

"*Nunca mais!* Never again!"

And Chabotte left.

Because she'd immediately twigged that the novel wasn't his. Thian, who'd never read two books in his life apart from when at school and studying to be a copper (he didn't include the hours spent reading out J. L. B.), wondered how such a thing was possible. But apparently it was. "He had done something worse than all my father's enemies put together, sir. *He had stolen someone else's work!* My son had stolen another person's identity!"

But the best was still to come.

Thian warmed his hands in the sleeping Verdun's hair. Yes, recently little Verdun's hair had started to grow like wild fire.

What happened next . . .

Chabotte paid no attention to his mother's orders. Each evening, at the same time, he kept coming and sitting down in front of her on that chair. He kept confiding in her. But he didn't lie to her any more. And he no longer said *tu* to her. "The *vous* seems more appropriate to the arctic feelings you have always inspired in me." He laughed. "Not bad that, 'arctic feelings', is it 'writerly' enough for you, mother? Sufficiently *identitarist*?" Jabs of torture. But she'd chosen her weapon: silence. Sixteen years of silence! It had made Chabotte as crazy as his grandfather, the mad poet. Like all lunatics, he made a clean breast of it, told the entire truth: "Do you remember that young prison governor whom you found so appealing, so distinguished, so authentic, Clarence de Saint-Hiver? Well, it is one of his inmates that writes my books. On a life sentence and as prolific as the very devil! A huge fortune in prospect, mother dear. All of us are profiting from it nicely, Saint-Hiver, me, and a handful of middlemen. The prisoner, of course, is absolutely in the dark. He works from his love of art, the grandson whom you should have given to the memory of your father, Paolo Quissapaolo . . ."

One day, Chabotte burst into his mother's room with one of his "handful of middlemen", a certain Benjamin Malaussène, a funny little fellow with a pot belly and a three-piece suit, "a fake fat man tarted up like a cosmetics salesman". Chabotte pointed out his mother to Malaussène, and yelled:

"My mother! Madame Nazaré Quissapaolo Chabotte!"

Then added:

"She always tried to stop me from writing!"

Later that evening, straddling his little chair, he explained everything to his old mother:

"This Malaussène is going to take my role in the limelight. If anything goes wrong, then he will be the one to pay. You see, poor old Saint-Hiver has been murdered, my author has escaped and death is now stalking the streets. All rather exciting, don't you think so, mother dear?"

*

Malaussène had been killed first. Then her son.

"A good job, too."

*

Thian had asked her just one question. A good five minutes after she'd said her last word.

"Why tell me all this?"

At first he thought she wouldn't answer. She was no longer even a tree-trunk on a riverside. She was a mere stone in the darkness of the night. A river must have flowed by there. Long ago.

Then he finally heard her murmur:

"Because you are going to kill my son's murderer."

*

"Oh I am, am I?"

The child-bearing copper walked on through the night.

"You are going to kill my son's murderer . . ."

The child-bearing copper soliloquised in Paris's night air.

214

"The idea people have of the police force . . ."

Hitmen, in fact . . . That old biddy, driven mad by her father's and her son's words, thought Thian was the Holy Ghost for hire.

"You are going to kill my son's murderer . . ."

Not that I wouldn't like to, mind you . . . He did stick a bullet in Benjamin's brains . . . I'd just love to whack him . . . but, dear lady, vengeance is a dish which is forbidden to the police force . . . untouched . . . uneaten . . . don't even think about it . . . otherwise, dear lady, there'd be no justice any more . . . each to his own, your thing is the honour of Literature and mine is the ethics of the Truncheon . . . we all have our cross to bear . . .

The two-headed copper talked to himself through the night. Unless what he was doing was talking to that second head, snuggled up fast asleep in the hollow of his shoulder.

"So, it seems like if I put you down on the ground, I've had it . . . You'd leave me, would you? . . . You reckon that's really true? . . . You'd abandon me, as well?"

Words, like guns, sometimes go off on their own. These ones hit the child-bearing cop right in the guts. Completely out of the blue. He'd been playing around with it, and the thing had gone off. He stopped in his tracks. He had a clear vision of that little girl trotting along that pavement in front of him. It took his breath away. The visions multiplied. Big Janine on her death-bed. Gervaise, Janine's daughter, and as good as his own, in her novice's robes, dumping him for God. "Would you rather I became a whore, Thianie, like Mum?" Whyever not? No! And here's why: "God's an illness you're called to, Thianie, and its incurable." And Gervaise disappeared into God. Now Pastor, the old cop's last object of affection, had gone too. Head over heels in love with ma Malaussène. "A silent woman, Thian, a vision . . ." Pastor was in Venice, lovingly grilling that vision's silence.

And Thian here.

On the pavement.

"That old biddy's done my head in . . ."

Change of direction.

"You know what? We'll pop into the Station. Report to the boss. There are some things you shouldn't keep to yourself too long. What do you reckon?"

Another departure. Different images. Coudrier's face when he finds out the part Malaussène played in all this business! Amazing, when you think about it . . . Coudrier calls Malaussène in, packs him off to play as far as possible away from the Saint-Hiver case and our lad finds himself right up to his neck in it.

Malaussène . . .

Chief Superintendent Coudrier's boomerang . . .

Benjamin . . .

"If you want my opinion, your big bro's better out of it . . ."

Incredible!

"Because if he knew the part they'd written for him in all this, then he'd come down with something even worse . . ."

Chapter 39

A LL THE SAME, brain death does have a weird reputation . . . even among the most broad-minded people . . . comfort, if you like, or mental comfort at least . . . the good side of consciousness . . . the dream side . . . detachment . . . a slide down the black velvet of oblivion . . . that sort of idea . . . just because the brain's gone quiet . . . preconceptions . . . cerebrocentrism . . . as if the other sixty billion cells were just peanuts . . . sixty billion little molecular factories, that's right . . . making up one single body . . . super Babel . . . Babel the superb . . . and you reckon that all of that dies when it goes quiet . . . all of a sudden, just like that . . . but with sixty billion cells, it dies slowly . . . an hourglass which leaves you time enough to assess the situation . . . before becoming a heap of dead cells . . . dead cells in a heap, like an old woman forgotten by her window . . . that was now the image floating through Benjamin's night, that terrible old woman, with her terrible stare fixed on the top . . . But Benjamin could also picture Saint-Hiver's prison and, in particular, one cell in that lovely prison, a cell with a high ceiling, as deep as a monk's knowledge, entirely lined with books . . . oh! there was nothing wonderful in that library, just works of reference: dictionaries, encyclopaedias, a complete set of the National Geographic, Larousse, Britannica, Who's Who, *Robert, Littré, Alpha, Quid,* not a single novel, not a single newspaper, elementary handbooks of economics, sociology, ethnology, biology, the history of religion, of science and technology, not a single dream, just the raw materials of dreams . . . and at the bottom of this well of knowledge, the dreamer in person, young and ageless, well-preserved good looks, a hesitant smile for Clara the photographer's lens, eager to get back to his work, to plunge once more into his papers, to abandon himself once more in that neat, reassuring, cramped hand-writing, as though it were not so much a question of filling up the pages as of simply covering them with words (on both sides, no margins, crossings-out done with a ruler) . . . and Saint-Hiver's voice coming through the half-open door: "Come on, Clara, let Alexander get on with his work." . . . and Clara's final snaps of the writer's wastepaper bin, brimming over with unrumpled pages . . . and, in one of Clara's blow-ups, that elusive sentence he'd been after for so long: "*Death is an on-coming process.*" . . . all alone among its competitors which had carefully been crossed out, the chosen one: "*Death is an on-coming process.*" . . . hanging up in Clara's darkroom.

So, Alexander, did you write that famous sentence?

And did they pinch it from you?

And all your other ones, as well?

Then disguised me with them?

And did you cross me out with a bullet, shot straight along the edge of a ruler? Is that it?

That was it, washed up in Benjamin by a tide of memories . . . the first visit to Champrond's model prison, Clara and Clarence's eyes meeting for the first time . . . "I don't want Clara to get married." . . . Clarence at the dinner table, talking about his lags: "I just try to make them bear their own existences and that much, I think, I succeed in doing." . . . Clarence . . . Clarence's white mop . . . so convincing . . . did you kill Clarence, Alexander? . . . the slaughter of Saint-Hiver was your handiwork? . . . and Chabotte . . . and Gauthier . . . and you wounded Calignac . . . because they'd nicked your writings . . . that I can understand . . . "They kill," said Saint-Hiver, "not as others do, in order to destroy themselves, but rather to *affirm their existence,* just as one would knock down a wall." . . . oh yes . . . or just as one would write a book . . . "*most of them are gifted with what can be called a creative temperament.*" . . . "what can be called a creative temperament" . . . so, obviously, if you rob them of a word . . . a line . . . a book . . . what would Dostoievsky have done if he'd found his *Idiot* published with Turgenev's name on the cover? . . . Flaubert, if his girlfriend Collet had pinched his Emma? . . . that lot were big enough to slaughter such thieves . . . they wrote like murderers . . .

Thus did Benjamin's cells run on . . . little arguable points splintering up until there was nothing left to be argued about . . . powdered images . . . sudden halts . . . something indigestible . . . like a clot of consciousness . . . what Clara had said, for example: "I've done something behind Clarence's back." . . . "Behind Clarence's back, Clara?" . . . "My first secret . . . I've lent Alexander a novel." . . . "Alexander?" . . . "You know, the one who spends his life writing . . . I took him in one of J. L. B.'s novels." What? . . . What? . . . .WHAT? . . . Clara? . . . it was Clara's fault that all this happened? . . . that bullet in my brains . . . that avalanche of corpses? . . . Jesus Christ! . . and Clarence's voice once again: "*Indeed, the sole element from the outside world which my lodgers accept within our walls is Clara.*" . . . Clara within our walls . . . Clara innocently putting one of J. L. B.'s novels into the hands of the *real* J. L. B . . . "Do you think I did wrong, Benjamin?" . . . wolves are innocent . . . it isn't hunger, it isn't their cunning, it isn't murder that lets the wolves into the sweetest of sheepfolds, it's their innocence . . . Clara in the sheepfold . . .

Thus did Benjamin's cells run on . . . off and on . . . such a shock, just now, that the encephalographic trace itself suddenly flashed like lightning across the pale screen . . . but a lightning flash that nobody sees will never be a lightning flash for anybody . . . and death became a straight line once more . . . have pity for writers, said Benjamin's cells as they slipped through the hourglass . . . have pity for writers . . . never show them a mirror . . . don't change them into images . . . don't give them a name . . . it will only make them crazy.

Chapter 40

"KRÄMER."

"Krämer?"

"Krämer. His name's Alexander Krämer."

Silence from Inspector Van Thian. Whispers from Chief Superintendent Coudrier. Don't wake up Verdun. Don't open those eyes.

"Old mute women are not the only things that suddenly start talking, Thian. Severed fingers do, as well."

"There was enough skin left on them to reconstitute his dabs?"

"Affirmative."

"Who is this Krämer, then?"

"Your colleagues are here to tell you."

Chief Superintendent Coudrier handed over to the three inspectors there present. Krämer's three arrests, three files, three coppers. The first, an old pipe-smoking officer, spoke with one eye fixed cautiously on the sleeping Verdun.

"Nothing much the first time, Thian. A cheeky little bit of swindling. Krämer had left home. He was eighteen. He joined the Blanchet School of Dramatic Art here in Paris. The sort of thing kids study when they don't know what to do, see what I mean? Anyway, according to his teachers, he was a lousy actor ... good-looking, but with no stage presence. But he wouldn't let up. He wanted to prove himself, and then ram the proof right down old man Blanchet's throat. During the month of July, Blanchet and his family went away. So he gained access to their flat, ran an ad. in the papers and sold the place to a dentist. Incredible, Thian. The notary was completely taken in by the fake title-deeds and the sale was duly registered. When our acting master comes home, he finds our dentist has moved in. Just imagine his face ... Then Krämer turns up all smiles and goes: 'So, Mr Blanchet, I'm a lousy actor, am I?' I thought the whole thing was a bit of a laugh and tried to hush it up. The dentist decided to let the matter drop, but the school head was a right bastard and insisted on pressing charges. The notary, too. The result was that little Krämer went down for six months. He'd turned eighteen just one month before pulling off his little caper."

"What about his family?"

"Wine merchants in Bernheim, Alsace, who made an honest business of passing off their Sylvaner as Gros Plant from Nantes. They disinherited Krämer in favour of his two elder brothers. Except for the legal minimum, of course, which they gave him in the shape of a rundown hovel. Lovely people . . . "

"What was your opinion of Krämer?"

"Nice. Really, at the time he was a nice kid. God knows how many others I've had to deal with since then, but him I can still remember, which is saying something! A bit of a shy lad who spoke like a book, with subjunctives, the works . . . He told me that the only time he'd really felt alive was during that sting."

"Meaning he was bound to start again as soon as he was out the can."

"Yes and no. Because there was Caroline."

"Caroline?"

"A girlfriend he'd met during his acting classes and who came to pick him up when he was released. She had a good influence over him, you see. He introduced her to his family, he married her, they even renovated that wreck of a hovel."

All of which didn't stop young Krämer from having the con trick in his blood, the thrill of being someone else. A vocation which filled out his dense second file. Life-insurance swindles, false tax returns, wine *appellation* scams, more fraudulent property sales . . . this time, he went down for five years. When the judge asked him to justify his crimes, "hard to explain in a child that wanted for nothing", Krämer very politely replied:

"Quite right, your Honour, it is a question of upbringing. I come from an unimpeachable background, and so cannot be blamed for applying what it taught me."

Silence.

There was a strange gentleness in those five policemen's voices as, in the middle of the night, they talked over the long-ago case of Alexander Krämer, their tone hushed by the fear of waking up that baby sleeping on their Vietnamese colleague's belly. Existence sounded like a whisper . . .

"When he came out of prison, Krämer went straight home, where he killed Caroline and his two brothers, Bernard and Wolfgang Krämer."

"His two brothers?"

"Twins. The two of them had moved in with her. Krämer gunned down all three of them, set fire to the house, then turned himself in. It took him just that round trip."

There.

The nocturnal breathing of the city under those men's murmurs . . .

There.

"And he was in prison when he came to Saint-Hiver's notice?"

Yes. Krämer had started to write. Fictional biographies of financial whizz-kids. He was transferred to Champrond, where he was a model prisoner for fifteen years. Until the murder of Saint-Hiver.

"When he realised they were nicking his books, why didn't he kick up a stink, instead of snuffing Saint-Hiver . . . ?"

Someone asked.

And everyone thought about it.

Inspector Van Thian's answer:

"Kicked up a stink with who?"

He went on:

"Put yourself in his shoes . . . During his first stay in the slammer, his parents pinch his inheritance . . . During his second stay, his brothers make off with his wife . . . During his third stay, his entire literary output gets ripped off. Fifteen years' work! Stolen by his benefactor . . . Who do you reckon a bloke like that could turn to? Who the hell could he trust?"

Silence.

"All a bloke like that thinks of doing is blowing away anything that isn't nailed to the floor. Revenge . . . that's what he got life for, isn't it?"

"Talking about blowing people away, my dear Thian, this Krämer has something in common with you . . ."

Chief Superintendent Coudrier wrinkled his brow as he flicked through the third file . . .

"You are both excellent marksmen. Caroline's father, his father-in-law, was a gunsmith on Rue Réaumur. He wanted to enter Krämer in the French championships. One moment, I read something of interest concerning that point . . ."

But, giving up trying to find the right page amid that heap of psycho-babble:

"Well, anyway, one of the psychiatrists that studied Krämer's case came up with a rather strange theory about brilliant marksmen . . . it is as if the best of them create a sort of double personality, when they shoot they are at once the gunman and the target, here and over yonder, hence that extraordinary accuracy which cannot be explained by the keenness of their eyesight alone . . . What do you say to that, Thian?"

("It's just the same for bad marksman," Inspector Van Thian thought. "Except they miss themselves.")

"There's some truth in that."

The conclusion belonged to the Chief Superintendent:

"From this moment on, gentlemen, you know whom you are up against, a marksman as good as Thian, and one that has become accustomed to killing. Seven murders in all, if we include the fellow prisoner whose throat he cut before escaping."

End of the meeting.

Everyone got up, with Inspector Van Thian holding the sleeping child's head against his chest.

"Thian, you arrived after the news reached us, but it would seem that we are now to have an eighth corpse on our hands."

"Julie Corrençon?"

"No, the head of the Vendetta Press."

"Queen Zabo?"

"Precisely. Queen Zabo. She has now been missing for three days."

Chapter 41

"THREE DAYS AND three nights, shit-for-brains."

(...)

"I didn't tell you before so as not to worry you."

(...)

"What with all those machines sprouting out everywhere, you must have enough on your plate as it is."

(...)

"But this evening, I can't take it any more. Complete insomnia. I'm sorry."

(...)

"Your Julie has struck again."

(*Bushi Julie, Loussa!* It isn't Julie, Loussa!)

"She's kidnapped my Isabelle."

(*Bushi Julie*, for crying out loud!)

"On Wednesday, Isabelle called me into her office and, between two or three items of business, she told me that the coppers had got it wrong on Julie's score."

(*Ta shuo de dui!* She's right!)

"That she'd spoken to her on the phone and arranged a meeting."

(*Nar? Weishenme?* Where? Why?)

"She wouldn't tell me where or why."

(*Made!* Shit!)

"And she didn't want me to go with her."

(...)

"In fact she was all in a tizzy. She swore by all that's holy that there was no risk, except for being followed by the two inspectors who'd been assigned to protect her. 'But I'll lose them, Loussa, you know me!' Her eyes were sparkling, just as if she was going undercover all over again."

(*Houlai!* And then?)

"Have I ever told you how wonderful she was in the Resistance?"

(*Houlai! Houlai!*)

"Clandestine paper-mills, clandestine print-works, clandestine distribution networks, clandestine bookshops, novels, newspapers, she printed everything the Bosch banned."

(...)

"On August 25 1944, on the very evening of the liberation of Paris, the Great Charles told her in person: 'Madame, you are an honour to French publishing'..."

(...)

"And you know what she said?"

(...)

"She said: 'What are you reading at the moment?'"

(...)

...

(...)

...

(...)

"I'll tell you what it is, Isabelle ... Isabelle is the *zeitgeist* transformed into books ... a magical transmutation ... the philosopher's stone ..."

(...)

"That's a real publisher for you, shit-for-brains! Isabelle is THE publisher."

(...)

...

(...)

"So obviously I don't want your Julie making a mess of her."

(*BUSHI JULIE*, FOR FUCK'S SAKE! How loud do I have to shout, Loussa? It isn't Julie! It's a tall fair-haired bloke who was one of Saint-Hiver's prisoners, it's the real J. L. B., *KEKAODE J. L. B.*, FOR CHRIST'S SAKE! A mad penman who covered his pages without leaving a margin, a crazy killer who's framing up Julie! What are you waiting for? Go and tell the boys in blue, instead of sitting there reminiscing! The police, Loussa! *Jingchaju! JINGCHAJU!* THE POLICE!)

VII

THE QUEEN AND THE NIGHTINGALE

The Queen could tuck up in bed even a murderer.

Chapter 42

Aʟʟ ᴛʜᴇ ᴄʟᴏᴜᴅs of the Vercors had gathered above the roof of the farmhouse. A black sky in the blackness of night. But the thunderstorm was already there in the Queen's voice. The Queen's chubby finger was beating out her anger as it pointed at the manuscript she'd just thrown down onto the table in front of Krämer.

"This is all about *you*, Krämer, this is your autobiography, not one of your usual heroes, not a man of paper! Be a good chap and rewrite the whole thing in the first person singular. You're not here to serve us up some more J. L. B.!"

"I've never written in the first person."

"So what? If everyone was afraid of doing something for the first time . . ."

"I couldn't."

"*I couldn't?* What does that mean? Nowadays we have machines that can do that very nicely, you replace the 'he' by an 'I', put it into the memory, press a button, and Bob's your uncle. Listen, Krämer, you're not going to tell me that you're thicker than a machine, are you?"

Julie caught the sparks flying off that voice. The Queen's voice was shrill, her words rusty. The Queen was just as Benjamin had described. The Queen wasn't afraid of anything. Sheltered in her father's bedroom, Julie could follow that woman's work word by word as, downstairs in the kitchen, she was carpeting a killer.

"And what's all this heroic rhetoric to justify your killings doing here, Krämer? Does shooting little Gauthier's brains out really make you as proud of yourself as that?"

The words rose up through the chimney hood which, in winter, was large enough to heat the Governor's bedroom.

"Why did you kill Gauthier, Krämer?"

Krämer fell silent. All around, the forest creaked in the wind.

"If I give credit to what I've just read, your character knows perfectly well why he killed Gauthier. A crusader on the warpath against the infidels of Publishing.

229

That's the sort of hero you're hiding behind. And you call that a confession? There aren't any crusaders in the real world, Krämer, there are only killers. Like you. Why did you kill Gauthier?"

The service automatic was slumbering under Julie's pillow.

"Because you suspected that he was involved in the Chabotte scam?"

"No."

"No?"

"No, that didn't matter any more."

"What do you mean it didn't matter any more? You didn't kill him because you suspected him of having stolen your books?"

"No. Nor Chabotte either."

Krämer sounded like a schoolboy who'd been caught red-handed, lies . . . silences . . . then spurts of truth. The heavens cracked. It suddenly started to rain. From way up yonder.

"All right Krämer, now you listen to me: I've undertaken a long journey and I hate travelling, so this is the bottom line, either you scratch your head a bit and then write down, in black and white, the real reasons for your murders, or else I'll pack my bags and head straight back to Paris. Right now! In a thunderstorm!"

"I wanted to . . ."

(But, so Benjamin said, Queen Zabo could also sing the midwife's beguiling song.)

"Let's be clear about this, Alexander, you're a brilliant novelist. If the smartarses ever say that you aren't, then don't kill the smartarses, let them make fun of your stereotypes, leave them the little pleasure that their intelligence gives them and keep on quietly writing. You are one of those novelists who tidies up the world, like others tidy their bedrooms. Realism isn't your ball game, and that's an end to it. A spick-and-span bedroom, that's what your novels have to offer your readers. And it's something they are in dire need of, if your success is anything to go by."

The Queen's voice was now the easing-up of the sky, the murmuring of the gutters. Benjamin was right, the Queen sometimes had Yasmina's voice. The Queen could bathe Krämer, soap down what there was to be soaped down, then coddle him in a warm towel. The Queen could tuck up in bed even a murderer.

"The only thing is, Alexander, circumstances have made you leave your bedroom. The world's out there now. You'll have to look that monster in its eyes and tell me why you killed Chabotte. And Gauthier."

The tall, blond killer, pale and rather stiff – how old must he be? – finally said:

"I wanted to avenge Saint-Hiver."

The Queen answered, with a sort of persuasive caution:

"Avenge Saint-Hiver? But Alexander, you *killed* Saint-Hiver . . ."

He fell silent.

Then he said:

"It's a bit complicated."

Chapter 43

H E'D STARTED WRITING sixteen years before, after the triple killing of Caroline and the twins. Nothing autobiographical, though. "He" – the character that came most naturally to his pen, that fast-drawing hero in an international financial western – was diametrically the opposite of himself. A brand-new stranger to be explored; the ideal cell-mate.

Alexander had received a life sentence.

He wrote with a sort of concentrated distraction, as though he was doodling on a telephone message pad, listening with less and less attention until the drawing completely took over. That's how Alexander wrote, taking refuge in the loops and curls of his neat handwriting, of his industrious doodles.

Saint-Hiver had been struck by so much industry.

By the pages piling up.

Saint-Hiver had taken him in, to Champrond prison.

There or anywhere else . . . Alexander wrote.

In fact, those sketches of golden boys which blossomed under his pen were not pure products of his imagination, but his father's favourite topic of conversation. Precocious kids . . . Old man Krämer had always dreamt of other people's children. Other people's precocious children. "Lhermitier's son wasn't even thirty when he took charge of the French Coal Board." "Müller is sending his youngest boy off to cut his teeth at Harvard. He's only just turned seventeen. Quite something, don't you think?" "You remember young Metressié? Well, he's the person behind the take-over of S. L. V. . . . he now has a majority stake in the world's biggest yeast group . . . At just twenty-three!" At each and every family dinner, old man Krämer reeled off a legion of exemplary sons. Carefully worded, implicit comparisons at a table around which the twins were struggling to pass their law diplomas and Alexander had dropped out of school at the age of fifteen. But old man Krämer found his own consolation: "That doesn't mean a thing. Young Perrin, who never lifted a finger at school, is now doing very nicely for himself. His ball-bearings are selling like hot cakes and he's just set up a plant in Japan . . . "

Alexander wrote.

Alexander traced out the patterns woven into his father's flying carpet. Strictly speaking, they were not memories. More like disembodied reminiscences which allowed his methodical, literal imagination to take off. Alexander's fancies were orderly ones. He didn't rebel against the established order of things, he described things in the order in which they appeared. Alexander was soothed by this well-ordered world, in which his heroes never failed. If he crossed out a sentence – which he always did with a ruler – this was seldom to modify the content but more to improve its calligraphy. His pages piled up into rectangular parallelepipeds which, each evening, he carefully tamped down until their edges were immaculate.

Alexander was one of the first guinea-pigs of Saint-Hiver's experiment.

"If it hadn't been for you," Saint-Hiver told him, "Champrond would never have existed."

"You can consider yourself as being one of your prison's founder members."

That observation came from Chabotte, a live-wire personal private secretary with a sharp mind and a safe pair of hands, whose report had made it possible for Champrond to receive the public funding it needed.

Alexander wrote.

His cell was a circular room, in which he had had the window bricked up and replaced by a dormer, making it look like a light shaft lined with books.

Sixteen years of happiness.

Until that morning when Saint-Hiver's extremely young fiancée had innocently placed a J. L. B. novel on his desk.

A good fortnight went by before Krämer opened the book. If Saint-Hiver's wedding, which was due to take place the next day, hadn't reminded him of its existence, he would probably never have opened it at all. Alexander didn't read novels. All Alexander read was background information for his own novels: teach yourself books, encyclopaedias, the building blocks of dreams.

He didn't recognise himself in the first few lines of that J. L. B. He didn't recognise his own work. The neatness of the printed word, the rhythm of the paragraphs, the whiteness of the margins, the very material nature of the book and the glossiness of its dust jacket put him off the scent. The title – *Last Kiss on Wall Street* – meant nothing to him. (He wrote without worrying about dotting his books' final full stops or giving them titles. The end of each volume was determined by its overall balance, an intimate familiarity stood in place of a title. Without stopping, he then went straight into the beginning of his next story.) So, he read himself without recognising himself, having never in fact

233

reread what he'd written. The names of the characters and some of the locations had changed. It had been cut up into chapters without any respect for the pacing he'd given it.

Then, at last, he recognised himself.

An Alexander Krämer in strange fancy-dress.

He was neither struck by surprise nor ablaze with fury.

That night, when he'd left his cell and was going towards Saint-Hiver's rooms, all he had in mind was a list of questions. Extremely precise ones. Just to satisfy his curiosity, nothing more. Was it really Saint-Hiver who had stolen his novel? And the others, too? Why? Was it possible that people were earning money by publishing such childish nonsense? For Alexander was no fool. To his mind, his infantile tales had no more market value than the murals in a nursery school. They were merely the dreamlike expression of his penitential bliss. Not for a moment did he see himself as being a novelist in exile. Rather, in the chair of a seamstress, joyfully going back again and again over the same pattern. That sort of bliss. The sort which all of Saint-Hiver's prisoners shared. All of them, painters, sculptors, musicians, lived in the same eternity as Alexander. There was even a Yugoslav, a certain Stojilkovicz, who was busy translating Virgil into Serbo-Croat and thinking about asking them to double his sentence. To which Saint-Hiver had replied with a laugh: "Don't worry about details such as that, Stojil, when you are released we shall keep you on as an honorary member."

No, the person walking that night towards Saint-Hiver's rooms was no murderer.

*

"As a matter of fact, I don't see why you killed Saint-Hiver," said the Queen, in that farmhouse shaken by the fury of the Vercors. "You set off towards his office without the slightest murderous intent, you metamorphosed on the way, then it was a Rambo-Rimbaud who knocked at Saint-Hiver's door. As if the 'he' of your books had come to claim its own. I don't believe all that for a minute, Alexander. What *really* happened?"

*

Really? As usual, Alexander opened the door without knocking. He was holding the book in his hand. Saint-Hiver, in black trousers and a white shirt, was trying on his bridegroom's suit in front of the mirror. He was shaking his head. He was slim, with a supple figure, used to old tweed jackets and corduroy trousers. That morning suit wasn't him. A dubious penguin stuck into the pack-icing of a wedding cake. When he turned round and saw the book in Alexander's hand, he turned into something utterly different. A suit-and-tie bastard who'd been caught with his hand in the till.

"What are you doing here, Krämer?"

A reaction, words, a wanness that was so unlike Saint-Hiver. Which was more like a run-of-the-mill prison governor who'd just realised that he was trapped in his office by a run-of-the-mill armed convict. And Krämer suddenly realised that all he had ever been was that convict. Being plundered when inside, just as he had also been plundered on the outside. And what happened was precisely the same as what had happened another night, when he had caught Caroline in bed with the twins. The lampstand which hit Saint-Hiver's temple killed him outright.

Then Krämer butchered him.

Methodically.

To make it look like he'd been attacked by a gang. And the police were taken in.

The next day, standing in the prison yard, Krämer wept at the news of Saint-Hiver's death along with all the others. For weeks he, too, underwent the police's impotent questioning. Then life began again. A new governor. Same old direction. The prison was to be run exactly as it had been before. Alexander had gone back to work. He'd rediscovered the pleasure of calligraphy, the refuge of his clear-cut pages filled in from top to bottom and from side to side, which he left unnumbered. But this time, he'd decided to tell his own story, the life of a person who seemed to have been born to be plundered. From the murder of his two brothers, to the killing of Saint-Hiver, including the sacrifice of Caroline, all he'd done was execute the plunderers. He made up his mind to write his confession (but the Queen was quite right, "confession" wasn't the correct term, since he'd written it in the detachment of the third person).

He started by describing his operation.

Yes, that piece of surgical barbarity had been the beginning and the end of it all.

Until the day of the operation, Alexander had been a happy child, a perfect playmate for the twins, but occasionally subject to attacks of breathlessness. These were at the same time atrocious and delicious, the lack of oxygen in his lungs made him beat his arms about as though he was drowning, but also gave him a heady lucidity, such a clear vision of people and of things that he would have been quite content to spend the rest of his life flaying around like a crazed windmill. Old man Krämer and surgery didn't agree with this view. One day, when a giggling fit had degenerated into death-bed gasps, little Alexander was taken to a clinic where a series of x-rays revealed the presence of a foreign body in his chest. The ball of flesh and hair which the surgeons removed was the withered embryo of a twin who had coiled up round his heart. Cases of embryo-anthropophagy were not that rare, but sufficiently spectacular for a herd of junior doctors and medical students to stand gawping at the freak in the little boy's room.

"A classic case," said a voice. "The scallywag gobbled up his little brother."

When they took the jar away, Alexander thought he could see a tooth glinting inside it, like the last flash of a vanishing smile.

Alexander went home with the vicious scar of a crab that had been cracked open by a pair of secateurs. He was ten years old.

Half of him had been amputated.

Chapter 44

THE QUEEN ATE little. The Queen said that she nurtured her skinniness like a bonsai. The tiny mouthfuls which she slipped in between her massive cheeks were just enough to keep her alive. When she swallowed one mouthful too many, she quite simply went off to the toilet and made herself sick it up. Julie cooked too well. Julie felt responsible for the extra mouthfuls. She decided to make up for this by not making a tart the next evening. With or without the tart, while Julie was changing Krämer's dressing, she still heard the Queen pruning her personal bonsai. Krämer's wound had healed up. The two missing fingers also looked as if they'd been pruned. His hand blossomed around the wound. A callus on an old tree. Krämer's hands alone revealed that he was a grown man. The rest of him was like an eternal adolescent.

"Time to stop the antibiotics," Julie said.

The Queen gingerly came downstairs, her inexplicably chubby hand gripping the wooden banister rail.

"By the way," she said. "Jeremy Malaussène, your Benjamin's brother, has decided to burn down our warehouses."

She took a seat.

"I could do with some lime-blossom tea."

Julie made infusions.

"I'm going to tell you all about publishing houses, Krämer. How they work. Or how mine does, in any case . . . After all, I am your publisher . . ."

They rose early. Weather permitting, they started the day with a walk. At that time of year in the Vercors, there was no danger of running into anybody. The Queen led, leaning on Krämer's arm. Julie followed, the automatic weighing down the Governor's raincoat. Dawn came up over the valley of Loscence.

"Why didn't you escape immediately, Alexander?"

"I wanted to write my confession in peace."

"So why did you escape later on?"

"They'd sent someone to kill me."

A pianist. This pianist had won everyone's heart in Champrond. He gave concerts. He played without using a score, while mumbling away merrily like Glenn Gould. The prisoners loved that. But Krämer had sworn to be wary of any newcomers. The night when the pianist tried to strangle him, Krämer stuck twenty centimetres of steel into his throat. Then escaped, taking with him as much money as he could find and the pages of his third-person confession.

It wasn't particularly difficult to escape from a prison which no inmate had ever wanted to leave.

But surviving in the outside world certainly was.

Cities reproduce themselves by parthenogenesis. In sixteen years, Paris had produced a city whose birth Krämer had missed. Clothes, cars and buildings had changed shape. There was no longer the same hum in the air. Métro tickets had remained the same, but now had to be put into slots which were a mystery to him. Airlines and tour operators advertised low-price international jaunts, but people no longer looked upwards toward their billboards. Krämer surprised himself by imagining the story of a young advertising executive who ingeniously leaves all the walls to his competitors while taking over the ground, all of it, platforms, pavements and runways covered with ads, dreams lying at your feet all over the world. Yes, he'd write about that, once he'd finished telling his own story. But the walls of Paris also told a part of Krämer's story. He lifted his head. He read the posters. Most of them made large claims for articles he wouldn't even know how to use. But some of them were about him. J. L. B. OR FREE-MARKET REALISM: ONE MAN, ONE CONVICTION, ONE CREATION! – 225 MILLION COPIES SOLD. And that face. His own face, in fact. So Saint-Hiver had simply been the middleman ... The posters started to multiply around Krämer. Soon, Paris spoke to him of nothing else. Krämer was certainly not alone in that city. His double stared at him on every street corner. Once more, he experienced that feeling of almost amused stupefaction which had been aroused in him by that book Clara had given him. He should have exploded with rage, metamorphosed at once into a wild beast thirsting for blood. But that only happened later. His first feeling was of curiosity. This business *interested* him. He asked questions in bookshops: "What? You've never heard of J. L. B.?" There was unanimous astonishment. Where had he been, if he hadn't heard of J. L. B.? 225 million copies sold worldwide in the last fifteen years! Did he have the slightest idea of what 225 million copies meant? No, not the slightest. They even went so far as to calculate his royalties. They added onto that a rough estimate of his earnings from film rights. J. L. B. was an empire. Who published him? There lay the real trick of it: no name, no face, no publisher. Books that had been washed up by the *zeitgeist*. Or conceived by any one of their readers. There was, in fact, something of that in the "urge to buy". His customers would often say: "He writes well and thinks just the way I do." Yup, quite a marketing triumph! That said, sales had fallen away slightly, hence the decision to reveal who J. L. B. really was. The public launch of his latest novel, *The Lord of the Currencies*, was going to be one hell of a beanfeast!

In a corridor of the Métro, a kid had stuck a lump of gum between J. L. B.'s lips. Krämer, who'd been ambling by in a daydream, was rooted to the spot. It was the glint of that tooth, taken away along with the ball of flesh and hair by his childhood surgeons. Krämer had to lean back against the wall opposite. When his heart had regained its normal beat, he meticulously scratched away the gum.

He started looking at that face. For hours, he would remain sitting on a bench in front of an advertising hoarding. It was the face of a man with chubby cheeks, a piercing stare coming out from beneath a powerful brow, an ironic sensual mouth, a fleshy chin, hair greased back from his forehead, giving him the vaguely Faustian look of a creator who'd sold his soul to his era. But at other times of the day, and in a different light, Krämer noticed an innocent amusement lurking in those eyes whose stare never left him. The posters no longer took him by surprise. He anticipated their presence. He and his double were playing cat and mouse. "Got you this time," he murmured after spotting one behind a revolving billboard. "Well played!" he exclaimed as a bus passed by, taking his smiling image with it. They were playing tricks on each other.

Every evening in his hotel room – he'd registered under the name of Krusmayer, a German businessman with only a smattering of French – he rapidly jotted down his daily impressions which, when the time was ripe, could be used in the appropriate section of his confession. Before going to sleep, he reread a few pages of his works. As they appeared in the shops. Real books. Glossy dust jackets, huge titles, the author's initials at the top: J. L. B. in enigmatic, all-conquering capitals; the same initials at the bottom: *j. l. b.* in modest lower-case italics, the discretion of the publisher, like a sculptor placing his initials on the plinth of his own genius. That's how he discovered he was a writer. He found what he read powerful. A basic, elementary, chthonic force which produced books like so many unmovable blocks of stone. In which 225 million readers had found their roots, the true meaning of their lives. There was nothing very surprising about that, in fact. In German, his surname "*Krämer*" meant "shopkeeper", and he had the first name of a conqueror: Alexander! Alexander Krämer! And what else had he written, if not the epic tale of all-conquering commerce? In other words, the tale of this century. He wondered why he'd found his work childish during all those years spent in prison. The question then answered itself: it was Saint-Hiver who had made him stay like a child. Him and all his pals at Champrond. His *pals* ... he was still speaking like a schoolboy, a lousy little boarding-school boy.

He went back over the pages of his confession which dealt with Saint-Hiver's murder. He wrote a second version. The metamorphosis had occurred in the corridor, Krämer had become an adult within a couple of strides and it was Faust who'd killed Saint-Hiver. Faust had settled his score with the devil.

He would kill this J. L. B. who had, by stealing his writings, opened his crab chest once too often. He didn't look at the posters any more.

He prepared the execution.

He wanted it to be a public one.

He'd kill J. L. B. on the evening of his appearance at Bercy's Palais Omnisport. What J. L. B. was in fact doing was making an appointment with him by means of this advertising campaign, which provided him with the day, the time and the place of the sacrifice. J. L. B.'s *Playboy* interview only made him more determined. The smug stupidity of the answers merited an exemplary punishment.

He acquired the weapon from his father-in-law's gunshop on Rue Réaumur. He knew the place inside out. He couldn't go in like a normal customer, but the owner's flat communicated with the shop. He went into action on one of those beautiful Sundays when Paris empties itself out into the countryside. He chose a Swinley .22, equipped with a telescopic sight, plus two hand guns in case he needed to defend himself afterwards. The cash which he found in the flat (Caroline's mother, distrusting the abstract nature of banks, kept all her ready money between her sheets, where Caroline as a teenager used to cream off her weekly pocket money) came in extremely handy. There was almost nothing left of what he'd taken with him from Champrond.

Then he began staking out his target.

In the Palais Omnisport, the killer's lair he chose was a metal gangplank running between two spotlights, whose intensity would dazzle anyone trying to look in his direction.

So, on the evening of the execution, there he lay, on the gangplank, between the spotlights, the rifle in front of him. He'd slid a Smith & Wesson into his trouser belt. The second revolver, wrapped up in a plastic bag, was buried in the Jardin du Luxembourg, a public hiding place which was safer by far than his hotel room.

Beneath him, the Palais Omnisport filled up. That was when he first set eyes on the Beauty.

Chapter 45

WHEN THE BEAUTY appeared in his telescopic sight, it gave him a shock. He saw that she was beautiful and surrounded by men, not one of whom dared to enter the circle which their admiration had drawn around her. He recognised in her the paradox of beauty: to rule over an empire locked shut by covetousness. He had experienced that during his childhood. Too good-looking to make friends. The truly beautiful were a race apart. And this Beauty was a member of that race. He'd described her so many times in his novels! And now there she was, standing amid that circle of men, right in his telescopic sight!

When he had gunned down J. L. B. and the Beauty threw her guts up right in the middle of the crowd, he hailed the evacuation of that body as the most marvellous declaration of love. She thought he was dead. She was honouring him with a sumptuously volcanic expression of mourning. She didn't know that it hadn't been him up there on the stage, but a mere pathetic caricature. She thought she'd lost her favourite writer, while, on the contrary, her favourite writer had just discovered her!

Those were the sentences which, word for word, he jotted down in his notebook that evening.

He let the Palais Omnisport empty itself out and left a few paces behind his Beauty. He got into the same Métro carriage. He followed her to her block, spotted which floor she lived on and the door to her flat. He changed hotels and took a room near her windows. And, that night, just like any other night, he wrote. He'd reached the point of describing the pianist. The murder of the pianist. "He", his hero, knew exactly what he was doing. "He" was going to get back his identity, unmask the publishers, force them to reveal themselves, then claim what was his. Then, and only then, would he present himself to his Beauty. And that was also what Alexander Krämer intended to do.

But he wanted to see her once again before setting out on his hunting trip. Despite the wig, he recognised her at once. He recognised the extraordinary determination in her stride. He couldn't tear himself away from her. He wanted to know why she was wearing that wig and where that determination was leading her. He watched her hiring cars, dogged her to the doors of her various bedsits, familiarised himself with her collection of wigs. As for him, he drove around in a little Renault, rented under the name of Krusmayer. He watched the way she staked out that mansion on Rue de la Pompe. The three hire cars forming a triangle around the target. She went from one to the other, and from one disguise to another, thus keeping up a constant watch in front of that mansion. She left the keys on the dashboards, presumably so as to be able to make a rapid getaway if necessary. He had no idea why she was surrounding this house. But when he recognised Chabotte, when he saw her push a revolver up into Chabotte's guts and disappear with him into the Mercedes she'd just crashed into, then he understood. It all happened so quickly that he was left standing there on the pavement. He ran over to the BMW, which she'd left parked at a nearby crossroads, and had one hell of a job catching up with the Mercedes. Fortunately, it was driving at a funereal speed. When it stopped at the edge of the Bois de Boulogne, he parked near it, slipped into the undergrowth and approached it. Yes, it was definitely Chabotte, that vivacious private secretary who had been so enthusiastic about his work, seventeen years before. Chabotte had a dry temperament, which life leaves untouched. Easily recognisable. But how did his Beauty come to know Chabotte? It was something he'd ask the ex-minister, assuming she didn't kill him. She didn't. She made him get out into the dusk, and the Mercedes drove off. Krämer pinned Chabotte down onto the ground in a thicket, his nose in the moss, and stuck his revolver into the nape of his neck.

"Twice in five minutes is at least once too often," the politician calmly protested.

Krämer turned him over.

"So it's you, is it, Krämer? And it was you at Bercy, too? Well done . . . You are more co-operative as a killer than as a victim."

Not the slightest trace of fear.

And cards straight down on the table.

Yes, Chabotte had stolen his writings, yes, now he had no alternative, he admitted that much. But a part, at least, of his intentions was laudable: a large percentage of the profits paid for the running of Champrond.

"By the bye, you were wrong to kill Saint-Hiver. The poor soul had nothing to do with all this, he kept not a single penny for himself. A genuine saint. But we live in a world where even saints have to face economic realities. It was that, or a normal prison for his inmates."

Chabotte misread Krämer's silence.

"Does that astonish you, Krämer? What, did you really imagine that Champrond

242

Prison was paid for by public funding? Can you imagine a state opening up its coffers so that murderers might play at being artists? And the French State, at that?"

Krämer asked him who the Beauty was.

"I haven't the slightest idea. She wanted to know why I had had that clown who was playing your part on stage gunned down. Which really takes the biscuit, don't you think? Very well, Krämer. Shall we now get down to the serious business? What I suggest is . . ."

He turned Chabotte back onto his face and killed him.

*

"To avenge Saint-Hiver?"

Sitting next to the saddened Queen, Krämer nodded.

"Poor old Krämer, the number of reasons you come up with for killing people . . ."

They spoke in whispers. A long, brown and ochre grass-snake was slithering between the stalks of the hollyhocks towards a saucer of milk which Julie had put out for it under the shelter of a flat stone.

"And what about Gauthier?"

"I wanted to wipe out the entire publishing house."

"Why?"

"Perhaps because, after the death of Saint-Hiver, I have become a real killer . . ."

"What do you mean by that, a *real* killer? Don't you think you were sufficiently *real* before?"

The grass-snake advanced slowly, but each of its coils was sliding forwards with the speed of a whiplash. Its force was contained. Like an imminent decision.

"There was a grass-snake just like this one which nested in exactly the same place in my father's day," Julie told them.

*

He killed Gauthier because he'd appeared in one of the *Playboy* photos as J. L. B.'s personal assistant. When the Beauty (in a brown wig, this time) had left Gauthier on Rue Gazan, just by Parc Montsouris, he killed him at once without even asking him anything. In the same way, he was out to execute everyone who had, by stealing his work, destroyed the work of Saint-Hiver. Now, for some reason that was beyond him, his Beauty was leading him to his targets. They were acting as a team. It was a good bet that, sooner or later, she would lead him to that giant who was built like a prop-forward and stood grinning broadly next to J. L. B. in another one of the *Playboy* photos. The Beauty was his pilot fish. She was conducting her

243

own inquiries, and they coincided with his. She had spared Chabotte and Gauthier after they had presumably pointed her towards the brains behind the whole set-up. On her way up to the top, he, Krämer, wouldn't spare a single soul.

A brilliant idea occurred to him after the thrill he'd experienced at killing Chabotte. He'd compromise his Beauty! Put the police on her trail. There were two reasons for this, which he enumerated: 1st to have a free hand for his executions; 2nd to save her when she was arrested. He was so looking forward to that moment. The moment when he'd turn himself in for her. The moment when, by confessing, he would clear her. This prospect kept him bowling along in a mood of lucid delight, which turned him into a sort of merry killer, incredibly instinctive, untouchable. He saw the world with the same clarity which had cast a halo round people and things during his long-lost fits of suffocation. He knew what he'd say to his Beauty when he saved her. Perhaps they would be together only during a brief confrontation, but he'd still have time to say it to her. He'd point to her with a smile and tell her:

"You . . . you . . . I love you *precisely*."

Maybe he'd leave a pause between verb and adverb.

"I love you . . . *precisely*".

Or maybe not.

*

"And sure enough, that's the first thing he said to me when he came to."

"What?"

"That, 'I love you precisely.'"

"No kidding?"

"His very words."

The Queen and Julie were talking softly. Krämer was asleep in the room next to the kitchen. The Queen had indeed tucked the murderer up in bed. For they were going to have to be up at dawn. A massive task was awaiting them: rewriting the entirety of Krämer's confession, putting it all back into the first person singular and reworking those passages where his pen had wandered off into the purple prose of epic. "You do still agree, Alexander?" He nodded. "Fine, now go off and get some sleep." The Queen laid her chubby hand on the murderer's brow. The last man whom the Queen had touched like that was Malaussène, a few minutes before the killer shot him. Krämer fell asleep under the Queen's chubby hand.

"All the same, this is an odd situation," the Queen said to Julie over her evening cup of lime-blossom tea. "Two women, lost in the middle of the Vercors, busy preparing a murderer's rehabilitation . . . his rehabilitation into prison."

That's what had been decided. They would iron out Krämer's confession, then hand it over to Chief Superintendent Coudrier so that he would put his pack of bloodhounds back on the leash. Otherwise, Krämer would be shot dead as soon as he was spotted in Paris. The Queen and the journalist were working on the nightingale's rehabilitation. So that he could return to the peacefulness of his cage and slip once more into the nest of his writing. The Queen was interested in every kind of literature.

"So this is where you spent your childhood with your father, the Governor."

"Yes," Julie replied. "I was born in this house, in this very kitchen."

"Quite a character . . ."

The Queen spoke between scalding sips.

"The decolonising Colonial Governor . . ."

Julie nodded. She, too, had found her father to be "quite a character".

"You've never been tempted by the idea of writing a book about him?"

"That's out of the question."

"We'll talk about it again later."

The two women fell silent. In the neo-colonial jumble in the attic, mice could be heard performing their nocturnal saraband on tiny paws.

"And what did you say in reply?"

"Sorry?"

"To Krämer. When he made his declaration of love . . ."

*

As soon as he saw his Beauty, he fainted. Partly, of course, because of all the blood he'd lost, but mostly because of his emotional state. He fainted as though he was letting himself go. He pulled over a little chest of drawers as he fell. The pages of his third-person confession showered down about him.

When he came to, he was naked, laid out on the bed, strapped up, and on a drip. Sitting on a desk chair, which had mossy growths jutting out of its ruined leatherette upholstery, the Beauty was busy reading his confession.

"You . . ." he said.

She raised her eyes.

"You . . . I love you *precisely.*"

Immediately, she was on her knees beside him, pressing the barrel of the service automatic against his temple.

"Another word and I'll blow your lousy little brains out."

He didn't doubt for a moment that she'd carry out her threat. He shut up. Her reaction did not cause a wave of sorrow to break over him which should, in the logic of love, have finished him off. Once again, it was his curiosity that had the upper hand. Why should a woman who'd just saved your life then threaten to blow your brains out? The question *interested* him. He asked her why a little later, when she'd calmed down and got him to tell her the rest of his story.

"At Bercy, you killed the man I loved."

That suit-and-tie jerk on the stage of the Palais Omnisport was the man she loved? In some ways, the Beauty's answer only added to her mystery. Krämer wanted to know what kind of man he had been, when not playing at being someone else in a tawdry pseudo-literary jamboree. The Beauty went laconic on him:

"The kind I love."

But then she added:

"The only one of his kind."

And when he asked her why such a lovable man had accepted such a shameful role – pretending to be a writer that he wasn't – she replied at once:

"To comfort his sister, to put aside a nest egg for his sister's child, to entertain his family and have some fun himself, because his was a tragic temperament which played at having fun, but never really had any, in fact, all he ever had was a good laugh . . . a jerk who ended up being killed by dint of not being a killer!"

"He stole my writings."

"He stole nothing at all from you. He sincerely believed that Chabotte was J. L. B."

("An image," Krämer thought. "That night, I shot down an image . . .")

"And all of the staff of the Vendetta Press thought so too, Gauthier included!"

She was trembling with fury. Krämer was expecting her to grab the service automatic again. Instead of which, she barked at him:

"Now shut it. I have to change your dressing."

She worked with the dexterous brutality of a surgeon.

They left Paris as soon as he could stand. They went at night. She stuck a blue flashing light on top of a white Renault and made him put on a male nurse's outfit.

"They're looking for a wounded man. They won't suspect a nurse."

At dawn, they arrived in a little farmhouse in the Vercors. Clouds, pine trees, cliffs and hollyhocks.

"You can sleep there."

She pointed at a sofa bed in a room panelled with off-white pine. A Chinese lantern hung from the ceiling.

"You can write on that table, just by the window."

The window overlooked a wood of young oaks.

"I'll call the head of the Vendetta Press when you've made enough progress."

That was her plan: for him to complete his confession. It was so full of mitigating circumstances that it was bound to argue in his favour. They wouldn't go back to Paris until Chief Superintendent Coudrier had read it.

"Why are you doing this?"

Good question. After all, he had killed her man . . .

"Because I'm not a killer," she answered. "I don't solve problems by wiping them out."

He also wanted to know why she was so keen on the idea of having his confession published and widely distributed.

"Transparency. They won't be able to lock you up and throw away the key, nor send someone else to kill you. Perhaps we'll even be able to save Champrond Prison."

During all the time he spent in her company, Krämer felt not the slightest emotion for his Beauty. Her precision numbed him. He let her fix his destiny for him because his destiny now left him indifferent. As ever, he was curious about what was going to happen, but indifferent about the consequences. He didn't care any more if they saved Champrond or not. It was all a show. The Beauty was a show girl. She was no more real to him than the characters that came into being under his pen. Whose run-of-the-mill imagination had dreamt up this infallible woman? She was good at everything, disguising cars, using a gun, passing herself off as anybody she wanted, nursing a hand that had lost two of its fingers . . . She managed it all, acquiring antibiotics without a prescription, getting hold of three litres of blood for a clandestine transfusion, changing cars whenever she wanted, unearthing an isolated house in the Vercors . . . Okay, she was beautiful, but her beauty was so *blatant* . . . His Beauty was a stereotype. But a modern-day stereotype, convinced that she was unique.

"And what do you think of my novels?" Krämer asked her, between two endless silences.

"A heap of bullshit."

On the other hand, he felt close to the Queen as soon as he set eyes on her. The Queen treated him roughly, but she spoke the true language of books. Under her absolute authority, he worked fervently. He wrung the third person's neck to come up with an "I" who could write in his name. He then discovered that he was not the idealistic avenger he'd taken himself for (and whose moods he'd obligingly described), but an impulsive killer, completely under the sway of the present indicative.

"Do you still think about Saint-Hiver sometimes, Alexander? Stop before you answer. Do you still think about Saint-Hiver from time to time?"

"No."

"And about your life in Champrond Prison?"

"No, never."

"But you were happy in Champrond, weren't you?"

"I think so, yes."

"Does the fate of your fellow inmates concern you?"

"Not really."

"How do you explain that?"

"I don't know. I'm here now, with you."

"Do you sometimes think about Caroline?"

"Caroline?"

"Caroline, your wife . . ."

"No."

"Alexander, why did you really kill Saint-Hiver?"

"I don't know. I suddenly saw myself as a prisoner, I reckon, and him as a prison governor."

"What about Chabotte?"

"To avenge Saint-Hiver."

"The prison governor?"

"No, the other Saint-Hiver, the founder of Champrond."

"But, if you never thought about him . . ."

"Chabotte talked to me about him, made fun of him, it was awful."

"*Awful?*"

"Yes, awful. It was brutal. I couldn't stand that brutality."

"And Gauthier?"

"I had to avenge a man and I had to avenge a dream."

"That's what you wrote in the third person. But it isn't really you. It's just J. L. B. speak. Why did you kill Gauthier?"

"It seemed that that was why I was there."

"Not good enough."

. . .

. . .

"I wanted to . . ."

. . .

"I wanted to compromise Julie."

"And be her saviour when you gave yourself up after she'd been arrested?"

"Yes."

248

"Write that down. Then put the whole thing into the present indicative, if you wouldn't mind."

The Queen had helped him to work over his confession. In the present indicative, which is the only tense in which murders are committed, and in the first person singular, which belongs to the murderer. A hundred-odd pages, no more, but the first ones that were really about *him*, which were really him. The Queen didn't scoop crabs' meat out, she refilled them with their own flesh and rubbed away the scars.

*

Then came the morning when the Queen and the Beauty went back to Paris in order to plead his case before the police. He stayed on alone in the house in the Vercors.

"Don't move till we come and fetch you."

"In the meantime, write, Alexander. Why not start that story about an advertising executive who buys up the ground? It's a great beginning."

But the Vercors had given him a different idea: the story of a little ten-year-old woodcutter who, on July 21 1944, witnesses the massacre of his entire family by the S.S., which had just arrived on the Vassieux plateau, and who then swears to locate them all and punish them one by one. In the process, the little wood-cutter was to save the Amazon rainforest, which had fallen into the hands of those self-same executioners, and become the world's biggest manufacturer of pulp, a friend to both publishers and writers, the man who allows books to take wing.

As Queen Zabo was closing the car door, he asked her:

"When you come back to fetch me, would you be so good as to bring along a complete documentation concerning the printing and paper markets?"

And, when the car pulled away, he shouted after it:

"I'm going to write this one in the first person singular of the present tense!"

VIII

WHAT AN ANGEL

We're calling him "What An Angel".

Chapter 46

"NO BEATING ABOUT the bush, Berthold. You've been emptying Malaussène out like an oyster!"

Professor Marty was back from Japan and the hospital corridors were echoing with the news.

"All you said, Marty, was that I shouldn't unplug him!"

On his spindly legs, Berthold was having trouble keeping up with Marty's rage.

"When I've finished with you, Berthold . . . you're going to wish you were in the same boat as Malaussène!"

Berthold didn't doubt that.

The corridors froze as the small furious one and the tall pitiful one hurried onwards.

"Your problem is that you're incurable, Berthold."

They were heading for Malaussène's room.

"For crying out loud, all I did was remove a little piece of his liver!"

"I know, to graft onto a case of cirrhotic hepato-carcinoma who died the next day."

"It was an experimental graft, Marty. It might have worked."

"There was no way it was ever going to work and you knew that. Some experiments should never be attempted."

"To save a patient! Experiments that should never be attempted? Is that really your idea of medicine?"

"Exactly. As far as I'm concerned, Berthold, you are an experiment that should never have been attempted!"

"Watch what you're saying!"

"If you start to watch what you're doing!"

"What about the double kidney transplant, and the double lung and heart transplant? Weren't they a success?"

"You had the family's authorisation?"

"What family? The Malaussènes? Don't talk to me about the family! A load of shit-stirrers, half of them are Arab, and who spend their lives getting in our way. Yes, what a lovely little family are the Malaussènes! And speak of the devil, here they are! Take a good look at them, Marty, just take a good look!"

Berthold had flung open the patient's door with a victorious gesture of Q.E.D.

*

They were all there in Benjamin's room. There was Thérèse, Clara, Jeremy, Half Pint, Thian and Verdun, Louna, her husband and the twins, Amar, Hadouch and Yasmina, there was Nourdine and Leila, Black Mo and Simon the Berber out on special leave, there was Julius the Dog and there was Julie, there was Loussa de Casamance and there was Queen Zabo, there was even a copper in a pilot's jacket with a fur-lined collar, and Chief Superintendent Coudrier, his boss.

Twenty-three visitors.

Twenty-four, including Marty.

The Malaussène family.

The Subject's tribe.

Whose birthday they were celebrating.

"Stay out of this, Berthold," Doctor Marty ordered. "This is a party and you're not invited."

There was a cake with candles and champagne for everyone. There was even a pile of presents, in the shape of various bits of good news, which Jeremy unwrapped one by one into Benjamin's ear.

"Julius is better, Ben, which is a good sign, and Half Pint's stopped having nightmares, Marty's back, Julie's found the real killer, I didn't burn down the Vendetta Press's warehouses, everything's hunky-dory, Ben, there's light at the end of the tunnel, you'll be up and about any day now, you do believe me, don't you?"

*

I do believe you, Jeremy, and it's a great birthday, thanks, brilliant presents, thanks, Julie and Marty are back, thanks again, but as far as resurrecting me is concerned, don't call me, I'll call you, so thanks anyway, it's the thought that counts, and, Jeremy, all that doesn't matter really, because the best present of all is on its way, how come you lot here, standing upright on your humanoid trotters, with your ears and eyes agape, all so very much alive, so very sensitive, how come you lot always miss what's really important in this century of clear-sightedness, why is it that I'm the one who copped on at once, even though I'm only the envelope of myself, a helpless fax machine plugged into the world, can't you hear Clara's double heart beat, Jeremy?

254

Clara's about to give birth!

Julie, Hadouch, Yasmina, Clara's about to give birth!

Marty! Doctor! My sister is on the point of giving birth!

And her little lodger is in one hell of a panic, judging from the heart beat I can hear it! He's been fed, watered, housed, walked, cosseted for nine months and now he's about to be dropped without warning, or a parachute, into a minefield! It's like watching a .22 high-penetration bullet entering your field of vision. Bergson was right about that much: when it comes to life, both the new arrival and the departing can hear the trumpet blast of no return, and it puts exactly the same shits up them, exactly the same, dying or being born is much of a muchness when you haven't been that way before, a radical change of routine, and man is a creature that tries to hang on – in the shadow of the secateurs, the poor sod.

Doctor Marty, I know my family's a bit of a handful, but I'd be undyingly grateful to you if you could take the time out to welcome my Clara's little squatter, really I would, I reckon he'd be less frightened, sure not to be born with three feet and six ears, and it'd be a human being rolling out the red carpet for him, something to perk up a beginner like him and, on the other side of the door, he won't meet that many human-humans like you . . .

*

The first outward sign was the mother discreetly fainting. An eggwhite, beaten till stiff, then collapsing in on itself. A sigh.

"Clara!"

But Clara was already in the arms of a copper wearing a pilot's jacket, and "this way" said the doctor, upon which the twenty-three members of the Malaussène tribe followed Marty down the hospital corridors (twenty-two, to be precise, Julie having stayed with Benjamin), and the corridors shot past them until they reached the table where everything begins, where Clara came to, where, sleeves hiked up, the doctor started angling for the living, and the tribe closed in like a scrum around the ball, an international pack pushing and breathing with Clara, because they'd all trained with her, all of them, during the last few months, breathing in, holding it, pushing and breathing out, even the backs joined in, those who hadn't been warned, the outsiders, uncertain about life, not really concerned, they too found themselves breathing in all the air they could swallow, Queen Zabo ("but what on earth am I doing? I must be going completely soft . . .") pushing fit to pop her champagne cork of a head, as though a book was about to emerge from between those thighs, the Black breathing in, the Berber holding it, and the Chief Superintendent in person ("oh well, I might get some peace and quiet tomorrow . . ."), Leila, Nourdine, Jeremy and Half Pint shuffling round the scrum without any fear of being offside, looking for where the ball was going to come out, to be the first onto it, that was all that mattered . . .

But the ball came out way over their heads . . .

Brandished in Marty's victorious hands.

And the scrum broke apart, heads up, distancing themselves as if for a line-out, waiting to see what the doctor was going to reintroduce into the game.

It looked just like a usual new-born baby and, as usual, was unique.

To start off with, it didn't cry.

And it was looking. The crowd felt slightly embarrassed, given that they were there to look and not to be looked at.

And it didn't seem the slightest bit scared. Pensive, even. As if it was wondering what the hell all these rugby players were doing there.

Then it decided to smile at them.

A new-born baby's smile is an extremely rare commodity. In general, you have to wait a bit for the first smile, until it's formed its first illusions. But here, no. A smile straight from the kick-off. And which went perfectly with the rest. The rest was Clara Malaussène and was Clarence de Saint-Hiver. It was Clara's oval with Clarence's mop, it was Saint-Hiver's blond whiteness above the Mediterranean Malaussène, it was matt and luminous, it had just been born but was already scrupulous, careful not to upset anyone, not to forget either the father or the mother in the sharing-out of resemblances . . . But what best united Clara's dreamy attentiveness and Clarence's thoughtful enthusiasm was that smile, with a little personal touch all the same, one side of the lips pulled up slightly higher than the other, a hint of jollity in an overflow of seriousness, as if it reckoned that, after all, lads, things aren't that bad . . . we'll make do . . . just you see if we don't . . .

"What an angel," Jeremy said.

Then added, after a moment's thought:

"That's what we're calling him."

"What, Angel? You want to call him Angel?"

It was always Jeremy who baptised.

And it was always Thérèse who disagreed.

"No," said Jeremy. "We're calling him 'What An Angel'."

"In one word? Whatanangel?"

"No, with all his words and all his capitals."

"What An Angel?"

"What An Angel."

*

What happened next (when Clara had gone to sleep and Doctor Marty had put What An Angel in his crib) was to show how Inspector Van Thian's life was predestined. As if to inaugurate that name, which was now going to stick, What An Angel gave a graceful Saint-Hiverish flick of his hair, then went to sleep as well, like an angel folding its wings. "Angels go to sleep as soon as they land," Jeremy observed. This sentence flopped out into a motionless silence, which resembled catatonic astonishment or mystical communion. No-one even felt like budging his little finger. That was the moment that Verdun decided to start wriggling around in her leather harness. Old Thian thought that the little girl was starting to get fed up and tried to comfort her by stroking her head. But Verdun brusquely pushed the inspector's hand away and, grabbing firmly hold of the edges of her harness, pushed hard on her elbows until she'd extracted herself completely from it. Thian just had time to catch her before she fell to the floor. But, with a twist of her tiny frame, the little girl escaped from him and headed off with a determined, almost straight toddle towards What An Angel's crib. When she had reached it, had stared long and hard at the sleeping baby, then turned back towards the assembled tribe, everyone knew that wild horses wouldn't drag Verdun away from her sentry post. "Verdun can walk," thought Jeremy. "Don't forget to tell Benjamin that Verdun can walk." But Inspector Van Thian had silently moved away. Three steps back which had taken him into the hospital corridor.

He was now walking towards the exit. Inspector Van Thian's quiet delivery had been an unshared agony.

Chapter 47

THE PRESENT INDICATIVE didn't do anything for Krämer. It took him just one night in that house in the Vercors to be sure of that fact. After the women had gone, he sat down at his desk, but the words wouldn't come. What was worse, he'd even lost the desire to find them. He remained empty in front of that infamous blank page. This had never happened to him before.

At first, he didn't find this feeling of emptiness unpleasant. It was interesting, like everything which surprised him. "In the end, the present indicative doesn't do anything for me." But the desire to write in the past seemed to have vanished as well. "Nor does the past." Sitting at his desk, he let the day glide by until nightfall. When the grove of oak trees was no more than an impenetrable wall in front of him, he went to bed. It felt as if the bed was slipping away from under him. "As for the future, there's no point even considering it." The idea that anybody could attribute a future to him gave him such a fit of hysterical laughter that the bed swayed about even more. His arms shot forwards to break his fall, but that sliding sensation remained. The bolster, which he clutched at with his fingers, was no more stable than the rest. So he let himself roll down onto the floorboards. "Get out of this old tub and sharpish." Bad idea. The floor sailed away from him, too. "Time and tenses, it's a never-ending collapse . . . " He saw himself walking upstream on a conveyor belt without advancing a single step. Grabbing hold as best as he could of the moving bed, the receding corner of the table and the decidedly dodgy back of the chair, he managed to sit up, get one knee onto the floor, then finally stand. Stable. "On my feet." "The world needs perpendiculars."

He wrapped himself up in the eiderdown and went out to sit on the bench which had been set up near the back door. A plank of elm wood, weathered into whiteness, propped up by a few flat stones. "There. Just about stable." Leaning back on the farmhouse's uneven wall, he thought for a moment about that Queen Zabo, who had put the idea of tenses into his head. And so had emptied it of everything else. Reducing it to the instant. "Not to the present, to the instant, which isn't quite the same thing." A perfectly white half-moon cast a halo around the hollyhocks. He wanted to know more about the nocturnal landscape behind them. Dropping his eiderdown, he armed himself with the scythe which hung from the frame of the wood shed then set about mowing down that wall. Above the Beauty's bed there was a photo of a man wearing a white uniform, which had been taken amid that wild undergrowth. Naked in the moonlight, Krämer freed the Governor at last. The Beauty seemed to love the Governor. As he mowed on methodically, Krämer felt close to that absolutely unmethodical love which the Beauty seemed to have for the men in her life. She let weeds smother her loves. (The Queen had said so: winding creepers were shooting up around Malaussène's bed . . . medical vegetation.) Behind the wall of hollyhocks stood a rampart of nettles. Krämer continued mowing until daybreak. The sun discovered him, naked, "extremely upright", cutting down the last of the weeds with a precise twist of his body, his feet and calves insensitive to the stings.

He got dressed. He filled up the grass-snake's saucer with fresh milk. He then added a sprinkling of those red poison pellets intended for the mice in the attic. Tame animals should be spared the torture of loneliness.

He slipped though the clump of young oaks as far as the edge of the neighbouring farm. When the postman went in to deliver the mail, he slid behind the wheel of his yellow post-office van.

In Grenoble, he took the high-speed express to Paris.

In Paris, he took the Métro to the Jardin du Luxembourg.

*

The man with three fingers was digging a hole in the Jardin du Luxembourg.

"Are you looking for buried treasure?"

The man with three fingers turned round. Two puzzled children, aged between four and seven – he knew nothing about children's ages – were watching him.

"I'm looking for an Easter egg."

The boy shook his head. So did the girl.

"Easter was last holidays," said the boy.

"And the bunny leaves its eggs in people's gardens," said the girl. "Not in the park."

"The bunny leaves its eggs all over the place," said the man with three fingers. "That's why you can find eggs anywhere and at any time of the year."

"Shall we help you?" said the little girl, who was equipped with a bucket and spade.

"Yes please," said the man with three fingers.

He pointed to the plinth of a statue about ten yards away and a horse-chestnut tree in the opposite direction.

"You," he said to the little girl, "go and dig under that tree. And you under that statue."

The children dug away diligently, but didn't find any eggs. "Just what I thought," they said to themselves and each other. When they decided to go and explain to the man with three fingers that he'd made a mistake, he'd disappeared. In his place was a hole. And at the bottom of the hole, a plastic bag.

"He found one," said the little girl.

*

In the taxi which was taking him to Saint-Louis Hospital, Krämer examined the revolver while making sure that he couldn't be seen in the rear-view mirror. It was in perfect working order. It gleamed. It was a beautiful weapon, the sort which Caroline's father adored. A chrome-plated Smith and Wesson. The cylinder clicked smoothly. Like the door of an expensive car when closed slowly. The plastic bag, despite being very thin, had protected it nicely. "Did you know that the French invented plastic?" Old man Krämer loved this story. He often used to tell it over the dinner table. "It was a young Frenchman who discovered the technique: Henri Préaux, a Northern lad, not even thirty. The only thing is that he went into partnership with a swine who sold off his secret to the Americans on the sly. And Préaux lost the patent war." *Not even thirty.* Old man Krämer's ideal son was always under that age. Krämer wondered how old Malaussène – the Beauty's second love – must have been when he gunned him down at the Palais Omnisport. It didn't matter. From that evening on, Malaussène no longer had an age. The prisoner of that *instant* when the bullet had lodged in his brains. Coma. The Queen had painted a touching portrait of him. "I'm going to be able to see him now," the Beauty had replied. And Krämer was quite sure that he'd find her there with him. She did everything better than everybody else. She was quite capable of spending the rest of her life at the bedside of that instant. But Krämer was going to free Malaussène and the Beauty, just as he had freed the Governor and the grass-snake. Then he, too, would quit that never-ending instant which had started with the removal of that ball of flesh and hair and gone on with the death of Caroline, of the twins, Saint-Hiver, the pianist, Chabotte and Gauthier, but wasn't it incredible that such a tiny lump of sugar refused to dissolve in such a scaldingly hot cup?

"Are you a doctor?" the cabby asked him.

"I'm a nurse," Krämer replied, to explain away his white coat.

"Oh, right . . ."

"Do you know," Krämer said when the driver had stopped the car and announced the fare. "Do you know that I sold 225 million copies?"

"Oh, right?" said the cabby.

"I started very young," Krämer explained as he held out a two-hundred-franc note.

Then added:

"Please, keep the change."

*

He wasn't wrong. The Beauty was there all right, crouched at Malaussène's bedside, holding Malaussène's hand, letting her head fall onto Malaussène's chest, that beautiful head whose hair had grown back, but which was now entangled in that web of hospital tentacles which plunged into Malaussène's body. She didn't hear Krämer come into the room. It looked as if she was asleep, her legs doubled under her, the graceful curve of her back pointing her entirely towards Malaussène.

He didn't want to wake her.

Being extremely careful not to break the silence, he released the safety catch on his revolver.

Chapter 48

"**K**RÄMER!"

Thian instinctively pushed away little Verdun's sling so as to draw his service automatic. With no child in it, it didn't put up the usual resistance. A split second's surprise which allowed Krämer to turn and open fire. Both revolvers fired simultaneously.

Inspector Van Thian experienced that fragment of eternity with a sensation made up of professional exasperation (a good copper shouldn't let his habits get the better of him), of incredulous admiration (no doubt about it, widow Chabotte's predictions were coming out spot on: Verdun had left him and he was killing her son's murderer), of gratitude to Krämer (who, by exchanging bullets with him, was sparing him the interminable agony of retirement), of extraordinary relief (he wasn't going to have to mourn for his little Verdun) and of mystical hope (if Gervaise hadn't got it wrong when she took the veil, then Thian would surely come to in Big Janine's arms up there, on God's couch). Added to all that was also the satisfaction of having passed in front of Benjamin's room at the right moment, mixed with the certainty that he, Benjamin, would definitely live to the age of ninety-three if only he, Thian, managed to plug a second bullet into Krämer's head, who was in urgent need of it.

Three rapid gunshots echoed down the corridors of that huge hospital, until they reached the ears of the Malaussène tribe, whose countless heads were soon peering through the door into that room.

Krämer's body was lying, almost completely hidden under the bed, while Thian's had been thrown out into the corridor, had slid down the wall and wound up crouched on its heels, feet flat on the floor, like a Thai peasant meditating.

They leant over him.

Carotid . . .

Thian was no more.

"Angels go to sleep as soon as they land," Jeremy repeated to himself when the white sheet had folded its wings over old Thian's body. And the little boy would have let his tears flow, if Half Pint hadn't cried out:

"Look! Benjamin's speaking!"

All of them turned round towards Malaussène. But Malaussène, of course, wasn't saying anything as usual, was just lying there in an enviable indifference under Julie's protective body.

"No, there, Julie! Look!"

Julie finally lifted her head and saw what everyone else was looking for in the direction indicated by Half Pint. There, behind that profusion of translucent creepers which she, too, was caught up in, the electroencephalogram was quivering gently, like a clearing in a shaft of sunlight. Benjamin's brain was crossing that clearing in frantic leaps.

"Jesus Christ!" someone said.

"It's obviously a short-circuit!"

In three strides, Berthold was across the room, bending over the machine and wittering on about how people shouldn't lean on patients when they're connected to delicate apparatus. He put his ear to it, twiddled with its buttons, lights flashed . . . no getting away from it: Benjamin kept on filling up the screen.

"What's he saying?" Jeremy asked.

And, as no-one answered:

"What's he saying?" Jeremy repeated.

Berthold was now banging on the machine, first with the flat of his hand, then with his fist, more skeptical about this sign of cerebral rebirth than a Roman Catholic official in front of blossoming stigmata.

"You can't even bleeding well tell us what he's saying?"

Jeremy now addressed himself directly to Marty.

Marty's and Thérèse's eyes had just met.

Nothing to hope for from that quarter. Thérèse was Thérèse. Not the slightest astonishment.

"Is that it?" Jeremy persisted.

Berthold had picked up the machine and was shaking it.

"The Malaussène family . . . "

Head down, the resurrected Benjamin was not in a very good mood. The screen was now black with fury.

"I mean, for fuck's sake, what's that screen on about?" Jeremy bawled. "You can't even sodding well explain it, that's it, isn't it? Benjamin's better, isn't he? It obviously means Benjamin's better! That we're going to take away all that plumbing, then bring him home . . . Marty, doctor, I'm talking to you! Can you or can't you tell us if Benjamin's better? Is there one single medic in the world who knows how to say 'yes' or 'no'?"

Jeremy's voice had now reached a sufficient height to awaken Marty on his cloud of stupefaction. Marty turned to him, with a look that Jeremy knew only too well, and said:

"Jeremy, if you're looking for a clip round the ear, then you're going the right way about it."

After which, he added:

"Everyone out."

Then, sweetly:

"Please."

Finally, with a hungry lick of his lips:

"Leave me alone with Doctor Berthold . . ."

IX

I-HE

*"Lazarus, come forth!" and it is the whole world
which emerges from the tomb.*

Chapter 49

"THE CARAFE'S EMPTY and I'm thirsty! Where's the waiter? Tell him to fill the damn thing up!"

There was no waiter, just half-a-dozen students leaping forward, taking Professor Berthold's chair by storm, grappling up the first rungs of the professorial ladder, fighting over that water jug.

"Doctor!" one of the journalists bawled into his mike.

"Professor!" Berthold corrected him. "I didn't come here to be downgraded!"

"Professor, how many hours did the operation last?"

"Anybody other than me would have taken till kingdom come, my lad, but a good surgeon works faster than his own fingers."

Under the auspices of the annual medical junket known as "The Bichat Symposium", the Pitié-Salpêtrière teaching hospital was celebrating Professor Berthold's unbelievable exploit: a quadruple kidney-pancreas-heart-lung transplant on a patient who had been in a coma for months, a spectacular success, not the slightest sign of rejection, so that a mere ten days after the operation the patient had regained all his normal bodily functions, had gone home and was back at work. A true resurrection!

"Thanks to our technical capacities and to a multi-disciplinary approach," Professor Berthold went on, "I was able to operate for eight consecutive hours, the use of a laminar flow to avoid any risk of infection enabled me to perform a sternolaparotomy, thus providing myself with a sufficiently broad field of manoeuvre to operate on every front!"

"Did anyone assist you?" asked a radiant hackette, who seemed to be having problems handling her mike, notepad, pencil and enthusiasm all at the same time.

"In this sort of business, assistants count for nothing," Professor Berthold proclaimed. "A few hands serving one sole brain. That's what surgery has in common with *haute couture*, Mademoiselle!"

"In what order did you carry them out?"

"I started with the heart-lung unit, but had to finish it sharpish because

267

a pancreas must be transplanted no more than five hours after excision."

"So you finished off with the kidneys?"

"The kidneys were a piece of cake! . . . In fact the rest wasn't that hard, either . . . for me, that is . . . I insisted on most of the anastomoses being done by automatic clamps . . . You have to move with the times."

"How do you explain the extraordinary lack of rejection in the patient?"

"That's my secret."

*

Everything has already been said about the delights of convalescence: the body awakening in the clean sheets of existence, the familiar surprise of finding yourself still there, feeling each day more like yourself, and yet so new that you touch yourself with kid gloves . . . oh, the first taste of creamed potatoes, with an atom of ham between your cautious molars . . . oh, the first steps to break you in again for life . . . then, suddenly, Belleville in your lungs, so good that you'd take wing and fly if you weren't still as weighty as a sick man . . . oh, the sweet shelter of your bed to wear out the little strength you yet have . . . and those smiles tucking you in . . . hands touching you like you were bone china . . . the shadow stretched across your slumbers . . . long convalescent slumbers . . . oh, the morning sunshine!

Everything has already been said about the delights of convalescence.

But resurrection . . .

It's true. Berthold resurrected me. Under Marty's threats, admittedly, but he did resurrect me. Incising and excising in Krämer's body, grafting and stitching in mine, Berthold resurrected me. From the murderer and the murderee, Berthold has made one body . . . which has one or two things to say regarding resurrection. Firstly, that the most fervent believers believe in it without any real belief. Like Clara and Jeremy, for instance. The look in their eyes when my eyes opened! Even Thérèse! I wouldn't swear to it, but I reckon I saw a flicker of surprise pass fleetingly over Thérèse's face when she saw me on my feet for the first time. They looked at me with eyes that were so new . . . It was almost as if they were the ones that had been resurrected! Oh, Lazarus, old cousin of Bethany, is that the greatest surprise of all? When brought back to life, *it's life itself which is resurrected!* It's Martha and Mary created all over again for you by that fair walker on the waters! More than that, even, it's the entirety of Judaea which has been resurrected for you, for you alone, Judaea summoned back to life! "Lazarus, come forth!" and it is the whole world which emerges from the tomb, totally familiar and utterly new. That's the real miracle! Those you thought you'd never see again and who are there, freshly hatched out but with a hint of eternity: Julie, Clara, Thérèse, Julius, Jeremy and Half Pint, Louna, Verdun, Hadouch, Amar and Yasmina . . . oh, that delicious litany of names . . . Loussa, Calignac, Zabo, Marty and Coudrier . . . oh, that clutch of resurrected names . . . and the resurrected repeating your name, Benjamin! Benjamin! as though pinching themselves to make sure they were really alive . . .

*

Yes, and that amazing atmosphere of resurrection still dominated the Vendetta Press, in Calignac's massive office, a fortnight after I'd left hospital, after my delightful convalescence, to celebrate my return to the fold, champagne flowing, friendship on everyone's faces, and our eyes converging on that bright television screen, over there between the two windows, on which Berthold, the pirate with the magic cutlass, was occupying the entirety of the One o'clock News. Berthold gesticulating like a presidential candidate, Berthold answering all the questions at the same time, Berthold thirstily draining his cup of glory.

Question: What are the difficulties that are most frequently encountered during this sort of operation?

Answer: One's fellow doctors' preconceptions, obstruction from the family, unwilling donors, out-dated equipment, the National Union of Nurses, and the persistent hatred of an inferior practitioner whose name I shan't mention. But surgery is an apostleship that demands everything from its adulators.

"Just listen to the fucker!" Jeremy growled, anger still lurking in the back of his throat.

"'Adulators of an apostleship', a daring image," grinned Queen Zabo, ever the close reader.

And Marty, holding high his glass of bubbly, chuckling away to himself:

"How do you manage to make so many people so happy, Benjamin?"

Question: Professor, could you possibly reveal the identity of the donor?

Answer: A forty-year-old convict, but well nourished, in perfect condition, the kidneys of an eight-year-old, without the slightest trace of hyperlipidemy in his blood, a total lack of arteriosclerosis . . . and some people still criticise the food in French prisons!

The television news, that hour of total communion. While the cameras and satellites were broadcasting Berthold's feat across the planet – and making God the Father look like a hick farmer in comparison – I slid my arm under Marty's.

"Can I ask you something, doctor?"

And, without giving him the choice:

"About rejection . . . how come my body has so easily accepted Krämer's little presents?"

Marty thought for a couple of seconds while watching Half Pint giving Julius the Dog a glass of champagne.

"Do you want the technical answer?"

"Just something I can pretend to understand."

A violent twitching of Julius's snout as the bubbles hit it.

"Krämer and you were histocompatible."

"Which means?"

And lap, lap, a cautious tasting.

"That Krämer's tissue antigens were identical to yours."

"Does that often happen?"

"Never. Except in identical twins."

"And you don't even sound surprised."

Julius had become a convert. After a single twist of his tongue Half Pint was left holding an empty glass. He went off for a refill.

"When it comes to you and your family," the medic finally replied, "I'm so used to surprises that I don't waste my time being astonished any more. Hang on, though, isn't your dog walking strangely . . . Do you think it's the champagne?"

"The after-effects of his epileptic fit, a little stiffness in his neck and front legs . . . And what about my brain, doctor, what about that sudden reawakening?"

"I'll just take a look," said Marty going over to the wine-tasting pooch. "Give me your paw, please, Julius."

Won round by such politeness, Julius offered the medic a paw which was as stiff as a stiff middle finger.

"Yes, indeed," he murmured as he knelt down. "Now, sit, if you wouldn't mind."

And Julius slumped down onto his fat arse, his two tetanised legs shooting up to land on Marty's shoulders.

"Hmmm," said the doctor absorbed in his examination.

"Hmmm, hmmm . . ."

"The vet says there's nothing he can do," intervened Jeremy, who hadn't taken his eyes or ears off Marty, his hero, his demigod, the source of his recent medical vocation. ("I'm going to be a doctor when I grow up, just like Marty!" "A doctor, oh really, Jeremy?" "Yeah, to screw up the likes of Berthold!")

"Well," said Marty, getting to his feet. "We'll entrust Julius to that fellow on the screen over there. He's an excellent plumber who does everything I ask him to."

The "excellent plumber" was still filling up the screen where, in a fit of divine justice, he was now raging against the ingratitude of his walking miracle "who should now have been here by my side, paying due homage to medical science!"

That's what happens to gods, Berthold. They all get cheated on. Their creatures go off and play somewhere else. It's inevitable . . .

"As for your brain . . ." Marty murmured pensively. "In the present state of our knowledge . . ."

A wink in his eye.

"You'd do better to go and ask Thérèse."

Chapter 50

A SUGGESTION WHICH gave me pause for thought, until Loussa's and Calignac's voices brought me back to the land of the living.

"There's a bloke waiting for you in your office, shit-for-brains," said the former.

"What sort of bloke?"

"The sort of bloke who waits for you in your office," chuckled the latter. "Obsessed and impatient!"

Resurrection also means going back to the grind.

Should have thought of that . . .

*

"Good afternoon, Monsieur Malaussène!"

I didn't recognise him at first. A strange impression on my freshly awakened senses: I'd seen our man somewhere before, that much was certain, and his suit as well, that much was certain too, but never one in the other. Nor his fat Texan's attaché case. On my mother's life, I hadn't.

"Quite a turn-up for the book, eh?" said he, crushing my fingers in his enthusiastic fist.

A jolly rubicund giant, a redwood in its Sunday best, speaking in merry riddles:

"You just can't credit how much someone can change, can you? And don't say you can! It's written all over your face!"

I escaped from his clutches and slid behind my desk. Protection! Sanctuary!

Life teaches caution – death even more so.

"Maybe you'll recognise me now!"

In one stride he was across the carpet, which had been separating me from him, leant his massive bulk over my desk, grabbed the armrests of my chair and placed both chair and me face to face with him on the table, which did indeed set bells ringing: my mad giant! Jesus Christ, my despairing hulk! The one who smashed my office to smithereens! But now as happy as an ogre, as inflated as a zeppelin, not a trace left of his skeleton, a pneumatic colossus laughing fit to send all of the Queen's books flying to kingdom come. But what had happened to his wild boar's crop? Where had the good mood come from? And why did that suit, as grey as a pimp's conscience, look so familiar?

"I've come to tell you two things, Monsieur Malaussène."

The laughter had suddenly stopped.

"Two things."

Which he emphasised by unfolding two massive fingers under my measly snout.

"Firstly . . ."

He opened his attaché case, removed the manuscript I'd leant him and threw it down onto my lap.

"I read your novel, my poor chap, and I'm afraid it really is quite hopeless. Give up writing at once, you're only heading for some bitter disappointments."

(Well done! I should take a leaf out of his book!)

"Secondly . . ."

His hands on my shoulders, his eyes staring into mine, the inevitable pregnant pause. Then:

"Have you been following this J. L. B. business, Monsieur Malaussène?"

(Well, how can I put it . . . ?)

"Off and on."

"That isn't sufficient. I've been following it extremely attentively. Have you ever read one of J. L. B.'s novels?"

(Not really "read" one, no . . .)

"No, you haven't, have you? Neither had I, before the recent events . . . Too lowbrow for such lofty souls as ours, isn't that right?"

He fell silent. He fell silent so as to make me understand that the most important bit was coming next. Talk of any kind can be interrupted, but not silences such as this one.

"We are children, you and I, Monsieur Malaussène . . . little, tiny children . . ."

A last moment's reflection. The final limbering-up of the champ before he leaps into the ring.

"When a man is gunned down while presenting his latest novel before an audience of millions, the least one can do is to read it. Which is just what I did, Monsieur Malaussène. I read *The Lord of the Currencies* and the penny dropped."

And so it had, alas, for me. I suddenly realised what fire was blazing down below, beneath my colossus's hints. They were working like crazy in the engine room. The last shovelfuls of enthusiasm had pressurised his nerves. His heart's cauldron was boiling over. His muscles were tightening, his fists clenched, his cheeks went the colour of baked sheet metal, and I then recognised that suit, it was J. L. B.'s, the very suit I'd been wearing at the Palais Omnisport, only five or six sizes larger, and his haircut was the same as J. L. B.'s – cropped, combed and plastered onto his head like a huge Concorde with its all-conquering nose-cone! And I knew what he was going to say, and he said it: he sounded the trumpets of the arriving cavalry, *he was the new J. L. B.*, he'd caught onto all the preceding one's tricks, he'd apply them religiously until he'd broken the bank of the international publishing world, that's the way it was and no arguing, he'd adopted *free-market realism*, he didn't give a toss about "the navel-gazing subjectivism of our native Gallic literature" (sic), he was all for novels being quoted on the Stock Market and nothing was going to stand in his way because "*Will power, Monsieur Malaussène, is the power to will what you want!*"

Said he, bringing down his massive fist onto the telephone, which had just started ringing.

Sitting on your chair, which is itself sitting on your desk, it is possible to take the waves of sorrow issuing from a rejected writer, it's do-able, I've done it. But the hurricane emanating from a writer convinced of his imminent wealth . . . get your head down! Nothing in the world can stop illusions from bursting a dam – we just can't live without them. Don't stand up against that torrent, stay sitting down, keep your strength for later . . . wait for the moment of consolation.

Which is what I did.

I let my giant bawl out the commandments of free-market realism at the top of his voice: "*my main strength: enterprise! my main weakness: that I don't always succeed!*" Shame on me, he knew all of J. L. B.'s interviews off by heart: "*I have lost battles, Monsieur Malaussène, but this has always taught me what I needed to know to win the war.*"

At each line, a button popped off his waistcoat, which was too stiff for such massive jubilation.

"Writing means *counting*, Monsieur Malaussène, not *recounting!*"

He tore the portrait of Talleyrand-Périgord (huge fortune in real estate) off the wall, gave it a big sloppy kiss, then, holding it at arm's length:

"My dear prince, we're going to make loadsa, loadsa, loadsa money!"

His Concorde plumes were standing up on his head and his shirt had a life force of its own.

"People who don't read read only one author, Monsieur Malaussène, and *I shall be that author!*"

He shed tears of joy. He'd become that unkempt wild boar once again.

As for me . . .

On my throne . . .

Like a shamefaced king . . .

I watched that shipwreck which was mistaking itself for an ascension.

Chapter 51

" *H*AIZIMEN YE AN, *manman shui.*" (Good night, children, sleep well.)
"*Manman shuiba, Benjamin.*" (You too, Benjamin.)

There. The children slid into bed after their nightly Chinese lesson. One of Jeremy's ideas: "Don't tell us any more stories, Ben, teach us Loussa's Chinese instead." And the following profound thought from Clara: "There are all the stories in the world in a language you don't know." A taste for languages which is welcome in a Belleville where carefully lacquered ducks hang in the very shop windows from which, only yesterday, sheep's heads used to watch us pass by. Loussa was right. Belleville was becoming Chinese. Queen Zabo had made no mistake, the Chinese were there and their literature had woven a nest for their souls in the *Herbes Sauvages* bookstore. Belleville was Geography given over to History: a nostalgia factory . . . And Benjamin Malaussène, sitting on old Thian's stool, taught his children the three tones of that new exiles' music. The children listened, the children repeated, the children learnt. There had been only one interruption that evening: Thérèse had suddenly risen up in the midst of us. She hadn't stood up, but risen, like a monolith, rigid on departure, rigid on arrival, she wobbled dangerously on her base, her eyes swivelled three times round her head, then, when she'd recovered her balance, she said in the wan voice she has at such times:

"Uncle Thian wants you to know that he's arrived safely."

To which Jeremy observed:

"A fortnight later? He certainly took his time!"

Thérèse said:

"There were people he had to see."

Before concluding:

"He and Big Janine send you their love."

*

276

There. What An Angel was sleeping as befits his name. His future was assured and he had nothing to fear from the night: little Verdun was patrolling his slumbers and Julius the Dog has always slept in the shadow of the crib.

*

Julie and I closed the children's door on our mutual desire. Like every night for the last fortnight, we couldn't wait to reach our fifth floor before reuniting again. (One of resurrection's side-effects.)

*

"*Ban bian tian!*" Half Pint yelled out in his first dream of the night.

"*BAN BIAN TIAN!*" his cry echoed around the central courtyard. "*BAN BIAN TIAN! The woman carries half of the sky!*" God knows why, but I thought of Queen Zabo, and the way she whisked off my giant ("So you're the new J. L. B. then, are you? Come and tell me all about it . . ."), a gigantic chick under the Queen's down ("And you have an idea for a novel? Several? A good ten? Wonderful!"), heading off for the heights ("We'll be more comfortable in my office . . ."), with its four bare walls ("I just know that we're going to get on like a house on fire!"), the hatcher-out of everyone's dreams . . .

And to me, through the half-open door:

"It's all over, Malaussène, I shall no longer discourage anybody's vocation. If Hitler had been given the Prix de Rome, then he would never have gone into politics . . ."

*

There. Julie had fallen asleep as well. She was a ball of warmth. Never seen such a comfortable retriever before. With curves all my own. As though, each night, I curled up in a cello case. And it was there, lying against the warm velvet of her skin, my murderer's virginal heart beating in my breast, that I whispered into Julie's ear the most beautiful declaration of love ever spoken:

I said:

"Julie . . ."

. . .

"Julie, I love you *precisely.*"

POST-SCRIPT

Life is not a novel. I know that only too well ... But the novelistic is the only thing that makes it livable. My friend Dinko Stamback died while I was telling this story. He was the old Stojil of my Malaussène tribe. In reality he was poetry, that elixir of the novel. He was a delightful reason to go on living. And writing. And describing him. I should like these pages to wing their way to him; they were written in the impatient expectation of his reading them.

D. P.

14/10/99